Property of Nueces County
Keach Family Library
1000 Terry Shamsie Blvd.
Robstown, TX 78.

D0290508

WITHDRAWN

ONE
NIGHT
STAND

ALSO BY ROLAND S. JEFFERSON

The School on 103rd Street

A Card for the Players

559 to Damascus

Damaged Goods

ONE NIGHT STAND

A NOVEL

ROLAND S. JEFFERSON

Property of Nueces County
Keach Family Library
1000 Terry Shamsie Blvd.
Robstown, TX 78380

ATRIA BOOKS

New York London Toronto Sydney

ATRIA BOOKS
1230 Avenue of the Americas
New York, NY 10020

This book is a work of fiction. Names, characters, places and
incidents are products of the author's imagination or are used
fictitiously. Any resemblance to actual events or locales or persons,
living or dead, is entirely coincidental.

Copyright © 2006 by Roland S. Jefferson

All rights reserved, including the right to reproduce
this book or portions thereof in any form whatsoever.
For information address Atria Books, 1230 Avenue
of the Americas, New York, NY 10020

ISBN-13: 978-0-7432-6888-2
ISBN-10:   0-7432-6888-1

First Atria Books hardcover edition May 2006

10 9 8 7 6 5 4 3 2 1

ATRIA BOOKS is a trademark of Simon & Schuster, Inc.

Manufactured in the United States of America

For information regarding special discounts for bulk purchases, please contact
Simon & Schuster Special Sales at 1-800-456-6798 or
business@simonandschuster.com

For Shannon

ACKNOWLEDGMENTS

I would like to thank my agent, Manie Barron, for his wonderful motivation. My editor, Malaika Adero, for her incredible patience in dealing with this "old school" writer stuck in his ways. And Irwin Evans, whose input helped guide the manuscript's legal premise through proper procedure.

ONE
NIGHT
STAND

Property of Nueces County
Keach Family Library
1000 Terry Shamsie Blvd.
Robstown, TX 78380

CHAPTER 1

THE MUSTANG 5.0 ROARED out of the darkness on tires grown accustomed to the brutality of decaying asphalt. The car was followed by the banshee scream of LAPD sirens, flashing red and blue lights of a half dozen black and whites in dogged pursuit.

Overhead drama. The familiar low-pitched coughing drone of an LAPD helicopter playing hopscotch with its halogen beam spotlight joined in the chase, followed by the higher-pitched whine of news helicopters approaching in the distance. Without braking, the driver attempted a tire-punishing right turn onto a one-way street. His lights off, he misjudged his speed and plowed into the side of a parked car, shearing off its door and sending it flying through the air like a Frisbee. The explosive force of the collision sent the Mustang skidding sideways across the street. The driver manhandled the wheel, brakes, and gearshift all in a single motion, careened into the glaring headlights of an oncoming pickup truck, near-certain lethal impact in the making. But skill and luck were still with the driver. He regained a measure of last-second control and prevented a head-on collision, but not the slamming impact with a parked car that left the mangled white door with streaks of blue. The chase continued—with the shrill, ear-splitting squeal of tortured rubber, whiffs of smoke from rear wheel wells, and a whining transmission through five forward gears of acceleration down the one-way obstacle course—as the Mustang approached a spike strip visible at the corner.

Show-and-tell.

The driver downshifted, avoided the spike strip, hit the curb

1

and sidewalk, and took a shortcut across a vacant lot that kicked up clouds of dust and clipped the rear fender of another parked car as it exited, sending pieces of metal, red plastic, and shards of glass clattering across the pavement. Tires screamed for relief. Near-deserted Market Street an LAX runway as the Mustang approached liftoff speed. Suddenly the halogen light of the helicopter caught up to the pony, painted it in a circle of daylight like the tractor beam of the *Enterprise*.

Inglewood.

Family Bloods.

Hard choice: spike strip or Bloods. Both lethal.

He gambled on Inglewood, made a tight last-second tire-shredding turn onto a tree-lined street of graffiti-covered apartment buildings. Hoping to become invisible in a world of infrared sensors and global positioning satellites, the driver raced down a darkened corridor toward the next intersection. But there was no intersection.

There was a cul-de-sac.

Downshifting and locking disc brakes put the muscle car in a screeching, out-of-control skid that destroyed a pair of expensive twenty-inch rims with all the blunt force of its five thousand pounds slamming headfirst into a curb, up, over, and into the immovable mass of a concrete light pole that brought the 5.0 to a crashing, bone-jarring stop. A swirling cloud of coolant hissed and seeped from the radiator like steam from a teapot.

One way in. No way out—unless the Mustang could fly. Black and whites swarmed in like a flock of helicopter gunships on a search-and-destroy mission.

All they needed was a declaration of war.

Bail or assume the position. Only partial halogen sunlight through the trees. He could've run for it, lost himself in the massive apartment complex, found a sympathetic tenant who didn't like cops. Waited it out till the K-9 squad gave up. Only problem: graffiti-covered apartments were not friendly. Driver read the gang

2

graffiti, knew his blue scarf was the wrong color to wear in a Blood neighborhood. Bloods in a war with LAPD on a daily basis, battling Crips on a second front. Driver figured his odds were better with the cops.

Tractor beam of the helicopter, blinding spotlights on top of a dozen black and whites turned the battered Mustang into a show car, optical reflections from whirling spinners on damaged rims bathing the perimeter like strobe lights in a disco. Drawing beads on the driver with their nine-millimeters, twice as many cops cautiously approached the car from all sides like hunters on safari stalking their prey.

The chase was over. Five-O won. Ignition key off, deep-throated mufflers fell silent, all too familiar command on the charged-up bullhorn barking orders. He knew the routine. Both hands out of the window, open the door from the outside, step out slowly. Don't make any sudden moves. Don't even sneeze. Cops on edge after a chase, adrenaline rush, hair-trigger index fingers itching for exercise. Hands over his head, walk to the center of the tractor beam. Slowly. Down on both knees, then flat on the pavement with both arms outstretched, wait for the pat-down, wrists handcuffed behind his back.

Sleepy-eyed South Central LA residents fell out of bed, crowded into barred front windows, porches, and litter-filled streets to see the latest inner-city reality show as if on cue from a Marine Corps drill sergeant. A group of curious residents, some men, more women, ten times as many teenagers, all wearing red in some combination—shirts, scarves, sweats—began hurling insults across the street, as much at the driver as at the police, his blue head scarf to the growing crowd what a red cape is to a bull. Angry youths gave the finger to helicopters above, hitting up gang signs behind arriving TV commentators who were interviewing police and spectators. Drifting in and out of the tractor beam, shouting profanities over the loud popping of helicopters circling overhead like buzzards waiting their turn to feed, amid the constant chatter of police traffic on radios and walkie-talkies, the gathering crowd began to make a block party out of the event. The aroma of blunts, primos, and weed daring police to say a word or risk Rodney King time. Boom boxes started to blare. Teenage girls wearing scarcely more than hair curlers began wiggling, bouncing, and dancing in a wild sexual frenzy to the beats as if auditioning for a Dr. Dre music video. Gangbangers rapping along with 50 Cent, Jay-Z, OutKast. A few got out lawn chairs, ice chest full of forties. All they needed was barbecue. Three o'clock in the morning. Someone should've sold tickets.

A pair of hands jerked the driver roughly to his feet, brought him eye level with a small white face, blond mustache, name tag that read MONROE. Rifling the driver's wallet, he asked, "Your name Napoleon Booker?" looking first at the photo on the driver's license and car registration, then at the driver.

"If that's what it says."

"I can't read. Suppose you tell me. I run a check, what name's coming back?"

"You can't read, go take a special-ed class."

The cop shook his head and mumbled to no one in particular. "Comedian, huh? Okay, Napoleon, here we go," he said, and he withdrew a small card from his shirt pocket. "You are now under arrest," he began formally. "Anything you say can and will be used against you in a court of law. Do you understand these rights?"

Napoleon shook his head and said, "Whatever, but whose court and whose law?"

"Got any warrants, Napoleon?" Monroe said, ignoring the comment.

"What do you care, muthafucka. You can't read!"

"Smart-ass, huh," the cop spit out, not really looking at Napoleon, expecting little more, like it would be unusual if he cooperated. He ripped the blue scarf from Napoleon's head, revealing a field of cornrows in need of attention. "What set are you in, Napoleon?" the cop droned on, fingering gold chains

4

around Napoleon's neck, going through zippered pockets of baggy pants hanging miraculously at his butt line as if by some unseen force, lifting up his shirt, turning him around, inspecting prison tattoos on both arms. "Who do you bang with—Fruit Town Crips? Rolling Sixties? Hoover Crips? What do they call you? What do you go by?"

"Fuck you."

"That's good," Monroe said, then called out to the clan, "Hey, fellas, says his name is Fuck You, but his license says Napoleon, if you can believe that. Any you guys know him, what set he belongs to, his gang name?" Several cops walked over, took cursory looks at Napoleon, shook their heads, drifted away.

"You Mirandize him?" The name tag said CALVIN. The razor-bumped face was black, nose broad, the beady penetrating eyes cold and deep-set, a vicious mouth that snarled like a rabid dog when it opened. Attitude pure Gestapo. Not waiting for Monroe to answer and not really caring, he said to Napoleon, "Homeboys never learn, do you? Trying to drive like Mario Andretti. Don't you know you can't outrun a computer, or the ghetto-bird up there?" He pointed toward the helicopter, nine-millimeter still in his hand. "Or did you keep your black ass in school long enough to learn that?!" he said, attitude on full throttle, words hostile and venomous, absent any kinship with the suspect. "You don't have three strikes," he went on, face inches from Napoleon's, spray of spit a fountain between them. "You will when we get through with you. Won't need them gold chains on your neck where you're going. Know what I'm saying? You feelin' me, homey?" The cop slammed the nine-millimeter into his chest several times, like Tarzan declaring himself king of the jungle. Only thing missing was the yell.

Napoleon said, "Why don't you get the fuck outta my face!"

Calvin bristled at the challenge, put both hands on his belt, brought his broad nose, razor-bumped face, malignant stare, and rabid dog's mouth a hair's breadth from Napoleon's, like he was

Mike Tyson squaring off with an opponent in the ring, and said, "'Cause I don't want to. So what you gonna do about it? Huh? I'll *tell* you what you're gonna do—nothing! You ain't gonna do a god-damn muthafucking thing 'cause I'm the man, see." He waved his nine-millimeter in Napoleon's face like a flag. "And *you* ain't nothin' but a little punk-ass bitch. Know what I'm saying, homey? You feeling me?"

Mindful of news commentators broadcasting live, restless crowd watching the exchange, Monroe thought it best to intercede before Tarzan lost control. He said to Napoleon, "Why'd you run, Napoleon?"

"Why'd you stop me?"

"'Cause you were driving with no lights and had no plates."

"I just bought the car!"

"I can understand the plates," Monroe said. "What happened, they forget to install the lights?"

"Whatever."

Calvin looked over at the mangled muscle car, back to Napoleon. He laughed.

"Really? You just bought it, and you with no visible means of sup-port," he said, knowing from instinct and experience he spoke the truth. "Let me see that," he said, and without asking he snatched the registration from Monroe's hands. "Who's Mary Booker?"

"My moms."

"That's what I thought." Calvin handed the registration back to Monroe and said, "How's a little punk-ass gangbanger like you gonna pay for a new car—legitimately?"

"Negro, suck my muthafuckin' dick, why don't you!"

Calvin smiled, said to Monroe, "Hard little punk-ass nigga, isn't he. Wants me to suck his brains." In his face with it—*nigga*, what they call black cops behind their backs.

Monroe said, "Man's name is Fuck You, what'd you expect?"

Calvin said to Monroe, "Not very creative, was she, his mom . . . name her kid Fuck You." And with an expression of utter disdain, beady eyes looking Napoleon up and down as if appraising a contaminated rat, he said, "Then again I can see why. I mean what else do you call garbage. Know what I'm saying." And he stepped back, wiping his hands on his uniform as if he had just touched a dirty rag. "Just look at him."

Monroe's face brightened with amusement but he didn't comment. What he saw was a black youth in his mid-twenties, muscular, well conditioned, skin the color of night. His cherub-looking unshaven face was sprinkled with hair and anchored by a wide mouth enhanced by large African lips that exposed two rows of crooked teeth when it opened. A large, flat nose, heavy lids struggling to stay open over hard brown eyes grown suspicious beyond their years, and a low forehead buttressed by flat ears, pierced with small diamond studs, rounded out its contour. The brown baggy pants with a dozen zippered pockets and matching sweatshirt were generic. But the blue head scarf said who and what he was.

"You still haven't answered the man's question, homey," Calvin went on, trace of foam at the edges of the snarling mouth. "Why'd you run?"

"'Cause I ain't white, *popo*! That's why!"

Calvin half laughed, half grunted, said that answer was played out, suggested Napoleon try something a little more original. "Naw," he said, "that ain't why you ran." And the cop took Napoleon's car registration from Monroe a second time, waved it in front of his face, saying, "Nice car like that, all torn up . . . half a dozen other cars totaled." Calvin shook his head and said, "You one of these little thugs that ran 'cause you got something to hide. Wanna tell us what it is, or we gotta find it?"

"I ain't tellin' you shit, you cracker-ass nigga! Fuck you."

Calvin laughed for the third time in as many minutes, gave the registration back to Monroe. He said, "Right. Retard with a limited vocabulary and poor memory. Keeps repeating his name so he won't forget it." Calvin holstered his nine-millimeter, walked away in another fit of laughter. "Have it your way, Fuck You."

Gesturing toward the crowd in red, Monroe said, "Maybe I ought to let *them* question you. Bet they could find out the four-one-one . . . what set you're in? Gang name? What do you think, Napoleon? Yeah? No?"

Napoleon didn't say anything right then because he knew this tactic to be true, knew cops threatened to drop a suspect from one gang into the neighborhood of rival gangs if they didn't talk, and sometimes did exactly that even when they did talk. But he knew that was unlikely this time. He'd run, they'd chased him down, and it was on the news. No way they were going to let him go after this much drama.

Napoleon said, "I think you should kiss my ass, white boy. Know what I'm saying?"

Monroe said, "Well, your eyesight's good. Can't say the same about your choice in names."

Napoleon said, "Fuck you."

Monroe smiled for the first time. He said, "I'll be damned. He was right—only way you remember your name is repeat it. Have it your way then, Napoleon. We'll go with what it says here while we're waiting for your sheet to come back. Meantime, we search your car, what are we gonna find?"

"Whatever you plant, muthafucka," Napoleon said in truth, knowing from personal experience the way LAPD can frame suspects. "That's what you'll find."

"You got a weapon in there?" another cop with crooked teeth asked, knowing from instinct there probably was and hoping to save time in the search.

"Hell no, I ain't got no weapon," Napoleon said, knowing it was a lie, knowing too that if they didn't find the trapdoor compartment behind the dash where he kept his Glock and if they were angry enough and wanted him bad enough, they'd plant one. Plant dope too if it suited them. They'd find the half-empty fifth of Johnnie Walker Red, his dime bag of weed, crow about that. They'd charge him with an open container, possession, try to charge him with sales if they thought they could get away with it.

The cop with crooked teeth just looked at him, fingered the blue scarf, then called out to the team checking the Mustang. "Hey, guys. Napoleon here says he hasn't got a weapon, but he's wearing Crip colors, so what does that tell you? It tells you he's either the bravest Crip I know, traveling in a Blood neighborhood without packing, or he's the dumbest wannabe I've ever met. And looking at him, way he's dressed and all, I don't figure him for a wannabe. Either way, we get back to the shop, you go through that buggy with a fine-tooth comb and find me something, 'cause it's there, somewhere."

Find me something. That said it all. Code name for a setup.

"Like I said, ain't nothing to find less you put it there," Napoleon said again, knowing he should be quiet but helpless to control his anger, his explosive temper, letting the cops get next to him like that. Especially the black cop. Knew black cops always had something to prove, were harder and more brutal than white cops.

"And the money," Calvin's voice blurted from somewhere in the pack. "Don't forget that."

"Money?" Napoleon said, twisting around to face Calvin's voice, see if he could read the cop's face, see if he was just baiting him to make him talk or if there was another agenda. But all he saw was a group of blue shirts gathered around the crippled Mustang. Napoleon was suddenly feeling uneasy about the situation, knowing his only money was the hundred and twenty dollars in his wallet Monroe had already counted. "What money you talking about?" he shouted to the knot of blue shirts.

Monroe continued the inquisition. "What about dope, *Na-po-le-on*," he said, pronouncing his name with as much derisiveness as he could muster. "We gonna find any dope in your car? Any Sherm? Rocks? Weed? Primos? Blunts?"

"Wait a minute," Napoleon said. "What is this? What money . . . ?"

"I wouldn't worry about money now, Napoleon," Monroe said. "From the looks of things, Calvin was right . . . where you're going you won't have any use for money either." But Monroe knew this was not true, that jailed inmates always had money on the books to negotiate favors and privileges. Napoleon knew this too. Still, he wondered why the black cop had brought it up.

"You got all my money right there in your hand," Napoleon said to Monroe. "No coins. Six dubs . . . hundred and twenty dollars all total. You *can* count, can't you?" Street smarts still in hiding.

The cop cut intolerant eyes at Napoleon, could understand why Calvin's patience wore thin with hoodlums like Napoleon.

"Talk to me about dope, Napoleon," Monroe said, his own patience waning.

"Naw, muthafucka," Napoleon spit out angrily, "you talk to me about money!" he said, continuing to press the issue. "What money you looking for I'm supposed to have?" Napoleon said, watching a sea of blue around the Mustang suddenly part as a police flatbed arrived, backed up, began to hook up chains and braces.

Monroe said, "I'd like to say you cooperated in my report, Napoleon, giving us the heads-up on what's in the car . . . ?"

"What's in the car? Ain't nothing in the car," Napoleon said. "I told you, *popo*, whatever you planted is what you'll find. You illiterate *and* deaf too?" Arrogance still ruling the day. Anger. Temper out of control, the way it had been all his life.

With tremendous reserve Monroe said, "All of the above . . . none of the above. Take your pick. At least I know my own name. You, on the other hand, wanna go for bad. Your car's all jacked up, you're standing here in handcuffs not offering an ounce of cooperation, looking at more strikes than the law allows, knowing you're gonna do some time . . . and you call *me* illiterate?"

"Listen," Napoleon said, touch of reality finally creeping into his voice, street smarts coming out of deep freeze. "I don't know anything about any money. What kind of game you playing?" Napoleon was used to the games played by cops. Knew from past experience just how far they'd go, Rampart far, if necessary. He knew they planted dope. And guns. Sometimes both . . . if they didn't kill you first. He had in fact been set up before by LAPD who'd planted a gun used in a homicide, knowing too they'd be out to get him once his sheet came back and they found out who he was, that he beat the 187, beat their setup. Murder or drugs—he could see that, understood that kind of frame, how it worked, and knew there was a way to beat it if you had a good lawyer. He knew they wouldn't plant anything in front of a crowd, news commentators, TV cameras. They'd wait until they had the car secured in police impound, plant whatever they wanted. But why money? What would that get them? A gun . . . dope, he could see that. But the cop had said money. What money? Whose money? From a dope dealer? Evidence room? If that was the case they wouldn't be advertising, they'd be helping themselves and keeping very quiet about it. Whatever cops were about, honesty wasn't included. Extortion? Gambling? Counterfeiting? No, that wasn't him. They'd know that once his sheet came back. He couldn't see them setting him up on a counterfeiting case. Murder . . . carjacking, maybe. Not counterfeiting. And absolutely not bank robbery! He could beat that blindfolded. Street smarts back in high gear now, but they weren't working on all fours. He just couldn't figure the angle about money. Then maybe it was just a cop trick after all. He was just too paranoid, reading more into it. Had to be the drugs . . . driving a new car with no plates and no lights. No wonder they flagged him. Jesus, what was he thinking about? He *was* wired from hits on the freebase pipe, he had to admit that. Which is why he took off when they flagged him. He wouldn't have run like that if he wasn't high. Stupid. Stupid. Stupid. Still, the cop did say to find the money . . . ?

With the Mustang secured on the flatbed, the driver followed several black and whites out of the artificial sunlight of the tractor beam, signaling the party was over. Army of occupation started piling into black and whites, began their orderly but well-practiced retreat from hostile territory. News commentators and broadcast technicians packed up their gear just as fast, filed out behind the police ground units and headed to the next hot spot. Helicopters faded away one by one in search of tomorrow's news today. With lawn chairs folded, boom boxes silent, residents returning to their apartments, the tractor beam shut off, plunging the street back into darkness. The inner-city reality show was over—for the moment. Tune in tomorrow night for a new episode.

Monroe walked Napoleon over to a nearby black and white, put him in the backseat with a white female cop whose close-cut, slicked-down ash-blond hair was her only saving grace. Her severely acne-scarred, pockmarked Elephant Man face so distorted her features it was hard to tell if her mouth was open or closed. Her name tag said TAYLOR, and after getting settled on uncomfortable manacled hands, Napoleon asked if Taylor was her first name or last. She didn't open her mouth to answer him. But when her robot head rotated to face him, her eyes raked across him with the cold, impassive hardness he'd seen on female cops that was far more intimidating than that of their male counterparts. He figured the wedding ring was just for show, couldn't imagine anyone so ugly with such hard eyes ever being married. He wanted to ask her if she had children and if they were just as hideous-looking as she was, decided it was prudent to stay silent.

"Right," said Napoleon after a moment, guessing conversation was not one of her strong points.

Monroe rode shotgun next to the driver, a white cop he called Darryl who had a knack for chewing gum despite missing half his teeth.

"We'll book him at Seventy-seventh Division," Monroe said after they'd joined the parade of black and whites leaving the fire zone, turning his attention to the car's computer. They drove east out of Inglewood on Century Boulevard in silence, passed Hollywood Park racetrack, crossed over Crenshaw, turned north on Normandie for the run to Seventy-seventh.

Monroe said, "Well, well, well. What have we got here?" He was looking at the computer screen. "Napoleon T. Booker, aka Little Dog Nine—what's the Nine, Napoleon, type of piece you use or how many gangbangers you've killed?"

"Fuck you."

He should have expected it. The elbow that rammed into Napoleon's rib cage knocked the wind out of him, caused him to double over with pain, his chin almost to his knees. He looked up at the Frankenstein face responsible, started to speak, doubled over again with the second blow she unleashed, tried to catch his breath, knew a third blow was coming and tried to protect himself by turning away from the sadist. No good. It caught him just below the kidney. Napoleon thought he'd pass out.

"Says here you've been in and out of jail since you were ten," Monroe droned on, ignoring the rear seat action. "B and E's, burglary, assaults, GTA, theft, one eighty-seven—a one eighty-seven . . . ?" It sounded like he'd just discovered gold. The cop hesitated, typed on keys, mumbled to himself as he read green lines that rolled down the screen. Momentarily he turned around, spoke to Napoleon's doubled-over form: "How'd you beat a one eighty-seven three years ago?"

Napoleon didn't answer. Couldn't answer. Couldn't catch his breath, but managed to spit out a weak "fuck you" a second time. Suddenly the gargoyle reached over, grabbed a fistful of loose cornrows, snapped his head up and around to face Monroe, and spoke for the first time. "Officer asked you a question. Be to your advantage to answer him." The voice was surprisingly feminine, but it was just as cold and hard as the eyes stuck on the face.

"I was set up," he said truthfully after a moment, remembering the harrowing trial that threatened to put him on death row at twenty-three.

Monroe and Darryl both laughed. Frankenstein too.

"That's what they all say," Darryl said over his shoulders. "I was set up—give me a muthafucking break, why don't you."

"Don't take my word for it," Napoleon said, trying to shake loose from the fingers attached to his cornrows, his head feeling like a trophy held up by cannibals victorious in battle. "Read the transcript, you don't believe me," he went on, tether of fingers still attached to his hair. "My PD proved the gun had been planted 'cause there were no prints, the ballistics didn't match, and the only witness was a basehead informant for LAPD."

"PD did all that?" Monroe said somewhat incredulously. "Who represented you?"

"White lady, Myra Cross."

"Myra Cross," Darryl said, excitement in his voice. "The hottie. Built like a—"

"Down, boy," Frankenstein interrupted from the backseat. "There's a lady present." Lady? Napoleon wondered who she was talking about.

"She's a good lawyer, way I hear it," Monroe said. "Was cross-examined by her on a burglary case once. Don't remember much about the case, but I sure remember Ms. Cross. Hard to pay attention to details when you're staring at her rack all the time." He tried to stifle the laugh but it slipped out. And still snickering, he turned to the figure in the backseat and said, "No offense, Lila. You have a nice rack too." Patronizing her. Just like that, questioning her femininity. Good-old-boys' club alive and well in the LAPD. No women, niggers, or dogs need apply. Not necessarily in that order.

Lila. The name fit the voice, but not the Frankenstein image.

Lila grunted deep in her throat and said, "My, aren't we in a patronizing mood tonight." Neanderthal man. All he needed was a club.

Half turning in his seat, eyes taking in Monroe, trying to catch Lila's and start damage control, Darryl said, "He didn't mean anything by it, Lila." Lying politely, almost sounding like he meant it.

"I know what he meant," Lila said. "Watch the road, please."

Concrete hardness of words matching the icy stare of a pair of blinking shell-holes in the cratered face.

A no-win situation for the good old boys.

Six and a half blocks of frosty silence before Monroe's courage returned. He said to Napoleon, "You're going back to the joint, Little Dog Nine . . ." It sounded as if he almost regretted saying it. "On top of your priors we'll add felony hit-and-run . . . that's a strike. Felony evasion . . . that's a strike. Resisting arrest, parole violation . . . two strikes there. Plus whatever we find in your car."

Napoleon shook his head violently, got rid of the tether of fingers. "You mean whatever you *plant* in the car."

Darryl said, "We don't need to plant anything in your car to put your little gangbanging ass away. You're a TV star. Made the eleven o'clock news, remember?"

Napoleon knew they were right. They didn't need to plant anything. He'd fucked up. Still, it pissed him off to have the cops remind him. Unable to rein in his seething anger, he said, "Fuck you, *popo*. Fuck all you white cocksuckers!"

Monroe said, "Race card."

Darryl said, "Yeah."

As if on cue, Lila's pile-driving elbow returned to Napoleon's rib cage, his nose dropping down to meet his knees. "Muthafuckin' bitch, you!"

"It's Officer Taylor," Lila said through the hole that passed as a mouth, "since you asked. Remember that, why don't you—Officer Lila Taylor." And almost immediately one fist grabbed the other, and like a jackhammer she rammed another elbow into Napoleon's side so hard he cried out in pain and toppled over on the seat, his head hitting the armrest of the door.

It took great effort for Napoleon to speak. He said, "I'm gonna sue your assess for police brutality!"

The trio of cops all laughed in unison. Monroe said, "I don't see any police brutality. Darryl? Lila? You see any brutality?" A hairy

15

white arm reached over the front seat, inspected Napoleon's neck, lifted up his sweatshirt, inspected his chest. "I don't see anything on your neck, your chest. No cuts, bruises. What police brutality you talking about, Napoleon?"

"Man, fuck you, *popo*," Napoleon said, bracing for the elbow, surprised when it didn't come.

"We get through with you, Napoleon," Monroe said, turning back around, fingers working the keyboard, "you won't need Myra Cross—you'll need Houdini himself."

Napoleon said, "Houdini's dead."

Monroe said, "My point exactly." The explosive laughter of the trio sounded prerecorded, like the laugh track for a TV sitcom.

The pain in his side unbearable, Napoleon lay crumpled over on the seat in silence. He thought about what the cop had said, about needing Houdini instead of Myra Cross. If it wasn't for the pain he would have laughed. Myra Cross.

Houdini incarnate.

CHAPTER 2

MYRA CROSS STEPPED OUT of her flossy burnt-orange Mercedes Benz 500 SE the way a supermodel steps onto a Versace runway—with all the attitude and arrogance her green eyes, flaming-red *Basic Instinct* haircut, and Cancún-tanned 118-pound frame could command. Only she wasn't a supermodel. Not yet. But she was working on it. What she was was a thirty-one-year-old divorcée doing time as a public defender. She popped the trunk, withdrew the portable carry-on that held two feet of legal briefs, and beeped on her alarm. Expensive Tony Valentine boots carried her across the twenty or so yards of P-3's underground concrete to the elevators that serviced the Los Angeles County Criminal Courthouse. Conservatively dressed in a blue Ann Taylor business suit, with its not too short, not too tight skirt, she was a cyclone of shameless sexuality. Snug waist-bound jacket that failed miserably at concealing the ample bulge of her chest, salmon-colored wide-collar blouse only pretending to cover a delicate neck freshly decorated with monkey bites—Myra Cross, if she was anything, was stunning to look at on her worst day. It was no exaggeration to say that on her best day you'd need sunglasses.

The parking elevators brought her to a lobby filled with black and brown members of the dispossessed. She followed the guilty, the innocent, and the families of both through the security barrier and headed for the elevators.

Dillon Lester, DA's office. Three-piece pin-striped suit, button-down shirt, *L.A. Law* power tie—reached past her, pounded the elevator button without taking his eyes off Myra's neck.

He said, "Whoa, Myra. Cancún was good, eh?" They stepped back from the gathering crowd, found a pocket of space in which to talk.

Myra smiled shamelessly, played at the collar of her blouse in pretense and said, "They show, do they?"

Dillon smiled. "I was talking about your tan," he said, winking, leaving the pocket to pound the elevator button again, then returning.

"Yeah, right," Myra said, still pretending modesty with the blouse.

Dillon asked enviously, "Who'd you go with?"

"Somebody you know, probably."

"Have fun?"

"Ask him."

"When's it gonna be my turn?"

"That the word on me in the DA's office—everyone gets a turn?"

Dillon said, "What do they know. I'm talking about you and me, Myra. Hawaii. Cabo maybe. Three days in paradise. What do you say?"

Myra wanted to say he wasn't bright enough and had crooked teeth. She could work around the crooked teeth, but not matching her intellect was a deal breaker. Instead she said, "I say you're not my type. Elevator's here."

They rode the elevator with cops, felons, ex-felons, parole officers, lawyers, witnesses, and spectators. Dillon asked Myra about Cancún. Myra said it was a lot like Puerto Vallarta, only more developed. She said it was like the movie *10* with Bo Derek, but the piano player sucked. Dillon said he hadn't seen the movie but he'd rent it this weekend. They could watch it together. Myra said she never saw the same movie twice.

The elevator was not quite empty by the time it reached the Seventeenth floor. Only Dillon, Myra, and a couple arguing in Spanish who'd gotten on at the ninth floor. Assuming the couple didn't know much English and not really caring, Dillon turned to Myra as he stepped off and said, "Keep in mind what we discussed earlier." He cocked his finger like a gun and pointed. "You and me—sun, sand, and romance."

She wanted to say "in your dreams," but decided not to be cruel and said, "Got some dirt on your collar."

Dillon frowned, reached absently over his shoulder and said, "Where?" as a closing elevator door came to Myra's rescue.

Myra stepped into the busy nineteenth-floor corridor of high ceilings, polished marble floors, and thick teakwood doors with frosted glass panels lettered in black. She turned the corner and three doors down brought herself to a stop just long enough to play feebly with her collar before entering the noisy office of the public defender. The crowded windowless waiting room of faded pea-green floor-to-ceiling walls was broken by a thick, riveted steel door adjacent to a two-inch-thick single bulletproof window with a built-in microphone. Behind it sat Clara, the obese cornrowed black receptionist with dagger-shaped multicolored fingernails who considered the PD's office her own personal fiefdom.

The waiting room of uncomfortable steel chairs was filled to capacity by mostly young, mostly black and brown defendants, the standing overflow of desperate faces stretching out against the walls like suspects in a police lineup. Myra glanced around for familiar faces and, seeing none, waited for Clara to hit the buzzer. Clara didn't appreciate the interruption of her donut breakfast, spit out plenty of South Central attitude with hostile eyes as the door popped open.

As Myra pranced through, Clara said, "The vacation lady returns. And look at you . . . brown as a berry." Clara reached out her arm, put it next to Myra's. She said, "Any more time in the sun you be lookin' like me."

Myra said, "Not really. I don't like donuts."

Clara frowned, drew back angry lips, and said, "Low blow, *Miss* Cross. Low blow." Myra learned early on whenever Clara called her

Miss Cross, it was attitude time. "Got a slew of messages on your desk, *Miss* Cross," Clara said gruffly, then laughed suddenly, adding, "They see that neck, you gonna have a lot more."

"And we're paying you to spread the word, right?"

"You, *Miss* Cross, ain't payin' me a dime. My paycheck comes from the County of Los Angeles, *thank you very much.*" Clara brought her eyes back to the donut and added, "But you could make me an offer . . . ?"

Myra said, "Blackmail is a felony."

Moving full painted lips to the donut in her left hand, dismissing Myra with a flash of FloJo fingernails on her right, she said, "Whatever, *Miss* Cross."

Myra knew when to quit. Knew too that by the time she'd reach her office her neck would be public gossip. Legal briefs in tow, she swept past the typing pool to her closet at the end of the corridor, settled into the familiar discomfort of a squeaky steel chair just as the button on line three lit up. It was Marty French, her boss. Bright. Straight teeth. Balls. Gay. Too bad. She could go for him.

"I'd like to see you, Myra, when you get a moment," he said plainly, no feminine affectation in his voice, though she could tell he was struggling to keep from asking about her neck.

"Anything urgent?"

"No, Myra. Nothing urgent. You've been out two weeks. Just want to bring you up to date. Like I said, when you get a moment."

"Sounds like a plan," Myra said, clicking off, turning on her computer. Waiting for it to boot up, she began leafing through Clara's stack of phone calls, wondering how Clara could write, much less hold a pen with cumbersome appendages passing as nails. Looking for one call in particular and not seeing it, she checked her e-mail.

There it was—*Photos ready. Call when you get back. Jason.*

Dialing his number, goose bumps sweeping over her skin as she waited for him to answer, she felt giddy as a schoolgirl on her first date.

"Jason Rice."

"Jason. Myra Cross. Got your e-mail."

"How was it after I left?"

"Got a tan finally. Maybe we should go back, shoot some more?"

"Not really. Uneven colors distract the eye. Better to be tanned all over or not at all. But don't sweat it. You photograph like a natural. Wait'll you see what I've got. When can you come by?"

Myra said she'd be there after work, clicked off just as line two lit up.

"Myra. Good to have you back." The booming voice belonged to Craig McInnis, the attorney covering her cases during her absence. Sight unseen you'd think he was the size of Hulk Hogan. Willie Shoemaker was more like it. He was smart and aggressive, but his ego blocked the door. "Heard you have a fabulous tan," he said. He may have had the "little man" syndrome, but he was as lecherous as they came.

"Jesus," Myra said. "Why don't I just sell tickets, then everyone can see my neck and I can recover the cost of my trip!"

Craig said, "You never paid for a trip in your life, Myra."

"You my travel agent, Craig?"

"Now, Myra. Just welcoming you back. That's all." She could hear him drooling through the phone. Wondered if he was masturbating. Down, boy.

"Yeah, right," Myra said, ending it. "Call you back later." She clicked off as line one lit up. Clara's line.

"Line four, *Miss Cross*," Clara said, her words wrapped in the frost of attitude like cold meat from a butcher. "Roderick Cole from downstairs." Downstairs was the code word for the DA's office. Clara clicked off before Myra could thank her.

"Mr. Cole," Myra said, turning professional, knowing he was calling about cases, but knowing too he wanted to fuck her, wanted "his turn," as Dillon had so succinctly put it. "To what do I owe this honor?"

"You might say hello, Myra, or did we miss you while you were gone." He sounded pitiful, like a small child looking for sympathy because he stubbed his toe, the awkward silence that followed his way of pleading for Myra to give him some play without his having to come right out with it. "We" didn't mean the DA's office. "We" meant Roderick, or Rod, as he was known among colleagues, was jealous but didn't have the balls to speak up. That too was a deal breaker, not having any balls. And Myra regretted that in a way because Roderick was a real hunk. Perfect teeth. And intelligent. But he wasn't aggressive or assertive enough professionally or socially, and that would keep him out of her bed.

Myra said, "Sorry, Rod. Both of the above. Now, any offers on the table?" Not having any balls, he'd fold and get right to the point, and she waited for him to shuffle papers and collect his thoughts.

"You talk to Craig yet?" Roderick asked.

Myra said she hadn't. Roderick said Craig had handled just about all her misdemeanors, then read off the dispositions. He'd left the felonies for her. Craig had the smarts all right, but he didn't know how to play poker. Myra, on the other hand, was a pro.

"Let's discuss the Newton case," Roderick said.

"Which Newton?" Myra said, her memory waking up, shaking off the sand of Cancún. "I've got three."

Roderick shuffled more papers. "Billy Newton. Street name Long Dog. Kid he shot's gonna live but he won't testify. Forensics couldn't match the slug with the gun they found, and the only other witness who could place Newton at the scene is a crackhead with a sheet a mile long. So we'll probably kick it out as a reject."

"All right. Who's on second?"

More shuffling of papers. "The Brady girl."

"Brady? Brady?" Myra's memory not quite off the beaches of Cancún yet.

"Solicitation—"

"Of a vice officer, yes," Myra cut in. "Entrapment, Rod. Get real, why don't you. My client was sitting in a bar minding her own business. So you tell me, just who solicited who?"

"Doesn't matter. She mentioned money."

"We both heard the same tape. She said, 'That's fifty bucks.' Who wouldn't mention money, *after* it was dropped in front of your nose with no comment. Hell, I'd mention money too if someone I didn't know just walked up to me, *interrupted* my lunch, and dropped fifty bucks on my plate. Fifty bucks buys a lot of daiquiris. I'd think they were looking for a drinking buddy. And that's what a jury will think."

Roderick half laughed, half coughed and said, "Interrupted your lunch. Give me a fuckin' break. I can't believe you're gonna take this to trial. Christ, Myra, she's a hooker with priors that go back ten years! It's a wonder she's not dead!"

"Maybe so," Myra said, still not quite up to speed, half of her photographic memory somewhere in Cancún, the other half scrolling down the rap sheet as if reading it on her computer screen. "But none for soliciting in a bar. She may be a streetwalker, Rod, but she wasn't working the night Vice set her up."

"*You* say Vice set her up. But we both know different, don't we?"

"I only know my client is innocent, *Counselor*." She pronounced "counselor" with such derision she could feel him bristle at the other end.

Roderick coughed again in exasperation. He said, "I just can't believe you're gonna waste taxpayer money on this!"

"*You're* the one forcing it to trial."

After a long pause Roderick coughed and said, "She must have an asshole of a pimp since he wouldn't bail her out. Suppose we give her time served, let's see . . . that's forty-two days . . . give her eighteen months' probation with community service, save the taxpayers some dough. What do you say, Myra?"

Time to get out of Cancún entirely, start playing poker. Myra said, "No deal, Counselor. My client was minding her own business. Nothing on the wire but her comment about the fifty dollars. Not what it was for, when, where, or how long. Nothing. Vice came to her. She didn't go to them. Entrapment, Rod. I'll go to trial."

23

She heard Roderick take a long, deep breath through his nose, pen tapping nervously on papers, hoping his decision would help land him between her legs.

"All right, Myra," Roderick said, anger framing his words. "I'll kick her out this time. She gets busted again, taxpayers will pay for a trial. Trust me!"

No balls. God, how she loved this game. She leaned back in the chair, smiling, carefully inspected the fresh gloss on her nails, and for a moment lamented the fact they weren't as long or stylish as Clara's. But only for a moment. She said, "I can live with that, Rod," making it sound as if she were genuinely appreciative. "Who's on third?"

The poker game lasted another twenty minutes. She bluffed some hands and won, got called on a few and lost, knew when to compromise on others. When it was over she'd won the pot. Four of her clients would go to trial: one for a drug-related homicide Myra knew she couldn't win; two who'd been looking at twenty-five years to life on a third strike for separate armed robberies—but Myra had plea-bargained to a lesser charge of simple theft because no weapon was ever produced; a repeat child molester who would get twenty-five to life, which meant he'd do sixteen and a half years of the twenty-five before eligible for parole. Three more would plead down from felonies to misdemeanors and do up to a year or less in county jail. Four more would be DA rejects.

Myra knew from experience that not all her clients would like the results. They were young thugs who had long histories with the criminal justice system and previous PDs who they were right in believing had sold them out, because they had. But in the end, when all was said and done and they'd looked at the options, they would consider Myra Cross a miracle worker.

Negotiating was a great turn-on. Court appearances and the jousting with her DA adversaries produced an even greater high. But nothing, not even a not-guilty verdict on a client she *knew* was guilty, compared to the high of good sex. Nothing excited her more. Absolutely nothing.

But the high came at a price, and at day's end it always left her tense and agitated, with a feeling she might explode if she couldn't bring herself down. She could see the slight tremor in her hands, could feel beads of perspiration forming on her neck, feel the dryness in her throat, the craving in her brain, and knew she needed something to settle her nerves. Not a tranquilizer. Not Valium or Xanax. Not just anything. No, what she needed was another joint. She'd had two before leaving her west side Barrington Avenue condo but realized it was too soon. She knew too her perfume, powerful as it was, wouldn't mask the odor. No. She'd have to suffer through this day like dozens before it. And so to take her mind off the craving, she spent the balance of the day buried in paperwork, returning calls, answering e-mails, and reviewing clients' jackets. By the time she'd finished, some of the edge was gone. She looked at her watch. Not really looking forward to it but knowing it was necessary and feeling ready to brace the firestorm she knew was waiting, she went to see Marty French.

Marty French's office was a testament to his feminine traits. Myra could never decide if it was a law office or sitting room. Though only slightly larger than her own, Marty's office seemed spacious by comparison. When he took over as chief counsel of the public defender's office, Marty, at his own expense, hired an interior decorator to outfit his office. The end result was something akin to a retro seventies art deco lounge. A mint-green deep-pile carpet supported an economy of furniture. Other than a thick cushioned winged Louis XIV chair behind a single glass-topped chrome-legged desk, there was only a large vinyl-covered sectional strewn with pastel-colored oversized pillows. Behind the desk, wood-paneled walls were fronted by faux orange-crate boxes that stacked themselves one on top of the other between the ends of floor-to-ceiling shelves of law books, the contents of which Marty constantly reminded his staff he had committed to memory. Gay, yes. Bright, exceptionally.

Marty's secretary was Lorna, a very tall, gangly unattractive brunette who'd come to the PD's office straight from business college. In the twenty-five years since her arrival she'd never missed a day of work, and without exception maintained a daily routine of early arrival and late departure. She was loyal, efficient, did not socialize and did not gossip. With no husband, no children, and fading prospects for either, she lived frugally and schooled herself in managing her meager salary. Myra was the only one in the office who sensed that Lorna's frugality had made her rich. Though she never discussed her personal business with anyone, she became despondent following her mother's death and came sobbing to Myra for someone to talk to. Only then did a hint about the enormity of her wealth slip out. Myra wondered why she still continued to work, guessed her solitary life knew nothing else.

Lorna flashed a toothy smile as Myra walked in, asked about her vacation, had too much class to comment about her neck. She rang through to her boss, announcing Myra's presence, brought her enormous six-foot frame out of the chair and over to the door, opening it for Myra to pass.

Tom Mesereau was the only other lawyer Myra knew who was as impeccably dressed as Marty French. Giorgio Armani suits, Van Heusen pin-striped shirts, silk ties, and matching suspenders were a daily ensemble that never repeated itself in the same month. Seated at his desk with eyes buried in paperwork, he did not look up or acknowledge Myra until she'd crossed the room and dropped down on the sectional. Only then did he bring his steel-gray eyes off the desk and onto her face. Myra got the impression it was almost an effort.

"Myra. Enjoy your vacation?" Marty asked matter-of-factly, eyes seeking out her neck, trying not to be obvious.

"Got a tan," Myra said, rubbing it in.

"I've often wanted to go to Cancún. Never seemed to manage it. I don't suppose you were ready to come back."

"Who wants to leave when you're enjoying yourself. Especially in Cancún. Never seems to be enough time."

"Vacations are like that," Marty said, dropping his eyes back to the paperwork, giving up on Myra's neck. "Well," he went on, change of tone to the formal, signaling the end of banter, beginning of business. "Good to have you back, Myra."

"Can't say I'm overjoyed," Myra said, trace of impatience in her voice, last vestiges of blue water, sun-drenched white sand beaches fading rapidly with the change in mood. The edge had faded for the most part, but not entirely. She still needed a hit of something, hoped it didn't show, played it off by kicking off her shoes, stretching out full length on the sectional like she was relaxing at home.

The steel-gray eyes and movie-star face didn't appreciate Myra's informal presumption. "Vacation's over, Myra," Marty said frostily.

Myra made no apology. She cut her eyes at Marty, sucked air through disgusted teeth, and sat up. Swinging her legs back to the floor and realizing Marty would see her neck, she braced for the comments she knew were coming. Marty French was nothing if not a fanatic about proper dress and appearance on the part of his staff. Particularly his female PDs. He did not like tight-fitting short skirts, revealing blouses, or makeup beyond a thin application of lipstick. Anything more got you the riot act. Maybe fired. The PD's office was not a democracy. Marty French was president for life.

Myra slipped on her shoes, straightened up for the lecture.

But he didn't mention her neck. He wasn't looking at her at all. He was perusing case jackets on his desk.

"Let's go over your cases, Myra," Marty said.

"All right, chief. Who's on first?"

"You talk to Craig?"

Myra said she had.

"You satisfied?"

Myra said she was. Told him about her conversation with Roderick, disposition of her cases. Marty listened dispassionately, nodded his head in approval when she'd finished.

"You and Craig make a good team." The comment caught her off guard. Then it dawned on her why he hadn't mentioned her neck. Craig McInnis had worked a deal of some kind in her absence, the midget motherfucker. Without asking, she knew what was coming.

"You've got to be kidding!"

"Look at the results if you don't believe me. You and Craig have the highest acquittal rate in the office."

"So?"

"Soooo . . ." Marty reached into a drawer, pulled out a stack of files, pushed them across the desk to Myra. "I want you and Craig to work on these together. There are some constitutional issues we can bring to the table, especially in light of the Rampart scandal."

"What's all this teamwork about, Marty? Why not just separate them—half to Craig, half to me?"

"This office has always been a team, Myra, or have you lost sight of that?"

Myra bristled. "What's that supposed to mean?"

"Just what I said, Myra. This office is a team. Any one defendant belongs to all of us. You and Craig are very skilled defense attorneys. Your understanding of case law and the thorough preparation you undertake is why you two have been so successful. And with the client population we have to serve, that's no easy matter. But you act as if Myra Cross is the only attorney in this office. You following me, Myra?"

Only too well, Myra thought. Marty was guarding his ego *and* his power base. The news articles about her in the local papers must be getting next to him. She wondered what he would say if he knew what she was really planning. No matter. She'd be gone by then anyway. But for now she was pissed that Craig had exploited Marty's weak side.

"And when did I not consult any senior staff when it was necessary?"

"But you do it grudgingly, Myra. That's what I'm talking about. This 'when it's necessary' attitude of yours."

She couldn't argue that one. She'd become a standout almost from the beginning when she'd won an acquittal in the Raymond case, a very high-profile case in which movie actor Ralph Raymond was killed by his supposed lover in a jealous rage. The DA's office presented an airtight case with DNA matches and videotape from a surveillance camera. But from the beginning Myra's gut feeling that her client was innocent drove her to investigate well beyond Marty's recommendation, with the admonition that using the PD's resources on such a hopeless case, especially a high-profile case, could well mean the end of her public service. But Myra was dogged in her investigation, and what she uncovered and presented to the jury read like a movie. Her client had a twin separated at birth whom she'd never met. A slew of investigators were able to locate the twin. Myra proved she was mentally ill, had stolen her twin's identity, and was in the area at the time of the homicide with no verifiable alibi. This explained the matching DNA and likeness on the videotape.

Myra became a minor celebrity with the acquittal, turned down lucrative offers to join prestigious Century City law firms because she astutely recognized she'd lose her autonomy in hundred-member firms, enjoyed being a big fish in a small pond. Knew too they'd see her success as a fluke, begin demanding sexual favors as the price of partnership. She wouldn't mind the sex necessarily, but not as a bargaining chip for the use of her intellect.

But if the Raymond case had made Myra a celebrity, it had also made her arrogant. Not in a boastful or obnoxious way, but in swelling her self-confidence to a fault. She began feeling if not actually believing it unnecessary to consult with colleagues or peers except in rare instances. This was what Marty meant. And if it was just between her and Marty she could deal with it. But Craig McInnis?

"Why do I have to partner with Craig?" she asked, knowing it was Craig's idea from the get-go, that the teamwork idea was bull-shit. "Why not Janice or Melvin or Ignacio?"

"Why not with Craig? He's bright. Aggressive."

"And Janice isn't?"

"Of course she is. So is Melvin and Ignacio and a host of others around here. But you two are exceptions. I'd like to take advantage of that, put together a dream team of my own. Bring in Janice and the others if you want," Marty added reluctantly as a concession. "But I want to start with you two."

"This something Craig thought up?"

Marty cut his eyes at Myra. He said, "This is something I want, Myra. You on board or not?"

Poker time. Myra didn't miss the veiled threat in Marty's voice. She wasn't ready to leave the PD's office just yet. Not until she talked with Jason Rice. Better fold on this hand. She stood abruptly, scooped the files from Marty's desk.

"Absolutely, Marty. Teamwork can only make things better for our clients. I'll hook up with Craig first thing tomorrow, get right on top of things."

Marty smiled and flashed his steel-gray eyes in victory. He said, "Knew you'd see the wisdom of the idea." He gestured to the files with polished nails and added, "One of the defendants there requested you personally, Myra. Ought to make him feel pretty good to know he's got not one but two PDs working his case, wouldn't you think?"

Myra glanced at the files, frowned. "Who?"

Marty looked away, thinking. "Three-striker. Booker something or other . . ." Then he snapped his fingers and said, "Napoleon, right. Napoleon T. Booker. What mother in her right mind would name a child Napoleon?" He said it as if insulted.

"Napoleon was a general."

"Who caught his third strike at Waterloo and was banished for life. What does that tell you?"

"That his mother wanted a role model, a chance for her son to make the history books instead of the eleven o'clock news."

It was one of the few times she'd ever heard Marty laugh. "Role model? This Napoleon's a drug dealer looking at twenty-five years in Soledad, only he doesn't have rank on his shoulders." Marty was having fun and still laughing. "I wouldn't bet against him making the news. But I guarantee you, Myra, absolutely guarantee you, no one will ever read about him in the history books. You helped him beat a one eighty-seven three years ago. Figures you're his get-out-of-jail ticket. Name familiar?"

Myra thought it was. "And he wants me?"

"Everybody wants you, Myra." Marty couldn't stop the smile that came and went from his lips. "That's why I'm pairing you with Craig—so you don't get overloaded. I'm sure you can appreciate that."

It took great effort for Myra to rein in her anger, then realized his remark, as tactless as it was, was not entirely without truth. Biting the bullet, she turned to go without comment. Just as she reached the door, Marty's voice came across her shoulder, demanding and flushed with control. "Glad to have you back, Myra. But make sure your neck is covered when you go to court tomorrow. It's already a circus—no reason to turn it into a soap opera. Ask Lorna to step in, won't you. Thanks."

Marty French didn't miss a thing—waiting till the end to twist the knife, the cocksucker. She didn't bother to turn around, thought it prudent to let Marty have the pot, wait for the next deal of the cards and a better hand. She felt the edge returning now, knew she needed a hit or she'd explode. Nodding to Lorna in Marty's direction as she closed the door, she left the office and headed for the elevators. If Jason Rice was right, her time in the PD's office would soon be nothing but a memory. Her reputation, however, would be an entirely different matter.

CHAPTER 3

FOR FORTY-TWO of his sixty-three years Jason Rice had photographed some of the world's most glamorous women for just about every magazine in which they were featured. Having started out submitting his work freelance, he was soon under contract with *Playboy*, where he built his reputation as a photographer who understood the subtleties of light and shadows that framed the female form. Over time he was hired away by *Penthouse*, who lost him to *Hustler* and a succession of other magazines from the prestigious to the sleazy. He had a knack for making homely women look attractive and attractive women look gorgeous. He was professional at all times and lived with his gay lover of ten years in the apartment over his Argyle Street studio in Hollywood.

Myra Cross was drop-dead gorgeous. He could tell that when he first saw the Polaroids she'd sent him: a series of photos of her sitting on a window ledge, modestly dressed in a cleavage-revealing halter top and pleated dress falling across her waist, exposing bare fleshy legs. He sensed she might be a natural. Confirmed it when he met her in person and realized she was a photographer's dream—that rare creature whose beauty needs no enhancement. It wasn't her chest that impressed him. It was the way her face caught the light, threw its rays across her emerald eyes into the strands of luminous red hair.

They'd shot some studio poses to submit around, got first bite from *Playboy*, who wanted Myra in their upcoming Professional Women's issue. They had a surgeon from Virginia, an accountant from Chicago, an engineer from Dallas, a dentist from Miami, a magazine editor from New York, an architect from Birmingham, and several college professors from around the country. Myra would be the lawyer. But time was of the essence. They needed the pics yesterday.

Timing. The first four days of Myra's Cancún vacation were spent in front of Jason Rice's lens, the remaining time with her flavor of the moment, Assistant District Attorney Bruce Marshall. He'd planned to join Myra three days after her departure. Soon as his trial was over, he said. Besides, no sense in raising eyebrows among the gossips in the DA's office who knew how to add. But Myra asked if he could make it five, buying herself more time in front of the camera, not ready to tell him or anyone for that matter about the *Playboy* spread. This was more important than sex . . . for the moment.

She would've gotten more of a tan than she did, but Bruce wanted to make up for lost time, kept her in bed the first few days he was there. Not that Myra had objected. She loved the sex. She didn't love Bruce particularly, but he was a hunk to look at, with a Brad Pitt chin and a Schwarzenegger physique. He was intelligent and had a sense of humor that kept her laughing. She just wished she could've gotten a better tan.

She arrived at Jason's studio as soon as rush-hour traffic spit her out of the Hollywood freeway's parking lot onto the Vine Street exit. She was sweating when she walked in his studio and knew why. So did the photographer.

Myra said, "I need something to take the edge off, Jason."

Jason said, "What's your poison?"

"Got any blow?"

"In the john, Myra."

There weren't many places you could hide a stash in the thimble that passed for a bathroom. Myra found it inside the toilet bowl, sucked up three lines, came out feeling like the fifty-foot woman.

Wiping white residue from her nose, Myra said, "Thanks."

"Glad I could oblige your nose," he said. Jason frowned on drug users, but knew enough to keep some of everything on hand so the whole shoot wouldn't be wasted on clients so wired he couldn't get a decent shot.

The walls of Jason's studio were covered with signed photos of clients. Some famous, some just photogenic. One wall was covered with numerous shots of a bare-chested man half Jason's age. Myra figured that first day in his studio that it was his lover and said so. He never answered her, of course. He just smiled, brushed back the shock of wavy gray hair from his forehead, and started twirling the waxed ends of the handlebar mustache that supported his nose.

"You ready now, Myra?"

Expecting to see large prints of her own photo shoot pasted up on the walls, she was disappointed to find only proof sheets, tried to adjust to looking through a magnifying glass, see if Cancún was really there. Jason assured her it was, that what she was looking at was history in the making.

He explained the spread would include five poses. A three-quarter-page close-up of her face with a byline would introduce her. On the other side would be the remaining four: one of her dressed in her professional attire, which they had shot in front of a bookcase made to resemble a law library where Myra was posed studying a law book; and the other three would be nude shots of her in Cancún. Jason had marked his favorites with a grease pencil. One of her walking out of the surf backlit by the silhouette of a golden sunset. Another of Myra on the sand, a wanton, sexy pose of her sitting up, head thrown back, hands running through her hair, lips parted, laughing. The last shot: Myra stretched out on wet sand, head cradled in one arm, the forefinger of the other hand in her mouth like Babydoll.

Myra liked them all but wanted two others. One lying in the surf, her back arched, body slightly twisted toward the camera as water washed over her, hand on her crotch, face contorted in ecstasy. The other pose more provocative, almost pornographic: a shot of her lying on her back, both knees pulled up to her chest and wide apart, one hand on her crotch, her face toward the camera, sucking on her forefinger as if it were a lollipop. Jason said *Playboy* would never publish them because they weren't in good taste. Myra said she figured that, agreed on his choices but wanted copies of the others for herself.

"I suspect you'll get lots of offers once the spread appears."

Myra laughed. "I can imagine what kind too."

Jason said, "Never know. Issue they did a couple years ago sprung a couple of teachers into their own talk shows."

Myra said, "I could do talk shows. Call it *Myra's One Night Stand.* Format with men and women talking about the best fuck they'd ever had. Bring on their partners to either refute it or agree. If they disagreed, I'd set 'em up with new partners, have them come back after a one night stand, and tell how the sex was. Guarantee you the ratings would bury Oprah *and* Jerry Springer."

"Myra's One Night Stand," Jason said with some amusement, repeating it once again, getting the feel if it. "Myra, you're shameless. Absolutely shameless."

"No truer words were ever spoken."

Jason laughed. "You'll draw a crowd with that subject."

"Sex sells."

"Always has."

"Ever thought your might have had a life before this one?"

"A courtesan?" Myra laughed in delight. "If so I bet I was the best lay any king ever had. The way I see it, Cleopatra didn't know how to treat a man. She should've fucked Mark Anthony's brains out and then some. Continent of Europe would be much different today if she had. Trust me."

Jason said, "You intend to have gays on your talk show?"

Myra said, "Why not. Maybe bring you on . . . show you what you're missing. Tempted to do you myself, if you want to know the truth about it. You're still quite a hunk for a man your age, case you don't know it, Jason." Myra's eyes appraising him up and down, showing their disappointment at the fact he was gay.

Jason laughed hard. He said, "Men tell me that all the time." He looked fondly, almost reverently at the photo of his lover on the wall, started playing with the locks of hair gracing his forehead. "You're a gorgeous woman, Myra," he went on, twisting the ends of his mustache. "I suspect straight men really enjoy you, with your red hair, big tits, and all." He shook his head. "But not me. There's nothing you can do for me, as unbelievable as that may sound."

Wasn't that the truth. Myra couldn't imagine any man ever telling her that. She sucked air between her teeth, shook her head. "What a waste. Hunk like you. Don't know what you're missing."

Jason looked at the photo again, raised his eyebrows in approval. "Nothing," he said. "I'm not missing a thing. Be happy to come on your show, though. Show some of my work. Get my fifteen minutes of fame."

Myra said, "So long as you bring your lover and talk about sex."

Jason said, "Is there anything else?"

"Not really. Money, I guess, if you're into that."

"And power. Don't forget power," the photographer said.

Myra said, "The big three—money, sex, and power, not necessarily in that order."

Jason laughed. "These shots are gonna change your life, Myra. Hope you understand that. They're gonna make you a star."

Same thing her father had said that day he pulled two-year-old Myra out of her playpen, smeared a fingertip of her mother's rouge on her cheeks, swiped a thumb of lipstick across her lips, gave Myra a sixteen-year advance on her femininity. "You, young lady, are going to be a star," he'd said. "It's your destiny." And started Myra on the path that very same day. She began piano lessons. Singing lessons. Dancing lessons. He entered Myra in every fashion show and junior-miss beauty pageant there was. Wiping away the tears when she lost. Enthusiastic and encouraging whenever she won.

He was present at every piano and dance recital Myra had. From day one Myra's father was her biggest fan.

Not so her mother. She thought it was nonsense and refused to participate in her grooming for a career in entertainment. School was the only thing that mattered. Myra was smart. Gifted. She needed to get her education. Not to waste the gift of her superior intellect on the frivolity and pie-in-the-sky wishful thinking of entertainment. She seldom if ever attended the recitals and never came to fashion shows or beauty pageants. But that was okay with Myra, because it was Daddy who was there. It was Daddy behind her, always pushing her toward her destiny.

Until he suddenly left. Disappeared on her tenth birthday with another woman and never returned. And the dream died. Right then and there. The dancing lessons stopped. Singing lessons. Piano lessons. Fashion shows. Beauty pageants. All of it stopped. Her mother, open in her bitterness at the abandonment, destroying in Myra everything that reminded her of the betrayal. Absolutely everything.

Except the idea. It may have been smothered by her mother, but it never completely died. And though her mother's insistence that Myra pursue a professional career prevailed, the idea of a pre-ordained destiny her father had planted so deeply in Myra's psychic lay percolating just below the surface. It may have taken twenty years to break through, but it finally did. Myra Cross was destined to be a star, and the time was now.

Myra's face brightened. She said, "God, I hope so."

"Well," said Jason more seriously, expression of levity gone from his face. "Your reputation might be the first to change. Sure you want that?"

"Other women in the issue worried about their reputations?"

The photographer didn't know. He guessed not.

"Appreciate your concern, Jason," Myra said after a moment. "But I've had a reputation as a slut since I was fifteen, and I'm still considered a slut even though I was Phi Beta Kappa all through college and law school." She went on rather lamely, cocaine beginning to take over. "So what's a reputation, really, in the grand scheme of things?"

"Was me, Myra, I'd start worrying about my lawyer's license," Jason said, eyebrows raised, fanning his face with the proof sheet. "This stuff is hot. I can't imagine they'll take you seriously as a lawyer once this hits the newsstands, accuse you of perverting the legal system, making a mockery of the scales of justice. How can they permit you to represent people with this image? And you're a high-profile gal. Don't think there won't be pressure to get you disbarred . . . !"

Myra laughed and said, "I can tell you don't watch much TV. They've got legal shows with female attorneys so anorexic they're almost invisible and some so big they belong in a circus. Doesn't interfere with their brainpower in the courtroom, though. And besides," Myra went on, ringed fingers smoothing back wisps of red hair, "in France they do TV commercials in the nude, so what's a spread in *Playboy*? Go figure!"

"True," Jason said, "but that's France. They're in the real world. Over here everyone's still living in the dark ages and fully dressed in prime time. You'll be butt naked for the whole world to see. How's that gonna play Myra, you walk into a courtroom after the spread hits. No one's gonna see you dressed, only that picture in the magazine."

Myra said, "And you don't think I won't have the jury's complete and undivided attention? Why, after the spread comes out I could get a serial killer off a murder beef if the entire jury had been present during commission of the crime."

"That would be a gross miscarriage of justice, Myra. I can see the headlines, '*Playboy* Centerfold Gets Not Guilty Verdict for Serial Killer, Nudity Definitely a Factor in Jury's Verdict According to Prosecution.' Won't do much to instill faith in the criminal justice system. Sell a hell of a lot of magazines, though."

"May as well be in one now, way they stare at me in court," Myra said, hands brushing her chest. "Looking at me like they have X-ray vision . . . undressing me head to toe . . . eyes fixed on my boobs like they were crystal balls in a fortune-teller's tent."

Jason said, "They can't help it, Myra. Your sexuality jumps right out at people. No one's fault really. You are who you are. A natural."

And just who *was* Myra Cross. That question had plagued her since birth. She was a woman whose sexuality was not easily explained. It wasn't how she dressed, the dozen or so ways she styled her red hair, or the swatches of color on full lips that spoke volumes when they parted in ecstasy or in anger. It wasn't how she walked on firm, shapely legs or the subtle, unpretentious wiggle to her hips leading the cart of legal briefs. And it wasn't the raspy June Allyson voice that was so soft and controlled as to be nearly inaudible on some occasions, so shrill as to be heard a block away on others. Nor was it her brilliant analytical mind and genius-level intellect that so intimidated courtroom adversaries, could charm a jury box of twelve strangers, or enrapture lovers in the bedroom. No, it wasn't any of those things that explained her sexuality. It was divined.

Myra Cross was a throwback. A dinosaur. A woman born to be a trophy in a time and place that rendered trophy women obsolete and powerless. And while she may have been many things, power-less was not one of them. Her power was an inherited intellectual genius and an uncanny sexual essence. Both first noticed in infancy, both developed without persuasion or encouragement in childhood until blossoming as an adult into a hypersensual woman of unimaginable presence with absolutely no effort on her part. There was really no other way to explain it. No matter what effort or steps she might take to diminish this gift, this curse—and over the course of her life she had come to see it more as a curse than a gift—it was futile.

The photographer was right. Her sexuality jumped out as if it had a mind of its own. And for all intents and purposes it did. Whatever its source, Myra Cross, thirty-one-year-old divorcée and honored member of the bar was indeed, if she was nothing else, a natural.

"The bar," Myra said derisively after a moment, making a futile effort to suck back drivel forming at her nose, cocaine working its way into her reasoning. "Just who the hell is the bar, Jason?" And before Jason could open his mouth she added, "I'll tell you who the bar is . . . the bar is a group of hypocritical lawyers who sit in judgment of everyone but themselves. And to a man . . . and woman, they'd give their eyeteeth to get between my legs," and she knew this was true because several had tried. "Trust me on that."

Jason said, "Oh, I do, Myra. I do. If anyone would know, it'd be you."

"'He who is without sin cast the first stone.' Isn't that what the Bible says?"

"I'm an atheist."

"No matter. I'm not doing anything immoral. There's no man in the photos. What's the bar going to say . . . I can't practice 'cause I posed nude in a magazine they jack off to?"

"They might!"

"What?" Myra went on, knowing her argument was moot and naive, that it was cocaine speaking on her behalf, and not really caring. "You can be a lawyer if you're an alcoholic or a drug addict. Bar doesn't mind that. But if you appear nude in *Playboy*—oh no, can't have that! You can't be a lawyer because you don't fit the image. What a bunch of horseshit!"

"In your profession I imagine image is everything."

Drivel from her nose washing her upper lip, Myra said pointedly, "You mean in *your* profession image is everything. In mine it's many shades of gray. Ever see *The Verdict*, movie with Paul Newman?"

He hadn't.

Fueled by cocaine, her reasoning somewhere in space, Myra withdrew a handkerchief from her purse, wiped the drivel from her nose, and said stupidly, "Newman was an alcoholic lawyer who came back from the brink to win a case. He wasn't disbarred!"

Jason reminded her she was still on earth. He said, "That was a movie, Myra."

"No matter. Real-world lawyers coached the actors. So what does that tell you about the legal system?"

Jason sighed through a smile. He said, "It tells me Paul Newman has aged well. Too bad he's not gay. But we're talking real-world stuff here, Myra. Not Hollywood make-believe. Society gets rather sensitive about the image of its public servants."

Myra couldn't resist. She said, "You mean public servants like Bill Clinton?"

Jason shook his head in defeat, laughed softly. "You're good, Myra."

Myra winked, put the handkerchief away. "Men tell me that all the time."

"They tell me that too," Jason said, sheepish grin on his face, eyebrows raised in sly truth. "But I don't have a license to lose— you do. I'm just watching out for your interests, that's all," the photographer said, genuine concern behind the words.

Myra said, "I appreciate that, Jason, but I'm trying to make a point here. Is there really any difference between a lawyer who's a lush and one who's nude in a magazine?"

"One's got bigger tits," Jason said. He returned the proofs to the file cabinet, walked Myra to her car. "All I'm saying, Myra, once I turn these in, all hell's gonna break loose. Hate to think my work ended your legal career."

"If it does, I'll thank you personally," Myra said, her remote beeping off the alarm before she opened the door, slipped into soft leather. "Stop looking at the glass half empty. Your pictures might jump-start my entertainment career, get me signed with William Morris, my own TV show."

Myra started the engine, lowered the window, put the car in gear. She said, "Way I see it, Jason, legal briefs and condoms go hand in hand in my business. Call me, you beautiful hunk of wasted manhood."

Jason said he would, kissed Myra on the forehead, waved as she drove off, and knew the next time he saw her she'd be famous.

Or infamous . . .

CHAPTER 4

RUSH-HOUR TRAFFIC to Brentwood from Hollywood was not for the impatient. And Myra, still wired on cocaine, decided a shorter trip and a place to relax a better way to spend the ninety-minute drive time. So she doubled back almost as soon as she left Jason's office, took the I-5 freeway south toward downtown and Bruce Marshall's eleventh-floor condominium in Bunker Hill's Promenade Towers.

To say his face registered delight when he opened the door would be an understatement. Euphoria would be more like it. With his six-foot-four-inch frame filling the doorway, the Brad Pitt chin, bare, well-toned Schwarzenegger chest, six-pack abs dripping wet, towel around his waist, another one drying out locks of graying hair, Bruce Marshall belonged on the cover of *GQ*. Myra shivered. There ought to be a law, man this handsome. She knew this would not be the brief stopover she'd planned. He'd have to kick her out, if such a thing was possible.

"Stranger," he said, powerful arm going around her waist, pulling her into a room filled with Charlie Parker, closing the door. "Just got through working out and was on my way to dinner. Chinese?"

Myra took off her jacket, flung it on a couch, started undoing buttons on her blouse. She shook her head. "Later, maybe. Can we go to bed first?"

Her directness, one of the things he liked about Myra. And that voluptuous body of hers.

"You have to ask?"

"Well, a girl shouldn't be presumptuous, I always say."

"You may be as presumptuous as you want," he said, "but one day I'm going to say no." Helping her with the buttons, soft kisses on her lips and neck in the process, tongue probing her ear. Myra, eyes closed, relishing the moment.

"But not today," she said.

"No. Not today." Hands around her waist, underneath her panties, caressing her butt. Her tongue finding his, playing tag.

"And probably not tomorrow."

"Probably not tomorrow." Still kissing her, bringing hands around front, reaching under her bra, touching sensitive nipples that made her flinch.

"And probably not ever."

"You're right. I'm addicted to you," he said.

Myra slipped out of her skirt, stockings, and panties in a single motion and turned so he could unfasten her bra. She welcomed the feel of soft hands on liberated breasts, reached behind to feel his growing erection.

"Addiction is a serious illness," she said.

"Should I get treatment?"

"You could go into rehab."

"How long would it take?"

"The rest of your life."

"I could try cold turkey."

"You wouldn't like it."

"Then what do you suggest?"

"Guess you'll have to stay addicted."

"What do I do in the meantime?"

"Fuck me before I go crazy."

Bruce let the towel drop to the floor and turned Myra in his arms, pressing her close to his erection, kissing her about the face and neck, working down to her nipples before effortlessly scooping her up in his arms and laying her on the bed, his tongue working the entire length of her body, spending time on hardened nipples, even more time priming the pump between her legs. And it wouldn't take much more than that to get Myra aroused. He'd learned that about her in their on-again, off-again year together. She didn't need a lot of foreplay. It was her nipples, really. So sensitive that just a few kisses and caresses would turn them rock hard. And once that happened Myra was on autopilot.

She asked him to take her from behind so he could stimulate her G-spot. She'd discovered the pleasure of her G-spot during her brief marriage, the only good thing that came from her two years of conscription to a man who believed in ownership and the missionary position. Bruce, on the other hand, was open-minded and not afraid to experiment—except when it came to group sex, partner swapping, and orgies. He wasn't *that* open-minded. But he had one of the best tongues she'd ever felt. He was a good fuck buddy. And for Myra Cross, that was more than enough. Of course, it didn't hurt that he was a hunk as well as an intellectual equal who liked jazz.

Their movements, so tentative at first, so needy and desirous with excitement of penetration, reached the point of unbearable pleasure. Their breathing synchronous but harsh and broken, four eyes closed on two faces contorted in pleasure, fingers grasping and clawing violently at each other. Myra, body arching, twisting and turning in a race to her climax, finally screamed in ecstasy as her G-spot imploded in the rapture of orgasm, so paralyzing her with pleasure she couldn't move, didn't want to move. She felt the sudden weight on her back, knew they'd come together, like the uncontrollable spasms of Charlie Parker's frenzied exploding riffs. Their bodies awash in the intoxicating smell of their sex, exhausted and spent and wet with perspiration, they collapsed together on the bed like a bridge suddenly shaken off its foundation, prisoners of the lush aftermath of ecstasy. It was this moment, the aftermath, this cuddling that Myra enjoyed so much, seeking the comfort of arms that held her securely, soft hands that cupped her breast, Charlie Parker and company giving them a tour of Paris in April.

For Myra, sex had been a never-ending search for love, a search that began on her tenth birthday. Born and raised in the land of the Phoenix Suns, Myra and younger brother Nathan, two years her junior, had lived a relatively stable existence presided over by her schoolteacher mother and engineer father. Her mother, caring but somewhat limited in her ability to relate affectionately to Myra, could at times be aloof and unapproachable. Like the day nine-year-old Myra's period started and her mother gave her a box of pads and said, "Take care of it." No explanation, no instructions. Nothing. Her father, on the other hand, was quite the opposite. A warm, loving, and affectionate man who doted on both children from birth. "Daddy's little girl," "My little man," he called them. Myra the bright, precocious one. Nathan the athlete. But all that ended on Myra's tenth birthday. The memory of that awful day still burned in her mind like a hot brand on cowhide. The birthday party, the excitement and awe of a table full of ten-year-olds as each present was opened, the blowing out of the candles, the making of a wish. Her father arriving home late, arms carrying an enormous box, but saying he had to get back to work, staying just long enough to see her open the present, squeal with delight at the dollhouse, give kisses and hugs of appreciation. And he was gone.

She would never see her father again. A brief phone conversation the next day telling her he wouldn't be coming home anymore, but to be a good girl, do well in school, and mind her mother. Her mother in tears Myra didn't understand, thinking Daddy was going away on a job for a while. But her mother explained he'd found somebody else and was never coming back. And when it finally sunk in, that her father had abandoned her, she blamed herself. It had to be something she did. There was no other explanation. After all, she was Daddy's little girl. Why would he stop loving her like that unless she'd done something wrong? But what? Just up and leave her like that? Why?

And while three years later her mother would marry Edward, a man who would be a responsible and congenial stepfather, the abandonment by her own father was a blow from which neither she nor her brother would ever fully recover. For her brother it would lead to stealing, juvenile delinquency, and alcoholism. For Myra it would be sex and drugs.

The sex came first.

Six months after that awful day, Myra began to notice the change. Just as her mind had developed early, so did her body. Almost overnight it seemed. And before Myra was midway through her eleventh year she was as fully developed as she would be at thirty. Myra was not initially as preoccupied with sex as were her girlfriends, the majority of whom by the age of twelve had already dabbled in one form of sex or another, and because she hadn't, they'd made fun of Myra and accused her of being a lesbian. So to placate her detractors, and partially out of her own curiosity, she decided to experiment. Losing her virginity to a boy of fourteen she hardly knew. And because Myra never did anything halfway, once the experiment was over she was absolutely convinced she was pregnant, in her own mind a justified punishment for having caused her father to leave. She wasn't, of course, but the very idea kept her away from any sexual indulgence until she was fifteen.

That's when she met Bobby Robin. A nerd of the first order who was president of the math club, science club, engineering club, and chemistry club. He was a grossly overweight boy whose only saving grace besides his gifted intellect was perfectly straight teeth hidden under a sandpaper face of pimples. A fifteen-year-old boy genius who, because of his weight and pimples, had to endure derisive nicknames like "whale man," "blubber boy," and "body fat." Myra had always felt sorry for the underdog, and Bobby Robin was an underdog if she ever saw one. He had no friends to speak of, moving around every three years because his father was in the air force. And the idea that any girl would ever kiss him, let alone have sex with him, made him the butt of cruel jokes from one end of the campus to the other. And because he lived not far from Myra, and she had to pass his house to get to hers, they often found themselves walking home together after school. One day he asked if she wanted to come in and listen to records. There was nobody home and they could turn the music up as loud as they wanted. Which is how Myra came to like jazz, because the records Bobby was talking about were not pop records but his father's prized jazz collection. Listening to this strange music with this strangely gifted companion was exciting to Myra in an odd sort of way, and pretty soon stopping by his house after school became a ritual. Sometimes they would do homework together, other times work together on one school project or another, all the while Myra learning about jazz, the artists, their place in musical history.

One day, during John Coltrane's "My Favorite Things," Myra got the urge to have sex. She asked Bobby if he wanted to, but he became angry and asked her to leave, telling her, and understandably so, that she wasn't being serious, that she was teasing him and making fun of him like all the other girls. To prove he was wrong Myra suddenly took off all her clothes, her *Playboy* centerfold body standing butt naked in front of him and John Coltrane, asking was this enough proof she was serious. Bobby Robin nearly fainted, saying he'd never had sex and didn't know what to do. Myra said she'd show him and did. So besides homework, jazz, and science projects they added sex to their daily after-school routine.

Four months later Myra became pregnant. She wasn't surprised really, but had some sleepless nights at first. She didn't tell Bobby Robin or her mother, just forged her mother's name on the health clinic's permission slip and had an abortion, getting some birth control pills during a follow-up visit. Blaming her two-week school absence on the flu, Myra resumed her involvement with Bobby Robin for the rest of the school year. Then his father announced he was being transferred to Alaska and Bobby Robin left. As a memento he gave Myra a CD set of John Coltrane's favorite hits, saying he'd write every day and meaning it, Myra saying that whenever she heard "My Favorite Things" she'd think of him and meaning it. Myra's going-away present a card and a sexy picture of

herself taken with a Polaroid she signed "Love always," Myra saying she would write too.

And she did—for six weeks. After that Myra came to realize she
needed more than a letter and John Coltrane, she needed love—
the nearly yearlong routine of five-days-a-week sex triggering a
long dormant, unquenchable thirst for affection. So she became a
slut in search of love, running through high school athletic teams
like fire through dry grass. Strangely enough, however, sex with the
magnificently sculptured jocks wasn't nearly as satisfying as it had
been with the overweight, pimply-faced Bobby Robin. And it
wasn't until the end of her senior year that she finally came to
understand why. She'd never been in love with Bobby Robin. She
knew that. Yet she could have fulfilling and gratifying sex with a
boy others called ugly because in him she had a boy who loved and
worshiped her. Like her father. The jocks, on the other hand, just
wanted to fuck and tell. So she knew it wasn't about looks. It had
to be his intellect. The catalyst that stimulated her brain also made
sex with an unappealing boy far more fulfilling than with any team
captain. And from that moment on, when it finally dawned on
Myra she was turned on more by intellect than looks, she began
choosing her sexual partners by IQ instead of jersey numbers. The
one exception was Richard.

That's when the drugs started.

Having graduated with every honor her Phoenix high school
could offer and attending college on a full four-year scholarship,
she'd met Richard near the end of her freshman year at a sorority
party. A veteran from the Gulf War and five years her senior, he'd
gotten out of the army and was in college on the GI Bill. The thing
that struck her about him right off was his humor. The man was
out-and-out funny. She'd never met anyone like him. Not exceptionally good-looking and nowhere near her equal on the IQ scale.
But that didn't seem to matter. He was absolutely hysterical to be
around. Life of the party. Literally. And good in bed, especially
after he'd had a few beers and smoked a couple of joints. And while

Myra had experimented one or two times in high school with weed, it was not her recreational vehicle of choice. But Richard showed her how to tell the difference between good pot and bad, showed her how to cut open a blunt, fill it with weed, get the best buzz in the world. How to roll her own joint with Zig-Zags.

He insisted that Myra try PCP, gave her a Sherman, but Myra didn't like the strange and bizarre feeling it gave her. So he introduced her to the world of cocaine and the freebase pipe. First he showed her how to lay out the lines on a flat surface, suck them into her nose through a rolled dollar bill or a short straw. Then how to smoke primos and finally how to freebase it: smoke it with a pipe—dropping in the rock, lighting it, bringing the vapors into her lungs deep, holding it until her brain started to misfire. Myra couldn't believe something could feel that good. Better than sex at times. And when she added good Colombian weed to the menu, well then, there just wasn't anything else quite like it on earth. Except maybe good sex.

So she married Richard the beginning of her sophomore year, more for the good times and drugs than the sex, not really sure she was doing the right thing, telling herself she was "in love" and not meaning it. Not telling her mother until after the fact, knowing she wouldn't have approved, knowing too she wouldn't have approved no matter who she married.

She told Richard she was going to law school. Richard had said that was fine, he was going to be an engineer. But he flunked out after only one year because he stayed high all of the time. And absolutely paranoid about losing Myra. So much so he'd quit his part-time job as a mechanic to follow her to and from school. Finally Myra got tired of his jealousy and possessiveness and divorced him after two years of marriage. Richard said he'd never let her go, that he'd always be with her. And in a way he was right. For while the police and several stints in jail finally broke him of his obsession with Myra, he'd bequeathed Myra an addiction to drugs that clung to her like a tube of Super Glue.

"How was your first day back?" Bruce asked after a while, rapture beginning to slip away, need to talk replacing it. They'd just had great sex and he wanted to talk shop—Myra remembered this tendency as one of the things she didn't like about Bruce. With great effort she pulled herself out of the void, said it was the same as when she'd left, never-ending stream of defendants through a revolving door. She told him about her exchange with Clara, but didn't think it prudent to mention Marty French's change in staff assignments for ethical reasons. Bruce was, after all, an adversary in the DA's office. No reason to be Helen of Troy. But she did tell him she was planning to leave the PD's office and instantly regretted having done so.

"Get an offer from one of those Century City firms?" Bruce wanted to know.

"No."

"Where, then?"

"Nowhere, really. But I've decided to do something else with my life. Just not sure what it is yet," she said, lying, trying to sound casual, uncommitted.

"You mean something other than law?"

"Real estate, maybe. Go back to school, become a teacher. I don't know."

"Law can be hard on a woman," Bruce said honestly. "You burnt out, Myra, or are we talking biological clock here?" His voice energized with possibility.

Myra laughed in the darkness, hummed a few bars along with Parker's melody of "Autumn in New York," then, seeing an out, said, "At thirty-one my biological clock is quite healthy, thank you. But you're probably right about being burnt out. Time away from everything will do me some good. I could tell that in Cancún. You don't know how hard it was for me to come back," she said truthfully, memory of white sand beaches moving in and out of focus, Jason's camera working its magic.

Bruce said, "Who are you telling? My first day back was all about paperwork and questions."

"What kind of questions?" Myra asked, knowing exactly where the conversation was going but glad to be off the subject of her career change.

"About you."

Here we go. Reputation time.

Myra grunted. "I can imagine," she said. "Everybody wants their turn, huh?"

"I'm not into gossip, Myra," he said.

"Uh-huh . . ." Myra doubting him. "What about the others? They're not into gossip either? Give me a break, Bruce."

"So you went with a couple of guys in the office. So what?"

"A couple of guys, Bruce . . . ?" Myra drew in a deep breath, quite used to conversing about her favorite subject. "I slept with a whole bunch of guys in your office," Myra said, accepting the reality. "Why wouldn't they gossip?"

Bruce drew in a deep breath. He said, "Sounds like you're proud of it."

"I'm not apologizing, if that's what you're asking. I found them attractive or interesting, or both, and wanted to have sex. Plain and simple. End of story. Mature men keep their business private. Others want bragging rights. I would hope you're in the former category. But if not, so be it."

"Myra, I'm not into gossip," he repeated truthfully, needing her to believe him. To that end he said, "Look, why don't we move in together, put an end to whatever gossip's out there. My place, your place, doesn't make any difference. What do you say?"

Myra didn't say anything at first. She'd had these offers more times than she cared to remember. Knew in reality these offers were efforts to control her. Two years of marriage to a control freak was enough for her.

When she didn't answer, Bruce went on, saying, "I mean we've been an item more or less for the better part of a year, wouldn't you say?"

"More or less."

"And I'm not seeing anyone else. You?"

"Not at the moment, no."

"Well, then," he said, "what's to stop us from setting up house?"

Myra said, "Putting an end to gossip isn't much of a reason to move in together, Bruce."

Bruce said, "I agree. But we have so much in common. That's certainly a valid reason."

Myra said, "Yes, but you like to argue all the time. Look what happened in Cancún—argue, argue, argue."

"Points of law, Myra," Bruce said defensively, his memory of Cancún Myra's bodacious tits in his face, legs wrapped around his body, multiple orgasms. "Wasn't anything personal."

Myra said, "I didn't take it personally, Bruce." She lied efficiently, fleeting memories of Bruce humping her day and night, arguing about legal issues between rounds, still miffed at not having gotten a better tan. "But Cancún was supposed to be a vacation—you turned it into a courtroom. I hate it when a man likes to argue, have his own way all the time," she said, and finding his face in the shadows, fingers tracing frown lines around his mouth to soothe his damaged ego, she told him about her former husband, her intention never to be possessed, owned, or controlled by anyone again.

"I'm not like that, Myra," Bruce said when she'd finished, trying to prop up his bruised ego with a touch of pride in his voice. "And I do like to talk a lot," he admitted.

Myra laughed so loud she had to apologize, realized he was trying.

"That part is true," he went on with less enthusiasm now, knowing just how she felt. "Guess I'll just have to work on keeping my mouth shut. Sorry." He tried to laugh it off, draw Myra into his apology, get her sympathy vote, and he was failing. "But I really like you, Myra," he said. "I do. I just want us to be together on a regular basis."

"We are together on a regular basis."

"Once or twice a week, sure. But I'm talking twenty-four seven."

"So you want to smother me is what you're saying?"

Realizing he was losing the battle but not willing to concede just yet, Bruce sucked air in through his teeth. He said, "Myra, you know what I mean."

Myra knew exactly what he meant. Been there, done that.

"What about your son?" she asked after a moment.

"Keith? I have him every other weekend. You've met him. He's no problem. He likes you as much as I do."

"Ten-year-old boys can be very jealous of any woman Daddy brings home if they feel she'll replace their mother. Same thing with girls if there's a new man in Mommy's life," Myra said, speaking from experience, remembering her resentment of Edward when she first met him, found out he was going to be her new "daddy." "And besides," she went on, "I'm not so sure it's fair to take away the time you need to spend with him. I wouldn't want to come between you," she said honestly.

"I won't let you. Trust me."

I won't let you. There it was, that control thing. Not that she couldn't appreciate where he was coming from, protecting his father-son bond. She could respect that if what they had was a love connection. But they didn't. They had a sex connection, pure and simple. She knew it. And if Bruce didn't know it by now he never would. "On that matter I'd have to," she conceded, having no children or plans to have any, no immediate desire to begin playing mommy, not sure she had the temperament or know-how even if she did.

With the last of the cocaine working its way out of her system and as she began to feel the return of her old self, Myra sat up and stretched. Swinging big sexy legs up and over her embattled lover, she straddled Bruce, bent over and drove her tongue deep into his mouth. Covering his face with her breasts, teasing him with first one nipple then the other, Myra laughed and suddenly rolled away.

She slid off the bed and crossed the darkened room to the large bay window, pulling open curtains that brought into view the forest of high-rise buildings, ribbons of freeways that was downtown LA at night. As Charlie Parker's sax lit up the room with "Dancing in the Dark," she stood transfixed, looking down at the congested streams of slow-moving light feeding into and out of the 110 freeway near the Staples Center, remembered the Lakers were playing Phoenix.

Arms folded across her chest, she turned around to face Bruce, now partially visible in the shadows. Shameless in her nudity, her shapely frame was outlined against the night lights that filled the window and threw her silhouette across the void to the wall beyond.

Myra said, "We have a nice thing going, Bruce, why mess it up with a relationship?"

Confused, Bruce sat up as if on cue. After a moment of careful thought he said, "I thought what we had *was* a relationship."

It wouldn't be polite to laugh a second time.

Knowing Bruce's desire and passion for her was even more inflamed than before, Charlie Parker offering her a carpet of strings and soaring saxophone riffs on which to walk, Myra's silhouette left the window, brought its seductive form across the room in slow, measured steps. Thick, well-conditioned thighs straddled Bruce once again, as she pushed him gently back down on the pillow, bathing his face with her breasts, running ten delicate fingers through his hair as if combing it.

"No, my dear sir," she said softly. "Not a relationship. What we have is a game where everyone gets to play. It's your turn now. Enjoy it."

And he did.

CHAPTER 5

JUST EAST OF DOWNTOWN Los Angeles, across the wide expanse of a concrete viaduct that passes for the LA River when they aren't filming the *Terminator* movies, sits the massive new prison complex known as the Twin Towers, LA's version of the World Trade Center. Third World Trade Center would be more like it, given the majority population doing business there is black and brown. No discrimination allowed. Equal opportunity for all. Only one-fifth the height of its 9/11 namesake, the city fathers make no apology for a lack of aesthetics in its design. Built to be escape-proof, two windowless hexagonal towers rise up through the smog layer like parapets on a castle wall guarding the feudal king. Shotgun-toting alligators already in place, all they need is a drawbridge and moat. Presiding over a network of both adult and juvenile brutality centers, the towers divide the sexes into the good, the bad, and the ones guards use as piñatas. The only way out is by successful appeal or a body bag, whichever comes first. Suffice it to say this is not listed as a must-see location on anyone's travel brochure. And the buses that arrive daily are not filled with tourists out for a sightseeing adventure, photos, and lunch. They're bringing in permanent residents.

Directly across the street is the Men's Central Jail, an overcrowded, antiquated three-story dungeon built in the 1930s to house the ever-growing criminal population of a rapidly expanding white Los Angeles swelling with defeated and desperate refugees who were fleeing the dust-bowl poverty of the Great Depression in search of the American dream seen in Hollywood pictures.

And while 1930s LA may have disappointed some of them, the Men's Central Jail did not. It was just as James Cagney and Humphrey Bogart had portrayed on film: surrounded on all four sides by an electrified chain-link fence crowned by swirling coils of razor wire, its interior was a damp, filthy, vermin-infested, overcrowded domicile ruled by corrupt city officials who ruled a corrupt prison staff, who in turn were ruled by the corrupt and influential criminals who paid them. Underpaid, uneducated Neanderthal guards who lived for the brutality they could inflict ruled everyone else.

Seventy years and seven wars later finds nothing about the Men's Central Jail has changed except the age and color of its inmates: Black. Brown. Young. Video cameras, TV monitors, and metal detectors the only modern upgrades. Everything else about the Men's Central Jail is strictly Middle Ages. One pay phone, warmed-over food, dangerous showers, contract killings, and sadistic guards are the order of the day. Only the strong survive.

The Men's Central Jail visitors room is straight out of a 1940s dime novel: a high-ceilinged cavernous space built of concrete cinder blocks with unreachable narrow windows running the full length of two walls. In the center of the third wall, a four-inch-thick, shatterproof window shared by the guards' room is bracketed by two sets of electrically operated steel doors that control all traffic in and out of a room whose only furniture is a large wall clock mounted over the guards' window and a series of long picnic bench–type metal tables with attached bench seats bolted firmly to the cement floor. If it wasn't for the chest-high glass partition running down the middle of each table, you'd think it was a school cafeteria, only here there are no cooks in white hats filling trays with hot food. Tables set end to end, glass partitions peppered with holes so you don't have to shout or wear hearing aids. More video cameras than a TV studio. Signs on the wall in five prison languages—English, Spanish, Vietnamese, Filippino, and Cambodian—proclaim no smoking, drinking, cursing, spitting, fornication, or small children allowed. Parents, friends, and lawyers sit on one side, a sea of inmates in chains and prison-issue bright orange jumpsuits on the other. No touching, embracing, or kissing allowed, but lawyers are permitted to pass and receive documents over the top of the partition if nearby guards approve. Overhead fluorescent lights washing out color like bleach on a Sunday suit.

A woman screamed in Spanish and fell out on the floor. At another bench a woman started to cry. An inmate began cursing at a third, jumped up and demanded the guard take him back, his distraught wife imploring him to stay. Nobody paid any attention because there wasn't time. No one ever took their eyes away from the glass.

Hurry up and wait. Myra Cross knew the routine. The wall clock said four o'clock. Her client was due up thirty minutes ago. She sat patiently in familiar discomfort with a score of demanding inmates, equal number of noisy, hapless visitors. A lazy hand mechanically pressing out creases in her Calvin Klein skirt, the other thumbing absently through Napoleon Booker's jacket. Her memory still in Bruce's bed, last orgasm before drifting into sleep, she tried to clear the fog of amnesia, recall the circumstances and her defense of three years ago, familiarize herself with facts of the current charges, try to decipher Craig McInnis's chicken-scratch writing. The buzzer sounded. The red light over the steel door turned green just as it clanged open and a uniformed guard entered, motioned to the unseen figure behind him.

Napoleon Booker. Hands cuffed to waist chains, feet shackled in leg irons, he appeared in the door, caught Myra Cross's raised hand on the far side of the room, began his slow, noisy shuffle in her direction. Myra recognized him more from the color photo in the jacket than from memory of their time together three years earlier. He looked heavier but not necessarily older, his cherublike baby face retaining an uncharacteristic youthfulness that masked the aging hardness of criminal life. It started coming back to her: twenty-two-year-old gangbanger dope dealer arrested and charged with the homicide of a rival. But the alleged weapon had no prints and the ballistics didn't match, which meant the gun was planted. Prosecution's only witness was a known addict used as an informant by LAPD. Myra had destroyed the prosecution's case in the first hour of trial, and by the end of the first day they caved in, withdrew the charges, cut him loose. She remembered telling him they'd be out to get him in the future, advised him to tread carefully. Looking at the current charges, she guessed he didn't take her advice.

Something about the orange jumpsuit made him look out of place. It didn't go with the dissolving cornrows, slight beard trying to make a young face look older. Take away the irons, give him a parachute and helmet, he'd be a skydiver on the cover of *Sports Illustrated*.

"Wazzup, Miss Cross," Napoleon said, dropping down on the bench across from her, chains rattling noisily on the metal table, smile of relief playing across the brown face.

"Napoleon. Can't really say I'm glad to see you. Who does your hair?"

Napoleon bent forward, brought manacled hands to the loosened and frayed cornrows. He said, "Word. You a hard lady to catch up with. Been in this shithole two weeks already waiting for you. Your partner say you on vacation in Mexico."

Partner. Like she really needed one. Craig McInnis. His very name turned her mouth rancid. Out of habit Myra brought her hand up to her neck, drew the collar tight, hoping the monkey bites didn't show, that the makeup worked. It didn't.

"See by your neck Mexico was the bomb."

Myra let go of her collar, was tempted to ask what else Craig had said about her, decided to leave it alone.

"We gonna discuss my sex life or your case, Napoleon?"

"No disrespect intended, Miss Cross. Everyone entitled to a little R 'n' R. Just sayin' how long I been in this dump waiting for you, s'all."

"So it's my fault you're in here?"

"Naw. I'm just sayin', that's all. Sure glad to see you, though.

You still look good, Miss Cross," he said, eyes gazing through the glass, resting comfortably on the bulge in her unbuttoned blouse, its hint of cleavage, monkey bites in her neck, knowing the rumors about her were true, that she was a real freak of the first order. "You married yet?"

Myra's smirk answered before the words escaped.

"Thank you, no. Not yet. What about you?"

"Naw. Got a baby's mamma, though, since you seen me last. Boy, named after me, Napoleon the Second."

"Napoleon the Second. Sounds like royalty."

"It do, don't it."

"You living with your son's mother?"

Napoleon shrugged muscular shoulders with indifference. "For the moment." Casual, like he was doing her a favor for the inconvenience.

"Shaniqua. She young. Nineteen. Pussy's good, though."

Struggling to keep from smiling, knowing the baby mamma drama was little more than a booty call, Myra feigned insult.

"I beg your pardon?"

Napoleon didn't struggle with anything. He laughed and said, "Sorry, Miss Cross," playing the game, knowing she wasn't really offended, that she'd heard it all before and then some. "No disrespect. Just street talk, know what I mean?"

Myra did and said so, dropped her eyes down to the folder to signal the small talk was over. She flipped back and forth through several pages in silence.

"Got yourself in a lot of trouble, Napoleon."

"Nothing you can't handle."

"I'm not so sure about that. Armored car robbery. Homicide. Third strike. Parole violation. Priors. You could be looking at the death penalty, let alone life."

"This is bullshit," Napoleon said, raising his voice in indignation, manacled hands banging chains on the table. "I ain't ripped off anyone's armored car. I wouldn't even know how to go about doing that, know what I'm saying? And I sure as hell ain't killed no muthafucking guard either."

"At your preliminary hearing they produced a three fifty-seven found in your car. No prints, but a ballistics match that proved it was your gun that killed the guard."

"Ain't no prints 'cause I ain't never owned no three fifty-seven, know what I'm sayin'? Gun was planted. I can prove that."

Myra couldn't remember how many times and from how many defendants she'd heard that. She remembered too that he'd said the same thing three years ago, and she hadn't believed him until the evidence turned in his favor. This time she'd defer judgment until later.

"All right. What about the two hundred and fifty thousand cash they found in your spare tire? Serial numbers matched some of the seven million that was stolen. You saying that was planted too?"

Napoleon's baby face registered genuine shock. "Seven million? They didn't say nothin' 'bout no seven million in court. For real? Seven million dollars cash money?" He sounded like a child surprised by the revelation that Santa Claus was fake.

Myra nodded, painted nails on delicate fingers leafing through the file, holding first one page, then another. "Seven million, five hundred fifty-five thousand dollars and fourteen cents to be exact."

Napoleon took in a deep breath as if it was his last. "Goddamn muthafuckin' right it was planted. I ain't never had no seven figures of nothin' 'cept bad luck. Know what I'm sayin'? Give me a muthafuckin' break, lady! That kind of cheese, I sure as hell wouldn't be living on no Florence and Normandie, driving no Five Point 0. Have me a BMW or a Benz. I'd be legit, maybe running for president. Or I might be in Cancún like you, only I wouldn't be coming back. Have me a villa in the hills overlooking the ocean. Party with the hotties every night, smoking that good Mexican herb. You feel what I'm sayin', Miss Cross?" and Napoleon raised his manacled hands, pounded his chest, noisy chains drawing hostile stares from nearby guards. "I may be black and stupid, but I ain't dumb."

His comment about Cancún unnerved her for an instant. Craig, that cocksucker, discussing her personal business with defendants. She'd tell him about it just as soon as she saw him.

"Your words, Napoleon. Not mine. It's a good commonsense argument. But we can't get an acquittal on common sense. Jurys don't think in those terms. I need something solid to go on. Something to explain away a quarter million in cash in your possession. Something a jury will believe. Now, if it was dope money . . ."

Napoleon shook his head in short, rapid jerks. "Wasn't no dope money in my car, Miss Cross. I only—" He sat up, looked away in silence, eyes coming back to the glass, through the glass to Myra, to someplace past Myra, back again. "So that's . . ."

"What? Who? Talk to me, Napoleon." She leaned into him.

"Cop what arrested me. Said find the money 'cause it was there. Like they knew what they was gonna do, lay it off on me. Five-O muthafuckas!"

"Cop told you that?" Myra fumbled for a pen, poised it to write. "What was his name?"

"I dunno. Black cop. Oreo muthafucka with an attitude. I thought he was talking about planting dope money. Not no seven figures."

"Black cop, you say? Try to remember his name."

Napoleon shook his head, embarrassed. He said, "I can't remember shit, Miss Cross. I was so lit up, know what I'm sayin'. Shit was happening so fast and all." Napoleon's forefinger hit the glass, pointed to the file on the table. "Ain't it all there in the report?"

Myra's fingers turned pages, emerald eyes scanning down, memorizing the lines.

"Monroe, Taylor, and Brigham. Any of those names ring a bell?"

Napoleon mumbled the names to himself, shook his head.

"Lets start with the first one—Monroe. Gilbert Monroe. Sound familiar?"

"Monroe, maybe. Seems I remember seein' that on his shirt. White boy."

"What about Taylor? Lila Taylor?"

Napoleon's face brightened. "Yeah. Yeah, ugly-ass white girl. I do remember her. Bull dyke. Gave me an elevator ride. Didn't wait till we got to the station. Started on me in the car. I'm still sore behind that bitch," he said without apology.

"What about Brigham? Darryl Brigham?"

"First name. Called him by his first name. He the driver. He white too."

Myra lay her pen down, crossed her arms under the shelf of her chest, making her cleavage more evident. "You sure this was a black cop told you that?" Looking at him.

"Ain't color-blind, Miss Cross. I do know a nigga when I see one. All up in my face with his bad breath and attitude. Must have been twenty, thirty cops around me once I stopped. Regular *You-nited* Nations. Know what I mean?"

"Yeah, I do," Myra said honestly, "but why'd you run in the first place?"

"'Cause I was so lit up I couldn't think straight, that's why."

"Jury might believe that, they might not," Myra said. "Depends on the lab."

Napoleon said, "If that's the case, a DUI is a slam dunk 'cause that's all they got."

"Nothing's a slam dunk but the Lakers, Napoleon."

"I'm a Clippers fan myself," Napoleon said, manacled hands scratching cornrows.

"We're not here to discuss basketball, Napoleon. Talk to me. Give me something I can use."

"Your partner said this seven-figure armored car robbery was four years ago, ain't never been solved. That right?"

Myra leafed through the file, said the court transcript of his arraignment mentioned it but didn't go into details. It was an old case. She'd have to research it.

"I'm so dumb I'm gonna ride around in my car with a murder weapon and stolen cash from something I did four years ago?"

"Its been done before. What about the marijuana, Napoleon. That planted too?" Sounding cynical, doubt crowding out belief that didn't get past Napoleon.

He nodded. "Yeah. Nickel bag of weed was mine."

His admission helped some. The clock on the wall said four-fifty.

Myra stifled a yawn, closed the folder. She said, "Way I see it, Napoleon, we have three problems—one minor and two major. On the charge of possession with intent to sell, we can plea down to simple possession because of the small quantity. On the charges of felony evasion, resisting arrest, and reckless endangerment, we'll plea down to misdemeanor reckless endangerment. You tore up four cars, so we're talking restitution. But an ex-felon in possession of a weapon is a problem. That's a parole violation. Big problem. And the money. Bigger problems. So let's take the gun first. You said you could prove it was planted. How?"

Napoleon didn't answer right away, thinking about what he was going to say, getting it clear in his mind. He raised his hands, leaned close to the glass, and motioned for Myra to join him. Myra cut suspicious eyes at the request, moved reluctantly closer. When there was just a glass width between them, Napoleon spoke in a whisper barely audible over the room noise. He asked Myra, "Where did they find the gun?"

"Why are you whispering?"

"Just being careful," he said, and looked to both sides of the table repeatedly. "No telling who might be listening." Myra told him that was silly. She sat back up, opened the folder, thumbed through several pages, leaned back into the glass.

Her eyebrows raised, face flushed with the excitement of a childhood game where the object of the conspiracy was to keep a secret, patronizing him with a forced whisper that lacked any seriousness. She said, "According to this, it was in a trapdoor compartment behind the dashboard over the steering column." It was all she could do to keep from laughing.

Until she heard his response.

"Trapdoor compartment can't hold a three fifty-seven. Built for a nine-millimeter. They say anything about a Glock?"

Myra's desire to laugh drained away as fast as it came. She frowned, sat back up, leafed through more papers and leaned back into the glass, whispering, "Nothing about a Glock, Napoleon."

"Right. Where's my gun?"

Myra didn't say anything at first, but she didn't move from the glass. "You telling me you had a Glock under the dashboard?"

"Spent a whole weekend in Tijuana. Had them Mexicans design me a trapdoor, molded out of steel just for the Glock. Fits like a glove," he said, and raised his hands as far as the noisy chains would go, closed the fingers of one tightly around the fingers of the other. "Won't no other gun fit in the space. You can't force it, wedge it, or cram it in. And three fifty-seven so big you can't even get it up behind the dashboard, period. When I get out of here we'll go to impound, show you what I mean."

Myra sat back up, chewed on her lower lip, leaned back into the glass. "You tell this to Mr. McInnis?"

"Like I said, Miss Cross, black and stupid. Not dumb. What I wanna tell him for? You my lawyer."

Myra resisted the urge to smile and failed. Chalk one up for Napoleon. "This Glock of yours," she went on, "is it dirty?"

Napoleon thought about the question for an instant, ran his tongue between his upper lip and gums. He said finally, "Ain't sayin' it hasn't been fired, but I ain't killed nobody, if that's what you're asking. Least I don't think I have. And if they died ain't nobody told me about it. Know what I'm saying? I'm a businessman. Businessman always need protection. Ain't nothing on that nine-millimeter gonna come back to me."

Myra was impressed with his admission. She wanted to know about the gun's history before it came into his possession.

Napoleon surprised her. "Ain't no history but mine, Miss Cross," he whispered. "I stole it from a gun shop week before I got arrested. Three days after that I was in Tijuana with the Mexicans. It's a one-owner piece. Only prints on it mine."

A week before his arrest. Okay. Puzzle beginning to come together now. But there's still a lot of missing pieces.

Myra said, "Let me make sure I understand this, Napoleon. You're telling me you're willing to go into court and cop to possession of a stolen gun?"

"In a life-or-death situation, you muthafuckin' right I will. But I don't see no reason to bring it up. Once they see no three fifty-seven can fit the mold, case closed. 'If it don't fit, you must acquit!' Ain't that right, Miss Cross?"

They both laughed. Street smarts. Myra had to hand it to him. Thinking on his feet.

"All right. But if for some reason you had to, if the case hinged on it, why should they believe you? For all anybody knows you could be making up the story about the Glock."

Napoleon smiled, face still on the glass. He said to Myra, "But you know I'm tellin' the truth, don't you, Miss Cross?"

"Do I? Suppose you convince me. I don't want any surprises in court, DA presenting evidence the Glock was used in an old case."

Napoleon laughed for the third time. "Old case? What they gonna do, raise the dead, shoot a corpse?"

"They could. Look mighty stupid if they did. But you never know. Give me something else that'll prove you stole this Glock, that it was in your possession night you were arrested."

Napoleon thought about it for a moment. He fanned ten fingers on the table, sat back up, ran his tongue over his teeth, leaned back into the glass, continued whispering to Myra, "While I was in Mexico took a picture of myself with a Polaroid in front of my Five Point 0, posing like Pancho Villa and them Mexican bandits, ammunition belts across their chests and shit. Only I got my Glock instead, trying to look hard, throwing up Crip signs and all that. Got the idea from a movie, *City of God*—you see it?" Myra said she hadn't. Napoleon started to tell her the plot, Myra saying this meeting wasn't about movie reviews. Napoleon ignored her and went on, saying, "In *City of God* gangsters got their picture took with their guns, got on the front page of the papers. Made them famous. I was gonna do the same, send it to the *Times*. But I was all lit up that weekend, know what I'm sayin', smoking that good Mexican weed and shit. Got cold feet at the last minute, mailed it to myself instead."

Wannabe gangster. Myra shook her head in pity close to the glass, did the math on her fingers.

She whispered, "You're saying you took a picture of yourself with the gun only four days before you were arrested. That right?"

"In Tijuana. Yeah."

"Who's to say when the picture was taken?"

Napoleon whispered back, saying, "Holding a newspaper with the headlines. I was trying to impress the *Times*, thinkin' they might put it on the front page. Crazy, huh?"

Myra wanted to say she agreed, thought it best to keep her personal opinions to herself. But she had to give him credit—stupid with a big ego maybe, but he wasn't dumb by any stretch of the imagination. The Polaroid might just get him out of a murder charge.

She whispered to Napoleon, "Four days before your arrest is close enough. Doesn't prove it's your gun, though, unless it shows the serial number."

"Don't show that, but I got the serial number written down somewhere."

"Really? You have the serial number of a gun you stole?"

Napoleon nodded. "Wrote it down on a piece of paper and mailed it to myself. Got it hid along with the Polaroid. Prove I didn't rob no armored car, kill no guard."

Myra made no effort to hide the smile. She said, "It sure will. But we're still only halfway home. We've got one other big problem we're looking at. The money—quarter million dollars whose serial numbers tie you directly to the robbery."

"If you prove the gun was planted, don't that suggest the money was planted too?" Napoleon said.

"Suggestions go in the suggestion box, Napoleon. Talk to me. Give me something that'll convince a jury, because right now we've got nothing but your word."

Napoleon never moved from the glass. "Where they say they found the money?"

Myra sat back up, ringed fingers racing through pages, stopping on one. After a moment she returned to the glass and whispered, "Spare tire in the trunk."

Napoleon stayed glued to the glass. He shook his head slowly and said, "Didn't have no spare tire, Miss Cross. Took it out to make more space for sounds."

"Sounds?"

"Yeah. Sounds. You know, speakers." Myra nodded, remembered a VW pulling alongside her at a stoplight, bass so loud her car vibrated. Thinking something was wrong, she'd started to get out until she realized it was coming from the VW, wondered where the speakers were hidden. "Ain't no room in the trunk for no spare way I got it set up," Napoleon went on. "One big sound system. Like surround sound. And my shit be slamming too, know what I'm sayin'. I get a flat, oh well. Call the auto club."

Myra said, "Cops probably ripped them out. They'll say no speakers were present."

Napoleon seemed unusually calm. He said, "No matter. I got a receipt."

"Receipt?"

"Yeah."

"For what?"

"Installation."

"Of your speakers?"

"Day I was arrested."

"Day you were arrested? You had speakers put in the day of your arrest. Is that what you're telling me?" Myra felt like jumping over the glass and kissing Napoleon.

"Took all day. Didn't finish till nearly eight. Why I was so lit up. Smoked blunts and primos all the time I was waiting. S'a wonder I could even drive." He laughed at the recollection the way a comedian laughs at his own jokes, shaking his head at his own stupidity.

"What did you do with the spare?"

"Gave it to them Mexicans in Tijuana."

"Which means the cops substituted a spare."

"Man with a new car rip out a four-figure sound system for a beat-up spare?"

"We don't know it's an old spare. Could be a new one."

"If it is, won't match the batch number of the other four."

"Batch number?" Knowing she should see it, feeling stupid because she couldn't.

"Girl, don't you know nothin'?" School time. Educating white folks in ways of the streets. Napoleon brought his eyebrows together, shook his head in resignation. "New car get all new tires from the same batch, like they do when you buy Fritos or candy. You get sick they ask you for the batch number so they can trace which plant made it, shit like that. Tires made the same way."

The man had a PhD in street smarts. Myra didn't say anything for a moment. She sat back, shook her head, computer brain beginning to plan defense strategy, anticipate her opponent's moves. Countermoves. Dangerous moves.

"Way I figure it," Napoleon said, "we got enough to prove I didn't rip off no armored car or kill no guard. Plain and simple. Know what I'm sayin', Miss Cross."

Pieces of the puzzle in place now. She could see the picture clearly and it wasn't a pretty one. It was a scary one. In a voice filled with just a trace of apprehension, Myra whispered with cautious satisfaction, "I know you didn't, Napoleon. But it means we're dealing with dirty cops who pulled off a seven-million-dollar armored car robbery, killed a guard, and will do anything—I repeat, *anything*—to protect themselves. Think Rampart, Napoleon. Dirty cops are the most dangerous kind. Once they realize the gun switch points directly to them, all hell's going to break loose. Your life might not be worth the cost of a Fubu outfit. You feeling me on this, Mr. Booker?" she said, letting him know she believed in him, was up to the job, and wouldn't be intimidated by DA strategy.

"Why I got to get out of here."

Myra opened the file for the last time that day, raised penciled eyebrows, shaking her head in doubt, saying, "Can you make bail?"

"Not at three million."

"I get the gun squashed in a pretrial motion, your bail drops to a million."

"Walk out the same day," Napoleon said. "Business partner will put it up."

Business partner. Yeah, right. More like a drug dealer or addict. Or both. Myra ran six rings on ten fingers through locks of red hair. At the risk of offending her client, she reminded him that bail bond companies wouldn't accept money from questionable sources.

Napoleon was not offended. He said, "They will from him. White boy. Lawyer in Century City. I just have to figure best way to go about it."

Lawyer. That said it all. Any reputable lawyer a street thug could con into putting up a hundred thousand dollars bail money on a million dollar bond had to be an addict who didn't want to lose his connection. She raised her hand, signaled the guard. They stood at the same time, ignored protocol and shook hands over the top of the glass. "Well," she said, "that's on you," having serious doubts Napoleon and his "business partner" could pull off a hat trick. "I'll get my investigator on the case first thing in the morning." She looked at her watch, matched it with the one on the wall.

Both said five o'clock. She suddenly felt very tired. "I'm out of here, Napoleon."

"Hope you enjoyed Cancún," he said as if it might be the last vacation she'd ever take. Myra didn't say anything, but she cut him a smile and a wink that said she did, disappeared through the first of two steel doors, and headed for the parking garage elevator.

The meeting with Napoleon Booker had been draining, perhaps because she hadn't gotten much sleep the night before. Or because she hadn't eaten all day. Or both. Then there was the fact she'd gone the entire day without a snort of blow, her "energy boost," she liked to call it. She wasn't back on her routine just yet, stuck somewhere between the beaches of Cancún and the fourth dimension.

Myra Cross left the crowded elevator, said her good-byes to familiar colleagues, and stepped into the late afternoon chill of the third-floor rooftop parking level attached to the Men's Central Jail. Dying rays of a five o'clock sun poured through the breech in the Twin Towers, splashed remnants of gold across oil-spattered concrete. Pulling her cart of legal briefs behind, she smiled as she caught sight of MYRA'S BEAU, the vanity license plate of Bruce's cream-colored Mercedes 500 SE, wondered what he'd change it to if they ever broke up. She stopped just long enough to slip her business card under his wiper, the words "call me" scribbled on the back.

It was a good walk from the elevator to Myra's parking spot at the far end of the rooftop. And at five o'clock the checkerboard of empty spaces that surrounded her Mercedes made it seem like an orphan that had been abandoned. The first thing she did was rummage through the glove compartment, looking for her vial of cocaine, and cursed loudly at the recollection she'd snorted the last line early that morning before her first court appearance.

She turned the key in the ignition.

Nothing.

Zero. Zip. Not even a hint of power.

Not again. Third time in as many weeks. Electrical short of some kind. Most likely her ignition, a Triple A driver had told her the first time she'd called them. Nothing wrong with her battery. She'd put off taking the Mercedes to the dealer because she'd found if she was patient and jiggled the key it would eventually catch. Not this time. Myra wasn't in any mood to be patient. It had been a long day, her nerves were on edge, and she needed a hit. God, how she needed a hit. After five minutes of doing just about everything short of breaking the key off in the ignition, her fingers raw from the effort, her cell phone brought Triple A to the rescue.

The tow-truck driver was Ernesto, a kid in his early twenties sporting a ponytail and a lilting East LA accent who, after jumper cables produced nothing but frustration, said it was an electrical problem, most likely something in the ignition. Then, sniffing the air, he said he smelled gas, asked Myra if she smelled it. Myra got out, sniffed the air, caught the whiff of gasoline in the developing breeze, asked Ernesto where he thought it was coming from. Ernesto sniffed under the hood, checked all the hoses for loose connections. Finding none, he walked around to the back, got down on all fours, rubbed his hand under the gas tank, sniffed his fingers, and got back up, shaking his head.

"I can't see anything," he told Myra. "Feels dry there and under the hood. My guess is you've got a leak somewhere in the fuel line or the fuel pump. You'd better take it in, have it checked out."

Myra said she would.

Ernesto said he knew a little about ignitions, asked Myra to let him fiddle with it for a minute and if he couldn't get it started he'd tow the car wherever she wanted. Myra said okay, was impressed with his professionalism as he spread a clean towel over the seat and steering wheel before starting to work.

Myra's cell phone, glued to her ear as she walked over to the far side of the roof, spit out a day's worth of unanswered messages. She looked down three levels to see if Bruce was among the five o'clock crowd pouring out of the Men's Central Jail and across the courtyard;

she'd spend the night at his place if Ernesto couldn't get it started, rent a car in the morning. But she didn't have the best view, so she moved over several feet and positioned herself between the front end of a tank-like Hummer H2 and the guardrail, tired eyes scanning the courtyard below.

It happened without warning.

She heard it and felt its force and searing heat blow past her in a fiery comet of flaming parts as the Mercedes Benz 500 SE exploded like a Roman candle. Myra was knocked off her feet. Her head slammed hard against the concrete wall before she hit the ground. Her head spun in a daze of confusion, lungs begged for air in the suffocating thickness of black smoke swirling on the ground. Myra had the presence of mind to drag herself to safety under the front wheels of the Hummer. There was no time to be frightened. No time to be sick. She pulled herself into a tight defensive knot, head and knees buried in her chest, eyes closed, trembling hands and arms covering her head. It was a move that saved her life, for at that instant flaming metal parts and debris rained down on and around the Hummer.

Myra Cross waited in a narrow prison of safety.

When the firestorm subsided, and the choking smoke, heat, and debris were picked up in light breezes, Myra dared to remove her hands from her head and open her eyes. Only then did she fully realize the magnitude of what had happened. She knew it because in front of the Hummer, on the ground where she had stood only moments before, lay the crumpled and seared remains of a license plate.

MYRA'S BENZ

CHAPTER 6

MYRA CROSS EXPERIENCED bouts of insomnia only three times in her life. The first was at age twelve when she thought she was pregnant. The second was at fifteen when she knew she was pregnant. And the third was during the 9/11 attacks when her mother and stepfather, visiting in New York, hadn't been able to contact her from the train they were on because the Verizon antenna had gone down with the South Tower. Now a fourth wave of insomnia was sweeping over her in the days following the explosion on the rooftop of the Men's Central Jail parking structure. In truth it was Ernesto that really got to her, the first thing she saw once she climbed out from under the safety of the Hummer H2, the horrifying image of his incinerated remains, charred and unrecognizable in the spot where her Mercedes had been parked. Stumbling not quite dazed through a surreal landscape painted with gusts of smoke, pockets of still-burning wreckage, blackened carcasses of burnt-out cars and trucks, shocked and disbelieving faces of bystanders, distant scream of a dozen sirens, drone of approaching helicopters. It reminded Myra of now-familiar television images of carnage that lay scattered on the road to Basra in the final days of the Gulf War.

In general the rooftop had pretty much contained the eruption. And as luck would have it, there was a lull in people leaving the Men's Central Jail at the instant of the explosion, so the flaming debris that did manage to extend beyond the rooftop fell in a haphazard shower to the relatively empty courtyard three floors below.

Myra had escaped any real injury save for the bump on her head where she'd hit the wall when the force of the blast had knocked her to the ground. Because it was so late in the day, many cars had already vacated the parking structure. Only two other people had sustained any significant injuries: a man cut on the face by flying glass while walking to his car, and a woman driver burned on the arm while trying to get out of her SUV as it erupted in flames. Seven cars had been totally destroyed, another ten damaged.

Bruce's Mercedes was showered with glass but otherwise undamaged. He and several others were in the elevator, heard the explosion, exited onto a rooftop shrouded in smoke, flaming metal debris raining down. No one left the elevator until there was a sense it was safe to do so. They picked their way cautiously through a blanket of choking smoke, a carpet of smoldering metal debris, toward vehicles or what was left of them. Bruce had found Myra staring hypnotically at the remains of the tow-truck driver, pulled her away to the safety of his car to await the arrival of authorities, her statement to police. He agreed with paramedics suggesting she have the swelling knot on her forehead checked at the hospital. Myra refused, saying all she needed was a joint and some rest. So he took her to his Bunker Hill apartment. But he found no pleasure in her company—the nights of mechanical, unresponsive, roboticlike sex she occasionally submitted to, days of silence that followed one after another.

Upon learning it was Myra's car that had exploded, Marty French gave Myra two days off, another three if she felt she needed it. Myra took a week. Needed all seven days and then some. The insomnia, mostly. And on those occasions when she could sleep, the nightmares. Always the same one—a nauseating image of Ernesto, his charred face glaring at her, grinning at her, like the skeletal remains of a mummy in a horror film. Long, bony fingers beckoning for her to follow, his skeleton arm with burning flesh peeling away as it reached slowly out to caress her face, going around her waist, pulling her to him for a mating of the damned. And every time she braced to kiss the smoldering, faceless skull, she would wake up screaming in terror, dripping wet with perspiration, gasping for air, heart pounding in her chest like the bass drum in a marching band.

Miles Davis, Dexter Gordon, and Nat King Cole among a chorus of legends that made days and nights seamless as Myra struggled with the shock, rode out its impact on a river of jazz. She smoked one joint after another, taking herself back to Cancún, the warm waters of the Gulf of Mexico, cavorting up and down the crystal-white sand beach in her barely-there bikini—the fantasy a way of anesthetizing herself against the terrifying nightmares settling in, and the stabbing sense of guilt and responsibility at the tow-truck driver's death.

Maybe it was the jazz. Or the dope. Or the sex. Or maybe just being away from the office. Myra didn't know. But eventually the nightmares began to fade, the insomnia became less frequent, and by the end of the week Myra was beginning to feel like her old self. Her grieving was over.

In truth Bruce was beginning to bore her. His apartment had become a jail of claustrophobic sameness, of waking up every day to the same face, same familiar routine of housekeeping: cooking, cleaning, laundry, and watching Jay Leno before retiring. Though under the circumstances there really was no same routine other than Bruce's impressive collection of jazz CDs she played around the clock. And to be fair to Bruce, he was really quite understanding, letting each day dictate itself, placing no demands on Myra save for an occasional request for sex to which Myra agreed, hoping it would relieve her nightmares. But Myra could see why living with Bruce, with any man really, was still out of the question. It meant being accountable, and she'd learned that lesson the hard way during two years of marriage to Richard, an insecure man who believed possession was nine-tenths of the law.

"Where are you going, Myra? . . . I'm going to the store, Richard! . . . It shouldn't take you more than fifteen minutes! . . . It might take me twenty, Richard! . . . Why should it take you twenty, Myra? You

can drive there in five! . . . Yes, Richard, but there might be traffic, or there might be a crowd! . . . Or you might be meeting a man? . . . Richard, why don't you come with me if you're worried about my meeting someone? . . . I think I will. And another thing, Myra, I don't like you spending so much time after school! . . . I'm in college, Richard. I have to use the library! . . . I want you here with me in the evenings, Myra! . . . I know that, Richard, but I have finals coming up! . . . I want you home right after your last class, Myra. It takes you thirty minutes. I'll call the house. If you're not here I'm leaving work and coming up there to see who you're meeting! . . . I'm not meeting anyone, Richard. I'm in the library studying for finals! . . . You're meeting someone, Myra. You can't fool me! . . . I'm not trying to fool you, Richard. I'm in the library! . . . I don't believe you, Myra! You belong to me! . . . Nobody owns me, Richard! I don't belong to anyone! . . . Yes you do, Myra. We're married! . . . I can remedy that tomorrow, Richard! . . . You wouldn't dare, Myra! . . . Try me, Richard!" And he did. The little shit actually came up on campus, found her in the library, and started a ruckus, demanding to know which student was her lover. Myra filed for divorce the next day, moved back home with her mother and stepfather, and got a restraining order against him. And despite all of Richard's drama and threats of drama, she still aced her finals. She was too driven and independent to let something like an insecure husband intimidate her, or a divorce change her focus. And for all that she was or was not, Myra Cross never missed a beat.

No, the seven days of cloistered living on Bunker Hill let her know she could never again be accountable to anyone, not even a trusted fuck buddy like Bruce, sincere in wanting to help her. A week with him in Cancún was different. It was fun and games, *Fast Times at Ridgemont High.* But welded together for a week in his Bunker Hill apartment was like *The Mummy's Tomb,* only with good jazz instead of eerie special effects. She was genuinely grateful for his assistance and told him so. But by week's end she was ready to go, knew if she stayed a day longer she'd lose all feeling for him.

Bruce was cool about it, knew his plea that she stay longer was futile, and he dropped her off in Brentwood, where she rented a car from Enterprise, returned to her Barrington Avenue condo just long enough to check her mail, pay bills, wash some clothes, and began what she knew would be a long battle with her insurance company for a payout on the Mercedes.

Her return to the public defender's office was even more difficult than when she'd returned from Cancún. Myra just didn't want to do this anymore. And in the wake of what had just happened she felt this even more intensely. It took considerable effort to force her concentration back on track, slip into the backlog of work with the same prowess and intensity as if nothing had happened. But she did. She was a professional. And her demand that Craig McInnis not discuss any aspects of her personal life with clients was the first order of business. It produced a reluctant apology, but it didn't make a dent in his ego. And collaborating with his ego took every bit of Myra's willpower, more than her usual snorts of lunchtime cocaine to keep her disdain for him from showing. She wondered when Jason Rice would call, free her from this hell.

Myra's investigator was Raymond Watanabe, a seasoned and skilled member of the PD's office. She gave him Napoleon Booker's story about the gun rack, speakers, and spare tire filled with money, told him to run with it, see what he could turn up.

Myra had been back at work for nearly three weeks, her time divided between an unwieldy caseload, arguments with the insurance company, and daily sparring with Clara. She'd just finished a conference call with the DA's office, Dillon Lester agreeing to a plea bargain on a mentally ill arson defendant, slipping in his invitation to dinner at Perinos, suggestion of sexual dessert at his place. Myra declined his invitation, said she was on a diet, that premarital sex was against her religion. She was about to leave for lunch when line three lit up. Lorna asked her to hold for Marty French. Marty French said he wanted to see her in his office. Now.

They were all standing.

Marty French behind his desk. And flanked on either side in front of the chrome legs, two men whose identical plain black suits looked shabby in the shadow of Marty French's pin-striped Giorgio Armani. They wore white JC Penney button-down shirts, matching black ties, black thick-soled Timberland shoes, and close-cropped Marine Corps haircuts. If they had ray guns and sunglasses they'd be *Men in Black* clones. The taller, older one needed orthodontics to match the crooked nose, a pair of large antenna ears, and an upper lip slightly distorted by a harelip. The shorter, heavier, younger one had enormous gray eyes magnified by thick horn-rimmed glasses, bushy Martin Scorsese eyebrows, a neatly trimmed mustache, and a dimpled chin so prominent Myra was sure it was a second mouth.

Marty French beckoned for Myra to enter and said, "Myra, these gentlemen are from—"

"The FBI, Miss Cross," the taller one said, interrupting Marty French, dismissing him over his shoulder without turning around, flashing Myra a wallet of credentials like the high-speed opening and closing of a flip-top cell phone, the shorter one doing the same. "I'm agent Chester Barton." Pointing to the shorter man, he said, "This is agent Keith Lansing." Myra didn't know if she was supposed to shake their hands or curtsy. When no hand came out to greet hers, she guessed the protocol was different, looked past them to Marty for clues, but Marty had been demoted. She could sense the rage hidden behind his clenched teeth as he dropped into his chair, clasped his hands behind his head, and leaned back.

"We'd like to ask you some questions about the events a few weeks back, if you don't mind," Barton went on, picking up a folder from the desk, opening it slowly, turning pages as his eyes shifted from the folder to Myra, down to her chest, back to the folder, letting her know he wasn't impressed, that she had no choice. The shorter one, Lansing, pulled out a notepad and pen from his coat, licked his finger, turned several pages, poised his pen to write.

"Have a seat, Myra," Marty French said, gambling he still had some authority, waving her to the sectional, Myra obliging, dropping down stiffly on the edge, pulling her Liz Claiborne skirt down to tightly closed knees, extreme effort at modesty.

Barton said, "How long have you owned the Mercedes, Miss Cross?"

Myra said, "About three years."

"Buying or leasing?" Lansing said, second mouth moving in tandem with the first, forest of eyebrows waving on his forehead.

"Buying," Myra said. Lansing's pen scribbled noisily on the pad, and he looked up when he'd finished, waiting for the next question from Barton, as if they'd rehearsed it.

Barton's eyes moved back to Myra. He said, "Any problems with the car since you've had it?" Myra wondered why he didn't grow a mustache, cover the harelip.

"None until about two, three weeks ago," Myra said. "Ignition. At least that's what I think it was. Sometimes it'd start. Other times you had to finesse it, you know, play with it until it kicked over. I was going to take it in first chance I got."

"Why didn't you?" Marty French asked.

Barton said tersely, "We'll conduct the interview, Mr. French." Without turning around to look at him. Immediate demotion. Just like that. FBI show all the way. "It's a good question, Miss Cross," Barton continued. "Why didn't you?"

Myra said, "Just lazy, I guess."

Barton nodded, seemed to accept Myra's explanation. He continued leafing through the folder, withdrew a sheet, looked at it for a few seconds, then said, "Let's see, you've had it serviced only twice. The first time at the fifty-thousand-mile checkup and the second . . ." He paused, scanned the sheet a few seconds, then continued, saying, " . . . about six months ago." He looked up at Myra. "That sound about right?" Myra said it was, impressed they had the service records, and asked why the FBI was so interested in her car.

They didn't answer her. Didn't make any lascivious eye movements that focused on her chest. Myra didn't know if that was a compliment or insult. They were all business. They didn't move from the spots they were standing in. Didn't turn or twist, not even toward each other. She looked past them to Marty, but Marty just raised his eyebrows, shrugged his shoulders as he brought both hands up in a gesture of ignorance, then returned them to a clasp behind his head.

Barton returned the sheet to the folder, withdrew another one, scanned it slowly before he spoke. "What can you tell us about Ernesto?"

Myra frowned. "Who?"

"Ernesto Ruiz. Tow-truck driver that was killed. You told the police his name was Ernesto. How did you know that?"

"It was embroidered on his uniform as I remember." Myra paused. "Ruiz, you said. I didn't know his last name until you mentioned it."

"So you'd never seen him before that day?" Barton said. "No previous contact with him?" Looking at her.

Myra said she hadn't, asked again why the FBI was so interested in her car.

And again they ignored her.

Reading from the sheet, Barton said, "According to the police report you said he, Ernesto that is, told you he smelled gasoline. That true, you smelled gasoline?"

"When he brought it to my attention, yes," Myra said, praying her nose wouldn't start running, let on cocaine was already destroying her sense of smell.

"But not before then?"

"No. Not before."

"And that he told you he knew where it was coming from?"

Myra said, "That's not what he said. He was guessing. He said he *thought* it could be a fuel line or a fuel pump because there was no leak under the gas tank or the front hood."

"How did he know that? Did he check under the hood?" Lan-

sing asked, FBI man's pen writing on the pad in sync with big gray
eyes blinking rapidly behind thick lenses. Myra had to work at not
staring at the dimple.

"When he finished trying to jump-start it, I guess," Myra said.
"I'm not a mechanic and to be honest with you I really wasn't paying much attention at the time. I was in the seat trying to turn the
key when he would tell me to."

Barton said, "And he knew there was no gas coming from the
tank? How did he know that?"

The FBI men were either stupid or playing with her. Myra took
in a deep breath of exasperation. It was lunchtime, past lunchtime;
she was hungry and needed a hit.

Myra said, "Because he got down on the ground and ran his
hands under the gas tank to see if it was leaking."

"On the ground, you say. You mean like this," he said, and the
one and only time Barton ever moved he lowered himself to Marty
French's green deep-pile rug on his hands and knees. "Like this,
Miss Cross?" he said, lowering his head, turning it and looking up,
as if he was looking under something.

Vaudeville time. Front-row seats. All she needed was the pop-
corn.

It wouldn't have been polite to laugh. Myra caught Marty's
smile behind them, wondered if Barton knew just how stupid he
looked, FBI man down on all fours, head bobbing up and down like
a lapdog. All he needed was a tail and a leash. She was surprised he
was looking at her face and not between her legs like most lawyers
did whenever she was sitting opposite them. She guessed FBI
agents were better disciplined than lawyers, realized she wouldn't
win any cases if he was on the jury. Myra nodded, said his pan-
tomine was accurate.

For some reason his abrupt change in position made her aware
she hadn't moved from the edge of the sectional, that she'd been
sitting almost unnaturally erect like a stuffed animal on display at a
shooting gallery. She suddenly noticed stiffness developing in her

back, so she repositioned herself against the pillow and, trying not to draw attention to herself, carefully and slowly crossed her legs and pulled down the Liz Claiborne skirt to its limit.

She may as well have been naked. No response from the Men in Black if in fact they had even noticed. She wondered whether they would even stare at her chest if her blouse was unbuttoned. Even in the midst of an FBI investigation Myra's vanity was working overtime.

"He have anything in his hands, any tools or instruments of any kind?" Barton went on as he stood back up, shoes returning to their exact spot on the rug. Myra said no. She told them how he rubbed his hand under the tank and when he stood up he smelled his fingers and said it was dry.

"How long was he down on the ground, by your gas tank?" Lansing asked.

"Few seconds, if that. Just long enough to see if there was any leak."

"And you saw him do that," Barton went on, Lansing writing furiously. "Get down on the ground, on all fours like I just did, nothing in his hands, and rub the gas tank and get back up in just a few seconds. You still insist that's what you saw?"

Insist? Myra wondered if he was hard of hearing. "I'm not insisting anything, Mr. Barton. I was standing right next to him. The man got down on the ground, looked at my gas tank, got back up, and said it was dry. End of story," she answered, resenting the questioning of her truthfulness, nerves on edge, and needing a hit before she broke out in a sweat. "But I wasn't going to smell his fingers, if that's what you mean."

"Nothing personal, Miss Cross," Barton said, sensing Myra's irritation. "We just have to be sure of our facts. That's all."

Sergeant Joe Friday time.

Myra not picking up where the FBI was headed. Paying more attention to where their eyes were looking than to what they were saying, trying to tell her. She was tired, hoping they didn't see, mis-

interpret the trace of perspiration beginning to show on her forehead.

"All right then, Miss Cross," Barton said. "Let's move on, shall
we." Subtle change in direction, tone of his voice that Myra
missed.

Barton continued with the inquisition, brought her out of the
daydream. He said, "You told police he offered to try and help start
your car after he couldn't get it started with jumper cables?"

"That's right," Myra said. "Said he knew something about ignitions, as I recall. Offered to try and fix the problem and if he
couldn't he'd tow it. He was very professional. Spread a cloth over
the seat and the steering wheel so there wouldn't be any dirt or
grease marks."

"He have any tools with him?" Lansing wanted to know, pen
scratching across the pad between questions, Myra's answers.

"You asked me that," Myra said.

"I mean when he went to work on your ignition?"

Myra said, "I wouldn't know. That's when I walked over to the
guardrail."

"Why?" Lansing asked, bushy eyebrows waving, pen grating on
the pad.

"Why . . . ?" Myra thought it was a silly question and said so.
Lansing said maybe it was but he insisted she answer, so she said,
"Get out of his way so he could work. Why do you think. What am
I supposed to do, stand there asking dumb questions?"

Neither man seemed bothered by Myra's sarcasm. Lansing said
between noisy flurries on the pad, "So you have no idea what happened after that. You told police you didn't see your car explode?"

Myra said, "That's right. I was on the other side of the lot looking over the guardrail when it happened."

"Looking at what?" Barton wanted to know.

"People leaving the courthouse. See if I recognized anyone."

"Did you?" Lansing asked.

Myra said, "Did I what?"

Lansing said, "Recognize anyone?"

Myra said no, glanced at her watch, not really caring what time it was. Just so her displeasure was obvious. She said, "How much longer will this last? Court's over at four and I've got some pretrial motions to file before—"

Barton cut her off, saying, "You're a public defender attorney, are you not?"

Changing up now, his tone softer, more conciliatory. As if they were long-lost friends having a conversation about old times. Casual like.

"For seven years, yes."

"With this office?" Barton asked.

"With this office," Myra said. She smiled briefly, caught Marty's disgusted eye, letting him know she was on his team.

"I suppose you see all kinds of people in your line of work," Barton said, friendly and concerned, signaling the interview/interrogation was at an end, trying to put her at ease, learn how lawyers operate, the mystique of law. "My guess is you represent some clients who might express all kinds of views, even antigovernment views." Throwing it out there. Right in her face. Myra missing it altogether. Flattered, thinking he was impressed with her position as a female PD.

Myra laughed, saw Marty smother a smile, second smile since his demotion.

"They all do, Mr. Barton," Myra said, trying to talk and laugh at the same time. "They're in jail and blame the system for being there."

The FBI men didn't laugh. They realized then the redhead didn't see it, girl that bright with the nice body hadn't picked up where their questions were going. Amazing.

"Any clients ever blame you personally?" Barton asked.

Myra's ego as big as Marty French's, neither one seeing what the

FBI man was getting at. The guy had no idea who she was, her string of victories, high-profile reputation. She smiled, shook her head and said no, asked why should they.

"Maybe dissatisfied with your representation?" Lansing suggested.

"All the time," Marty said, leaning forward, elbows on the desktop bracing a cathedral of fingers under his chin. "If we win, and we win a lot, trust me . . . we're the greatest lawyers in the world. If we lose, and we do lose, then we're the worst sons of a bitches on the planet. We sold them out. But we didn't put 'em in jail. That's on them."

Myra had to agree, supporting her boss trying for a promotion, acknowledging they were a team. "Our clients are black, brown, and poor," she said. "They come to us on a wing and a prayer and no evidence to help their cases but hope."

"We have a very high acquittal rate," Marty French interjected proudly.

"Any recent threats on your life?" Barton asked, question directed at Myra, ignoring Marty French altogether, his bid for recognition, Myra's team support.

Barton's question caught her by surprise, its meaning going right over her head. All she had to do was reach up and grab it. But she didn't. Myra thought about it for a moment, remembered Richard's barrage of empty threats ten years ago, guessed they didn't qualify as recent.

"Recent?" Myra paused. "Never is more like it. Look," Myra said, face filling with a luminous smile. "Only lawyers I know get threatened represent the Mafia." She laughed, ran five fingers through a crown of red hair. "This office deals with the down and out," she went on. "We're the only hope these people have. Why would they threaten us?" Saying "us," assuming the FBI man was talking about the PD's office in general, her in particular. Myra bragging, offering Marty French his props, letting him know they were a team, not seeing where the FBI man was going with it.

Barton looked at Lansing, waited for him to finish writing, put the pad away, catch his eye. And when he did, Barton gave him the nod, looked back to Myra, and closed the folder. He could see she didn't get it, wondered whether it was just a put-on act or that she was really that dumb. She was brains and a cover-girl face attached to a pair of tits that had something to prove. Blinded by her high IQ, need to compete with men, he guessed. Redhead was right up on it, so full of herself she couldn't see the forest for the trees. *Why would they threaten us?* Jesus, he couldn't believe she'd said that. Incredible. He decided she really was that dumb, that he'd have to spell it out for her own good.

"You're a very lucky young woman, Miss Cross," Barton said, bringing it to her easy, trying not to scare her. "Being lazy probably saved your life."

"I beg your pardon!" Myra said, bristling, moving forward to the edge of the sectional, ready to stand, take on the FBI man insulting her like that. And drawing the back of her hand across her forehead casually to wipe away the layer of dampness, mustache of perspiration on her upper lip, trying not to be too obvious. Nose sending her a message it was about ready to run, that it needed to be fed. Now.

Lansing said, "Ignition. You said you didn't have it fixed because you were lazy. Isn't that what you said?"

She couldn't argue with truth. Myra moved back to the pillow.

She said, "Oh. Yes, I did say that, didn't I." Feeling on edge, like she would come apart at the seams, nose ready to run, fighting the urge to suck it back, make a spectacle of herself. She just looked at Lansing, her face blank and expressionless. Waiting. No idea where he's going with it and not really caring so long as he gets it over with. If she didn't get to the ladies' room.

Barton said, "Your car didn't explode because of a gasoline leak, Miss Cross." Cutting right to the chase. Spelling it out. "The explosion was the result of an IED."

Myra's face still empty, still not seeing it. FBI man talking Greek. Forehead turning into Niagara Falls, nose beginning to run. Another minute she'd need soap and towel.

Lansing said, "Why you're still alive. The ignition."

Myra said, "What's an IED?"

Lansing said, "Attached to your starter."

Myra said, "What was attached to the starter?"

Barton said, "A bomb."

CHAPTER 7

TWENTY-SIX MILES off the coast of Los Angeles sits Catalina Island. Twelve hundred feet high, three miles long, one mile wide, a population of two thousand permanent residents, a Rotary club, a Kiwanis, and a high school with just enough students to field a football team. Tourism is the engine that drives the economy and Avalon Harbor, with its yachts, fishing boats, sightseeing vessels, and vintage 1930s domed ballroom, is usually the first stop.

Unless you arrive by plane.

Darryl Brigham had flown over to Catalina Island's mountain-top airport more times than he could remember in the some twenty years he'd been licensed as a pilot. Taking flying lessons on a dare during his four-year stint in the army, he discovered he enjoyed it just about as much as bashing in heads as an MP. After his discharge from the army he moved west, joined the LAPD, continued flying and bashing heads. Over the years he upgraded his skills in both, obtaining an instrument rating as a pilot, and a reputation as a sadistic cop who played by his own rules. No wives, but several live-in girlfriends. One with a kid she said was his, and probably was, who moved in with an artist and made him send three hundred a month for support in exchange for visitation. That notwithstanding, it was a good life, being a cop and flying, the latter a way to step out of the sewer of violence in which he thrived and to which he had become accustomed, if only for a few hours at a time.

And usually his flights across the twenty-six miles of Pacific Ocean to Catalina were enjoyable, a way of reducing the tension that had become the mistress of his daily existence. Taking off from

Santa Monica Airport, where he kept the Cessna 172 on which he'd finally made the last payment, soaring into the sky and leveling off at three thousand feet, feeling the jostling of thermals under the 172's wing during the brief twenty-minute flight to the island, the three-thousand-foot runway clear and visible below, stretched out across the entire width of the mountain like a Band-Aid on a broken arm, steep thousand-foot drop-offs at both ends leaving no margin for error. Circling at the approach, dropping a thousand feet downwind, dog-leg down another five hundred, correcting for the crosswind on final, flaps down, reducing power, the challenge of touching down at the very edge of the slightly downhill runway—give yourself the entire three thousand feet to stop before the thousand-foot drop-off at the end and if you can't, power on, flaps up, and go around for another try, get it right.

But not today. Today's flight would be troubling because of the panic call he'd received from Sanford, telling him they had to meet. Not a request, an order—Thursday. The Mountaintop Restaurant, Catalina Island. One P.M. Day off, sick leave, or vacation time. It didn't matter. Just be there. All of them: Calvin James, Gilbert Monroe, Neil Sanford, Paul Stepolini, and Darryl Brigham. Rejects from Rampart Division's CRASH antigang squad because they were considered too "over the top," they bonded together in secret out of frustration and anger, became the Seventy-seventh Division's most notorious if not infamous cops who collectively had more police brutality civil suits, IA investigations for "officer involved shootings" than any similar group at any other LAPD division, except maybe Rampart. They managed to survive in the LAPD because of the police culture. How they survived one another was an entirely different matter. They even had a savings account, each man gave ten dollars a month, all five signatures required to withdraw the twenty-four hundred dollars they'd saved, access to the safe-deposit box, combination to the vault that for the past four years held seven million dollars blood money. The name they gave themselves said it all. The Gang of Five.

Stepolini said he hadn't been on the water in a while, would make the four-hour crossing in his thirty-foot sailboat he docked at Marina del Rey.

Darryl offered to fly his buddy over, but Monroe said small planes were too dangerous, that he'd pay the $44.50 for a round-trip ticket on the tour boat out of San Pedro, make the ninety-minute crossing through choppy seas with Sanford and Calvin.

It may have been the reason Monroe didn't stay in the air force, where, like Brigham, he'd been functioning MP. He absolutely loved working the bars at overseas bases, going in, busting up brawls already under way, starting fights with drunk and rowdy airmen just so he'd have some action, use his club to draw blood. He didn't mind working the stockade, except it was boring most of the time. He didn't mind going TDY to Panama or Japan or Alaska to escort an AWOL prisoner back for court-martial. But working security on the flight lines, having to secure crash sites soured him on flying to the point he couldn't get on a plane, any plane. He became so fearful of flying it made no sense to stay in the air force, so he took his DD 214 discharge at Mather Field in Sacramento, caught a Trailways bus down to LA, became a cop, and never got on a plane again.

Scattered clouds and good visibility but windy on the mountaintop. The wheels of the 172 touched down too far down the runway to stop, so Darryl powered up, made a second go-around for another try, dropped the plane on the runway right at the markers, tied up next to a Beechcraft Bonanza on an airport apron that was otherwise deserted. Catalina airport was dead midweek, first-come first-serve on the weekends. Darryl grabbed his *Flying* magazine in case he was early and headed for the restaurant.

The Mountaintop was nearly empty. A few customers at the lunch counter, others scattered about at tables, U-shaped booths below a wall of windows with an unbroken view of the runways, a solitary waitress on duty fighting a war with obesity and good manners. A big picture of the Wright Flyer anchored the wall behind the counter, along with signed photographs of celebrities posing with their planes. The restaurant was set for lunch, napkins with pictures of the island, place mats with various pictures of the island saying "Catalina Island" in each spot, elevator music spilling out from hidden speakers.

Darryl was not the first to arrive. The Italian waved from a booth in the back, beer in the hand that didn't wave. Stepolini: black hair, narrow face, even narrower features, and deceptively small but rock-solid build—had the kind of looks that could have made him a movie star. Except for his temper. Brought about the end of two marriages and destroyed every job he had. Except as a cop. It was ideal as a cop. Ideal too for the five years he served in the marines. But they court-martialed him for assaulting an officer. He was acquitted when it came out he'd been unreasonably provoked by a man who'd seen *The Godfather* one too many times and didn't like Italians. Stepolini could have stayed in the marines, made a career of it, but figured any potential for advancement was essentially over. So he returned to LA, tried a number of jobs: salesman for water softeners, driver for UPS, cable installer for the phone company, and bouncer. He liked being a bouncer. Enjoyed the confrontation. He never backed down. Never, ever backed down. But the club had to let him go when he nearly killed a guy who was drunk and wanted to fight. Someone told him LAPD was hiring, that he should take the test. He passed with flying colors. Just what LAPD needed: an aggressive, doesn't-back-down kind of guy. He fit right in, just like the three other cops entering the restaurant, sliding into the booth shoulder to shoulder, placing orders for drinks and lunch.

Neil Sanford, at forty-eight, had been a cop too long. You could see it in the spiderweb of frown lines that mapped his tired face, the drooping, deep-set watery eyes that gave the impression he was either just waking up or drunk. And Neil Sanford did like to drink. A receding hairline of gray drew attention to thinning eyebrows, cauliflower nose, and tiny ears that looked as if they had been added to the skull at the last minute to fill in dead space. An army vet, Sanford was the only one who'd seen combat. At sixteen he had looked twenty because of his solid, six-foot-three, all-conference linebacker frame. He fought daily battles with alcoholic parents so desperate to get him out of the house that they willingly forged his birth certificate so he could join the army. In Vietnam he was a natural leader who, after their lieutenant was killed on a search-and-destroy mission in Quang Tri Province, managed to bring the entire platoon through one firefight after another unscathed. His leadership brought him a chestful of medals, all the liquor he could drink. If they'd known he was only sixteen they'd have made him a general. Vietnam had made him a killer and he liked the feeling. He was going to reenlist, but during a period of R and R in the states he was diagnosed with TB and spent nearly nine months in a sanitorium. By the time they released him, Vietnam was winding down, the fall of Saigon expected in ten months or less. He'd gotten one of the nurses pregnant, so he took his discharge and played daddy for a couple of years, didn't like it and thought about going back into the army. And he would have too if he hadn't seen the LAPD recruitment booth at a job fair at the college where he was taking night courses in business. It wasn't Vietnam, but it was close enough.

Calvin James rounded out the Gang of Five. He was the token black cop. They knew it and he knew it, and everybody laughed about it when they were together, called him nigger when he wasn't around, to his face when he was. He was raised in a group home because his mother was an addict who physically abused him until Child Protective Services removed him from her custody. They put him in a group home where it was either fight or die. So Calvin James learned to fight and was good at it. So good, in fact, he was encouraged to take up boxing. He was disciplined and trained rigorously, but had so much uncontrolled explosive rage built up that when he was in the ring and got hit, he turned Mike Tyson on them. He didn't bite them but would grab his opponents, throw them to the ground, start kicking them like Dennis Rodman until the referee and corner men pulled him off. They banned him from boxing when he refused to take the Thorazine prescribed by the Boxing Commission's psychiatrist. He tried joining the army but couldn't pass the psychological exam. But his profile was perfect for the LAPD, where they let him kick people without having to play basketball, see a shrink, or take medication.

The Gang of Five all present and accounted for.

Waiting for their food, everyone nursing a beer, Darryl a Pepsi because he was flying, they talked about things in general: how rough the water was on the ride over, disaffected wives, women they'd screwed, movies they'd seen—Monroe saying he didn't think *The Matrix Revolutions* was as good as the first two installments. Stepolini saying his mother was sick, that he might have to go back to New Jersey to see about her if his sister couldn't bring herself to put her in a nursing home. Darryl Brigham saying he had a root canal in an effort to save his few remaining teeth, Calvin saying if he stopped chewing gum and flossed every day he wouldn't need a root canal. They talked about family and friends, who died, vacations they'd been on, fellow officers who'd retired. Small talk. Because there really wasn't anything else to talk about until Neil Sanford was ready.

"You blew up the wrong car," Neil Sanford said after their food arrived, not looking up, eyes focused on the cube steak, covering it with A.1.

Stepolini said, "How was I to know the guy couldn't read. I gave him a picture of the guy, the car, license plate. Jesus! I couldn't believe it. All he had to do was follow him, pick the right place, and *boom*." Not looking up either, twirling spaghetti around a fork, bread following the fork into his mouth.

"A tow-truck driver. Can you imagine that," Neil Sanford said, still looking at his plate, mixing the mashed potatoes around in the gravy, head shaking in disgust.

"I just can't see how he got the wrong car. I mean, Christ, he had the goddamn license plate! How hard is that?" Stepolini said, fork twirling the spaghetti.

"A second license plate," Sanford said, concentrating on the sauerkraut now, shoveling it onto his fork, mixing it with the gravy.

"Can't be a second plate," Stepolini said, working more spaghetti onto his fork, following it with a sip of beer. "It was one of those vanity plates, you know, personalized. DMV won't allow any duplicates."

"What did the plate say?"

Stepolini paused, thought about it. He said, "Myra's Beau."

"Myra's Benz," Sanford said. "Second plate. Why he missed it."

"Really," Stepolini said, eyebrows going up at the revelation. "Myra's Benz. Same model and color?"

"Same model. Different color. Burnt orange."

Stepolini took a long sip of beer and said, "Myra's Benz, Myra's Beau. Never figured on that—vanity plates that close. Guy don't speak much English and can't read, I can see how he'd miss it."

Darryl's fork filled a mouth of missing teeth with romaine lettuce. "Papers said FBI hasn't ruled out the tow-truck driver as a suicide bomber." Darryl's head up, looking around, seeing who agrees, chewing salad with difficulty, lower jaw moving from side to side like a cow chewing cud.

"What they're supposed to say," Neil Sanford said. "FBI isn't stupid. Knows it wasn't any suicide bomber. Wrongful death suit against the city for ten million dollars sound like something a suicide bomber's family would do?"

"What it sounds like," Calvin said, teeth in the snarling mouth ripping through corned beef and rye bread, "is a dead Mexican. One less wetback we don't have to worry about," and he started laughing, choking it off with more corned beef and rye bread.

"No, Calvin," Neil Sanford said, "what it sounds like is a mistake that has to be corrected."

Calvin said, "So. We correct it. Blow up the right car next time." Looking at Stepolini, heads nodding in agreement. "Don't see why you had to drag us way over here to tell us that. Phone call do just as well." Looking right at Neil Sanford, then to the others in turn, snarling mouth back to the corned beef and rye bread.

Neil Sanford finished off his beer, brought a napkin to his mouth.

"Not that simple, Calvin. We blew up the wrong car." Bothered they didn't see the urgency, not taking it seriously.

"You're repeating yourself," Calvin said. "Tell us something we don't know. Something explains why I'm here in Catalina 'stead of home."

"All right." Neil Sanford paused, opened another beer, filled his glass. "Car we blew up, one with the Myra's Benz plate, any idea whose it was? Yes? No? Anyone?"

Blank faces looking at one another, lost in lunch, light buzz of beer. Waiting.

"Car belonged to a PD," Neil Sanford said after a moment of silence, waiting to see if it registered yet, realized it hadn't.

"Yeah," said Calvin finally. "Someone named Myra." And he exploded in another spasm of laughter choked off with another sip of beer. "No matter who they work for, insurance company gonna total it out, buy the owner a new one. No sweat off my balls." Calvin laughing again, not taking it seriously.

Darryl's face brightened. He brought his head up from a plate of salmon, red beans, and rice. He said, "Wait a minute. *Wait. A. Minute* . . . PD's office. Yeah. Myra—Myra Cross. Little redheaded hottie with the nice rack." Pair of hands going out, fingers cupped like he was holding something heavy. "That Myra?" Looking at Neil Sanford like he'd won *The Price Is Right*, waiting for the key to a new car or a refrigerator.

Neil Sanford seemed relieved. He nodded and said, "That Myra."

"Really?" said Stepolini, like he was surprised but not taking it seriously, seeing a different picture. "You're thinking she's the DA's old lady?"

Neil Sanford nodded his head and said yes. But blowing up the PD's car by mistake had alerted the DA now. He thought that might prompt him to tell her about the arrangement.

Through a mouth of red beans and rice Darryl said, "Sure wish it was me. Pillow talk. Boy, would I like to drill her. Word is she turns a guy every which way but loose."

Calvin said, "High-maintenance pussy, Darryl. You can't afford her till we split that seven mil we got coming. Then you stand in line."

"Right. Like you'd really have a chance."

"Blacker the berry, sweeter the juice."

"There you go with that racial thing again," Monroe said. "Why do you niggers always go there when you can't think of anything else to say?"

There. Right in his face with it. Like he was invisible. Calvin laughing right along with the white boys like he was a card-carrying member of the Klan, not enough sense to realize he'd just been insulted, telling them niggas always had it going on with white girls, they pay him he'd be glad to give lessons.

Stepolini cut his laughter short. He said to Neil Sanford, "You don't think we should go back to the DA, remind him he can't change the terms of the agreement?"

Neil Sanford put the last of the cube steak in his mouth, followed it with a sip of beer, napkin, and said, "Bomb in the right car this time will do. But I'm not worried about him as much as I am about the reason we're here—the seven million Calvin mentioned."

Darryl said, "What about the seven million?" Missing teeth working overtime on romaine lettuce.

"Guess who Myra Cross represents?"

Another round of blank faces. No *Price Is Right* winners this time.

"Myra Cross represents one Napoleon Booker," Neil Sanford said, sure they'd see it now. "That name sound familiar?" It did of course, but no one seemed overly concerned.

"Really?" said Stepolini. "Little gangbanger we set up."

"One and the same."

"So?" Calvin said. "Nigga ain't got no money. Gonna do twenty-five to life, I don't care what color the PD's hair is."

"You'd better. Everyone at this table," Neil Sanford said. The deep-set watery eyes opened, closed, and opened again, began a slow-moving trek around the horseshoe, taking in each man separately.

"Why don't you cut to the chase, Neil," Stepolini said. "You've been dancing ever since we got here."

"All right." Neil Sanford took a sip of beer, moved his empty plate to the side, and leaned forward, both elbows on the table, slow-moving eyes closing and opening, taking in the group. "Two days ago I get a call from the DA's office," Neil Sanford began, speaking in soft, hushed tones so it wouldn't carry beyond the booth. "Prosecutor wants to talk about the Napoleon Booker case. He wants to know if all the evidence is good. I told him of course it was good, why wouldn't it be. He says Booker's PD, Myra Cross, the same Myra Cross with the red hair and big rack whose car we blew up by mistake, has filed a pretrial motion to get the gun thrown out as evidence. He wants to know why she would do that, what about the gun would make her confident enough to try and get a judge to declare it inadmissible as evidence. I told him he should know her well as anybody, that was her style—challenge the evidence good or bad, try and intimidate you. I told him she's probably just blowing smoke up his ass, that the gun was solid. We went back over everything—chase, little gangbanger's arrest, search of his car at impound, where the gun was found, who found the gun. He wanted to know if Booker was Mirandized. I told him of course he was. I told him everything we did was legal," and on this Neil Sanford tried not to smile, but it broke through anyway. "We went over the forensic report," he went on, leaning back from time to time, straightening up, working the kinks out of his back, taking a sip of beer, leaning forward on the table, same soft methodical voice addressing the group. "Talked about the match on slugs that killed the guard as well as shell casings found at the scene. I told him if he didn't trust our guys, send the gun out to any forensic lab he wanted, get himself a second opinion. I asked him what it would mean to the case if the judge threw the gun out. He said it could mean everything, it could mean nothing."

"What kind of double-talk is that?" Monroe asked.

"Same question I asked him, Gil. What did he mean—everything or nothing. He said it would depend on the reason the judge threw it out: Did we have probable cause for the search? Was the gun obtained illegally? There was still the quarter mil, Booker's priors, parole violation. Says he's gonna do time regardless, but throwing the gun out weakens the case. He just doesn't want any surprises, says if I think of anything to call him."

Neil Sanford sat back up, one arm resting on the back of the booth, sipped his beer, and waited, sure they understood the implications of the DA's call, reason he'd called the meeting. Trouble was, he was dealing with morons. To a man, they just looked at him with dull, unresponsive eyes, continued eating, wondering why he was telling them.

Calvin decided someone should say something. "So the white girl files a motion to squash the gun. So fucking what?" he said. "Judge ain't gonna allow it. We had probable cause, set this little nigga up so good he'll never see the outside."

"Did we?" Neil Sanford looking right at Calvin.

"Did we what?"

"Set him up good as you say?"

"Sure we did," Monroe said, more relaxed now, sipping his Pepsi. "Little black muthafucka is going down for the count."

"Yeah," Darryl said, thinking about it, going along now, toying with the Mountaintop's daily special, buzz from the beer blinding him from reason. "Let the hottie file whatever motions she wants. It's not gonna change a thing."

Calvin finished off the last of his corned beef and rye, took a long sip of beer, belched without apology, and said, "Way I see it we got nothin' to worry about."

"You sure, Calvin?" Neil Sanford said.

"Sure I'm sure. Why wouldn't I be?" Calvin said.

"Was your three fifty-seven killed the guard, Calvin. You think of anything we might have missed. Anything that got by us?" Stepolini said.

"Hell no. We ain't missed shit. I told you!"

"Right, Calvin. You told us. But why don't you tell us again," Neil Sanford said. "Go over it one more time, see if anything comes up we didn't think of."

Calvin bristled at the insinuation. "Why I always gotta prove something to you vanilla-wafer muthafuckas? White boy only gotta explain something one time—nigga gotta repeat it all night long. My word ain't good enough? You don't believe me?"

They could believe him, they just didn't trust him. Neil Sanford could now see the mistake in overruling the others, bringing Calvin into the Gang of Five. He'd done so because he honestly believed Calvin fit right in with their take-no-prisoners philosophy. But clearly they had nothing in common beyond bashing heads. Calvin's racial paranoia was so volatile, it became more and more difficult to have a plain conversation without him turning Malcolm X on them, reading hidden racial agendas in everything anyone said or did. Having Calvin around was a chore. And Neil Sanford was tired of the task.

"Of course we believe you, Calvin. We're all in this together," Neil Sanford said in truth. "But it's been four years. Memories fade. Doesn't hurt to go over things from time to time, see that everything's in order. Right?" Neil Sanford tried to take the sting out of it.

"Ain't a muthafuckin' thing wrong with my memory." Calvin took another long sip of beer, drained his glass, slammed it down hard on the table, making plates and silverware bounce. Startled, they sat back, the noise drawing the attention of other diners. A waitress wanting to know if everything was fine, Neil Sanford playing it off, asking to see the dessert menu.

"One more time for you dumb-ass cracker muthafuckas," Calvin said. "Took the three fifty-seven off a drug dealer I busted almost twenty years ago. If it was used in a felony before then I couldn't say. If so, ain't never gonna come back to me. Up to four years ago only time I used it, New Year's Eve. You know, celebrating and shit. Last time, when I shot the guard. My job, remember? Security. Muthafucka gonna play hero, go for his weapon, protect the company's money. Sheeit!"

"Four years ago. And you haven't used it since?" Darryl said. "Not even once we don't know about—busting other drug dealers, gangbangers?"

Calvin took a deep breath of exasperation, like he had to work at it.

He said, "What the fuck's wrong with your hearing, white boy? Four years ago last time it was fired. Kept it stored ever since. Why I'm gonna keep a piece out that can send me to the joint? You crackers got eye problems—you can't see past black. Just 'cause I'm a nigga don't make me stupid!"

"And it's never been out of your possession since then. No one else had access to it? Borrowed it maybe?" Stepolini said, ignoring Calvin's Malcolm X posture.

Calvin shook his head and laughed, said to no one in particular, "This day and age, still hard to convince white boys a nigga can be trusted." And to Stepolini he said, "No, Don Corleone, not unless it was Houdini and he'd have to find it first."

Calvin's statement seemed to satisfy everyone. More or less. Neil Sanford drained his glass, filled it with another beer, brought his hunched form and elbows back on the table.

"All right, then," he said. "Let's not forget what brought this whole thing about. We set Napoleon Booker up to deflect the DA's heat away from us. And why did we have to do this? We had to do this because the DA's office got a letter from the administrator of a mental hospital with an incoherent note and some money from a *crazy* that the assistant DA assigned to the case traced to the armored car. And when it was finally determined the nutcase in the hospital who gave him the money was an LAPD informant—"

"Princess," Stepolini said, interrupting, sipping the last of his beer, opening another one.

"Right. Princess," Neil Sanford said, affirming it but not appreciating the interruption. "Well," he went on, "we got a break with the assistant DA. Lucky for us he was hungry. But something has changed. I can't talk to this guy anymore. And when I do, I don't like what I'm hearing. Which means we have to finish the job, get rid of him before they move forward with it, start talking about indictments? Why the PD's motion to exclude the gun scares me."

"I don't see why," Monroe said. "Calvin said the three fifty-seven's been out of circulation four years." Closest thing to an apology Calvin would ever get, Monroe believing him now because he had to. "Way I see it, forensic match to the slugs ought to get Booker the chair."

Stepolini said, "I agree. Let the PD file whatever motion she wants. We know for a fact the gun was used in the homicide. Booker can't get out of that."

"Good point," Darryl said. "The little redheaded hottie's just blowing hot air."

Neil Sanford sat back up with an abruptness that did not go unnoticed.

"Have I been talking in a vacuum? What part of this don't you guys understand? The DA is asking me if the gun is rock-solid evidence. He's asking me what possible new information about the gun might Booker's PD have. Now why would he be asking me that?" Neil Sanford paused long enough to open another beer, pour it in a glass, and take a long sip, see if anybody had figured it out. Blank faces all around saying they hadn't. "I'll tell you why," he continued. "The answer is, gentlemen, that he might already think the case against Booker is weak, that it's a setup."

"Why would he think that?" Monroe said.

Neil Sanford shrugged his shoulders. "Any number of reasons: gun surfacing suddenly after four years . . . gangbanger riding around town with a quarter mil of stolen cash in his tire . . ."

Calvin's face exploded in a map of frowns.

"Oh, please. Give me a fuckin' break, white boy." Malcolm X again. All he needed was a bow tie. "How many times we bust these little penny-ante dope dealers, find a fortune in cash hidden somewhere in their cars 'cause they can't put it in the bank. Ain't no DA gonna be surprised at that. And as far as it being from an armored car robbery . . . I was him, say I ripped off some other dope dealer, dropped a dime on one of my competitors, let him take the heat, prove he didn't have it." Low murmurs of agreement around the table, heads nodding in unison like movements from a hand puppet.

"And DAs do that all the time," Stepolini said to Neil Sanford. "Go back over evidence, make sure it holds up in court. Nothing unusual about that."

"No, no, no," Neil Sanford said, shaking his head in disagreement. "You're missing the point—all of you. Listen . . . Booker's PD gets the gun thrown out as evidence: procedure . . . probable cause . . . illegal search-and-seizure . . . wrong color, whatever. DA comes back to me, wants to know more about the gun, specifically where the gun came from. Don't you see? If he wants to know where the gun came from, it means he thinks it's planted. And let me tell you something, gentlemen, if he thinks it's planted—not saying he does, now—but if it turns out that's what the redhead has planned, whether she's got something or just blowing hot air like Charles Lindbergh here says, if the DA believes it, imagine what he'll think about the money. Because I can just about guarantee you, they throw out the gun, Booker's PD's gonna file a pretrial motion to squash the money. And you *know* what that'll mean . . . !"

A moment of silence. Not there yet, but almost. A horseshoe of blank faces putting it together.

Time for a little reality check.

"Hello? Knock, knock. Anybody home? Squash the gun," Neil Sanford said, "squash the money? Do not pass go. Do not collect seven million dollars. Go straight to jail!"

The light came on in all their minds. If they had any appetite left it was gone. Eating stopped. Beer sipping stopped. Monroe stared down at his salmon, red beans, and rice getting cold. Darryl lost his taste for romaine lettuce. Long, hard nails on Stepolini's fingers drummed the side of his half-empty glass, rhythm like a horse at full gallop. The waitress waddled over with the dessert menu. No one ordered.

It was the first time Neil Sanford had seen any real fear on the faces of the Gang of Five. No one seemed to have the courage to speak.

"Any way to stop the IA investigation?" Monroe said, beginning to appreciate the urgency of things now, that it might be something to worry about.

"Not the one we have to worry about," Neil Sanford said. And to Stepolini, "What about the Glock we found in Booker's car. Anything turn up?"

"Stolen," Stepolini said. "But it's clean. Ran it through ballistics but they haven't come up with anything so far."

Neil Sanford seemed disappointed. "So we can't use it."

"If we plant it in his home: ex-felon in possession of stolen property while on parole?" Stepolini offered.

Neil Sanford sucked air through clenched teeth, shook his head.

"No," he said, "I don't want to chance it. Not in this DA's frame of mind. Last-minute evidence might really make him suspicious. No, if we can't get a ballistics match on a prior homicide tied to the Glock, best let it stay invisible."

"All right," Stepolini said. "What do you suggest?"

Neil Sanford brought his aging frame, slow-moving watery eyes back to the table on a brace of elbows.

"We finish what we started. Get the DA's investigation off of us." Looking at Stepolini, who nodded in agreement. To the others he said, "We need to find out exactly what Booker's PD has, make sure it doesn't get to court."

"When you say make sure it doesn't get to court . . . ?" Darryl said.

"In Vietnam it was called search and destroy," Neil Sanford said.

"That include Booker, the hottie PD?" Monroe wanted to know.

Neil Sanford said, "Includes anyone who can point a finger at us. DA's office has evidence . . . PD's office has evidence . . . Princess has evidence. Far as I'm concerned, they're one and the same."

Calvin said, "Search and destroy. I like that."

Neil Sanford said to Calvin, "You would've loved Vietnam." And to the others, "Hearing on the motion to suppress the gun is in ten days," he continued on, general giving orders to his troops. "So we'll have to move quickly."

Speaking for all of them, Monroe said, "What happens if whatever Booker's PD has gets past us, winds up in court. What then?"

Neil Sanford straightened up, swung an arm up over the back of the booth, let his tired puffy eyes drift to the runway beyond the glass. He thought about the question for a moment. He decided there was really only one answer: truth. A truth he knew they would understand. He brought his attention back to the group but his eyes were still on the runway, a small plane clearing the markers, its wings catching the vortex of wind that lifted it into the cloudy afternoon sky.

To their dim reflections in the glass and without turning around, Neil Sanford gave the only truth he knew.

"Then the good guys win."

CHAPTER 8

THE NIGHT BEFORE the scheduled hearing on the motion to suppress evidence in the Napoleon Booker case, Myra worked at home until nearly midnight, much of that time on the telephone with Ray Watanabe, going over his findings and preparation of his testimony. When they finished she put on a CD of Sarah Vaughan's greatest hits, lit a joint of chronic, and dropped down into the recliner to kick back. She hadn't been able to relax like this since returning to work. She could deal with Craig McInnis's ego, not that she had any choice in the matter, even put up with Marty French's tyranny and Clara's feudal backstabbing gossip. But what she couldn't deal with was the gradual loss of interest in her work. She was still very good, but all the pleasure and enthusiasm had gone. Truth of the matter was she wanted a career in entertainment now more than ever. She couldn't believe it was taking *Playboy* so long to get the Professional Women's issue out. She didn't want to practice law anymore. And nothing had brought it home any clearer than the insulting FBI interrogation to which she'd been subjected two weeks earlier . . .

She was still smarting from the absurd allegation that her Mercedes had exploded because of a bomb, an IED—improvised explosive device—the FBI had called it. The kind insurgents use in Iraq. More incredible was the assertion that Ernesto Ruiz, the Mexican tow-truck driver, was most likely an operative in a Los Angeles–based Al Qaeda cell. Suggesting she might have known him before, implying she could have links to a terrorist group. Not coming right out and saying it like that, but suggesting it by inference and innuendo . . . that bit about their clients with anti-American views, and clients who threaten them. Oh, please. She'd felt insulted, and if she hadn't been so on edge when they told her, she would have laughed in their faces. And the image of the FBI man groveling around on Marty French's carpet like a dog brought a smile to her lips between hits on the joint. The nerve, FBI trying to cloud her reputation like that. And that bit about the gasoline—now, that was ridiculous. True, her nose may have been coked up, but it wasn't so far gone she couldn't smell gasoline, the FBI man saying the tow-truck driver could have planted the idea of gasoline in her mind, or may have had it on his hands, that she might have really believed she smelled gasoline. Oh, really? She was that dumb? She was expected to believe foreign terrorists had rigged her car to explode in a half-empty parking lot next to the Men's Central Jail. A real political statement, that one. How was anybody to know her movements, that her ignition was bad, who or where or when she would have to call Triple A. And logic seemed to escape them: if Ernesto Ruiz was a terrorist, it meant everyone employed by the company was in on the deal, just sitting by the phones day and night with nothing to do but wait for her call, handing it to Ruiz if and when it ever came in. Really? Just how dumb did the FBI think she was? And in a rare display of emotion, even the perpetually stoic Marty French had scoffed at the idea, in large part, Myra was sure, because the FBI had made him second fiddle, humiliated him in front of a subordinate staff member.

And the insurance company certainly didn't buy it. When they finally totaled out her car, it didn't say "due to terrorist explosion," it said "most likely a faulty gas line connection at the gas tank," and they sent Myra a check that she promptly used to buy another Mercedes: same make, same model, same personalized plates, but rust-colored instead of a burnt orange.

And Bruce. He really thought it was funny, started calling her nicknames, like the IED Girl, Bomber Freak, and Mad Myra. He even wore a bulletproof vest to bed one night, saying he wanted to protect himself in case Myra decided to explode. Myra didn't think it was very funny at first, until she realized the vest was perfect for their kinky sex games of bondage and subjugation, promised him all the sex he'd ever want if he'd bring one home for her to wear. So he brought her two.

No. If Ernesto Ruiz was a terrorist, so was everyone she knew— Marty French, Dillon Lester, Jason Rice, Bruce—everyone. She was beginning to feel more relaxed now, the vapors from the chronic draining away the tension of her new role as terrorist. She was feeling so relaxed that before she could get up from the recliner to get ready for bed, lay out clothes for tomorrow's court appearance, she drifted into a sound sleep.

Myra Cross arrived at the courthouse early, "Midnight Sun" and the syrupy voice of Sarah Vaughan still playing in her head. She had a light breakfast in the cafeteria with colleagues on both sides of the fence, and when finished she went to the women's room. From her purse she withdrew a razor blade and cocaine stash, laid out four lines on the flat top of her compact, which she snorted through a rolled Benjamin Franklin. She threw her head back, shook it violently, and shuddered at the rush that brought her alive. "Damn, this is some good blow," she said to no one in particular. She wiped cocaine residue from her nose, made several swipes with five ringed fingers through layers of red hair, and made sure buttons on the blouse under her smart navy blue Liz Claiborne jacket would keep her cleavage in check. A final once-over in front of the mirror, checking lipstick, shadow, and blusher, posing at different angles, practicing facial expressions as if on a Jason Rice photo shoot. Satisfied, she stuffed beauty products in her purse and left the women's room for Department 104 in the Los Angeles Criminal Courthouse.

Showtime.

The superior court's windowless mahogany-walled courtroom of Department 104, with its state seal and picture of the "governator" high on the wall behind the bench, was empty except for a few spectators, mostly journalists from local ethnic newspapers looking for a headline story on police brutality. The others, a ragtag conglomerate of paid employees who resembled refugees from gigs on Court TV and Judge Judy, included the court reporter, a middle-aged woman mumbling unintelligibly into a device that covered her face like an oxygen mask from World War II bomber pilots, and a clerk bantering with the four slow-moving bailiffs in Jolly Green Giant uniforms. Leonard Hoffler from the prosecutor's office was already there. He was a mousy-looking man made distinctively older by his receding hairline and the rather artificial way he tried to cover his baldness by combing thin graying strands from one side up and over the top. His looks were deceiving, however. Myra knew from personal experience he was not easily intimidated, that he seldom backed down unless overwhelmed with evidence that was incontestable. He gave Myra a nod of acknowledgment as she slid into her seat at the defense table across the aisle, asking if she'd tried the food at the cafeteria now that it was under new management, Myra saying yes though she hadn't noticed any difference. The usual banter among friendly adversaries who might have dined together the night before but who would be engaged in a fierce winner-take-all battle twelve hours later.

Moments later Napoleon Booker announced his presence with his usual "Wazzup, Miss Cross," dropped into the seat beside her. Guards had removed the waist chains and leg irons, but he was still in the prison-issue orange jumpsuit. They exchanged pleasantries, Myra saying Napoleon needed to do something about his hair, the cornrows fraying and loose. Napoleon telling Myra if she let her hair grow, she'd look good in braids, saying red braids on a white girl would be distinctive, like Bo Derek in the movie 10, but that he'd lost respect for her because she didn't give any screen credit to black folks who originated the style. Myra telling him she'd think about it, but who should get credit for the red hair. She was surprised Napoleon had seen 10, Napoleon saying she needed to break herself of the stereotype that black meant uncultured, that he went to movies as well as concerts, knew a little something about opera. Myra saying no disrespect was intended but she'd better quit while she was ahead, Napoleon agreeing, asking where was her partner.

Her partner. That horrible word again. Myra had suggested to Craig McInnis she handle the Napoleon Booker court appearance, he handle a deposition on another case scheduled at the same time so they wouldn't have to reschedule either one. To Myra's relief he didn't object, thinking Craig's ego liked to work alone as much as hers, that maybe it *was* Marty French's idea they work together after all.

Almost immediately she noticed the uncharacteristic absence of her investigator.

"Where's Watanabe?" Myra mumbled, looking at her watch.

"Who?" Napoleon wanted to know.

"Investigator," Myra said, looking nervously around, a few unrecognizable faces popping in and out of the door at the back of the courtroom, eyes going to her watch again. "This isn't like Raymond unless he's tied up in traffic."

"Man can't call you, tell you he's gonna be late?" Napoleon said.

"You would think," Myra said, punching in his number on her cell phone. She left a worried message on his answering machine, clicked off, and settled back to wait.

"All rise." The bailiff, like on *Judge Judy*, only he was short and scarecrow thin.

Cynthia Delacorte approached the bench with a posture and elegance befitting her position. A judge with a no-nonsense reputation. She was a woman in her late fifties whose face was beginning to show the telltale signs of age and who, Myra guessed, had been quite attractive at one time in her youth. Her trademark was a pair of herringbone-rimmed glasses that hung from her neck by a diamond-encrusted chain whose sparkle against her black robe matched the streaks of gray flowing back from graying temples. Myra had appeared before Cynthia Delacorte on numerous occasions. She wasn't Myra's intellectual equal, but Myra considered her fair. Myra called the investigator's number again, left another harried message, craned her neck to check the courtroom.

"In the matter of the People versus Napoleon Booker," Cynthia Delacorte said from her perch behind the bench, glasses going on, practiced fingers flipping papers one after another. "The defendant has brought a fifteen thirty-eight point five before this court to suppress certain evidence presented at his preliminary hearing. Is that right?" Cynthia Delacorte making sure she had the right case, the right parties before her bench. Hearing no objection and not expecting any, she continued on, saying, "The evidence in question before the court is—"

"Miss Cross!!!" the voice cried out, interrupting Cynthia Delacorte, drawing everyone's attention to the back of the courtroom, the tall, lanky woman running breathlessly down the aisle, eyes opened wide, frightened and tear streaked. Lorna reached the railing behind Myra, leaned over, and whispered frantically in her ear.

"Shot? My God!" Myra said loud enough for others to hear, her face suddenly gone pale, drained of its color.

"Miss Cross . . . ?" Cynthia Delacorte said from the bench, head lowered, eyes peering over the top of herringbone rims. "Problem?" Knowing there was because she heard what everyone else heard.

Visibly shaken, Myra Cross stood up on legs suddenly grown weak, saying to Cynthia Delacorte, "Uh, Your Honor. Uh . . . well, yes . . ."

Myra suddenly felt faint and nauseated. Unsteady on her feet, she dropped back into her seat, disorganized in her thinking and in shock, beads of perspiration beginning to form on her forehead, upper lip.

Napoleon said, "What this mean, Miss Cross?"

Myra said absently, "It means . . . Jesus. Shot!" Still in disbelief, trying hard to fathom the enormity of what Lorna had said.

Napoleon said, "You ain't got no other investigator you can call, prove I didn't kill no guard, prove I didn't—"

Myra touched Napoleon's arm, more to calm herself than him.

Cynthia Delacorte saying beneath the herringbone rims, "Miss Cross . . . ?"

Myra said, "Just a minute, Napoleon. I . . ." With great effort she brought herself upright, tried to hold herself together while she gathered splintered thoughts, planned a response, thought about what to do next. To Cynthia Delacorte she said, "I'm . . . uh . . . sorry, Your Honor . . ." Myra's voice suddenly going up several octaves, her words catching in a dry throat, eyes wandering around the room like a child lost in a park, not focusing on anything. Myra tried swallowing. "I've . . . Jesus. Well, Your Honor, I just this minute was advised our investigator on this matter, Mr. Watanabe, has apparently been seriously injured. I don't know any of the details or the severity of his injuries." She turned around to face Lorna, but Lorna had dropped down into a seat behind the railing, pale hands covering a tearful face lost in its own shock. Not looking up, she had nothing else to offer Myra, shrugging her shoulders and shaking her head. "Like I said," Myra went on, turning back around to face the judge, feeling faint again but leaning against the table to brace herself, stiff and rigid like a piece of lumber. "I was only just informed. But his testimony is material to this motion," she said, forcing herself to reorganize dismembered thoughts, feeling a headache coming on big-time. "And until such time as I can sort things out the defense is not prepared to move forward on the motion before the court at this time. We, uh . . . the defense"—Myra stammered, swallowing to bring moisture to a dry mouth—"the defense therefore respectfully asks the court to grant us a continuance on this motion." Myra amazed she could get it out.

Napoleon said, "What that mean, 'continuance'? I gotta go back to jail?"

Myra said, "Just a minute, Napoleon." Touched his arm again. No strength in her legs yet, lumber still braced by the table.

Cynthia Delacorte removed her glasses, let the diamond-encrusted chain take its weight over her black robe, and said, "Not being insensitive to tragedy, Miss Cross, but you said he was material to this motion. Are there not other witnesses material to the motion you can call to move this matter forward?"

"What I say," Napoleon Booker blurted out, head nodding in agreement.

Myra Cross said, "No, Your Honor. Mr. Watanabe was the only witness."

Cynthia Delacorte raised her eyebrows in surprise, returned the herringbone rims to the bridge of her nose, and leaned forward on the bench, sitting up straight on a wide pyramid of elbows.

"Really," she said. "A single witness on a matter this important, Miss Cross?"

Myra Cross said, "That's right, Your Honor." Careful not to overplay her hand, not appear arrogant or overconfident, just professional, beginning to think more clearly now, just barely, moving back from the table, standing under her own power.

Cynthia Delacorte looked at the folder, appeared to think about it for a minute, then said to Leonard Hoffler, "Do the People have an objection?"

Disappointed at having to wait to see Myra's evidence on the motion and concerned about her outburst, what bearing if any it had on the case, Leonard Hoffler rose from his seat and said, "No, Your Honor. The People have no objection."

Cynthia Delacorte leaned back, thought about it some more, and finally said, "Very well. Request for continuance on the motion to suppress evidence in the case of the People versus Napoleon Booker is granted for a period of twenty-four hours." And addressing the court reporter seated to the left of the bench, her face nearly hidden by the *Twelve O'Clock High* oxygen mask, she said, "The hearing on this fifteen thirty-eight point five will be rescheduled until nine a.m. tomorrow morning in this courtroom."

Myra said, "Thank you, Your Honor."

"All rise." The scarecrow bailiff announcing court was adjourned.

When Cynthia Delacorte disappeared through a door to her chambers, Myra sat back down weakly, her strength not yet fully returned. Knowing now what she had to do, that it wouldn't be pleasant, that she'd need a shock of dope to get her through it. She gathered up the file and tried to reassure her client.

"Minor setback, Napoleon," Myra said, lack of conviction in her voice not lost on Napoleon. "Unfortunate situation if it's true." Myra still struggling to believe it. She said, "But it shouldn't affect your case overall." And knowing she was lying, that it may have already destroyed Napoleon's chance at exoneration.

"Sure hope you right," Napoleon said, standing as the bailiff put on handcuffs and chains, and staring now at Myra. "What about a backup investigator?"

"If it becomes necessary, I'll get one," Myra answered tentatively because she couldn't think of anything else to say. "I'll know more later this afternoon." Myra lying again, and knowing Napoleon knew she was lying.

As the bailiff was escorting Napoleon Booker from the courtroom, Napoleon turned and said something to Myra over his shoulder, not loud or shouting. But Myra, only half listening, had turned her attention to Lorna, thanking her and suggesting she ask Marty French for the rest of the day off if she felt too stressed out. Lorna saying she'd be all right, that she didn't want to burden Marty French with finding a temp. Myra said that was nice of her and meant it, walked Lorna to the elevator. As soon as the doors closed she literally ran to the nearest women's room.

Fortified on a midmorning cocktail of narcotics, Myra found Raymond Watanabe hooked up to a life support system and dying in the surgical intensive care unit of Los Angeles County General Hospital—"Big General," they called it. Paramedics had taken him there because it was the trauma center closest to his house. Raymond Watanabe's eyes were covered with gauze pads, head swathed in a turban of bandages, breathing tube sticking out of his throat attached to a hissing respirator that moved a chest punctured by more tubes. He was not visibly recognizable. He'd been shot seven times—twice in the head, five times in the torso. Surgeons had stopped the bleeding, removed the nine-millimeter slugs from his chest and abdomen, but the shots to the head were fatal. He was essentially brain-dead. Myra wanted to know if he had said anything, the surgeons saying no, he never regained consciousness.

Myra vomited the moment she left the hospital. It was so horrible, seeing death like that up close and personal. Surreal, like something out of a horror movie—Raymond Watanabe lying in a hospital bed, unrecognizable, wrapped up in the bandages of death, like a mummy being prepared for burial. A victim. Somebody she knew. Somebody she'd spoken to only hours ago. Someone she'd dined with, exchanged gifts with on birthdays and Christmas, shared rides with to and from court, laughed with when they'd won, groaned with when they'd lost. Raymond Watanabe had been a good friend. Myra found it hard to use the past tense, hard to believe he was no longer alive. And good friends don't deserve to die like this. Myra couldn't help but believe he'd still be alive if she'd warned him it might be a dangerous assignment, given him the choice of taking it or not. But if not him, then who? Nothing about their work was guaranteed. Living with guilt over a professional decision gone bad wouldn't be something new for Myra. But it was the first time it had caused a death. She'd get through it. She'd have to. Myra had never run from the truth, and as painful as it was she wasn't about to start now.

She didn't know if she could finish the rest of the day, considered calling Marty French, telling him she wasn't up to coming back to the office tomorrow morning. Only the thought of surrendering to Craig McInnis kept her going. So with great reluctance she went to the crime scene. It wasn't anything like the prime-time CSI dramas on television. This was real.

Raymond Watanabe's hillside Silverlake house was a few miles east of the Greek Theatre and Griffith Park. Besides reams of yellow DO NOT CROSS police tape, there wasn't much to see, but what there was wasn't pretty—his Toyota Camry sitting in the driveway, driver's-side window shattered, glass scattered about the bloody headrest, blood-soaked passenger seat. The glove compartment was open and on the backseat his attaché case had been pried open, the blood-soaked contents scattered about. According to investigators, paramedics found him strapped in his seat-belt harness, his bloody form slumped over toward the passenger seat. Investigators saying in all probability it was a random carjacking, that he'd been shot through the window, causing the shattered glass to somehow jam the seat-belt mechanism, explaining why the carjackers couldn't move him out of the seat so they could drive. That turned it into a robbery. At least two assailants. Drug addicts most likely. They found discarded drug paraphernalia at the scene: a broken freebase pipe, near-empty bag of weed—the theory being they most likely happened upon him outside his home just as he was backing his car out of the garage, reminding Myra that Toyota Camrys were the most popular target for carjackers. Investigators said Raymond Watanabe's wife and other neighbors all heard the shots, but the high sloping walls on both sides of his driveway blocked any view from houses on his side of the street, his widow telling them that by the time she'd traversed the some fifty-odd steps down to the garage they were gone. And there were no houses across the street, just an unbroken panoramic view of beautiful downtown LA smog. They'd gone through his pockets, investigators said. According to his wife, they'd stolen his cameras, photos, and several rolls of unexposed film.

Photographs. That said it all.

Myra's leaden body climbed the fifty-odd steps to Ray Watanabe's house as she had done on several previous occasions for social functions held by the department and often hosted by Raymond and his wife, Ting. Once she reached the porch, it took every bit of effort she could muster to go through the door and into a darkened front room saturated with the soft, quiet sobbing of grief. Friends and family members Myra did not know sat on either side of Ting, a diminutive, small-boned woman not yet thirty and clearly six to seven months' pregnant. Even in the midst of her grief, Ting rose to greet Myra when she entered, proffering introductions to the assembled mourners despite a never-ending river of tears coursing down her face.

Myra said if she needed anything, all she had to do was ask, and she meant it.

"Thank you, Myra," Ting managed to say, the voice tiny and soft, nearly inaudible. "Ray always had nice things to say about you."

The words alone brought forth Myra's own tears, but she brushed them back and said to Ting, "He was good people, Ting. I can't say enough about him. He was just good people." Myra broke off for an instant, pushed back more tears, then said tentatively, "I know this may not be the time for it, Ting. And please forgive me for asking. I mean no disrespect, but your husband was working on a case for me. I need to clarify something you told investigators earlier today. If you're not up to it, I quite understand. But—"

Ting cut Myra off, saying, "No, Myra. You go ahead. Ray mentioned it when he left this morning." And with incredible strength of character, her trembling fingers dabbing a handkerchief at wet almond-shaped eyes, Ting waited.

"Well," Myra said, "how did you know what equipment had been stolen out of Ray's car?"

"I couldn't sleep last night," Ting said, placing both hands on her bloated abdomen. "The baby's kicking, so I couldn't get comfortable. So I came up front and kept Ray company, watched him pack his case. I saw every camera, the nine rolls of film, and the three envelopes of developed photos he packed."

"Do you know if he made any copies he might have left here?"

"No. Only what he packed. Ray didn't like to keep anything at the house."

"What about labs," Myra asked. "Do you know which ones he used by any chance?"

"Several," Ting said. "I'll have to go through the receipts later, try to find out for you. Have you checked your e-mail? I know he sends pictures by e-mail at times."

"Ray said his computer had crashed and his scanner was on the blink."

"That explains it."

"Explains what?"

"Why he didn't have the computer on last night. He's a computer geek in his spare time. He's working on developing some kind of software program. Who knows how long it'll take him to finish it. He runs that thing day and night. You should see our electric bill."

Who knows how long it'll take him to finish it.

Present tense.

That got to Myra—Ting talking like he'd be home from work any minute now, come walking through the door and go straight to the computer.

It was surreal and Myra had to leave before she started thinking like Ting—sit down with a cup of coffee or tea and wait for Ray to show up, talk about the baby they were about to have, ask him when he was going to get the computer fixed.

Who knows how long it'll take him to finish it. Never, that's how long.

Jesus, Ray Watanabe dead. It couldn't be true. It just couldn't be!

But it was. The software program would never be completed, the baby would never know the warmth of its father, and Napoleon Booker was going away for life.

She thanked Ting, repeated her offer of help, and exited gracefully, making her trek back down the fifty-odd steps to the street below.

Myra dropped back into the comfort and smell of new leather, new Mercedes, started the engine. Wynton Marsalis's trumpet soared on the radio. But she couldn't put the car in gear or step on the accelerator. Suddenly Myra cut the engine off and against all resistance burst into tears of uncontrollable grief. Jerking in the quick, rhythmic motion of her sobbing, Myra's head rested on a cradle of folded arms across the padded steering wheel, like a child in grade school at naptime. She couldn't remember crying this hard over anyone except maybe her grandmother. That was ten years ago, and she'd had time to prepare for it because her grandmother had been sick a long time. They knew the end was near. But Ray Watanabe—Jesus, she'd just talked to him.

When her crying finally tapered and Myra felt herself back in control, she brought the Mercedes out of Silverlake, headed back downtown, and began connecting the dots. The picture they produced was scary. She knew it wasn't a random carjacking turned robbery, as investigators theorized. It may have been set up to look that way, but seven shots said it was an assassination. Plain and simple. As for Napoleon Booker, well . . . ? She knew now, if she didn't before, that everything he'd told her was true. Knew too her theory about bad cops was also true—that they would stop at nothing to protect themselves. And if they were willing to eliminate an investigator, they would think nothing of eliminating her client.

Or his lawyer.

And now *they* had the evidence. Photographs. Myra hadn't seen them. But Raymond Watanabe had described them, evidence showing Napoleon Booker's custom-made trapdoor was so carefully crafted, the space so tight, there was no way any .357 could fit, no matter how positioned. Thirty-eight photographs in all. Raymond Watanabe told her he would've scanned them into his computer, e-mailed them to her, but there was something wrong with his scanner.

Now they, whoever "they" were, had the camera and negatives. And probably didn't care. They knew her strategy now, would be hard at work this very moment removing Napoleon Booker's trapdoor the way they did his Glock, replacing it with a crudely fashioned one of their own, one that would hold a .357, challenging any duplicate photographs Myra could come up with. Without Raymond Watanabe's sworn affidavit as to when and where they were taken, they'd be useless.

Myra was sad and demoralized, knowing tomorrow morning she'd have to request a further delay in her motion to suppress the gun and send out a new investigator who'd bring back useless photos. Myra needed time to think, to come up with a plan B. She found herself wondering if it was worth going forward. Maybe she should just let Napoleon Booker suffer his own fate for an exercise in bad judgment. Sell him out and let him hang. No big deal. Most of their clients believe that the PD's office is in league with "the system." They were convinced that you couldn't really get any justice if you didn't have money to hire the F. Lee Baileys of the world. Yes, that would be the easy way out. Even if she prevailed, at some time in the future Napoleon Booker's gangster lifestyle would get him another case, a third strike, and he'd disappear into the prison industrial slave labor complex for twenty-five years. Why even bother. Let Napoleon's predestined fate take care of itself. And for the first time Myra Cross became conscious of her thinking, thinking she knew was wrong. Knew it wasn't like her to cave in so completely so soon. No, she wouldn't sell him out, never sell any client out. She never had and never would. She was just depressed over Ray Watanabe's murder. That had to be it. She would regroup and move forward and would do so for one fundamental reason: Napoleon Booker was innocent. He was no choirboy, of course. But this is one time he was innocent. And wasn't it her job to defend the innocent? She'd taken an oath to do so. No matter the price.

It was then she remembered what Napoleon Booker had said to her earlier that morning as he was being led out of Cynthia Delacorte's courtroom . . .

"Watch your back!"

CHAPTER 9

"WHY I GOTTA GET MY ASS OUTTA HERE," Napoleon Booker was saying to Myra Cross, the visitors room of the Men's Central Jail a crowded ark going nowhere.

"If for no other reason than to get your hair done," Myra said. Napoleon's cornrows had become a loose and frazzled tangle of unattended hair in the nearly ten weeks of his incarceration. Her eyes still bloodshot and moist from crying, Myra trying to make light of bad news, telling him about Ray Watanabe's murder, delay in the pretrial motion to suppress the .357, her gut feeling it was going nowhere.

"You making a joke out of it, Miss Cross. But I'm telling you, get me outta here and I can help you 'cause this some Mafia shit going on." Napoleon lowering his head, bringing manacled hands up the short length of the waist chain, scratching loose cornrows on the other side of the glass.

"Thought you said one of them was black?"

Napoleon's head snapped back up, suddenly narrowed eyes caught hers through the glass.

"So?"

"Mafia is white."

"They eye-talians, Miss Cross."

"All right. Italians. Your man is black."

"You ain't never heard of the black Mafia?"

Myra hadn't and said so in a cynical way, like his opinion wasn't worth the energy it took to say it.

122

"Niggas just as bad as them eye-talians, Miss Cross. They into all kinda shit, know what I'm sayin'?"

Myra grunted. "So you think this is a black thing, this seven-million-dollar robbery homicide and the frame?" she said to Napoleon, knowing she was wrong when she did. She tried to express apology but failed at that too. Anything further she might say would only make it worse.

Classroom time for white folks.

Napoleon looked at Myra Cross, incredulous eyes still burning through the glass like a laser beam through paper. He sat back up. "What's so strange about that—niggas ain't smart enough to pull off nothin' that big?" he said.

"What I meant, Napoleon—"

"Naw. What you meant, Miss Cross," Napoleon said, interrupting, his voice more disappointed than angry, "was that niggas too dumb to pull off something requires any thinking."

"But I never—"

"Only white boys, uneducated folks like eye-talian Mafia can do that. Right?" Napoleon interrupting again, not letting her apologize and having fun with it. "That's what you meant, Miss Cross." And before Myra could mount a defense, Napoleon continued with the lesson plan, calling her on it. He said, "I ain't sayin' I was framed by no black Mafia, only that they got niggas out there do shit like that. Know what I'm sayin'?"

Myra's apology was genuine. She said, "I'm sorry I said that, Napoleon. I wasn't thinking. Really, I wasn't. I guess . . . well, Ray's death, maybe . . . I don't know . . ." Myra on the verge of tears again just saying his name. "I'm sorry."

A slight smile came to Napoleon's youthful face. Hands going back up to frazzled cornrows, he said, "I can see you upset. Figured it was that. Know you didn't mean no disrespect. Just read the wrong history books, that's all. You did, you'd know niggas invented the stoplight and air-conditioning." No one ever said educating white folks was easy. Just fun.

Myra said, "Really? Air-conditioning. I didn't know that." Having to give it to him once again, wondering what he'd be if it wasn't for the streets.

"Now you do." School was out. Fun was over. It was back to business. "What's the next move?"

The inquisition over, Myra relaxed, drew tired fingers through her mop of red hair, and said, "My plan is to send out a new investigator. But don't get your hopes up just yet. Now that they know about your trapdoor I can just about guarantee you they've changed it. That means I'll have to file a pretrial motion on the spare tire and money, try to get both suppressed." Myra telling him she didn't think it was as strong as the gun but still worth the effort. "I'll have the investigator check out the trunk, talk to the people who installed your stereo system," Myra went on. "See what he finds. You said you've got receipts, so that'll help some."

"Some?" Like the word was an insult. Napoleon's hands froze on cornrows, incredulous eyes caught Myra's through the glass and spoke louder than any voice that finally escaped. "I bail out, we go down to TJ, talk to the Mexicans what I sold the tire to, get their statements. Maybe even the tire." Cut right to the chase. Like that was all there was to it.

This time it was Myra's turn to smile.

"Oh, that'll go over real well—depos from south of the border." Myra facetious again, Napoleon not challenging it because class was out. "No, we'll need something else," Myra said. "Something stronger, something that'll hold up in court."

Napoleon said, "I bail out, I can help you get it, Miss Cross."

Over a loud core of screams and laughter, rattle of chains on metal tables, guards saying to hold it down, Myra said, "I'll ask for a hearing on your bail, Napoleon. See if we can get it reduced to a mil. Though quite honestly I wouldn't hold my breath if I were you. Bail is discretionary and without something tangible, more concrete . . ." Myra shook her head, brought green bloodshot eyes to the clock on the wall, back to the brown face on the other side of the glass. "It'll be an uphill battle."

Napoleon said, "How long that take?"

Myra said, "Depends on the judge. Could be a week. Could be a month. Maybe more."

Napoleon shook his head. "Week's too long," he said, more to himself than to Myra. He sat back from the glass, like he was thinking about something, eyes looking at Myra, someplace past Myra. Then he said, "Need a favor, Miss Cross," almost hesitant in the way he asked, but more a demand than a question, still not looking directly at her.

Myra said, "If I can . . ."

Napoleon said, "Need you to talk to someone for me. Tell how you know I'm innocent, how I'm being framed on some seven-figure bullshit. Know what I'm saying? Let 'em know I ain't robbed no armored car, killed no guard."

Myra said, "Be glad to, Napoleon. Give me your mother's number." And from her purse Myra pulled out a pen, Department of Water and Power envelope ready to write on.

Napoleon said, "Ain't Moms I want you to see. Shaniqua neither."

"Shaniqua?" Myra frowning, the frog of grief toying with her memory.

"Baby mamma."

"Right." Myra shaking her head, remembering. "Who, then?"

Again Napoleon seemed hesitant, like he was holding back, having second thoughts about it. Finally he said, "Business partner."

"The lawyer? Whoa." Myra put the pen and DWP envelope back in her purse, head shaking in a flurry of no's. "I'm your lawyer, Napoleon. Not a messenger service. You want to communicate with your business partner, get Shaniqua or one of your homeys to do it. Not me." Letting him know where her line in the sand was drawn.

"Ain't no one else I can trust, Miss Cross."

"Then I guess you're out of luck, aren't you," Myra said rather coldly. "Because if I can't get your bail reduced to a million, you'll have to ride it out. I mean, I can appreciate what you're going through, Napoleon. But—"

"You ain't got no idea what I'm going through, Miss Cross," Napoleon said, interrupting without apology. "You did, you'd handle this for me, get me out so we can work together."

"I'll go to the wall for you, Napoleon. Help you any way I can. But getting in your personal business is not something I do. Sorry."

"Even though you know I'm innocent?"

"Even though I know you're innocent. I have lots of other clients, Napoleon. Some innocent. Some guilty. I treat them all the same," Myra said in truth. "Give them everything I've got. But no one is special. Not even Napoleon Booker. Why should I treat you any different than the others?"

Napoleon didn't answer right away. He leaned back from the glass once again, eyes focused on the same distant place beyond Myra, thinking about his answer, getting his thoughts in order so that when he spoke she'd know where he was coming from.

"Don't make the mistake of thinkin' I'm just another dumb street nigga caught up in the mix what don't know shit, Miss Cross," Napoleon said, leaning into the glass now, his voice calm and restrained, trapping her evading green eyes with his own. "You be in for a rude awakening. Not saying I'm special, but I'm innocent. Straight up. And the way I see it, innocent man caught up in a seven-million-dollar frame your investigator died over ought to make me the most important client you got. It don't, then you fulla bullshit and I don't need my life in the hands of no coke-snorting, nymphomaniac lawyer fulla bullshit. Oh, yeah. I know all about you—all about how you get your little freak on, how you a base-head of the first order, sucking on that glass dick till you about to explode. Personally, I don't give a fuck. Your business. You feel you can represent your clients better when you all lit up, cool. But don't go patronizing me, tellin' me you appreciate what I'm goin' through on the one hand, but can't handle my personal business on the other, 'cause that makes you nothin' but Hollywood. And if that's all there is to you—real diplomas on the outside, fake-ass white-girl lawyer on the inside—then what good you gonna do me? I be better off handling my own case pro per. Know what I'm sayin'? So either you gonna represent this nigga right, be like one of Charlie's Angels and kick butt, or don't represent me at all . . . take your little skinny white ass and get the fuck outta here. You feeling me on this, Miss Cross?" Just like that. Napoleon Booker telling her like it was. Never raised his voice. Never took his eyes off her face.

Street smarts stopped Myra Cross dead in her tracks. Napoleon Booker had reached inside her brain and ripped out her essence, dangled it in front of her like an item for sale at an eBay auction. Was she that transparent—coke-snorting, nymphomaniac base-head little freak. Incredible. Man with no formal education reading her like a book with large print. Seven-million-dollar frame Ray Watanabe died over. Had a way with words, didn't he. She had to give him that, the motherfucker. Myra didn't say anything right away. She just sat there, stone-faced and expressionless like a figure on display in a wax museum. Moist green eyes the only thing moving in the wax, searching inside herself for truth. And behind the glass a foot away, truth was staring her right in the face. Its name was Napoleon Booker. And Napoleon Booker's truth was absolutely undeniable. He was indeed the most important client she had. Hands down. No competition. And he'd called it right—if she wasn't willing to go all the way with it, what good was she. He'd stand just as good a chance pro per. Jesus, where did he learn that? And that bit about the air conditioner? And patronizing—words the majority of her clients had never heard Napoleon Booker used like a scholar. She looked at his expression on the other side of the glass, the confident face that told her there was more to this guy than she'd given him credit for, that she may have misjudged him. And now it was on her. She either had to shit or get off the pot.

And Myra Cross never liked being constipated.

Slowly, not looking down, Myra's fingers brought out the pen and DWP envelope for the second time in as many minutes.

Myra said, "What's your business partner's name?"

Napoleon hesitated, still not sure he wanted to do this but knowing now he had no real choice. "Seymore. Gerald Seymore. Know him?"

Myra kicked the name around for a moment, told Napoleon it didn't ring any bells. "Your bail is three million, Napoleon," she said. "I seem to remember a million being your business partner's limit."

Hesitation still in his voice, Napoleon said, "Be more, you see him in person. Talk to him face-to-face, let him know I'm innocent, ain't robbed no armored car, killed no guard—check for three hundred grand be on the bail bondsman's desk nine o'clock next morning, straight up."

"You seem pretty sure about this."

Napoleon nodded. "Tell him 'scarecrow is down.' He know you for real."

Myra remembering her thoughts about the so-called business partner. Three hundred thousand dollars—her assumption the lawyer was an addict now more a certainty than assumption. And to be truthful about it, Myra was curious. A credentialed lawyer willing to put up more than a quarter million dollars for a street hustler just five years her junior. This was someone she had to meet.

Napoleon was saying through the glass, "Meet in your office noon the same day, we be on the road to Tijuana an hour later, get me some evidence hold up in court."

Like it was something he could order at a drive-thru, McDonald's only without the fries. And if she hadn't been so depressed over Ray Watanabe's murder, Myra would've laughed. Instead she reminded him that most important client didn't mean only client.

"Where's Gerald Seymore's office?" Myra asked.

"Century City somewhere."

"Somewhere? You don't have an address on your own business partner?"

"He a lawyer. Dial four-one-one or let your fingers do the walking."

"If you don't know his address, how do you conduct any business?"

Napoleon said icily, "Said handle my business, Miss Cross. Not get in it."

Just like that. Drew his own do-not-cross line in the sand.

Myra said, "Right." She returned the pen and DWP envelope to her purse and stood, signaling for the guard. "Okay. Napoleon. Just a minor setback. We'll get beyond it."

Napoleon rose to meet the approaching guard. "Know we will. I get outta here, things be moving fast. Know what I'm saying."

Myra turned to go just as the guard arrived, but her vanity stopped her in her tracks, turned her back around. She said to Napoleon, "By the way, Napoleon, you've got a serious problem with your eyesight."

"Say what?"

"Your eyes are bad. When's the last time you had them checked, got a prescription for glasses?"

Napoleon frowned. "Don't wear no glasses. What are you talking about?" Napoleon not seeing where she's going with it. That she's fucking with him.

The name tag on the guard's uniform read ROBERT, crew-cut hair, blue eyes, blond mustache, Jay Leno chin. Maya said, "Excuse me . . . Robert, right? Tell me, Robert, do you think I'm skinny? Just look at me. Tell me if you think I'm skinny . . ." Myra took a short step back from the bench and did a quick three-sixty. "Give me your honest opinion. Seriously." Even in the midst of tragedy, Myra's vanity demanded satisfaction.

The only thing that filled Robert's entire face besides the

uncharacteristic sudden blush was his toothy smile. Robert grunted and said to Napoleon, "She's kidding, right?" But Napoleon just stood there looking stupid, not knowing where this was going. So Robert turned to Myra and said, "Skinny?" and he laughed at the very word. "No, ma'am. Honestly, you are anything but."

Myra said, "That's what I thought," and winked, letting the guard know she wasn't coming on to him, that she was fucking with her client. To Napoleon she said, "See what I mean, Napoleon. First thing you do you get out, get you some contacts. Better yet, a seeing-eye dog. Man nearsighted as you might sign a document sending you back to jail, thinking it was a release order."

Napoleon said, "That's a joke. Right?"

Myra said, "Not by any stretch of the imagination." She laughed as she turned, walked toward the door, green light coming on as it opened. "Skinny. Now that's the joke."

• • •

MANUEL'S JUNKYARD was an East Los Angeles chop shop on Alameda Street off Vernon in a rundown industrial area dotted with body and fender shops, tune-up shops, occasional used car lots, public storage warehouses, and a few fenced-in abandoned gas stations. Surrounded by a makeshift tarp-covered chain-link fence, it was a large lot filled with stolen cars, parts of stolen cars, and a section of legitimate junk and scrap metal to justify the City of Los Angeles's business permit that let it operate as a junkyard. And it operated day and night—continuous sounds of power wrenches, clanging of metal tools, never-ending blare of Spanish-language radio playing mariachi music.

In one corner of the lot was a windowless aluminum storage container that functioned as both office and workshop, and because of its relative isolation, it made an ideal late-night meeting place for the Gang of Five.

Prisms of blue light from the carbon arc welder lit up the room, Darth Vader masks reflecting a sporadic shower of sparks that lived and died in the instant of their creation. Neil Sanford and Paul Stepolini stepped back from a workbench covered with eight-by-ten black-and-white photographs, removed their safety helmets, and turned away from the brilliance of the arc welder. Moments later the gloved hands of Darryl Brigham snapped off the welder, plunged the clutter-filled workroom into the semidarkness of a single unshaded lightbulb hanging freely near the door. He took off his helmet and, turning the metal object in calloused hands, muttered to no one in particular, "More like it."

Neil Sanford said, "How's it coming?"

Holding up the metal object, Darryl said, "See for yourself. Ain't pretty, but it'll hold a three fifty-seven."

Stepolini said, "I can't believe we didn't pick up on that. We hadn't seen the photos . . ."

Darryl said, "We'd be up a creek without a paddle. I'm just wondering what else we've missed . . ."

Neil Sanford said, "We'll know in the morning if she files another motion."

Stepolini said, "And if she does?"

Neil Sanford said, "Then we'll deal with it the way we did the gun. Plain and simple. And if she doesn't, then we're home free."

"Hope you're right," Darryl said. "I don't like sweating over last-minute details."

At that very instant the door to the shed swung open and a young olive-skinned Mexican burst into the room so fast he stumbled, nearly falling, going for bad in an oil-stained, sweat-soaked T-shirt, baggy pants, ponytailed hair, teardrop tattoo below his left eye, greasy hands holding Goodwrench power tools.

In a lilting East LA accent he said, "Say, *chota* . . . how long you gonna be in my shop, man? You know, customers keep seeing those black and whites, I don't get no business. Gonna ruin my reputation. You got to go, *chota*," he said. "You gotta go right now." Like he either wasn't afraid of the blue uniforms and holstered cowboy nine-millimeters or didn't know his place.

With speed that even surprised Neil Sanford, Stepolini's large hand suddenly grabbed the Mexican around the back of his neck, slammed his head down on top of Ray Watanabe's photographs so hard they jumped.

"Listen, Manuel," he said. "You don't tell us when to go. You don't tell us shit. We go when we want to go. Understand? Consider yourself lucky we don't close your Mexican ass down. We'll leave when we leave. End of conversation."

Drooling out of the side of his mouth onto the photographs, his hands dropping the tools, trying to get some leverage on the workbench, push himself up against the weight of Stepolini, Stepolini pushing him back down. His lips distorted against the photographs, Manuel said through a mouth of frothy spit, "Close me down? I pay you *chota* muthafuckas! Cash money. Every week I pay you."

"That's right, *esé*," Stepolini said. "You pay us. And you gonna keep on paying us every week just like you said, or you ain't gonna have no chop-shop business. You understand me?" And before Manuel could answer, Stepolini grabbed the ponytail with his free hand, raised up his head, and slammed it back down on the table as he said, "*Do . . . you . . . un . . . der . . . stand . . . me?*"

Manuel spit out something that sounded like a yes, head rotating up and down on his ear. Stepolini relaxed his hands just enough for Manuel to bolt upright, then pushed him down on the ground.

"Pick up your goddamn tools, *esé*," he said to Manuel, one hand still holding on to the ponytail, the other wrapped around his neck. "And besides," Stepolini was saying, Manuel picking up the tools, Stepolini bringing him back up on his feet slowly, his head at an awkward angle, not quite facing the cop because of his grip on the ponytail, but still seeing him out of the corner of his eye, the Mexican wanting to smash Stepolini in the face and knowing it would be suicide if he did. "Didn't we help you out, give you those nice sounds from the Mustang to sell, let you keep all the money for yourself. Right?" The Mexican not answering, not giving the *chota* any respect, just a venomous sideways glare that on the streets, if it was anyone but LAPD, would start a war. "Goddamn right we did," Stepolini said, "so you get your little Eighteenth Street gangbanging self outta here and leave us the fuck alone." And using his grip on the ponytail like the reins on a horse, he guided Manuel to the door, and once there he stuck the heel of his thick-soled Timberland in the small of Manuel's back, pushing him out of the room with the force of a jackhammer, saying, "You stick your ponytailed head back in here again, *esé*, I'm gonna fucking blow it off. You understand me?"

Stepolini looked at Neil Sanford and said, "That was fun. Where were we?"

Darryl looked at his watch. "Four-fifteen. I'd better get this over to the impound, get it installed before a new investigator comes snooping around. See you guys later," he said, and gathered up Ray Watanabe's photographs from the workbench and left. Neil Sanford and Stepolini lingered behind, Stepolini knowing Neil Sanford wanted to talk, Neil Sanford saying he liked the way the investigator was handled, wanting to know about Stepolini's plan for the DA, how that was coming, Stepolini laying it out for him in detail.

Neil Sanford said after Stepolini had finished, "Two birds with one stone. I like it. This is a two-step plan is what you're saying?"

Stepolini said, "Essentially."

"Who's going to handle the first step?"

"Calvin."

Neil Sanford said with some hesitancy, "Calvin. You trust him to do it right. Not fuck it up, go around flashing cash, shooting off his mouth like he did with Princess?"

"Speaking of Princess," Stepolini said, "I would've done her first. But the hospital presents a different set of problems I only just now worked out. As for trusting Calvin, I don't. He fucks this up, his membership in the Gang of Five is terminated. Permanently."

Neil Sanford's face turned thoughtful. "Thinking we might want to do that anyway."

Stepolini said, "Just say the word." Like it was already a done deal, something you ordered on layaway, picked up whenever you were ready.

Neil Sanford said after a moment, "You find a girl to handle the second part of this thing?"

Stepolini said, "Rose."

Neil Sanford thinking about it. "The redhead. Thought she was in rehab?"

"Why she owes us. It could've been fifteen years in Chow-chilla."

"She gonna hold up?"

"Share Calvin's casket if she doesn't."

Neil Sanford grinned at fond memories and said, "I rather liked Rose."

Stepolini said, "Everybody liked Rose. She handle this right, get herself cleaned up, I'm thinking maybe we should set her up in business, get a piece of the action. What do you think?"

"I like the part about a piece of the action," Neil Sanford said. "But in this case it might be too risky to keep her around. Follow me?"

Stepolini said, "If you think so." A real sense of regret in his voice.

Neil Sanford said, "What's the status of the gun?"

"Napoleon's Glock? Perfect for this," Stepolini said. "Mutha-fucka's prints all over it, but nothing turns up prior to this arrest."

Neil Sanford said, "Too bad he can't bail out, make it two pair."

"Still win the pot with three of a kind."

"Yeah, but only if you bluff."

"Why I don't like poker," Stepolini said. "I never bluff."

Neil Sanford said, "You said you figured out a way to deal with Princess?"

Stepolini said, "Latrice."

Neil Sanford said, somewhat startled, "The hooker? She's plain crazy!"

Stepolini smiled. "Why she's perfect."

CHAPTER 10

IN THE BUDDHIST TRADITION, Raymond Watanabe was eulogized for two days, the first night at the temple in downtown LA's Little Tokyo, where mourners could view the body while priests in robes delivered a series of spiritual and religious incantations. At the end of the second day he was to be cremated, and his ashes would be kept in the family home for forty-nine days before being taken to Rose Hills cemetery in Whittier for burial. Myra attended the first service, not understanding the Japanese spoken but getting the gist: they were saying nice things about him and wishing him well in his new life. She became too drained by her grief to return the second day; the thought of saying good-bye to a longtime friend whose death she felt partially responsible for was more than she could bear. She sent a note of condolence to Ting, telling her again to call if there was anything she could do.

Three days later she went to see Gerald Seymore.

Crutcher, Mason, Fifield, Dawson, and Seymore was a Century City law firm that occupied the entire ninth floor of a triangle-shaped high-rise on Avenue of the Stars, two blocks down from the Century Plaza Hotel and Spa. The elevator let Myra out on a deep-pile plush beige carpet that swept across the immense expanse of a waiting room richly appointed with handcrafted imported leather chairs and couches, custom-made rosewood center tables and matching end tables sporting priceless vases, their histories encased in laminated blocks at the base. The artwork alone on floor-to-ceiling mahogany-paneled walls was worth the price of admission. It wasn't a waiting room at all. It was a museum. Myra wondered if a docent was going to appear for a guided tour.

There was no docent. But in the center of the room there was a secretary, a perky, barely twenty-something barely brunette with highlighted shoulder-length hair, wide Nemo eyes that seemed to flutter automatically whenever she looked up, a healthy chest—which Myra was willing to bet cost her about four thousand dollars—wire braces on her lower teeth, and a face guaranteed to win an Oscar for underachievement in makeup. She was surrounded by a large granite-topped circular desk, on top of which was a name tag that read LONNIE. Next to it was a clipboard and chain-attached pen.

Myra signed in, gave Lonnie her card, said she was there to see Mr. Seymore, answered programmed questions: No, she didn't have an appointment. No, she wasn't a new client. No, she was not referred by anyone. Yes, she was from the public defender's office. Lonnie scrutinized the card like it was the Magna Carta, told Myra to have a seat, that Mr. Seymore was busy and seldom if ever met people without an appointment. But seeing as Myra was from the public defender's office, she'd see if he was available, and if he was, whether he'd be willing to make an exception in her case. She tossed her curls like Farah Fawcett, put the phone to her ear, Myra having to work at not asking Lonnie if she was a real secretary or just doing time until her big break at Paramount, playing cutesy airhead girlfriends in teen sex comedies.

Several minutes of unintelligible chatter before Lonnie told Myra Mr. Seymore would be tied up for the next thirty minutes. Could she wait? Myra said she would, asked if there was a restaurant or cafeteria in the building, Lonnie saying on the third floor, Myra saying she'd be back in half an hour.

Gerald Seymore, at sixty years of age, was one of the most handsome men Myra Cross had met in a long time. And the moment she saw him—coming through the paneled door to greet her in a tailor-made fifteen-hundred-dollar navy blue Canali suit draped around a broad-shouldered six-foot frame, Canali pin-striped shirt, gray silk tie matching a pair of steel-gray eyes scanning her from head to toe, lingering a second longer on the bulge in her jacket, impressed with the possibilities, full head of gray hair that crowned a face of soft, pleasant features, even softer smile that brought out dimples and showcased a mouth of straight teeth, extending his hand to greet her, soft fingers gripping hers more to hold it than shake it, holding it a second longer than might be expected, bowing slightly in a sort of formal politeness that was both charming and deceptive, saying "Miss Cross, I'm Gerald Seymore," Myra saying "Myra Cross, Mr. Seymore," entering his office a step ahead of him, Gerald Seymore's eyes finishing his appraisal on her butt—Myra knew they would be lovers sooner or later, gut feeling telling her it would be sooner.

Gerald Seymore's office was two and a half walls of floor-to-ceiling bookcases, a half wall of well-earned diplomas, and a fourth wall of glass that gave an unobstructed panoramic view west to the Pacific Ocean.

"And just how may I help you, Miss Cross," Gerald asked when they were seated, Myra casually unbuttoning the Anne Klein jacket so it would hang free, Myra in one of two leather chairs facing Gerald, who was framed by the Pacific Ocean in a high-backed swivel chair behind a massive teakwood desk whose size seemed to take up half the room, his fingers absently thumbing Myra's business card, his eyes having a hard time with the hint of cleavage in her blouse, Myra wanting to ask if there was an opening, that she was ready to leave the PD's office for the luxury of the Pacific Ocean at her back.

Instead, she sat back in the chair with just enough arch in her back to make the fullness of her breasts noticeable, bringing the cleavage into view and crossing her legs all in a single motion, making no effort to pull the skirt down. She said, "Napoleon Booker."

Cut right to the chase. No small talk about the weather, how long she'd been with the PD's office, Lakers' chances for another title, favorite reality TV show, or the war in Iraq.

Gerald didn't say anything at first, but the thumbing of Myra's card suddenly stopped as it fluttered to the ink blotter. And in Myra's world that meant he blinked. Gerald's face turned serious, his gray eyes narrowing, wandering all over the room as if he was putting forth a genuine effort to think about it. He said finally, "Who?"

Myra loved a good poker game. But having to work at keeping her mind on the cards. He was so unexpectedly handsome . . . in a fatherly way.

"Mr. Booker is charged with armed robbery and murder." Myra stopped, putting it out there to see what else she'd get. Nothing.

"Booker? Napoleon Booker . . . ?" Gerald's eyes continued to wander aimlessly about the room, always coming home to her blouse. He said, shaking his head, "Can't say the name is familiar."

"Mr. Booker asked me to contact you directly, Mr. Seymore," Myra went on. "His bail is three million. He seemed to think you might be willing to guarantee it."

Gerald Seymore showed his sense of humor. His smile made the dimples prominent. He said to Myra, "I've given to a lot of charities in my day, but bailing strangers out of jail is not tax deductible. I'm a tax attorney in case you didn't know. That's all this firm does. Tax law." The man was good. Myra had to give him that. And so handsome.

"Helping the wealthy avoid paying their fair share of the American Dream," Myra said, letting him run with it.

"You could say that." Gerald's dimples having as much fun with the game as Myra. He brought himself forward on the desk and braced on his elbows, picked up Myra's card and stared at it, sent his gray eyes back across the desk to play tag with their green counterparts. Suddenly his face brightened.

"The Ralph Raymond case," he said. "That was you, wasn't it?"

Myra said it was and Gerald, leaning back in the squeaky high-backed chair, said, "Thought I recognized the name."

Myra said, "But you don't recognize Napoleon Booker's name?" Bringing it to him the hard way. But he was cool about it. Just brought out the dimples and shook his head. Myra wondered if he was married, realized she didn't care if he was.

"Spend three hundred thousand dollars bailing out a drug dealer I've never heard of. Really now, Miss Cross."

Talk about blinking. Myra smiled. "Who said he was a drug dealer?"

The business card dropped to the blotter a second time in as many minutes. The dimples faded before the smile, and what was left of it was an effort.

"A generic assumption, Miss Cross," Gerald said. "You're with the PD's office. Isn't that just about all you handle—drug dealers, gangbangers, lowlifes . . . ?" Talk about thinking on his feet. Myra wondered if he had children. Grandchildren.

"Napoleon Booker may deal drugs," Myra said, thinking of a way to put it to him, a way she could get him to acknowledge his relationship with Booker without incriminating himself, "but the charge against him is murder during the commission of a robbery. A minuscule quantity of marijuana is the only drug charge against him. I can get that thrown out altogether. But his bail is based on the robbery and homicide charges. That's why it's so high. I thought I had a shot at getting it reduced, but the judge is a hard-ass."

"I'm not a criminal lawyer, Miss Cross," Gerald said, "but the felonies you're talking about, robbery and homicide, would warrant a high bail, would they not?" Gerald wanting to avoid any association with an acquaintance so charged, but not in any real hurry for Myra to leave. This redhead was bright. A killer body. Possibilities . . .

"Not if he's innocent."

Gerald Seymore's eyebrows raised in genuine surprise. "Innocent?"

"One hundred percent innocent, Mr. Seymore."

"Really?" Gerald leaning forward on the table, saying, "This Napoleon—what's his name . . . Booker, is it—is innocent, you say?" Still playing the game with Myra but his interest now beginning to surface.

"Completely."

"You know this for a fact?"

"Booker was set up, Mr. Seymore—"

"Call me Gerald, why don't you, Myra—may I call you Myra? Mr. Seymore makes me sound like a high school math instructor."

Myra looked at him and smiled. "All right. Gerald," she said, holding him with those green eyes that said he could be a lot more to her than a high school math teacher. "This crime took place four years ago. The real perpetrators were never caught. Booker just happened to be in the wrong place at the wrong time, got set up to take the fall. And while someone else is running around with seven million dollars of the taxpayers' money, Napoleon Booker is running up the state deficit."

"Seven million. That much?" Gerald's lips puckered as he whistled softly, did a three-sixty in his squeaky chair, coming back around to face Myra, saying, "Now, why couldn't I have a client like that, show him how to maximize available tax savings in IRS-approved shelters and at the same time protect his principal in offshore accounts."

"Protect? You mean hide it, don't you? Isn't that illegal?" Letting him know crooks come in all types of suits, especially those in fifteen-hundred-dollar Canali suits, wondering too what it was like to sleep with an older man, a much older man . . .

"Illegal is a relative term, Miss Cross. It all depends on the country you're dealing with. What may be illegal here may be perfectly legal elsewhere."

The man was just a crook. A very nice-looking crook. Older. Pleasant and charming. Just like her father. Only her father wasn't an addict. Still, the possibilities . . .

"You wouldn't want these people as clients, Gerald. Trust me."

"That kind, huh?" He seemed disappointed.

"That kind," Myra said, knowing if she mentioned Ray Watan-abe it would scare him—she was sure he'd already seen it on the news at eleven—and realizing now that Napoleon Booker's hesitance to involve Gerald Seymore may have had less to do with protecting the lawyer's reputation than it did with keeping him alive. Sacrifice his PD instead. Way to go, Napoleon. Wanting to tell Gerald she didn't blame him for playing dumb, that it was probably safer if he stayed out of it. Instead she said, "Nothing will come back on you, Gerald. As long as the source of bail money is legit, your name need never come up. I'll guarantee that." Myra not really sure she could but willing to try. "Napoleon didn't mention anything about your relationship, if that's what's worrying you." Talking to him like it was a done deal, that all he had to do was write the check.

And ask her out to dinner.

But Gerald Seymore was playing hardball. "Why would I worry about someone I don't know?" Letting his drug connection wither on the vine took balls, Myra had to give him that. Unless he had another one . . .

"All right. Worry about justice, then. Make a three-hundred-thousand-dollar charitable donation to a stranger in the name of justice if that'll ease your conscience."

"My conscience doesn't need easing."

"It will if your business partner is convicted and you know he's innocent."

"Business partner?" Like the term was in a foreign language.

" 'Just handle my business, Miss Cross . . . don't get in it,' was the way he put it, Gerald."

"Your client has a way with words, doesn't he?"

On this Myra had to laugh. "My thoughts exactly."

"Perhaps he'll become a jailhouse writer, get himself a book deal. Maybe even a movie deal."

"Be a lot easier if he was out on bail."

"As I said before, Myra, I'm not a criminal attorney. But I know enough criminal law to know that if he's innocent as you say, evidence to clear him would be presented at his preliminary hearing and the charges against him dropped. Am I right?"

"Except the evidence didn't surface until later. And some of it was destroyed before I could introduce a fifteen thirty-eight point five motion to suppress." Talking that lawyer talk, letting him know she was no dummy, how much she believed in her client.

"But not all of it was destroyed?" Gerald's eyes narrowing.

"No. Not all," Myra said, not really lying and not really being truthful. "But if Napoleon were out he could be a lot more helpful in his own defense."

"I'm sure he could," Gerald said. "But I'm afraid I can't help you. I'm sorry," and saying in his head, *The dumb-ass nigga, getting himself in this kind of jam and wanting to involve me. No way, José. But his redheaded PD . . .*

Myra read the lawyer's thoughts as if he'd spoken them out loud.

"He's not asking you to vouch for his character, Gerald. Just to bail him out."

Gerald fanned ten fingers on the broad expanse of the ink blotter, Myra noticing the absence of a wedding ring.

"Like I said, Myra, if it was someone I knew . . . But being charitable to strangers, especially criminals, is just not in my nature. I'm sorry," he said, and meant it, hoping Myra picked up on it, seeing them together in bed and wondering about the possibilities. She was so much younger—Sharon Stone body in the Ally McBeal outfit, *Basic Instinct* pose, boobs about to explode out of her blouse, dress riding up her thigh like an out-of-control elevator. Still . . .

And Myra wanted to say, *But you're a criminal as much as he is . . . offshore accounts. Give me a fucking break, Daddy.* Whoa, did she hear herself say "daddy?" Yes she did, and realized if they ever got together that's what she'd call him, that she wouldn't be able to help herself and wouldn't want to. Instead she said to Gerald Seymore, "Your final word on the matter?" Having to put forth a real effort not to say "daddy."

"I'm afraid so," Gerald said, but not as convincingly as he should have, hoping Myra picked up on it.

"Well, then," Myra said, throwing up delicate hands and green eyes in unaccustomed resignation, "I guess there's nothing else."

She uncrossed her legs and stood, Gerald coming around the desk, taking her arm just above the elbow, pushing in close and getting a sense of her breasts, escorting her to the door, and saying in a voice of soft measured tones, "Maybe dinner sometime. I'll tell you all about taxes, you tell me about lowlifes."

Myra turned toward him as they reached the door, both hesitating to open it, faces inches apart, Myra leaning into him, fullness of her chest pressed against his own, their eyes holding. "You mean lowlife business partners like Napoleon Booker?" The fragrance of his cologne reaching out, sending Myra on a high all its own.

The dimples again. "Tax law can be very interesting dinner conversation, Myra."

As Gerald Seymore's hand turned the doorknob, Myra lowered her hand on top of his and said as an afterthought, "I wouldn't accept a dinner invitation to discuss tax law, Gerald. But I would accept one to discuss 'scarecrow is down.' What do you say?"

Holding those dimples in place must have taken incredible effort. A tap with a small hammer and Gerald Seymore's stone face would have cracked in a thousand places. And in a move that did not go unnoticed by Myra, the hand beneath hers on the doorknob hesitated in midrotation an instant longer than it should have. Gerald Seymore, gentleman lawyer, addict, and crook, trapped in the radiance of her eyes, the fullness of her chest, soft feminine touch of a hand atop his own, had blinked. He didn't say anything as he opened the door for her to pass, but she could tell he was thinking about it. And in Myra's world, if you blinked three times it was all over.

• • •

MYRA'S FIRST THOUGHTS as she left Gerald Seymore's office was not about the two depositions scheduled for tomorrow, opening arguments for a drug possession trial the day after, or her speech before the Woman Trial Lawyers Association she was still working on. No, Myra's first thoughts were what she would wear to dinner when Gerald Seymore called. And he would call. She was utterly convinced of that. And that meant a new outfit. She could have walked to the Century City mall, decided instead to shop closer to home. So Myra brought the Mercedes south on Avenue of the Stars, crossed Olympic, and headed west out of Century City on Pico Boulevard to Overland Avenue and the Westside Pavilion. She had a veggie salad at McDonald's and spent the next three hours maxing out her Visa card at Nordstrom, Charles David, and Victoria's Secret, though the items she bought at the latter were a real waste of money, since she slept in the nude and had the kind of body that didn't need shielding to keep her lovers aroused.

The mall closed at nine and Myra, not yet ready to go home and start preparation for depositions, started to call Bruce, have him over for a good-night fuck. But after meeting Gerald Seymore, wondered if she and Bruce would ever have anything in common again besides jazz. So she decided on a movie instead, locking her items in the trunk of her Mercedes and sitting through two and a half hours of *Pride and Prejudice* and Keira Knightley, trying to imagine herself in bed with Matthew Macfadyen but seeing Gerald Seymore's face instead.

The eleven o'clock news was winding down by the time Myra pulled the Mercedes into the underground garage of her exclusive Brentwood Barrington Avenue condo. Arms laden with Nordstrom bags, cart of legal briefs in tow, she stepped off the elevator and trudged down the second-floor corridor to her unit, unlocked the door, and backed into a room of familiar darkness, the blinking green light of her phone alerting her to waiting messages, Myra wondering if one was from Gerald Seymore.

Perhaps it was this constant preoccupation with Gerald Seymore, her fantasy they'd somehow be together. Or because it was so late and she was tired. Or the replaying of *Pride and Prejudice* in her mind, imagining what it was like being a woman back in Jane Austen's time and realizing there wasn't much difference between then and now as far as women were concerned. Whatever it was, she failed to appreciate something was wrong, the uncharacteristic silence of her alarm, the high-pitched beeping that gave her thirty seconds to cut it off before security arrived, the vague smell of an unfamiliar odor in the room. When she finally did, when it dawned on her she was not alone, it was too late. The blow caught her just behind the ear, an explosive shower of lights the most magnificent fireworks display Myra had ever seen. Brilliant hues of blue, red, green, gold, orange, and yellow bursting all around her.

Then there was nothing.

CHAPTER 11

MYRA, GREETED BY THE STABBING PAIN of a ferocious headache unlike any she'd ever experienced, regained consciousness in the same veil of darkness that had ushered in the fireworks display. It took a while for her head to clear and when it did, when her confusion and disorientation began to subside, she came to realize she was in familiar surroundings and, in the grotesque posture of a gargoyle, lay spread-eagled on the floor of her living room just inside the door. Her right cheek was pressed against the rough fibers of a Persian rug, one arm folded beneath her, the other stretched above her head as if she was waving good-bye. Her torso was twisted to one side like a pretzel so that her legs looked as if she was in the middle of a pirouette.

Myra lay still, letting her eyes adjust to the ambient light that shone through unshuttered windows, the still-blinking green light of her phone. What had happened? She'd been assaulted? Hit? Shot? Raped? All of the above? None of the above? She didn't know which. But the headache was unbearable. She dared move the one arm that was free, felt the sticky wetness on the carpet, realized she'd been lying in a pool of blood. Myra rolled over on her back, freeing the other arm, now numb from loss of circulation. She tried to get up. But the one arm had no real strength yet, so she lay back down and waited. Even in the faint rays of streetlights she could tell her condo had been ransacked. Cushions from the couch and chairs strewn about, cabinet doors for dishware and home entertainment flung open, their contents broken and fragmented on the floor. She didn't want to think about the bedroom, knew it had been tossed the same. After a moment she tried sitting up again, managed to pull herself up to a sitting position, and realizing she was all in one piece but not steady enough to stand, she crawled slowly across the room on all fours to the blinking green light on the end table and dialed 911.

In Brentwood the police arrive in a heartbeat. The paramedics said Myra needed an X-ray and had a nasty cut that needed suturing, whisking her off to the emergency room at St. John's hospital in Santa Monica. Myra's elderly neighbor, Beatrice, agreed to watch her condo while the police conducted their investigation, as long as she could bring her cat, Fluffy, a gorgeous Siamese that Myra admired. Myra said Fluffy was always welcome.

The X-ray of Myra's head was negative for any sign of a skull fracture. So Myra, now covered by a thin surgical gown and strapped to a gurney, was wheeled back to the emergency room, where a detachment of police continued their investigation, comparing notes while the back of her head was being prepped for surgery, the doctor telling Myra he'd have to shave her head around the cut before suturing, Myra telling him she was vain, would he make it as small as possible so she could cover it with her hair instead of wearing a wig.

At first there was only one detective in the curtain enclosure while her head was being sutured. Myra flat on her stomach, hands at her side, her shoulders covered by a plastic bib, feeling the draft on the backs of bare legs partially exposed by the gown, her head on the pillow, wincing in pain as the doctor injected local anesthetic. She couldn't see the investigator behind her but heard his voice over her shoulder.

"Any idea how long you were unconscious?" the disembodied voice asked.

"I don't know," Myra said. "Show let out at eleven. I live about ten minutes away. Figured I got back somewhere between eleven-twenty, eleven-thirty. What time did I call nine-one-one?"

There was a rustling of papers and the voice said hesitantly, breaking up his words, "Eleven fifty-five. Which means . . . you'd been out for about twenty minutes."

"Were you raped, Miss Cross?" The voice belonged to a woman, low and masculine in modulation but female in tone.

"No, thank God," Myra said gratefully. "I was fully dressed when I came to and my clothes hadn't been disturbed or torn. Any idea who it might have been?"

"He was a professional," the female detective said. "Entered through your front door with a key. You lose your keys recently?"

"Not that I know of. No."

"He managed to disable your alarm system," the man's voice said, "so more than likely it's someone who works for an alarm company. Or did and knows all about them. You had any problems that required an on-site visit or routine service calls for maintenance?"

"Not since it's been installed. And that was over two, two and a half years ago."

"What about work done to your place?" another detective's voice said on the other side of the pillow. Male, young, tentative. "Any plumbers, electricians, carpet layers, painters . . . someone who might have cased your place?"

"Cable man," Myra said, remembering. "About six months ago. I wouldn't remember his name, though. You'd have to check with the cable company on that."

The woman investigator said, "The burglar seemed to know your routine . . . when you wouldn't be home. You notice any strange vehicles parked on the street when you left for work— service trucks, like the phone company, gas, water and power, cable, vehicles like that?"

Myra said, "It's a big complex. You see them all the time."

"What about phone conversations with telemarketers or people conducting opinion surveys wanting to know your schedule so they could arrange a meeting with you?" Another voice, another detective. An older man, calm and experienced.

"I never speak to telemarketers and don't believe in surveys," Myra said, and wondered how many more people could fit in the curtain-enclosed capsule—like there was an instructor demonstrating surgical techniques to medical students. All they'd need were long white coats instead of Brooks Brothers suits and ten more years of advanced education.

"You go to church, social events, parties, date often, or go to clubs frequently?" the same detective's voice went on. "Where you might have discussed your work schedule or mentioned some unusual or valuable possessions in your house?"

Myra took a deep breath and said over her shoulders to the gathering audience, "I'm not in the habit of discussing my personal business with anyone. That includes colleagues at work. I'm very careful about that. Especially in my line of work. I'm a public defender, in case you didn't know. We have to be very careful."

"Yes," the detective said. "You told us you were a PD when we first arrived."

"And no, I don't frequent bars or clubs," Myra lied pointedly, knowing she did between lovers, and sometimes without a lover's knowledge. "I have a boyfriend." And immediately heard the shuffling of feet behind her, the collective sigh of major disappointment from the men assigned to take her statement.

"Why are you asking such personal questions?" Myra said rather tersely, not thinking they were supposed to ask these kinds of questions and feeling stupid the moment the unmonitored words escaped her lips.

"Not trying to get in your business, Miss Cross," the woman detective said. "We're just trying to be thorough, make sure we cover all the bases."

"I know," Myra said apologetically. "I'm sorry. I'm just stressed out, that's all."

The doctor suddenly pulled the plastic bib from around her shoulders, sat Myra up on the gurney, helped rotate her legs over the side. That's when Myra realized how many detectives were in the room, the unseen faces attached to the voices that had taken her statement. At least seven men, one woman. All plainclothes. The woman indifferent. But the men lecherous. Looking not really at her face but lower, at the revealing impression of prominent nipples on the fullness of a chest clearly outlined by the clinging, near-transparent tissue-thin gown, the bare shapely legs dangling over the gurney's side.

One detective, Guy Pearce chin, Russell Crowe dimple, approached Myra, holding out a business card.

"Has to be hard on you, Miss Cross . . . being assaulted and robbed like this," he said. "In my experience it sometimes helps to talk about it. You ever need someone to talk to, day or night, call this number. I'm available to listen twenty-four seven."

Myra incredulous at his boldness, coming on to her like that and not once looking her in the eyes, but waiting for the gown to fall off, the peep show to start. Available to listen. Yeah, right. Even with a splitting headache Myra could see through that one.

One or two more questions from the gathering of disappointed detectives and they began filing out, the Guy Pearce chin, Russell Crowe dimple the last one to leave.

The doctor admired his handiwork and said to Myra, "It took four sutures. Your own doctor can remove them in five days. You'll be swollen back there for a day or so. Ice pack will help. Do not, I repeat, do not wash your hair, bend over, or do any strenuous exercise for the next week. Give it a chance to heal. Any questions?"

"I got a serious headache, Doc."

"I expect you do. I'll give you something for the pain. You allergic to anything?"

Myra said she wasn't and started to get off the gurney.

"Whoa," the doctor said, restraining her. "Not so fast. Wait for the wheelchair."

"Wheelchair? I don't need any wheelchair. I can walk. I'm not that helpless, Doctor."

"I'm sure you're not. But it's hospital policy, young lady. All patients with head injuries are taken to the entrance in wheel-chairs." The doctor calling her young lady because he saw her that way. His professional demeanor fatherly, but not much more than a day older than Myra and not her type. "Lawsuits," the doctor was saying. "You're a lawyer, right? So you understand."

Myra nodded and said she did.

Bruce had arrived at St. John's shortly after he'd received a call from the emergency room nurse. He'd tried to sleep in a noise-filled waiting room on uncomfortable plastic chairs for the six and a half hours Myra was there. He drove her back to the Brentwood condo just as the sun was coming up. Myra still wore the blood-soaked Anne Klein jacket, like Jackie Kennedy but riding in a Mercedes instead of a limousine. Bruce suggested Myra stay at his condo as a place of respite for as long as she wanted. He could keep a close eye on her, monitor her recovery like before.

Myra said, thinking about it, "I appreciate the offer, Bruce. But I think I'll pass. I don't want to put you out two times in as many weeks. Wear my welcome out."

Wear her welcome out—was she kidding? Bruce could scarcely contain himself.

"I like having company," Bruce said, remembering her last convalescence.

Myra read his thoughts as if he'd spoken them out loud.

"What you like," she said, "is all the kinky sex and the drugs."

"So do you."

"True. And I've had sex and done drugs under all kinds of conditions. But never with four stitches and a throbbing headache."

Myra walked into her condo just as the remnants of the forensics team were finishing up. Two rather tired uniformed officers and a female fingerprint technician packing her equipment. Beatrice was sleeping soundly on the sofa, Fluffy curled up next to her but wide awake.

The fingerprint technician said to Myra as she was leaving, "We get any hits on the fingerprint database, we'll let you know."

Myra told her she appreciated the information.

"Here, miss," said one of the cops, handing her a pair of business cards. "The detectives left these for you. They said to tell you they'd canvassed the neighborhood and spoke to your neighbors but nobody saw or heard anything. Said if any leads turned up they'd call, but you shouldn't hold your breath."

"Thanks," Myra said. "I don't plan to." And she followed the officers to the door, the cops removing the yellow crime scene tape as they left.

Myra roused the sleeping Beatrice with help from Fluffy, Fluffy suspicious and protective, hissing and baring her teeth.

"What do I owe you, Beatrice?" Myra asked, fishing in her purse for money.

"Nothing, my dear," Beatrice said, sitting up and yawning through the answer, hands waving at Myra, dismissing her effort at payment. "I'm just glad you're all right. You *are* all right, are you not?"

Myra tried to laugh lightly for the first time, but the headache cut it short.

"Yes, Beatrice. I'm quite all right, thank you. And thank you again for coming over on such short notice. I really appreciate it. Let me know when I can reciprocate."

Beatrice stood to leave, Fluffy jumping into her arms for the ride.

"The police behaved quite honorably," Beatrice said. "And they were nice to Fluffy too." Beatrice looked around. "Quite a mess, your place. Want me to stay and help you clean up?"

"No," Myra said, and ushered her housesitter to the door. "I can manage. Thanks anyway. I'll be in touch."

It was the first time Myra had seen the full extent of the robbery. Her condo had been thoroughly trashed. A large bloodstain that began at one end of the Persian rug had spread onto the hardwood floor in the living room. The contents of every cabinet and drawer in every room had been emptied onto the floor. Even the kitchen—dishes, silverware, cooking utensils. And the bath-room—toiletries, trash can, hamper of dirty laundry. The mattress in her bedroom had been moved off the box spring, the sheets, blankets, and feather quilt thrown back. Pictures on the walls in every room had been removed and thrown about as if they were Frisbees. The clothes in her closets were removed from their hang-ers and tossed about the room like so much rubbish on an aban-doned street. Jewelry cases were dumped on the floor, their contents scattered about like rocks in an unpaved alley.

Myra was so depressed after assessing the damage she wanted to cry. She was even more depressed when she finally checked her messages and saw that none of the three was from Gerald Seymore. Her mother had called, as well as SBC with a courtesy warning of a temporary disconnect if her bill wasn't paid by Friday, and a tele-marketer selling MCI long-distance service. She would call them all later. When she felt like talking. What she needed now, how-ever, more than anything else was something to lift her spirits. A hit. She wondered, given the extent of the burglar's search, if she dare look in the kitchen, in the nearly inaccessible alcove beneath the sink. There, undisturbed. Her stash of weed, blunts, cocaine rocks, Zig-Zags, Swisher Sweets, and freebase pipe. Myra breathed a near-euphoric sigh of relief, hearing herself say in her throbbing head, *There is a God*, wondering how the burglar missed it. Experi-enced addict—and it had to be an addict, tearing up her kitchen like that. Who keeps any money in the kitchen? You want money, you look under the mattress maybe, like old-school senior citizens who distrust banks. You tear up a kitchen, you're looking for drugs—usually check in unexpected places: toilet bowls, empty spray cans, garbage cans, dishwashers, outside a window where it might be hanging from a string. Myra thinking now for the first time that she was lucky. The cops could have found it, charged her with possession—that maybe it was time to change hiding places.

Myra crossed her legs, let herself drop to the floor, sat down right in front of the sink. She cleared out a spot on the floor in the midst of scattered silverware, pots, pans, the nauseating smell of day-old trash: chicken bones, rancid cheese, dirty napkins, rotten meat, pile of spoiled vegetables, spilled carton of sour milk, mound of half-dried Kleenex. She dropped a rock in the freebase pipe and lit it. Sucking repeatedly on the stem, she drew the pungent vapors deep into her lungs and waited for the glass dick to bring her relief. What it brought her was another headache. So she smoked three joints of chronic one after another and without moving dosed for a brief time on the kitchen-floor mattress of chicken bones, rancid meat, and rotten fruit.

Marty French told Myra he was glad she wasn't injured any more than she was and to take as much time off as she needed, that Craig McInnis would handle the depositions and her upcoming trial. Impressing upon Myra this was just the kind of situation that justified his decision to pair them together, that it allowed their respective cases to go forward without missing a beat. Myra telling Marty French yes, she never doubted his wisdom in this matter, but not meaning a single word.

It would take five days for Myra to reorganize her condo, ignoring the doctor's orders not to bend down or do any strenuous exercises, medicating her headache with Tylenol 3s and blunts. She took inventory of her scattered jewelry. Little if anything was missing. The thief, Myra thought, recognized costume jewelry when he saw it. She changed locks and alarm, remembering to write down the new installer's name in each case for future reference. She had the Persian rug shampooed, the bloodstain on the hardwood floor buffed out, and repolished. She took the Anne Klein jacket to the cleaners. She soaked every day in bubble bath, careful not to get her hair wet. By the fourth day her headache finally went away, so she used her vibrator and masturbated. And determined not to go to work with sutures in her head, she had them removed on the fifth day by her gynecologist when she couldn't schedule a same-day appointment with her personal physician. Still a little paranoid about the close call with the police and her stash—not sure they wouldn't return for more questions—she decided it was best to seal the stash in a Ziploc bag and hang it out the window on a string.

Myra Cross returned to the public defender's office six days later to a welcome back ceremony. Marty French made a short speech in front of the entire staff extolling Myra's brilliance and tenacity as a public defender, encouraging all PDs to work toward her level of performance. Clara presented Myra with a gift-wrapped Parker pen inscribed with her name.

Myra found two items, among many awaiting her attention, that she considered priority. The first was an e-mail from Jason Rice. Myra called him on her cell phone for privacy. He told her the *Playboy* issue would be on the stands in two weeks.

The second was an envelope of photographs from the new investigator assigned to the Napoleon Booker case. No surprises there. The photos showed a crudely fashioned gun rack hanging down from the dashboard with a .357 prop gun in place. Nothing even remotely resembling the custom-made nine-millimeter design Napoleon described. Photographs of the Mustang's trunk showed only a cavernous space of loose unconnected wires snaking out from behind the rear seat and a nearly balding spare tire with chalk marks and arrows pointing to the rim. Additional photographs showed several small holes in both fender wells and on the backseat that could be described as some kind of "attachment points" for some kind of apparatus, but nothing more. More photographs showed various parts of the Mustang's body damage, including close-up shots of the tires, showing lots of tread. Myra wondered if tire treads would be enough to keep her client out of prison for the next twenty-five years.

Line one lit up. Clara's line.

"Yes, Clara?" Myra listening, her eyebrows going up in amazement. "Really? Will wonders never cease. By all means—show Mr. Booker in."

• • •

"S'UP, MISS CROSS?" Napoleon Booker dropping down in front of Myra's desk in the only chair not occupied by files. Baggy pants, Lakers jersey with Kobe's number 8, baseball cap turned backward. Nike shoes. Arm thrown over the back. Attitude.

"Well," Myra said. "I see your business partner came through." Because there was really nothing else she could say.

Napoleon said, "Told you. See him in person, I'd be out. Been out three days now. Come by every day waiting for you to get back. Said you got robbed. How's your head? Heard you had stitches?"

Was nothing sacred? Myra's hand automatically went behind her ear, played with the red strands covering her bald spot. She said to Napoleon, "Four. Who told you about that?" Myra thought Craig McInnis. Or Clara. Or both.

Napoleon said, "Just office talk. I listen. Hear things. Know what I'm saying?"

Myra said, "Speaking of heads . . ." Looking at Napoleon, waiting for him to pull off the baseball cap, then seeing a head of freshly done cornrows, nodding her approval.

"Shaniqua. She do hair on the side," Napoleon said.

"Talented," Myra said. "She pretty?"

Napoleon said, "She aw'ite. Got big titties like you. Pretty legs. And she know how to cook."

"Not to mention the fact she has your son."

Napoleon smiled. "That too." He stopped for a moment, then said, "So, Miss Cross, now I'm out, get us some evidence hold up in court. What do you say?" Like the investigation was just beginning and now that he was out he was running the show.

Napoleon Booker, the black version of Craig McInnis, only taller.

"All right," Myra said, pushing the envelope with the photographs across the desk. "I guess we can start with these."

Napoleon sat up, went through the photographs slowly and carefully, discarding each one in turn as if they were useless cards in a poker hand. If he was surprised his face did not show it. But Myra could tell he was thinking about it. When finished, he sat back and resumed his pose.

"Why you have to interview them *esés* what put in my sounds."

"You mentioned a receipt?"

"Safe-deposit box. We going to Mexico too and—"

Myra cut him off, saying, "I think I mentioned, Napoleon, depositions from across the border will be about as useless as tits on a gander."

"I understand that," Napoleon said. "But there's another reason for going." He pointed to the pile of photographs. "You see that spare." Myra not searching through the pile but knowing the one he was referring to. "Bald as Vin Diesel. We go to TJ, see if they still got mine. They haven't sold it, we get it back. Help prove my case it was switched. Know what I'm sayin'?"

"All right. Let's say we do that," Myra said. "Say we can get the matching spare, show it's part of a set. What's to prove you didn't switch it, substitute the bald tire with the money before the police arrested you?"

Napoleon had all the answers. "Time frame. Receipt and photograph. Like I said before, *esés* didn't finish installing the sounds till late. Why I was so lit up, smoking blunts all day waitin' for them muthafuckas to get through. Why a nigga spend all day and five grand on new sounds and three hours later take 'em out for a fucked-up spare tire? Know what I'm sayin'?"

"You said something about a photograph. What photograph?"

"Yeah. Them *esés* got a lotta pride in they work. Take pictures when they finish up. Use 'em to advertise they work and shit."

Myra grabbed a pen, pad. "You're telling me there's a picture of your trunk with the speakers same day they were installed? Why didn't you tell me this before?"

Napoleon shrugged his shoulders in apology. "I was in jail. Can't expect me to remember everything."

"There's still the issue of the money."

On this Napoleon sat up. He said to Myra, "Seven million dollars. Why we gotta move on this now. Other shoe gettin' ready to drop and I don't need to be under it when it falls. 'Cause to be truthful, Miss Cross, I don't plan on spending nobody's twenty-five years in the joint behind seven million GWs I never saw. I'll bust a cap in somebody's head if that's what it takes. Know what I'm sayin'?"

Myra said, "I didn't hear you say that."

Napoleon said, "Just so you know. I'm lookin' out for both of us. Anything I have to do gonna be for that reason."

"Remember," Myra said, "you're out on bail. I'd exercise a little caution if I were you, Mr. Booker."

"Goes for you too, Miss Cross. Look what happened to your car and—"

"My car? How'd you hear about that?" Myra frowned in surprise.

"TV in the joint. Didn't know it was your car till I hear them talking in the office out there."

Myra's face softened. "Yeah," she said, "that FBI nonsense about terrorists was ridiculous. If they'd seen the insurance report they'd have known it was the gas tank. I guess with all the news about the war they're trying to scare people into being more vigilant. Leave it to the government, there's a terrorist on every block."

"You don't really believe that, do you?"

"About the terrorists?" Myra said. "No. Of course not. It was a crack in the gas tank like the insurance company said."

"And you said I needed glasses . . ." Napoleon sat up from the comfort of attitude, crossed his legs, and brought his right fist on top of his knee, his index finger sticking up, saying to Myra, "One—ain't no gas tank blew up your car, Miss Cross. These seven-million-dollar muthafuckas what framing me blew up your car." Holding up a second finger and saying, "Two—they killed your investigator." A third finger popping up and Napoleon saying, "Three—put four stitches in your head. And if you believe it was just coincidence then you a fool and I really don't need a fool for a lawyer. Know what I'm sayin'? How much clearer the picture gotta be for you to see it?"

Myra never argued with truth. She was not convinced by anything less. During the week of her convalescence she'd toyed with the possibility that Ray Watanabe's death and the break-in were related. But only toyed with it. If they wanted her dead, it would've happened during the break-in. So she wasn't totally convinced the two had any connection or that it was anything other than a random break-in she happened to interrupt. Neither was she convinced the destruction of her car was connected, simply because there was no way anyone could've known which PD would be assigned to his case. But Napoleon said trust him. Her car's explosion was related. And perhaps seeing it through his eyes was best because he had the most to lose, or because he was closer to the streets, too close perhaps. But he had a feel for just how these kinds of criminals operated. A nervous hand returned to the back of her head, fingers playing with loose strands shadowing the cut, a reminder of the price she paid for ignoring his warning, *Watch your back*. Wasn't that what he'd said?

"All right, Napoleon," she said after a moment, thinking about it. Being cool. Not letting on she wasn't totally convinced. "Let's say you're right—"

"Ain't no 'let's' about it, Miss Cross."

Myra said, "All right. Moving ahead, we still need to collect enough evidence by your trial date to refute whatever they throw at us."

"When's the trial?"

Flipping through her calendar, Myra said, "Four months from now."

Napoleon said with a grunt, "Four months. They know I bailed out, be lucky to live four weeks. Why I say we gotta get on this now, before the other shoe drops. We gotta find which one of them *popos* has my Glock before they use it to set me up on another one eighty-seven. We gotta go to Mexico too. And we gotta go now!"

"I do have other clients and responsibilities, Mr. Booker," Myra said calmly. "I'll arrange for the new investigator to go with you and—"

Napoleon Booker jumped up. Cool turning to rage. Not raising his voice, but growing intense, eyes narrowing, turning the baby face into a river of frown lines.

"Investigator? You ain't been listening, have you, Miss Cross! We in this together. You and me. They killed your boy, blew up your car. What they gonna blow up next? Your house? My house? My son? Shaniqua? My mamma? Yours? Oh yeah. They get desperate enough they do that, you know. Find out where yo mamma live, kill her too if they have to. No. We gonna do this together. 'Cause you my only hope to stay out of prison, and I'm the only chance you got of stayin' healthy. We move forward. Don't mean to scare you," Napoleon said, knowing he had, seeing the fear beginning to etch itself on her face, "or be disrespectful, Miss Cross. But you kinda ditzy, hitting the pipe and all. Know what I'm sayin'? Don't bother me none personally, 'cause I base every now and then myself. But you don't know how to take care of yourself. You lettin' all them diplomas and big-ass titties go to your head." Napoleon's arm swept a wide arc across the wall where Myra's diplomas hung. "But the people we dealing with don't give a shit about your diplomas. And in case you thinking them big legs and bodacious titties you got makes you immune from these muthafuckas just 'cause they white, don't kid yourself. Only color counts with them is green. Big legs, big titties, and red-haired pussy don't count for shit. Especially they have to make a choice between pussy and seven million dollars. Please! They fuck girls with big titties like you seven days a week. Kill your little narrow white ass without thinking twice, step over your remains on the way to the bank." Napoleon stopped, giving thought to what he was going to say next. He could tell he'd frightened her, hadn't meant to let his emotions get out of hand and, now that he had, was thinking about damage control. She was trying hard not to show fear. Cool about it. Poker face. Like he was talking about somebody else. "You the only one I trust, Miss Cross," Napoleon said in truth, his emotions reined in now, tone more conciliatory. "I can't make you do this for me. You gotta do it from the heart. You don't, I can understand, danger and all. But I always knew you to be someone who believed in her clients, someone never backed away from a fight when it came to truth. And you know I'm inno-cent of this bullshit. I figure that has to count for something. You don't feel this, want me to let you off the hook, I will. Straight up. Won't be no hard feelings. That be the case, I may as well go down-stairs to the DA's office, turn myself in, plead no contest and set up housekeeping at San Quentin 'cause without you I got no one else help prove me innocent. But if you feel me on this, Miss Cross, and I think you do, then I'm asking you roll the dice with me, expose the truth and run these muthafuckas into the ground. You do, I'll look out for you. Watch your back. Know what I'm saying?"

To stifle her fear more than anything else, Myra said, "What are you going to do—stand guard outside my house, follow me around like a shadow?"

Napoleon said, "Someone." Wondering if she could read between the lines.

Myra didn't say anything right off. She just sat there in disbe-lief, trying to digest all that he said. Calling her ditzy, saying she can't take care of herself. Some words clearer than others . . . *kill her mother if they had to*. She heard that loud and clear.

"You're asking me to put my mother's life at risk, Napoleon. I don't think I can do that. Not for you. Not for anybody."

"Last resort. We move on this quick, like the B1 stealth bomber, your moms ain't got nothing to worry about."

Myra shaking her head, patronizing him. She said to Napoleon, "Now, that's really comforting to know, Napoleon. You guaranteeing her safety like that."

Ignoring Myra's sarcasm, Napoleon said, "We send her away somewheres overseas."

"A vacation. Now, why didn't I think about that." Having fun with the absurdity of it all. "And what about your own mother? Shaniqua . . . I pronounce it right? Yes? And little Napoleon? Send them overseas too?"

Napoleon's face and tone not letting Myra get to him. He said, "If I have to."

"If you have to. Jesus, Napoleon." Like it was something you ordered from a catalog. Myra having to work at not laughing. "Of course," Myra said, shaking her head, her tone still derisive and cynical and patronizing. "Why not. Personally, I like Tahiti. Parade up and down the beach in a wrap skirt. Spend all day in a hammock. Napoleon—do you have any idea how absolutely silly you sound? Just choose a country. Make reservations. Fly off to paradise. Just like that."

Napoleon snapped his fingers and said, "Just like that." Still cool about it. Not letting her punch his buttons but surprised she hadn't picked up on it yet.

"No offense, Napoleon. But you're a small-time hustler who's gotten himself into big-time trouble. How do you propose to protect me much less your own family when you can't even protect yourself? I agree with you. We're looking at a dangerous situation here. But to handle it right, to put together the kind of defense that gets you off the hook and at the same time keeps us out of harm's way requires the involvement and coordination of a number of law enforcement professionals. Not some kind of pie-in-the-sky, movie-of-the-week scheme about invisible bodyguards and leaving the country." Myra trying to use logic, bring the conversation back to reality.

"You don't think I can?" Napoleon said.

"Be serious, Napoleon," Myra said.

"Business partner one what's serious."

Suddenly all the lights in Myra's head came on at once.

Business partner. Of course. Gerald Seymore.

The Godfather.

It was like a breath of oxygen to a suffocating man. Myra couldn't believe she hadn't seen it all along. Hadn't picked up where he was going with it. But there it was. The whole plan. All this time Myra thinking Napoleon's talking in a vacuum. That he's blowing smoke out his ass, running on adrenaline and bullshitting himself. All that talk about protecting her, watching her back, and sending her mother overseas if necessary. His mother. Baby's mother. Like it was something he could do just by picking up the telephone. Only he could. He'd been trying to tell her that from the beginning. She hadn't seen it because she wasn't looking for it, Napoleon Booker just another inner-city African-American client without resources. Wrong. This inner-city African-American client had a Godfather, a lawyer. A rich white lawyer. In Century City. If Napoleon had an MBA he'd be running Microsoft with Bill Gates.

There was really nothing she could say after that. Her involvement wasn't a slam dunk just yet, but she was thinking about it, not exactly sure just what she'd be getting herself into but knowing it would be a bumpy ride. But having Gerald Seymore along as God-father would make it a whole lot smoother. Myra thumbed absently through her calendar, ran a pencil down the margins.

"I'm in trial all day Monday, half of Tuesday, Napoleon. Will Tijuana still be there if we go Wednesday?"

"Question is, will we still be here," Napoleon said.

She brought her gaze up to meet his, giving him that disciplined poker face.

"Wednesday's the best I can do."

Napoleon thought about it. "Nine Wednesday," he said. "We'll go in your car. Aw'ite?"

Myra said, "Aw'ite," and sounded stupid saying it.

Napoleon opened the door to leave, suddenly turned around and said, "Oh. Almost forgot. Business partner said tell you to call. Something about you owe him dinner conversation."

Myra's face turned on like a neon sign at dusk.

"Really?"

"What he said."

"Uh, a question, Mr. Booker, before you leave." Myra hesitating, not quite sure how to phrase it, having to work at containing her enthusiasm. Napoleon looking at her, hand on the doorknob, waiting. Finally, "Uh, your business partner . . . does he like stage plays, opera, works of art. Things like that?"

Napoleon's baby face tried to hide the smile and failed.

"That you guys' dinner conversation—Shakespeare and shit? Nigga take a girl out to dinner, spending hard-earned cash on atmosphere, he gonna be conversatin' about gettin' hisself some pussy. Not about no Hamlet or King Lear. Know what I'm saying?" Napoleon half laughed, half grunted, saying, "Rembrandt . . . van Gogh . . . Cezanne . . ." He turned and walked through the door still laughing, shaking his head, taking his cool with him.

"White folks," he said.

CHAPTER 12

"*OH YES . . . YES . . . DADDY, yes . . . yes . . . oh Daddy . . . !*" Like the penetrating, high-pitched blaring of an air horn, Myra's scream erupted from deep in her chest through a mouth open just wide enough to emit sound. Her arms grasping at Gerald Seymore's back, holding tightly to his broad, muscular shoulders as her body twisted and writhed violently in the final uncontrolled spasms of orgasm, her cheek pressed firmly against the soft fabric of a down pillow, her neck muscles bulging in a head turned violently to the side as if she was trying to look over her shoulder. And locked at the ankles, firm fleshy legs wrapped tightly around her new lover's torso, keeping him inside as the deep-throated grunt and jerking seizure signaled the onset of his own release, Gerald saying, "Oh, Myra . . ." and collapsing exhausted and breathless into the willing embrace of waiting arms, unbelievable softness of wanton flesh half his age, sensual, delicate fingers that stroked his disarrayed locks of gray hair. And on the heels of a tongue probing his ears, soft lips bathing his face and neck with kisses, whispering to each other sweet nothings neither understood nor remembered, they would cling together for long periods of time, until the sweet narcotic of ecstasy had drained away and strength alone was no longer enough to sustain them. Lost in the luxuriating and indefinable moments of the erotic aftermath that bound them, their limp and exhausted bodies awash in the sweat and the smell of their sex was a spell neither wanted to break. And it had been that way with them from the very beginning, an almost uncanny attraction for each other that didn't have to be explained. It was natural. Myra Cross had known it that first day in his office. And so had the very handsome gentleman lawyer turned crook.

It had been a wonderful weekend. Unlike any Myra could ever remember. On Friday, prompted by Napoleon Booker, Myra had called the attorney's office, telling him absolutely, she most certainly did owe him dinner conversation.

For their first date Myra Cross slithered into a tight, chic ankle-length blue chiffon by Valentino that struggled somewhat unsuccessfully to contain her cleavage. Promptly at seven Gerald Seymore, wearing an Armani suit, picked Myra up from her condo in his black four-door Bentley Arnage RL, Myra guessing it cost as much as Napoleon Booker's bail but having too much class to ask. Reservations were for seven-thirty. On a tree-lined section of Robertson Boulevard north of Wilshire, the Ivy was a rather unassuming house converted to a restaurant known as much for its celebrity clientele as its cuisine, the perpetual knot of paparazzi camped across the street with long-lens cameras permanent residents claiming ownership of the sidewalk. Friday night their quarry was Angelina Jolie and Brad Pitt, Myra thinking, when she first saw them sitting together in a booth across the room, that Brad Pitt looked better on screen. And wondering too just how she'd look on camera.

Myra ordered rack of lamb, Gerald lobster tails. And while waiting, cocktails: for Myra a Grey Goose vodka martini. For Gerald a small glass of Johnnie Walker on the rocks. Myra had wondered just what their dinner conversation would be about: "Scarecrow is down" or sex and art, remembering Napoleon's comment, Myra hoping it would be about sex but prepared to discuss art if she had to. She let him take the lead but needed to know one thing before drinks, asking Gerald Seymore if he was married, bracing for the possibility he was, that she'd have to settle for being the other woman and not really sure she was up to it despite his looks.

Gerald Seymore, it turned out, was a widow. Edith, his wife of thirty-two years, had died from breast cancer not quite two years ago. He had three children. Two daughters: Shirley, the older, a psychologist. The younger one, Hadley, Myra's age, an architect. Both girls married, both with three children. His son a stockbroker in New York, living with an anesthesiologist who had a three-year-old son by a former marriage and was expecting Gerald's seventh grandchild in four months. Gerald had already been a very successful tax attorney five years before Myra's birth. He was Ivy League educated, well traveled, and conversant on a broad range of contemporary subjects, from art to politics, and liked classical music, racquetball, and sailing. The only drugs he indulged in: an occasional highball and pot.

There was no instrument that could have measured Myra's relief.

A widow. Unmarried. Cultured. Myra couldn't believe what she'd heard, had to restrain herself from asking him to repeat it. Instead she offered a toast, heard herself say "to us," Gerald saying "to us," and the two of them touching glasses, hooking their arms together the way newlyweds do.

They were the last to leave, Myra suggesting they go to the casino at the Hollywood Park racetrack and hear some live jazz, Gerald passing, telling her they were going sailing in the morning and needed to be well rested. Taking charge. Right off the bat. Myra liking that in some men. This man in particular. Telling her, not asking her, except whether or not she could swim. Myra said she could. Quite well in fact. She was on the girls' swim team in high school. There was no good-night kiss. No hint of sex. Myra somehow knowing this, not really surprised.

The perfect gentleman. A lost art.

Gerald Seymore's yacht was the *Prince*, a thirty-five-foot single-mast double-cabin sailboat he kept moored at Marina del Rey. Myra wearing jeans, a halter top that passed as a weak imitation sports bra, and a bulky life jacket, seated in the stern alongside Gerald, wearing a stiff-brimmed captain's cap, striped T-shirt, white bells, and deck shoes. Myra's face caught stinging wind and spray and loved it. Learning all about jibs and spinnakers and tacking into the wind, Gerald letting her play at steering when it was safe to do so. Myra wondered if they'd make love for the first time in one of the cabins when they docked.

What they did when they docked was not make love but go to dinner at the Warehouse restaurant in the marina. And cocktails: Myra toyed with another Grey Goose martini and Gerald a snifter of Courvoisier. They enjoyed seafood dinners of flounder and red snapper while enduring the hostile stares and bitter whispers of older women, envious stares of older men, curious stares from the younger crowd—and they danced slowly to the four-piece combo playing oldies but goodies.

When they finished and left, they knew it was time.

They drove home from the Warehouse in a speechless silence punctuated by the soaring trumpets of Jeremiah Clarke's "Trumpet Voluntary" on a stereo system that turned the Bentley's interior into a concert hall. They were going to his house. No discussion was necessary. It was the chemistry that spoke for them, that determined the time and place. Not Friday night after dinner at the Ivy. Not Saturday evening in the cabin of the *Prince*.

But Saturday night.

They discarded items of clothes in the silent climb up the sweeping circular stairway to the second-floor master bedroom of Gerald Seymore's twelve-room Beverly Hills mansion on Camden Avenue, the bedroom alone as large as Myra's entire condo. Five other bedrooms half the size, mini-suites with walk-in closets. Six rooms downstairs. Each one a museum of European furniture, wall art. Pictures of children covering a life span from playpens to cap and gowns to wedding portraits. Grandchildren. And Edith. Untouched elegance in an aging face still showing remnants of the beauty she once was. Recreation room with pool table, sixty-one-inch Hitachi wide-screen high-definition TV. State-of-the-art kitchen overlooking an Olympic-sized pool parallel to and surrounded by a high-netted Wimbledon-class tennis court.

Their coming together was natural, as if it had been ordained.

Gerald a little unsure of himself because of his age, lingering memories of Edith. Myra saying she understood, reassuring him it would be fine.

And it was. Better than either had anticipated. Chemistry.

They finally drifted off to sleep at sunup. Awoke eight hours later, never really getting out of bed, never really staying in. Myra touring the mansion after being assured no grandchildren would visit. Wearing one of Gerald's long-sleeved Canali shirts, which she fastened at her belly button. She played at chef, preparing a brunch of omelettes, a fruit bowl, and mimosas. She took a dip in the pool until shadows replaced the sun, then back to bed for more sex and a joint of chronic. She continued the evening watching TV: reruns of the Katrina disaster on CNN; Lakers coming apart at the seams on ESPN; TCM's *The Asphalt Jungle*, Marilyn Monroe calling Louis Calhern "Uncle Lon" and saying "Yipes!" and talking about how she'd look in a French-cut bikini. Myra thinking it would've sounded better if she'd called him "Daddy."

"You know," Myra said when the film was over and after they'd recovered from making love once again, "by today's standards Marilyn would be considered overweight. Isn't that the craziest thing you've ever heard?"

Gerald Seymore's fingers combed gracefully through Myra's red locks, her face nuzzled in the crook of his neck.

"You're probably right," he said, bringing up Myra's face, kissing her. "I was a teenager when I first saw her in *Bus Stop* and thought at that time she was the most beautiful woman I'd ever seen. And trust me, I'd have never kicked her out of bed no matter what she weighed. DiMaggio must've been insane, let a woman like that go. Hell, the man should've been grateful. After all, *she* chose him. And she could've chosen someone else."

Myra giggled. "Way I see it, whether a girl is skinny or fat, pretty or ugly doesn't really matter. I don't think any man would kick a woman out of bed if she's willing to fuck him. Well, maybe if he's gay he would."

Gerald said, "I don't know anything about being gay. But I guess pussy, like beauty, is in the eyes of the beholder."

Myra giggled again, her fingers tracing smile lines around his mouth.

"And just what are the beholder's eyes seeing now?"

"Why don't you let me show you," Gerald Seymore said. And he did.

"I'll have to tell Bruce," Myra said as they both toweled off after a shower, dressing to leave. "Unless you see things differently?"

"I wouldn't like it if I had to share you," Gerald said. "Even with Edith. I'd always been monogamous. Not always faithful, mind you. But monogamous nonetheless."

"Monogamous?" The word fell out of Myra's mouth with an incredulous laugh.

"My love for Edith, yes. It most certainly was monogamous. I never loved anyone else but Edith. I wouldn't have left her for anyone. There was no reason to. She hadn't done anything for me to leave. She was a woman who understood it was a dick thing. Not a love thing." Myra propped a leg on the edge of the vanity. Gerald Seymore's eyes followed the towel absorbing water from fleshy thighs and shapely calves, wondering now if the time was right for another woman in his life, if two years of mourning for a woman he'd truly loved was enough time. And Myra. So much like Edith: classy . . . bright . . . so very attractive. Wondering too if he'd be able to hold her against the challenges of younger men. Myra looking at him, sensing his insecurity and offering a smile of shameless reassurance, wondering where she'd stand if Edith was still alive. Gerald read the look and said, "That's right, Myra. Not for anyone. Present company included. We might be together, if you were so inclined . . . ?"

If she was so inclined. That honesty again. Myra finished the sentence. "You mean if I'd be receptive to going with a married man?"

"Something like that," Gerald said.

"I have in the past," Myra said. "Depended on the man, really."

"I suppose it's different with women. You know, the whole Venus and Mars concept. Way I see it, Myra, with women it's got to be a love thing. Or a power trip. A woman believing she has a 'superpussy,' so strong that it'll pull the husband away from the wife. You know, like the gal on *Sex and the City*, what's her name, the Cattrall woman. Sex as much for enjoyment as it is for power. But if a man leaves his wife for her, then he'll most likely leave her for someone else. So what do you have? Nothing. Why women refuse to accept the fact it's just a dick thing with men and nothing else is beyond me."

"So that's how you men rationalize cheating . . . saying it's just a dick thing. Never mind how the wife feels."

"I always cared how my wife felt," Gerald said. "I can't speak for other men."

"You don't have to. We're talking a double standard here. Right? You don't want to share *me*. But like Edith, I may have to share *you*. That what you're saying, Gerald?" Myra not really sure she wanted him to be this honest. "Give you a long leash because it's just a dick thing?"

"I was younger then."

"You were what, in your thirties . . . forties?"

"And fifties."

"Fifty is still young, Gerald." Myra shoring up his self-esteem, reading his reluctance at the admission, his concern about growing old. "But since when was age ever an excuse to fool around? Old habits die hard."

Gerald couldn't help but laugh. "Myra," he said, "be serious. Sixty-three years old, going on sixty-four—a girlfriend half my age with a genius mind and a body that belongs in *Playboy*, you honestly think I can handle more than one of you?"

Whoa. *Playboy*. And wondered just how he'd take it when it broke and decided now was just as good a time as any for him to find out.

"I've done a spread for *Playboy*, now that you mention it," Myra said, waiting to see his reaction. And when there was none she went on, saying, "Not a centerfold. But an issue with nothing but professional women—lawyers, doctors . . . women like that. It's due out on the stands any day now."

If Gerald Seymore was bothered it didn't show. "Taking your pubic hairs public, sort of."

Myra laughed. "Sort of. That bother you?" Myra thinking it might make him insecure, that she'd have to work on reassuring him. Letting Daddy know she wasn't going anywhere. But he surprised her.

"Should it?"

"Well, some men might get funny ideas about a girl posing like that, displaying her wares for all the world to see."

"They might. Personally, my concern is your career. Can't see the bar doing anything. But the PD's office is sure to let you go. You thought about that?"

"Same thing Jason said. Shouldn't I be worried about my legal career, my license to practice and all. Jason's the photographer, by the way. And he's gay," Myra said. "But to tell you the truth, Gerald, I really don't care much for the PD's office anymore. I've been thinking about leaving for quite some time now. What I really want is a career in show business. Ever since I was a kid. Be a TV talk show host like Oprah. I just need the right vehicle. And I think *Playboy* is it."

Gerald Seymore's face was comfortable with the smile that filled it.

"That spread hits the newsstands, I'll be the most envied man in America—going with a celebrity beauty half my age . . . ? Talk about being under the microscope! All the tabloids will be interested in is our sex life, can a man my age handle a younger woman like you?"

Myra's seductive, childlike giggle came again and she said, "Daddy, you've got nothing to worry about in that department. Let yourself enjoy being envied. The question they need to ask is, can I handle a man like you?"

"A man twice your age, I might add," Gerald said.

Myra said, "It's been done before—Sophia Loren, Céline Dion. They were all with older men. And Charlie Chaplin. My God!"

Gerald said, "His last wife. Forty years his junior. Wore her out. Imagine what would've happened if he'd had Viagra?"

Myra said, "They'd have declared his dick a lethal weapon." And when both had finished laughing, Myra went on, getting back on track. "All right, then, if I don't have to share you, I need to know if I'm expected to be like Edith. Or am I the trophy girlfriend with the *Playboy* body?"

"Don't forget that genius mind of yours."

Myra swiping her tongue across sensuous lips. "Right. I give good genius." But admittedly impressed with a man who saw beyond her tits and ass.

"Just be yourself, Myra."

Myra having to think about that, not really sure just who or what herself was.

"That what you expected of Edith, Gerald, be herself? Or did you mold her into what you wanted?"

"What you're asking," Gerald went on, wrapping a towel around his midsection, rolling on deodorant, "is will I try and make you into Edith. She was a good woman, Myra. And I'll always love her. Understand that about me. You don't forget thirty-two years overnight. But making you into her clone?" Gerald shaking his head and laughing. "No indeed. All that would do is drive you away. I want you to be comfortable in this relationship."

Myra looking at him, emerald eyes letting him know she was already comfortable. "All right," she said, "but I don't want to be possessed."

Gerald laughed. "Possession is nine-tenths of the law, Attorney Cross. How about a plea bargain, you let me have the one-tenth that's excluded?"

Myra had to think about that one. She said, "Depends on

which tenth you want. But I suppose I can live with the other nine. So long as you don't get too greedy. But you have to admit, three days is not much time to get to know someone." Myra thinking to herself he was Daddy, and that was all she really needed to know.

Gerald said, "It's time enough, as far as I'm concerned. Some things you just know. A feeling you have about someone. What about you?"

Myra wanted to say she had a feeling for him the moment she first laid eyes on him that day in his office. And knew once they were together she'd feel complete and whole again. Understood she'd felt like Humpty-Dumpty for more than twenty years of her life, having to live with the lingering pain of a thousand pieces of broken and fragmented emotions, waiting for all the king's horses and all the king's men—especially the men; Jesus, so many had passed between her legs she'd lost count—to put her back together, take away the pain, make her whole again. But it wouldn't be a king's army riding to her rescue on the Budweiser Clydesdales. It would be sixty-three-going-on-sixty-four-year-old Gerald Seymore, gentleman lawyer and crook in a Bentley Arnage RL. Oh God. At last. Daddy had finally returned.

Instead she heard herself say, "I'm fine with this if you are, Gerald. But I suppose your kids will have a lot to say about it. The age difference, I suppose."

Gerald said, "I can just about guarantee you they will. Thirty years *is* quite a gap."

"Thirty-two," Myra said. "But age is just a number—if you're right for each other."

Gerald said, "Are we, Myra—right for each other?"

She didn't have to think about that one. She said, "I think . . . no, I *know* we are, Gerald. But your kids might see it differently."

"They might."

"Will that cause a conflict?"

"It could for them. Not for me."

"And if it does?"

"Then we'll deal with it. Together. I'm not going to let them run you off."

Together. He said "together." It would be like "Uncle Lon" and "Yipes!" Only "Uncle Lon" would be "Daddy" and "Yipes!" would be the scream when she came. Myra hearing herself say in her own mind, Daddy this and Daddy that. The way it would be with them. And knowing it was meant to be and loving it. God, it was going to be so wonderful. Being with Daddy again. After all these years. She heard herself say, under a towel drying short locks of red hair, "I wouldn't want to create any problems for you."

Gerald said, "The only problem will be if you get cold feet about being seen with a man more than twice your age."

Myra smiled at him, her sparkling green eyes meeting his, giving him that needy, wanton, you-don't-have-a-thing-to-worry-about look. She ripped the towel from around his waist, threw it around his neck, and, backing him against the door, drew him down on the floor all in one motion. Her legs straddling him against the bathroom door, bathing his face with the suppleness of fleshy breasts, teasing him with the hardness of ripe nipples, her hands drawing his face to full pouty lips pressing tight against his, her tongue darting deep in his mouth like a snake.

Maya said finally, working his erection deep inside, "Being seen with a man twice my age . . . really. What about sleeping with one?" And her pelvis began stroking his hardness up and down. She mumbled childlike, burying her face in his neck, "Oh Daddy, you're so silly. Of all the things to worry about—cold feet . . ." Giggling and moaning deep in her throat like the little girl she once was and longed to be again. And as her moment exploded, *"Oh, yipes! . . . Daddy, yes . . . oh, Daddy, yes . . . yes . . . yes . . . yes . . ."*

And Gerald Seymore, intoxicated with the seizure of orgasm, heard himself whisper in Myra's ear in the waning moments of his own euphoria, "Yes, Myra. Daddy loves you."

• • •

THE REDHEAD ENTERED the empty lobby of Bunker Hill's Promenade Towers through the garage elevator at three-fifteen in the morning. Wearing white gloves, a large Gucci purse draped over one shoulder, both hands struggling with an extra-large, elaborately designed bouquet of white roses that, with the exception of glimpses of her striking red hair, all but shielded her face from view. Through the floral tower she asked the lone security guard to call Mr. Bruce Marshall and alert him she was coming back up, that she had something to give him. The security guard remembering the redhead from when she'd left, asking if she needed help, the girl saying thank you but no, she could manage, and backing into the penthouse elevator behind a shield of flowers for the ride to the eleventh floor.

Bruce Marshall was waiting for her. Barefoot and wearing jeans, arms folded across his bare chest like the Rock in a victory stance, only without the physique or the color. He was standing in the corridor just outside his door as she stepped off the elevator and began the slow trek toward him behind the huge mask of flowers. Perhaps because of the low-intensity lighting of the corridor, the fact he was still high from the buzz of stress, the half-finished snifter of Courvoisier, or just the anticipation of seeing her again . . . he didn't notice the thinness of her legs, the familiar but now ill-fitting beige skirt that hung loosely on hips that lacked their characteristic fullness, their subtle swaying in the way she walked, or the fact she was shorter. But he saw the red hair playing hide-and-seek, peeking out from behind the floral arrangement as she approached. He pushed open the door and held it, saying, "Changed your mind, huh?" Not waiting for her to answer but smirking behind her back as she passed, a whiff of familiar perfume tugging at his nose.

The girl entered an unfamiliar room crowded with the lingering odor of fried fish, the muted drone of a television in another room. And in a move the assistant DA failed to notice—perhaps again because of his vanity, his ego swelling at the belief he'd prevailed, that he was the better choice regardless—the girl seemed to hesitate for an instant longer than would be expected for one already familiar with the premises. She turned toward an open door through which she saw flickering shadows of light, pinpointed the source of the TV, and, assuming it was the bedroom, followed the lead of the bouquet through the door and into the void.

Locking the dead bolt, shutting off the light, and following her into the bedroom, Bruce said, "Thought you'd come to your senses. Realize we're a good match. Those for me? I'm impressed. Here, let me take 'em, put 'em in a vase, some water . . ."

The girl turned in the darkness, let Bruce take the flowers out of her hands and away from her face. She stepped back, and in the same motion reached into her purse and withdrew a gun. Holding it with both hands the way they'd practiced the night before in the Mexican's chop shop. It was heavier and unwieldy now because of its size, the long steel cylinder attached to the muzzle.

"Hey, you're not Myra. What the . . . ?" Bruce said, eyes blinking across an unfamiliar face—older, deep-set frown lines around a cruel mouth whose smile revealed two rows of decaying front teeth, eyes heavily made up with red iridescent shadow, thick Tammy Faye Bakker lashes, Joan Crawford eyebrows—fragments of light from a TV console in the corner, Larry King talking about Marlon Brando, replaying his 1997 interview with the star. She fired point blank. There was almost no sound, more like a water balloon bursting on the pavement. Bruce Marshall saw the tongue of flame leap from the muzzle, sliver of smoke that followed before realizing he'd been shot, the seep of blood leaking out from a hole just above his belly button. He dropped the flowers, saying, "Oh God. No . . . ! What . . . ?" Wanting to say more but the words stuck in his throat, cut off when a single round destroyed his windpipe and severed his carotid artery, sending a fountain of blood into the mirror. Another round into his mouth, two more plowing into his chest, sending him crashing into the chest of drawers, spinning wildly like an out-of-control top, limp arms flinging out like a pinwheel, futile in their grasping effort to support a body folding over on itself and collapsing lifeless on the floor amid a new floral arrangement of white roses and blood.

The redhead with decaying teeth and Joan Crawford eyebrows returned the gun to the purse and started to leave but stopped, caught momentarily by the stark black-and-white images playing on Bruce Marshall's body, familiar clip from *On the Waterfront*, voice of Brando saying, "I coulda been a contender . . ." And when the clip ended, she dropped down on the end of the bed to watch more of the Larry King interview, waiting for a clip from *The Godfather*. Absolutely unfazed by the dead body at the foot of the bed, she rummaged through the Gucci bag to see if she could find a joint, said "fuck" out loud, remembering their instructions not to have any dope with her. Their instructions too that she was to leave immediately for the rendezvous point. So when Larry King went to break she stood up and left the bedroom, stepping over Bruce Marshall's body as if trying to avoid a pile of dog poop. She walked out of the assistant DA's tomb with the same stealthy silence of her entrance. The large white herringbone-rimmed sunglasses that covered half her face wasn't as good a mask as the roses. So as she exited the penthouse elevator into the lobby and while waiting for the garage elevator, she covered her mouth with a handkerchief, pretending to sneeze repeatedly, turning away from the guard, giving him a good view of the back of her head so he'd remember the red hair, the Gucci shoulder bag, and saying thank you and have a good evening. Stepping out of the garage elevator thirty feet below sea level, she walked past her own aging and battered Honda Accord and trudged up the steep curving incline to Figueroa Street, thinking it made no sense—their insistence she leave it parked underground and walk the six or so blocks to Fourth Street and the five black spiral towers of the Bonaventure Hotel. She entered the lobby, passed the near-deserted registration desk, the two-level circular bar, and massive elevator console and crossed the hotel's remaining block-long width to the Flower Street exit. She stepped outside, dropped exhausted onto a bench, and waited.

"Hi, Rose." Neil Sanford in plainclothes, reaching over from the wheel, pushing open the heavy door of the Thunderbird, exchanging the twangy sound of country-and-western music for the redhead. Rose sliding in next to him, fastening her seat belt, head nodding to the familiar pair of cops seated in back, Stepolini and Calvin. The three of them looking strange out of uniform, the black cop even stranger wearing sunglasses at four in the morning.

"How'd it go?"

"Glasses killing me," Rose said, dropping them in the Gucci bag along with the gloves, which she worked off finger by finger, stripping off the blouse, sliding down the skirt to the sports bra and shorts underneath. Slipping on Fila sweats Neil Sanford handed her. Stepolini reaching over and taking the bag when she'd finished. In the dull glare of the Thunderbird's overhead light Rose's face looked haggard and worn well beyond her forty-six years of hard drinking, drugging, and whoring. Only the red hair, hastily cut short and unstyled, gave any hint of the brief arc of beauty she once possessed.

"I was asking how it went, not how the glasses fit, Rose." Neil Sanford pulling the Thunderbird away from the curb, the far lane of Flower Street a deserted concrete moonscape in the amber glow of streetlights still some two hours away from shutdown.

"Went all right. Don't see why I had to leave my car back there and walk."

"Walking the best exercise there is for a ho," said Calvin behind the sunglasses. "Get you off your back. Work your cardiovascular system."

"And fuck you too," Rose said, turning around, backing up her words with a fuck-you deadpan expression.

Calvin said, "Bad enough you a stinky-ass basehead ho. But your teeth! Jesus, Rose, don't you ever brush? Goddamn, I can't believe any muthafucka let you near his dick with a mouth like that. Give a muthafucka a disease just breathin' on him."

Rose said, "Then you got nothing to worry about, do you?"

"Just a precaution, Rose," Neil Sanford said, interrupting the exchange of insults.

"Precaution? What kind of precaution I have to walk six blocks for? Fuck, I need a goddamn joint."

"Later, Rose," Neil Sanford said. "Let's handle the business first. Anybody see you?"

"Security guard like you wanted."

"And upstairs?"

Rose said the corridor was deserted going in and coming out. Stepolini wanting to know how many shots she fired, Rose saying five and complaining how heavy the gun was, that it was nothing like when they practiced. Stepolini apologizing, saying they didn't get the silencer until late that same day and there wasn't time to rehearse, but figured she was smart enough to make the adjustment.

"You sure he's dead?" Neil Sanford asked.

"Unless he knows magic, he's dead." Describing the scene in detail, the layout of Bruce Marshall's condo. Saying they must have had red snapper for dinner, that they should've lit some incense to get rid of the odor. And describing the assistant DA's death. Talking about it without feeling or emotion, like it was a story she'd read or a movie she'd seen and not looking at anyone, eyes fixed on one object or another beyond the windshield. And when she'd finished, she said, "Can I get a joint now? Please?"

"Sure, Rose. Calvin, give Rose a joint, why don't you. I'd say she deserves it."

"Right," said Calvin. "The stinky-ass basehead ho with the bad teeth deserves one." He pulled out a bag of joints, passed one over her shoulder, and lit it for her.

Neil Sanford said, "Hey, guys, I'm hungry. What about you, Rose? You hungry for some breakfast?" And over his shoulder, "You guys okay for breakfast at the Pantry? What say we go by, pick up Rose's car. She can follow us."

Drawing on the herb, holding it in, exhaling slowly, Rose said,

"Pantry's kind of out of the way, isn't it? Pacific Dining Car is closer. Or King Taco. Yeah, why don't we eat there, pick up my car after?" Glassy eyes beginning to lose their focus.

Stepolini said behind a yawn, "You know, I'm really not up to Mexican this early."

Neil Sanford looked at his watch, calculated how much of the night they had left. Knowing what he had to do and not wanting to cut it too close.

With finality in his voice Neil Sanford said, "Same distance any way we cut it. We'll chow down at the Pantry. Pick up Rose's car on the way." End of conversation.

"First time I ever out-and-out killed someone," Rose said as the Thunderbird pulled to a stop, the stoplight on lazy. Rose pinched the roach, drawing the vapors in deep. A crescendo of laughter erupted from the backseat and Rose, reading behind the humor, turned around, exhaling. "That was self-defense," she said.

"Only because we said so, Rose," Stepolini said. "We hadn't, you'd be growing old in Chowchilla."

Rose remembering it now like it was yesterday, that terrifying night so long ago in her youth. Before the drugs, when she was new to the streets and had her looks—drop-dead gorgeous looks with an hourglass shape and flaming red hair she wore shoulder length like Maureen O'Hara. She remembered the trick who'd slapped her around because she wouldn't give him head a second time for free. Refusing to pay her, the trick was a large muscular athletic man in a drunken rage who threatened to kill her if she screamed or tried to leave, and he nearly did. Her face swollen and bruised, her ribs cracked, her lips cut and bleeding, she seized the only opportunity to escape when he passed out on the bed. But not before stabbing him four times in the neck with her switchblade. Rose, then too frightened to leave, watched the trick in his death throes. Clutching his neck with both hands and trying to talk, he staggered to his feet, coming toward her, but collapsed back down on the bed and died in a writhering shower of blood. And when it was over, when she was sure he was dead, she grabbed his wallet, found it stuffed with cash—five thousand dollars. Cash she had to give up to the Gang of Five, who investigated and lied in court, testifying it was self-defense. She'd bought her freedom for the price of an IOU. But with the Gang of Five you could never pay off an IOU.

"Which is why you owe us, Rose," Neil Sanford said, the light finally turning green, the Thunderbird moving across the intersection, settling down at twenty-five in a thirty-mile-an-hour zone.

"I'm reminded of that every day," Rose said, taking another deep drag on the joint. "Ain't I done everything you guys wanted? When does it end? Can't see this lasting forever." She thought about Brando in *The Godfather*, how you could never get out unless the Godfather said you were out. She asked Neil Sanford how much longer she'd owe them.

From the backseat Calvin said, "How long? Not long." Trying to sound like Martin Luther King but his imitation lacking the ear for the cadence. He sounded stupid. "Considering the circumstances, what it could've been, rest of your life, you stinky-ass white bitch!"

Rose, mellowing out on the weed now, said, "Oh, oh. The race card. Where's all this racial hatred coming from?"

Neil Sanford said, "Don't take it personally, Rose. Calvin's rehearsing. A school play called *Everything You Wanted to Know About Hating White People but Were Afraid to Ask*. Isn't that right, Calvin?"

"Yessa, massa. I's a re-*hearsin'* fo' the *min*-strel show." Saying it in a slow, dimwitted drawl like Steppin Fetchit. His imitation of a house nigger much better than his Martin Luther King. In fact, Calvin was a natural. Especially to play a nigger. Any kind of nigger.

Rose said, "Really." Giggling now, almost high enough to believe it.

Neil Sanford said, "We let him practice on us all the time. Get him ready for his debut. You ready for your debut, Calvin?"

"Oh yessa, massa. I's ready to sing an' dance fo' the white folks."

Rose wondered if he was going to try to shuffle his feet on the floor, get up on the seat and do a jig.

Stepolini spoke after a long period of silence. "Don't forget the Mexicans. He hates Mexicans too. Absolutely. But nothing like niggers. No one hates niggers like Calvin. I mean he's absolutely passionate about hating niggers."

Infected with the buzz of Colombian herb, their banter a false invitation into the good old boys' club, Rose giggled and said to Calvin, "You hate niggers too? Your own kind?"

Calvin said, "Yes'um, Miss Ann. I surely does hate them there *nigras*. I's always said, the only good *nigra* is a dead *nigra*." All he needed was some burnt cork and soap. She was surprised at his reaction—like he really didn't care. Surprised too at just how easy it was for her to call him that, not thinking she'd used the word her entire life.

Rose listened to them continue talking about each other in racial terms on the short ride back to her car. Calvin called Neil Sanford's kind white boys, rednecks, crackers, hillbillies, and hoogies—terms she'd heard before and knew to be derogatory. Rose not understanding how cops could insult each other and still work together. Street talk, she guessed. The black-white thing lost on her, except maybe OJ and Kobe—she could see it might have a place there. But for Rose—high on the vapors of good South American weed and laughing along with them as if she was one of the boys—the meaning went right over her head. It wasn't a joke. For what Rose missed, had she been really listening, was the ominous lethality that lay just below the surface of their exchange.

The Thunderbird made a sharp U-turn on Figueroa Street and came to a stop at the security gate entrance of the Bunker Hill Promenade Towers garage. Neil Sanford fumbled with a forged key card, waited for the gate to draw back. When it did, he eased the Thunderbird down the spiral ramp to the parking level below. Neil Sanford drove to the end of the garage where Rose said she was parked, brought the Thunderbird to a stop a car-length past the Honda, leaving the engine running.

Rose opened the heavy Thunderbird door herself, stumbled lazily out, saying, "Keys and license in my wallet, the bag there." Rose pointing to the large Gucci bag on the backseat between Calvin and Stepolini. Perhaps because she was so high from the weed, maybe even taken in by the flurry of good-old-boy insults, the laughter that went unchallenged, the hillbilly music that lulled her into complacency, or because she was just plain tired—Rose didn't appreciate the significance of the slow, methodical process with which Stepolini was putting on black leather gloves at four-thirty in the morning before heading off to breakfast at the Pantry, opening and closing his fist to work the stiffness out of the leather.

Neil Sanford said to Stepolini, pulling Rose's empty seat forward so he could pass, "Paul, be a gentleman, why don't you, and see Rose to her car." Stepolini saying he'd be glad to and easing himself out from the rear seat, bringing the large Gucci bag with him. He reached in the bag, brought out Rose's wallet and car keys, standing behind her as she got into the Honda, closed the door, and rolled down the window, securing her seat belt.

"You're right, Rose," Stepolini said, standing at the door, bending down to see Rose unlock the Club from the steering wheel, insert the key in the ignition, the engine taking its time before finally coming to life, belching out a cloud of dense black smoke.

"Right about what?" Not looking at him, but adjusting her rearview mirror.

"What you were saying in the car. That it has to end sometime. We agree with you, Rose—you've done everything we've asked. Can't ask any more than that. And like you said, this can't go on forever."

"Really!" Rose's ancient face looked up and brightened for the first time that evening, the smile putting two rows of decaying teeth on display like door prizes at a bingo game. Her eyes glazed and out of focus from the weed, looking at the Italian in the washed-out glare of wall-mounted garage lights, Rose not reading the practiced deception behind the broad smile, the spiderweb of frown lines showcasing a road map of lies.

And by the time she did—in the instant it took to regain her edge, when she detected the slight quiver at the edge of his mouth, the tip-off that his smile was a fraud—it was too late. The leather-gloved hand already bringing the gun out of the Gucci bag, the long steel cylinder approaching her forehead like the snout of a hungry rat sniffing at its prey. And flashing silently, capturing for a Kodak moment the cruel mouth holding the scream hostage behind a fortress of rotting teeth, Tammy Faye eyes opened wide in a face of stunned disbelief, awash with blood from the single hole in her forehead draining down onto Joan Crawford eyebrows. The executioner's gloved hand returned the gun to the Gucci bag, then moved through the window past Rose's lifeless body, trapped upright in the web of the Honda's seat belt, and shut off the engine. He walked over to and disappeared through the metal door with UTILITY EXIT printed in black letters, returned a moment later to the Thunderbird without the Gucci bag. He looked back somewhat impassively if not without some vague sense of regret, his memory of a younger, infinitely more attractive Rose, a Heidi Fleiss heir apparent providing the Gang of Five an unlimited supply of whores for their late-night parties with just a phone call. Yes, he would miss Rose. He had to admit that. But Neil Sanford was right. Business was business. And seven million dollars was worth a lot more than the pussy Rose and her cadre of sluts could offer. They might not be able to get ahold of another seven million in cash, but they could always get a replacement for Rose.

Always.

CHAPTER 13

"SEE, MUTHAFUCKA'S ripped out the bar used to brace the speakers. Top part. See it there in the picture? Scratches where it was bolted in . . . ?"

They'd been in the police impound yard on Figueroa Street since ten o'clock that morning, when Napoleon Booker's unexpected punctuality in the PD's office had begun their day. Their first stop was Sanchez Sounds, the auto stereo shop that had installed Napoleon Booker's elaborate speaker system. Sanchez took pride in his work, the wall of his cluttered office covered with photographs of satisfied customers. Sanchez was reluctant to give them the only copy he had, even more reluctant when Myra gave him her business card, telling her he wanted nothing to do with the police, asking Napoleon what kind of trouble he'd gotten himself into. Myra assured him it had nothing to do with him, that he had nothing to fear, and promised to return the original photograph undamaged after making a copy at Kinko's. Sanchez finally relented when Myra offered him fifty dollars, said she could keep it as long as she needed it but to keep his name out of it.

The battered Mustang 5.0 sat on four flat tires, bathed in a ten-week coat of thick dirt and grime, Napoleon Booker pointing to scratch marks around the periphery of the Mustang's trunk, Myra Cross holding Sanchez's small digital color photo while Napoleon Booker's index finger correlated the reference points. "Told you, I bail my black ass out, get us some evidence that holds up."

"Well," Myra said, thinking about it, "the photo certainly

helps. But it's still only circumstantial, Napoleon. Don't get your hopes up just yet. We have an uphill battle."

"Ain't it got the date and time on it? And the receipt. Don't that prove I had them sounds night I got arrested?"

"It proves you had them at" Myra peered closely at the photo—"eight-seventeen. It doesn't prove they were in the trunk six hours later when the cops stopped you. But they're both exculpatory in my book. Speakers and the receipt."

Napoleon frowned and said, "Ex . . . ? What that mean?"

"Exculpatory. It means the evidence in question could prove you're innocent."

"Goddamn muthafuckin' right I'm innocent. I'm so dumb I spent a whole day and five grand on speakers I tore out less than six hours after they were installed. Now you know that don't make no kinda sense, Miss Cross. I mean give me a muthafuckin' break." Myra reminded Napoleon he was repeating himself, rehashing his argument because it was the only one he had. Not that it wasn't a good one, but common sense and logic often goes right over the heads of illogical juries. "Replacing them with a tire. You believe this shit?"

"A tire, I might add, filled with a quarter million in stolen cash. Keep that in mind. The prosecution will argue you were on your way to make a big drug buy. Got the speakers installed to give yourself an alibi in case you got stopped."

Napoleon saw the flaw in that argument and said, "What's two hundred fifty thousand big faces gonna do for me, I got seven point five mil at home?"

"Seven million, three hundred thousand," Myra said.

"Whatever," Napoleon said, dismissing her correction. "What I need a drug buy for with that much cheese under my pillow? I got seven point five mil, I'm livin' next door to you, Miss Cross. Put little Napoleon in private school. Join the Kiwanis. The Rotary club. Get on the board of the LA Philharmonic. Make regular donations to the Dorothy Chandler Pavilion. Seven point five mil—this nigga be livin' real large. Know what I'm saying?"

Myra never challenged sound reasoning. But the Rotary club? LA Philharmonic? She continued to marvel at the knowledge slipping out of her client's mouth. Not really sure how comfortable she'd be living next to a client with seven and a half million in ill-gotten gains, but remembered Joe Kennedy was a bootlegger and his son became president. So she guessed they could be neighbors.

"Jury might see it as plain old-fashioned greed," Myra said.

There was a lot of cynicism in Napoleon's laugh. "Like Charles Keating, huh," he said. "White boys get greedy they just write a check and loot their bank. After all, it's their bank. They own it. Nigga get greedy he can't put no money in the bank 'cause he don't own no bank. Nigga gotta ride around all day long with it stuffed in the trunk of his car. Talk about the American Dream. What kinda shit is that?"

Myra said, "It's deep shit, Napoleon. And you're standing in the middle of it."

"Yeah? Well, muthafuckas what set me up for seven point five mil ones standing in the shit, I get my hands on 'em before the trial. We find the money, we find them. Ain't that the way it's done, Miss Cross—follow the money, you get to the root of the problem?"

"That's what they say." Myra looked at her watch and frowned. "It's almost noon, Napoleon. What say we go to Mexico. See what turns up. See if we can locate the original tire you say was part of the set."

Getting in the Mercedes, fastening his seat belt, sliding the seat back its full distance to accommodate long legs, lowering the seat back to accommodate his cool, Napoleon said, "Sounds like a plan. On the way you can tell me what you found out about that armored car robbery four years ago. We gonna follow the money, that's as good a place as any to start."

Once they were traveling south on the 110 freeway, leaving smog-shrouded downtown LA behind, Myra said, putting on Yves Saint Laurent sunglasses, "Four and a half years ago there was an armored car robbery that took place in Santa Monica. By all accounts it was a well-planned professional job. Criminals shadowed the route of an ASC armored car for an entire day, caught it at an S and L in Santa Monica on its last stop, where a tow truck and a van trapped the ASC vehicle in a narrow-access alley just as the guard was transferring the bank's cash. Investigators felt pretty sure it was an inside job. They theorized the guard killed might have gotten cold feet and wanted out at the last minute."

"Couldn't have that," Napoleon said.

"He was killed with the three fifty-seven they planted in your car. Five men were involved. All wore ski masks and gloves. Witnesses inside the S and L as well as the ASC driver all heard the shots, but none of them saw who killed the guard since it took place inside the truck. To a man they say the entire thing took less than two minutes."

"How long it takes the helicopter to arrive," said Napoleon, speaking from a core of street knowledge. "Probably monitored their radios."

Myra said, "It was so well organized and executed with such precision that detectives seemed to think the men, at least some of them, were ex-military or quite possibly retired law enforcement."

"Bet my money on LAPD to show every time."

"They cleared the ASC driver but he retired three months later on a disability pension for post-traumatic stress."

"Yeah," Napoleon said, "sight of losing that seven point five mil was more than he could bear."

"The investigation was kept open but going nowhere until they stumbled across you and, well, you know the rest."

Napoleon said, "Killed your investigator and knocked you in the head, try to scare you outta representin' me. Know what I'm sayin'."

Myra, still not totally convinced, said after a moment, "Right." She made the transition from the 110 freeway to the 405 South, set the Mercedes up in the far lane for the three-and-a-half-hour run to Tijuana. By habit she turned on the radio, a twenty-four-hour news station broadcasting news about congressional hearings on FEMA's delayed response to the Katrina disaster, Senator Tom Delay's indictment on money laundering charges. She turned to another station, KKJZ, early Louis Armstrong, his cornet soaring into the riff of a funky 1920s tune.

Without thinking, Myra said to Napoleon, "I can find a rap station if you like."

"Rap all right. Louis cool."

Myra said, "I'm into jazz. Have a thing for Louis Armstrong."

"Lotta people do. That's 'Cake Walking Babies from Home.' When he was with the Red Onion Jazz Babies. Charlie Irvis playin' trombone, Sidney Bechet on clarinet and soprano sax, Clarence Todd and Alberta Hunter vocals, but Alberta was singing under the name of Josephine Beatty at the time. They recorded it in New York, December twenty-second, nineteen twenty-four."

Beneath the Yves Saint Laurent sunglasses Myra's face twisted itself into a frown of utter amazement. Incredible. It had been building since he first mentioned the air conditioner. She'd thought that might have been a fluke. But that comment about Hamlet and King Lear. And Rembrandt . . . when she'd asked about his business partner. And just now, his comment about Louis Armstrong—information about a jazz impresario only a devotee would know. Information she herself was only vaguely familiar with, he'd committed to memory. She knew then it wasn't a fluke at all. He was either an idiot savant or Matt Damon's clone from *Good Will Hunting*. But Napoleon Booker wasn't an actor and this wasn't a movie. He was your ordinary garden-variety street criminal being framed for murder by a rogue group in the LAPD and looking at life in prison. Or worse. It didn't make sense. Napoleon Booker didn't make sense. The background just didn't match what was coming out of his mouth. Myra felt she was being conned. No—she knew she was being conned. It was sitting right there next to her. She just couldn't see it. Or didn't want to. Either way it pissed her off. As if Napoleon was toying with her. And Myra Cross, if she was anything, was not a woman to be toyed with.

"Where is all this coming from, Napoleon," Myra said, irritation in her voice making no effort to conceal itself. "What are you doing here? Just about all of the clients I represent are lucky if they can read and write their own names, remember their birthdays. You—you talk about Rembrandt and Shakespeare as if you're old friends, on speaking terms with the man who invented the air conditioner, kick it with the sidemen on a Louis Armstrong record, know when and where it was recorded. I don't understand this, Napoleon. I don't. One minute you sound like *Boyz in the Hood,* the next like Colin Powell. Why aren't you performing surgery? Practicing law. Or a professor in some university department? Instead you're a low-level street thug with a rap sheet and history from here to eternity. Here I am working in the dark with blinders on, can't see a goddamn thing in front of me, but you're pulling things out of the air like a soldier with night-vision goggles. What's with you, Napoleon?"

What it was with Napoleon Booker was rather extraordinary. He'd been born to a teenage mother of fourteen who'd been raised in the church and whose own mother had been fourteen when she was born and had sought solace and penance within the confines of religious dogma. Children having children. Napoleon got his good looks from his father, at least the man his mother said was his father. He was a suave, good-looking, small-time dope dealer who'd sensed his mother's sexual repression and seduced the adolescent in the church rectory. Six months after Napoleon's birth he was given a life sentence for the murder of a rival dope dealer. In the penitentiary he allegedly "found" himself, became a Muslim, and insisted on maintaining contact with his son. So Napoleon's mother and grandmother made the monthly trips up to Lompoc in those early years until his mother turned eighteen, got a driver's license, and made the trip without the grandmother. It was the drug dealer–turned–Muslim father who first noticed Napoleon's intellectual gifts—his ability to memorize and recite back in perfect order anything he saw. He would give Napoleon a "homework" assignment on each trip, discussing the results at the next visit. Required Napoleon spend his weekends in the library reading. He started him out with the Koran. Then assignments from the *Encyclopedia Brittanica*. It was incredible how fast he learned. His ability to absorb vast amounts of material like a sponge, spit it out days, weeks, months later as if he had only just read it. It was like being in school when he wasn't in school. Napoleon resented this at first, but finally capitulated and complied under the blistering pressure from the drug dealer–turned–Muslim father. And these assignments required Napoleon to read up on a variety of subjects—from history to science to music—and know them in detail. Minute detail. Minutiae and footnotes had to be included. If he didn't, the drug dealer–turned–Muslim father would fly into a castigating and humiliating rage, as if Napoleon's negligence or forgetfulness was a personal insult. Calling Napoleon names and suggesting he would wind up in jail like him. Napoleon resented being embarrassed in public and often rebelled by feigning illness to get out of the visits. But his father was unyielding if he was anything, insisting Napoleon's mother bring him to jail even on those occasions when Napoleon was legitimately sick. She did so, but reluctantly at times. Perhaps feeling intimidated by the threats from his father. Perhaps feeling guilty and shamed by her church members for having a child out of wedlock at such an early age.

Napoleon Booker was twelve when his father caught a shiv in the side and died. And while his mother would never say it, his father's death was a relief, for it freed her from the obligatory ritual of prison visits. Not just from visits to Lompoc, but also the church from which she beat a hasty retreat. She was working and pursuing various lovers in an effort to stabilize her life, so his grandmother, now sick and infirm, her eyesight and hearing failing, became the babysitter. This meant his education was left to the public school system. And because learning came so easily to him, Napoleon put forth little to no effort, which still generated a high school diploma and numerous college scholarships, none of which he ever accepted.

Because of the streets. Napoleon soon learned that being a genius was not an asset in the inner-city neighborhood in which he lived. He essentially had to apologize for being smart because it was embarrassing to his homeys, who viewed his intellect as his "trying to be white" and "trying to be better than everyone else." It got him laughed at and ridiculed by classmates. Got him beat up after school on a regular basis unless he turned athlete and ran home. But Napoleon Booker was tired of being made fun of and he was no athlete. He wanted to fit in. So he turned in his Jesse Owens track shoes and perfect attendance record and took to the streets.

He fit in, all right. Like a natural. He started missing class and hanging out with the gangbangers. They introduced him to dope, how to get it, how to sell it. Girls offered him more sex than he'd ever dreamed of because he was "so cute with his baby face." More than a few said he was their baby's daddy, wanted him to give them some money and gold chains.

Shaniqua. A booty call. A tall, full-breasted girl a shade over eighteen with distinctive African features and a deep ebony complexion who, a millennium of generations ago, would have been a queen to rival Nefertiti. She would have been raised in the splendor of royalty, worn gowns of silk and lace and necklaces weighted with sapphires, rubies, and diamonds, lived in a palace made of gold, worshiped and revered by millions. Instead she was raised on welfare, lived in the Nickerson Gardens projects, and wore cheap sweats bought at the local swap meet. The only diamond she wore was a cubic zirconia in her belly button. She wasn't worshiped—she was ridiculed. Castigated by a mother who cursed her birth as well as the man who impregnated her and who'd slipped out of her life four months into her pregnancy. Saw her only value as an unpaid slave/babysitter to the legions of half-siblings that would follow. And if she was revered for anything, it was the booty call that produced her only significant accomplishment, a son. Napoleon knew he was her baby's daddy, but he didn't seduce her in the rectory. He sensed she was the right girl when she suggested Napoleon II for his son's name. That, and the fact she got along well with his mother. After the baby was born she didn't ask him for anything at first, just that he come around when he had time. He remembered his father, did better than come around when he had time—he moved in with her and played baby's daddy.

And with the death of his father, his mother's religious convictions disintegrating under the weight of loneliness, and her frantic search for a partner, the umbrella of discipline that had shaped those first twelve years was gone. The streets were the only higher education Napoleon Booker would ever get. But the seed for reading planted by the drug dealer–turned–Muslim father had taken root. While the posse was kicking back, smoking dope and looking at the pictures in *Playboy*, *Hustler*, and *Players*, Napoleon was reading the interviews. When they were at Tower Records searching for the latest 50 Cent CD, Napoleon was reading the liner notes on jazz albums. In jail he found the library. And during long stretches he devoured entire shelves out of boredom. The knowledge base Napoleon had developed under the hand of his father during the twelve years of visits to the penitentiary wasn't lost on him. It just wasn't put to good use. His first arrest was for selling marijuana to an undercover cop on the school yard. It escalated from there. He was busted for possessing stolen guns, breaking and entering, drug possession with the intent to sell, petty theft, simple assault, grand theft auto, parole violation, the 187 frame by LAPD that Myra Cross got thrown out. Thirteen turns behind bars. Two days to two years. Two strikes and counting. Charged unfairly with a third that could effectively end life as he knew it.

Napoleon Booker. A twenty-six-year-old black man with a

gifted intellect, a girlfriend named Shaniqua, a baby's daddy with no vision beyond tomorrow.

"What a waste," Myra said, shaking her head slowly, the incredulity in her voice pushing out her words. "They offered you a scholarship and you turned it down? Napoleon, that's crazy. I don't understand!"

Napoleon seemed to be thinking about that one. His eyebrows and shoulders raised at the same time, like they were tied together.

"Most white folks don't," he said to Myra Cross. "You get used to something, you know, get comfortable. Don't really see yourself doing anything else. Like you, for example—raised in a *Leave It to Beaver* neighborhood. Growing up with dolls and Girl Scouts and birthday parties. Trying on your mamma's oversized high-heeled shoes, her dresses hanging off you, smearing your face with too much lipstick, pretending to be all grown up and knowing when you did, when your body caught up to your mind, you knew this was the way you would be—was what you were gonna be and the way you were gonna live 'cause you were use to that. That was all you saw. Sunup to sundown. You were raised like that, comfortable in the role that white skin created for you ever since you were a kid. You a lawyer 'cause you were raised to be one. Were expected to be one. A done deal." Napoleon half laughed and grunted deep in his throat, pleased with himself. He'd been guessing, of course, not really knowing the truth about Myra but taking her silence as a signal he'd come close. Louis Armstrong's trumpet blowing "Between the Devil and the Deep Blue Sea," Napoleon closing his eyes, nodding his head, body rocking in the plush leather seat, letting Louis take him wherever. "My neighborhood," he went on after a moment, almost regretting that he had to, his voice low, not wanting to drown out Louis's trumpet, "girl grow up to be a baby mamma, a ho, or do hair."

Myra was about to step on dangerous ground. She said to Napoleon, curious eyebrows raised behind the sunglasses, "You saying Shaniqua is a whore?"

"Slow."

Myra didn't understand.

Napoleon pointed to his head, made circles in the air with his finger.

"She's retarded?"

Napoleon shook his head. "Just slow. Never graduated. Spent all her time in special ed. Mixes her letters up."

"So she's dyslexic."

"Yeah. Slow," Napoleon said. "Pussy good, though."

From behind her sunglasses, eyes watching for the transition to the 5 South, the run down the coast, vistas of the Pacific Ocean coming in and out of view, Myra said, "So you've reminded me. She going back to school?"

"No reason to. School's hard for her. She's content to stay home, take care of Napoleon the Second."

Myra had to work at keeping her eyes on the ribbon of highway, said with a touch of anger slipping out from behind the sunglasses, "That's what *you* want. What about Shaniqua. What does *she* want? Dyslexia's no reason not to get her education. Look at Bill Cosby's son, the one who was killed, getting his PhD. He had dyslexia."

Napoleon said, "Bill Cosby had millions of dollars to spend on his son's education. You got that kind of bank, you don't have to go to school. Schools come to you. Money help you overcome a whole lotta problems."

Myra said she guessed he was right. Money couldn't hurt. But desire and motivation had to count for something. Napoleon said desire and motivation without money counted for nothing. Myra said he shouldn't be so cynical.

Napoleon grunted. He said, "Like I told you, girl comin' outta my neighborhood ain't got many choices. Every now and then one break the mold . . . become a Connie Rice, Marva Collins, Madame Walker, Judith Jameson, Oprah." Throwing out names like chips in a poker game. "Beyoncé, if you can sing and dance.

Not often. But every now and then, know what I'm saying. The talented tenth."

Like she really knew what he was talking about. Myra recognized three names, never heard of the rest. "Talented tenth?"

Napoleon smiled. Trying to explain it to someone with no frame of reference would be a waste of time. He let his eyes drift out to the expanse of the Pacific, tankers on the horizon, ears taking in Toni Braxton's "Another Sad Love Song." He said, "Black history. Know what I'm sayin'?" And knew even that would be a stretch.

Myra said, "Not really, Professor. But I'll take your word on it."

Napoleon laughed. He said, "Professor. Now, that's funny." But he liked the sound of it.

Myra said she didn't think it was funny at all. She hoped he'd take advantage of his intellect and go back to school. Napoleon said he might consider it but he'd have to be free first, reminded Myra that was why they were on their way to Mexico, to get evidence that would hold up in court.

Tijuana. A generation of picture postcards showing a town of narrow dirt roads, quaint adobe huts, and large sombreros covering the heads of slumbering villagers. But the siesta was over. Had been over since the beginning of the narco peso. The men wearing sombreros now carry AK-47s. The narrow dirt roads were now paved thoroughfares lined on both sides with shops selling brand-name American products to American tourists, only the labels read MADE IN MEXICO. Tijuana, land of the maquiladoras, where the greedy captains of American industry relocated for sweatshop labor, no unions, and no taxes. Tijuana. Little America with an accent. Everything and everyone for sale. For the right price you can have a ten-year-old girl clean your hotel room, or spend the night. Where you can buy the truth as easily as you can buy a lie.

But no amount of money could produce the Mustang 5.0's matching spare tire Napoleon Booker had left behind. The Mexicans who'd fabricated his nine-millimeter Glock gun rack were even better at fabricating stories. The only truth, they had sold the tire weeks ago. The one who remembered Napoleon, the only one who spoke English, said he didn't remember to whom. Asked his employees when Myra started handing out dollars. A farmer, one thought. Another said a laborer with a truck. A third thought it had been a policeman, and still a fourth thought it had been a tourist whose muffler they'd welded. The more dollars Myra peeled off, the more recollections changed. When one said it might have been a priest who needed it for his bus, Myra put her wallet away, realized it had become a game: dollars for false memories, who could remember what. But no tire. The one who spoke English offered to sell a tire off a Bronco he kept in the back. And failing that, asked Napoleon if he wanted another gun rack fabrication for the Mercedes. They could do a nice one, and admiring the dash and console, said he could possibly fit a second one behind the glove compartment. Napoleon said he was only interested in the tire, said the Mercedes was the lady's. Myra declined. Thanked them, gave each one twenty dollars for their time.

They found a McDonald's in downtown Tijuana for a late lunch and headed back across the border at twilight. Accompanied by CDs of Count Basie, Thelonious Monk, and Herbie Hancock, they didn't talk much on their return up the coast. It had been a disappointing trip, a waste of time as far as Myra was concerned, not even sure just how she'd have used the tire if they'd found it and thinking about her next move, if there was one, how to forestall what she was beginning to think was inevitable. For Napoleon Booker it was a sobering reality. Getting evidence that would hold up in court might not be as easy as he thought. A criminal force within the LAPD was sitting on seven and a half million of cold, hard cash at his expense. And if he was to have any chance at removing himself from this expense, it would mean a change in tactics. He'd have to begin thinking like those in the LAPD. Not like the cops. Like the criminals.

A big rig accident that tied up traffic on the 405 North put them into LA close to midnight. Myra dropped a discouraged

Napoleon off at the Blue Line in Hollywood, reached her Brentwood condo just seconds ahead of Freddie Hubbard's refrain in "Time After Time." Checking her mail, calls on her answering machine before undressing. Nothing urgent—Craig McInnis reminding her of a deposition at nine, her mother saying they were back from their cruise and would send pictures.

Myra settled into the comfort of silk sheets behind the mellow buzz of a joint and CNN, dozing off to the usual bad news: death of Richard Pryor; the rising body count in Iraq; Reggie Bush winning the Heisman; crude oil prices over sixty dollars. Perhaps asleep, maybe even dreaming, she wasn't sure which, when the name Bruce Marshall echoed distantly in her ear.

Again. Louder now. Several times. A voice saying, " . . . identified as Bruce Marshall, a deputy assistant prosecutor with the city attorney's office. The second victim, identified as Rosalie Roberts, was found shot to death in the parking garage below the exclusive Bunker Hill building in which Marshall resided. Investigators are being tight-lipped about the double homicide except to say there is strong evidence to suggest they are related. A gun found at the scene investigators say could be the murder weapon is now being processed in the lab for forensic evidence. Marshall, thirty-eight, had been with the DA's office for the past nine years and was considered one of their top prosecutors. This comes as quite a shock to the department, especially in light of the death of David Luna, the prosecutor with the Baltimore, Maryland, DA's office found shot to death two years ago outside Baltimore and whose murder remains unsolved. Investigators wouldn't speculate if Marshall's death was related, but are working on the assumption that . . ."

Myra's eyes opened and closed, opened again, seeing Bruce Marshall's picture fill the entire twenty-seven-inch TV screen as if on display in a photo gallery. Myra, laughing into her pillow, was used to dreams. Dreams about sex, usually. Sex with strangers. With men she knew. Bruce. Jason Rice. And more recently, lots of dreams about sex with Gerald Seymore. But this dream was different. She wasn't having sex with Bruce. In fact she wasn't even in the dream. Just Bruce. His picture staring at her with that familiar grin of his. And his voice. Inviting her into the TV. But no, wait, that wasn't Bruce's voice. Someone else's voice. A newscaster's voice telling her Bruce was dead. Myra's laughter stopped. What kind of nightmare was this?

The answer came when the picture faded to the crime scene, cordons of yellow tape, the newscaster interviewing police. Only then did Myra finally realize that, unpleasant as it was, nightmare and reality were now one and the same.

CHAPTER 14

"MYRA, I'D LIKE TO SEE YOU in my office, please," Marty French said after she and Craig McInnis returned from a trial that lasted half the day, line three lighting up almost the moment she dropped exhausted into the closest chair. And perhaps because of exhaustion, three sleepless nights in the shock of Bruce Marshall's murder, the lingering effects of a three-day binge of Colombian chronic, Myra failed to notice the subtle anger that tinged Marty French's voice.

"Craig and I just got back from trial, Marty," Myra said. And knowing Marty French had everyone's schedules down to the second, she added, "I haven't eaten all day. Can we do it after lunch?"

"Now, Myra! Immediately." And he clicked off. It wasn't a request. It was a demand. Myra hoping her discretion about Bruce Marshall hadn't been compromised, wasn't going to be a topic of admonishment. It shouldn't be. Myra had gone to great lengths to keep the names of her lovers out of the PD's purview. Sex with coworkers in the PD's office was strictly forbidden in her book. Not that there weren't temptations. God, were there ever. But she drew the line at work and held it. The DA's office, however, was an entirely different matter. "Everyone gets a turn." That was her reputation. And she wondered just how close to the truth it was. She couldn't prevent men from talking and didn't try. Every man in the DA's office she'd ever slept with had bragging rights for getting laid by Myra Cross. And there were a lot. Dozens, in fact. She didn't think Bruce Marshall had been any different. Hoping he'd been a little more discreet but not counting on it. So far her luck held.

Office talk about the assistant DA's death had seemed innocent enough, Myra's outrage mirroring that of the staff, each one offering their own theory as to who and why, no one tying them together.

Myra Cross walked into Marty French's office, suddenly grown small by the presence of four unfamiliar faces. Three men, one woman, all rising in silence as she entered. None offering her a seat, each staring at her with an unsmiling curiosity as if she was an object on display in a museum. Myra slowing her pace, nodding, saying a generic hello to no one in particular and then "Marty," to her boss seated behind the desk, chin resting on a brace of clasped hands.

"Sit down, Myra," Marty said, rising from his throne, his arm waving Myra to the familiar couch beyond the quartet, parting as she passed, dropped onto the couch, big sexy legs crossing by habit. Mindful of her skirt's tendency to ride up her thigh like a window shade, worked at pulling it down. But no one else sat down. Just standing there. The four of them staring at her as Marty said, "Myra," hesitating some, as if not really sure he wanted to go on.

And before Marty French continued, Myra said, looking at her watch, "Craig on his way?"

"This doesn't concern Craig, Myra," Marty French said, Myra failing to notice his voice colder and more aloof than usual. "Roy Fredricks is a detective with Rampart's homicide division." His arm swung out toward a Hulk Hogan clone, his bulky frame looking awkward in his too-small coat, unbuttoned shirt, and loosened tie, Myra guessing he dressed that way for effect. But he was show business right down to the sculptured mustache. All he needed was a headband. "Michael Pearson and Lance Baker are investigators with the DA's office," Marty French went on, his arm swinging in a narrow arc to a pair of Mutt and Jeff characters, one black, one white. Pearson, the black detective, short and skinny like Sammy Davis Jr. but without the gold jewelry and cigarette. Baker tall and awkward in a turtleneck sweater, long arms hanging out of coat sleeves cut too short for his height. Straight out of a Marvel comic book, gold badges from a Cracker Jack box and holstered guns hanging on thin leather belts. "And Cooper here, that is Miss Sheila Cooper"—Marty French dropping his eyes in apology, hating the need to accord her respect—"is with our alternate PD's office. She hasn't been with us very long so you may or may not know her." Myra shaking her head, saying she did not. Sheila Cooper was perhaps one of the thinnest women Myra had ever seen. Well, maybe the actress who played Ally McBeal was thinner. Sheila Cooper's pale pixie-face with razor-thin eyebrows hidden behind plain rimless glasses, absent any makeup, was the only attractive thing about her. And without makeup it was hard to determine just where her mouth was. Myra hoping she would smile so she could fix its location. Wearing a Marlena Dietrich pantsuit, vest, and tie, it was inconceivable her narrow, bony shoulders could support anything more than the weight of her skin. Myra wondered what kept the outfit, stylish as it was, from falling to the floor, thinking it must be sewn together and held up by the tie. Silent nods of acknowledgment between them, waiting for Marty French to wave his arm again when something dawned on her.

"Alternate PD's office," Myra said, her words meant for Marty French, but she was looking at the stick figure of Sheila Cooper, not wanting to miss the opening in her face when it revealed itself. "That's internal, Marty. Someone in our office in trouble?"

Marty French waving his arm to the quartet, saying it was all right for them to sit, only Sheila Cooper taking him up on it, finding comfort on the opposite end of Myra's couch, crossing her stick legs, her arm going up on the back of the couch in the same motion, space for two more between them, the mouth on the pixie-face still hidden.

"Why we're here, Myra," Marty French said frostily. "These gentlemen would—"

"We'll take it from here, Marty, if you don't mind." Roy Fredricks cutting him off, moving between Myra and Marty French, the move signaling Marty French's contribution was over, Marty French dropping back into the netherland of impotence behind his desk, chin returning to a brace of clasped hands. Roy Fredricks seemed somewhat startled, hesitant, his eyes exerting a major effort to avoid locking onto Myra's chest. He hadn't realized she was this stunning to look at. Jesus, she was beautiful. Red hair. Big legs. And those green eyes. "We're investigating Mr. Marshall's death," he managed to say, coming out of his trance, "the lawyer with the DA's office who was killed this week?"

Myra nodding, drawing a hissing breath through her teeth. And with genuine concern and sadness in her voice that no one in the room missed, she said, "Yes. That was terrible. I imagine you've got a big job ahead of you, interviewing everyone who knew him." Myra casting her arm aimlessly in the air. "We all knew Attorney Marshall. So I guess it's only protocol you consider everyone a suspect."

Fredricks pulled out a small notepad and pen from his coat pocket, Mutt and Jeff duplicating the action as if it had been rehearsed. "Quite right, Miss Cross. Everyone's a suspect." Eyes struggling to stay off Myra's chest, exposed sexy thighs.

Marty French said, his arm waving toward the anorexic seated two spaces from Myra, "Why Sheila Cooper's here, Myra. Make sure your rights aren't violated, that you're not denied due process during the investigation." Myra looking at Sheila Cooper, Sheila Cooper nodding but not speaking.

"You understand I'll have to Mirandize you, Miss Cross," Fredricks said, turning a page in his notebook.

Myra said, "Of course," and listened to his recitation, saying she understood her rights when he'd finished. Myra wondering if uncrossing her legs would distract him.

"Now, then," Fredricks began. "How well did you know Mr. Marshall, Miss Cross?" Back on track now. The hypnotic spell over. Almost.

Myra said, "About as well as anyone in the department." Lying and hoping it didn't show. "Just about every lawyer in this office has appeared opposite Bruce at one time or another." Careful to keep it from sounding personal, but knowing it was and not really sure how it sounded, calling him by his first name. If it revealed anything. "We often use first names around here regardless on which side of the fence they sit. It's a lawyer thing, you understand." If Fredricks and the toy soldiers with the Cracker Jack badges did, it didn't show. "He's considered, or *was* considered a worthy adversary," Myra went on, still finding it hard to think of Bruce in the past tense. "Wouldn't you say, Marty?" She tried to look around the Hulk Hogan twin to Marty French, Marty saying from behind the WWE look-alike that yes, Bruce Marshall was a worthy adversary, as if resenting having to concede it and with a patronizing tone Myra didn't pick up on.

"Did you know Mr. Marshall socially?"

Myra laughed. She said to Roy Fredricks, "Just because we're on opposite sides in the courtroom doesn't mean we hate each other. We don't take wins or losses personally," Myra said, lying, knowing full well Marty French was obsessed with court victories. "We may tear each other's throats out in the courtroom, but have lunch together after a trial. Like I said, it's a lawyer thing." She tried to laugh but got no action, so she stopped.

"Just lunch, Miss Cross?"

Uh-oh. Big mouth talked and Myra knew exactly where Fredricks was going with it. They knew something. Maybe everything. Maybe just fishing. Bruce, the cocksucker. She must've really pissed him off. Man wants her to move in, gets a Dear John visit instead. Myra organized her thoughts, got ready for the inquisition of truth or consequences. Decided to test the waters. Give them a little bit, see what they did or didn't know.

"Meaning?" Trying to act offended.

"Meaning, Miss Cross," Pearson said, chiming in, no Sammy Davis Jr. grin on his face, "was lunch the only thing you had together?"

"Mr. Marshall and I had a social relationship, if that's what you're asking. Yes."

"Was your relationship with Mr. Marshall a sexual one?"

Myra wondering if she could have a career as a psychic and get paid like Kenny Kingston, have her own psychic hot line like Dionne Warwick, then remembered they shut Dionne Warwick down because it was bogus.

"Yes." Give them only what they ask for. Don't volunteer anything was what she always told clients.

"Ever discuss cases?"

"That would be unethical and unprofessional."

"You're not answering the question, Miss Cross." Fredricks playing hardball investigator, working on his rep in case wrestling fell through.

Myra said, "No, Detective Fredricks. We never discussed our cases." Myra wondering what Marty French was thinking. Knew she'd get a good tongue lashing when this was over.

Fredricks said, not letting it go, "Not one time, Miss Cross. No pillow talk?"

"Oh, lots of pillow talk, Detective. But not about cases."

"I see," Fredricks said, pens of the Three Stooges scribbling ferociously on their pads. Myra thinking the titillation priceless, the Neilsen ratings on *Myra's One Night Stand* would be off the charts.

"Sleeping together but never once discussed your cases, Myra?" Marty French said, leaning around Fredricks to catch her eye. "Are you sure?" The tongue lashing starting early, Marty French straining to keep his cool, his disgust at Myra's behavior from showing.

"Quite sure, Marty," Myra said. "I never once compromised any client." Myra's green eyes holding Marty's grays until his skepticism seemed satisfied. She knew Marty wanted to believe her. Keep the PD's rep intact.

Before Fredricks finished scribbling on his pad, Baker said, "How long did you and Mr. Marshall live together?" What an ego.

Bruce must've been convinced she'd move in eventually, told his buddies it was a done deal. The arrogant son of a bitch.

"We dated for about a year. We never lived together."

"You do drugs together?" Pearson asked.

Now, that had to be a guess unless Bruce had infrared cameras in the bedroom.

"I don't do drugs, Detective." Myra struggling to keep a straight face. If they had any evidence they'd press the issue. If not, they'd fold on that one.

Flipping pages on the notepad, Fredricks said, "When was the last time you saw Mr. Marshall?" It was good to know Bruce hadn't told them everything. Or had he? Then again they were detectives . . .

"Monday night. I had dinner at his place."

"What time did you arrive at Mr. Marshall's condo?"

"Around eight-thirty."

"You cook or eat take-out?" Baker asked.

"Bruce, that is Mr. Marshall, was the cook. He fried some fish." Myra now wondering if it made any difference what name she called him.

"What time was that?" Baker taking over the inquisition.

"We ate around nine."

"You two have sex?"

"As a matter of fact we did not."

The trio suddenly stopped writing, raised their eyes in surprise. Baker said, "Really. Why not? You on your period?"

"That's a rather personal question, Detective . . . Baker, is it?"

"Murder is always personal with me, Miss Cross." The way he said it was not lost on Myra. Intimidation and authority. Showing her who was in control, telegraphing warnings about his ego.

"All right. If you must know, we didn't have sex because I went there to break up with Mr. Marshall. Not to fuck him." She looked over to see if the pixie face could handle her *Sex and the City* attitude. But there was no mouth. No blushing. Nothing. But there was a vague smile on the faces of the three detectives.

"Break up with him. Why?"

"Because I met someone else."

"Who?"

"None of your business, Detective."

Baker bristled and Myra, seeing the bulge in the sudden tightness of his cheek muscles, knew she'd gotten next to him, that he wanted to respond, put her in her place, tell her everything about her *was* his business. But she knew he wouldn't. She knew the type. Ego. Big ego. Wouldn't dare let out a signal he'd taken it personally, that she'd challenged his control. Myra could tell Baker was the nosy kind. He'd be the first one to watch *Myra's One Night Stand*. Still, she thought it best not to antagonize him.

"What time did you leave Mr. Marshall's condo?"

"Sometime between two and two-thirty in the morning."

"Where did you go when you left Mr. Marshall's condo?"

"Home."

"Which is"—Baker unfolded a piece of paper, reading it— "27274 Barrington Avenue. That correct?"

Myra said it was.

"Mr. Marshall follow you downstairs, see you to your car?"

And Myra, knowing they'd seen the building's surveillance video, said he did.

"And from there you drove straight home? Didn't stop anywhere along the way."

"Not even for gas." Myra having to work at not being flippant. But she was tired from court and needed a hit to keep her going the rest of the day.

Pearson must have sensed Baker was about to explode. He cleared his throat and before Baker's next question said to Myra Cross, "Do you know if Mr. Marshall had any other girlfriends?" Pearson taking over but not moving from his spot next to Baker, giving him a break, letting him regroup. Myra thinking Pearson might be shorter than Craig McInnis. Trying to imagine him in a jockey outfit and cap.

Myra said, "If he did I certainly didn't know about them."

Pearson said, "But if he did and you found out about it, how would you feel?"

Myra said, "I wouldn't feel anything one way or another. I didn't have any hold on Bruce, er, Mr. Marshall. I wasn't in love with him, if that's what he told his cronies. We had a thing going with each other, sure. But if he had someone else—he had someone else. End of story. Nothing I could do about it if he did. Nothing I'd want to do about it. Like I said, I wasn't in love with him, hadn't made Bruce any promises I couldn't break. I can assure you, Detectives, I'm not fighting over any man. I don't need to." Myra's vanity onstage, her emerald eyes taking them all in one by one. Trying to work their magic. And saying, "Personally, I don't think he did." Myra all but sure he couldn't handle anyone else, since he could barely handle her. Sure that her shit didn't stink. But felt it best not to tell them that.

Pearson said, "Do you know a woman named Rosalie Roberts?"

Myra thought about that for a moment. "Rosalie Roberts. Isn't that the name of the dead woman they found in Bruce's building?"

Pearson said, "In the garage, yes. You know her?"

Myra shook her head and said no.

"You're sure? You've never met her before. Had never seen her at Mr. Marshall's condo?"

Myra said, "I'm quite sure, Detective. We didn't go a lot of places socially. I only met a few of his close friends. Not many. And no one by the name of Rosalie Roberts comes to mind."

The little detective seemed as if he wanted to push the issue, but decided not to.

Fredricks, back on first, said, "You accompanied Mr. Marshall to Cancún a few months back. Is that not correct?"

What didn't that motherfucker tell the DA's office. Myra said she did, only they didn't travel together. They arrived five days apart.

"Why did he go to Grand Cayman first?"

"Grand Cayman? When did he go there?" Myra asked, surprise in her voice not lost on them.

The detectives looked up in unison. Then scribbled madly on notepads.

"You didn't know he flew to Grand Cayman before flying down to Cancún?"

"I did not. He said he couldn't get away for another two or three days. That he was in a trial and would join me down in Cancún, fly back together. He never told me anything about going to Grand Cayman."

Fredricks said, "So you don't know anything about Mr. Marshall's offshore bank accounts?"

Frown on her face, surprise in her voice genuine, Myra said, "Offshore bank accounts? In Grand Cayman? I'm sure I don't know anything about any offshore bank accounts. I didn't even know he went there."

More scribbling by all detectives in the room.

"And you're sure you don't know this Rosalie Roberts?" Pearson talking now, filling up his notepad. Myra convinced now more than ever that he was shorter than Craig McInnis, resisting the temptation to ask how tall he was.

Trying to remember her description from the newscasts but drawing a blank, Myra said, "You already asked me that, Detective. And I told you I don't know anyone by that name." Myra really beginning to feel the fatigue now and trying not to let it show.

Pearson, his ego barely more stable than his partner's, said, "And you're sure Mr. Marshall didn't have other girlfriends. Other women he was seeing?"

Myra was irritated at the midget's loss of memory and said so. Saying she meant no disrespect but the repetition was a bit much.

"That's not what I told you, Detective Pearson," Myra said. "I

211

said if he did, I didn't know about them. Why all these questions about my relationship with Bruce? Whether or not he had other lovers. What do they think, it was a crime of passion? That some other woman killed him in a jealous rage over me?"

Incredible how truth affects speech and motion. The room became silent. Pens stopped scribbling. No one moved, but the detectives all looked at one another. And if it wasn't for her fatigue, her preoccupation now with needing a hit, Myra wouldn't have missed the subtle telling communication between them. But she did.

"Because if that's the case," Myra went on, "it's really a tragedy, because it was over between Mr. Marshall and myself. Finis." And then said, after thinking about it for a moment, "That your theory, he was killed by some jealous woman? Or man?" She knew Bruce wasn't gay and told them so. Knew that for a fact if she knew nothing else about him.

"Why would you think that, Miss Cross?" Baker back on first. "That he was killed by a jealous lover?"

"I'm not thinking anything. You're the one who keeps asking me if he had other girlfriends. You must think there's something to it. That it has something to do with his death. Though for the love of me I can't imagine why you think Bruce would tell me if he did. With all these questions, you'd think I was the primary suspect in Bruce Marshall's death."

That paralyzing truth for the second time. Plunging the room into silence. No scribbling on notepads. Everyone holding their breaths again and not knowing it. Myra not picking up on it.

Until Marty French said, "You *are*, Myra."

Myra was so totally convinced she'd misunderstood Marty French, she asked him to repeat himself. But it wasn't Marty who answered. It was Fredricks, saying it appeared she was the last one to see Bruce Marshall alive. That there was developing evidence suggesting she might be implicated in his murder. And not just in Bruce Marshall's murder, but that of Rosalie Roberts as well. Marty

French adding he was sure it wasn't true but wanting to accord her good legal representation from the department. Reminded Myra that Sheila Cooper was here to represent her. Saying the PD's office guarantees the very best legal advice for one of their own if necessary.

"You have got to be kidding, Marty," Myra said when he'd finished, giggling in genuine disbelief. "You mean to tell me that just because I have an affair with Mr. Marshall, that makes me a suspect?"

Fredricks said, "Can you tell us why it wouldn't?"

"You don't have to answer that, Miss Cross." Myra turned in slow motion to the voice on her left, saw an opening in Sheila Cooper's pale pixie-face midway between the chin and nose, a dark hole like on a *South Park* cartoon character, with narrow rows of tiny teeth filling the space, the voice squeaky and high pitched, shrill like a school-yard whistle.

"*Don't have to . . . ?*" Myra let the words linger for a moment, so mesmerized by the sudden opening in the blank face, the unexpected emission of sound, that she temporarily forgot she was being questioned. Myra suddenly broke out in a laugh so loud and repetitious it caught everyone in the room by surprise. Without turning around, her voice coming across her shoulder, her green eyes still locked on Sheila Cooper's face, Myra said, "This is a joke, isn't it, Marty?" Myra suddenly whipping around to face the group, her forehead relaxed and without frown lines, full pouty lips drawing back into an infectious smile, not standing but sitting up straight, craning her neck to look around the room, her emerald eyes searching the entire periphery. "*Girls Behaving Badly*. Right," she said. "Where's the camera?" Myra suddenly collapsed back into the pillow of the couch, laughing hysterically, not waiting for him to answer. "Damn you, Marty French. Got me on this one, didn't you? Heard about your practical jokes. I figured I'd see it coming." Turning to Sheila Cooper and still laughing uncontrollably, Myra said, "You're pretty good, Miss. 'You don't have to answer . . . '" Myra still laughing and saying, "Almost had me there for a minute. Who coached you? Craig? Marty? 'You don't have to answer . . .' Yeah. You're good. Learn a few more phrases, practice enough, you'd pass for a lawyer. They ought to have you on *Law and Order. CSI.* At least give you a walk-on so you can get yourself a SAG card." Myra thinking now she might already have one. "'Cause you're good, like I said." Myra shaking her head in approval, giving Sheila Cooper, or whatever her name was, a compliment and meaning it. "You really are." Myra not as taken by her thinness now, the *South Park* face with the little opening and squeaky voice, waiting for her to speak in her normal tone. And while waiting she was sitting up now, bringing her laughter under a bare semblance of control, craning her head around again, focusing on Fredricks and Baker, somewhat more on Pearson, unrestrained temptation leading her to say to him, "If I may ask, just how tall are you?" And before he could answer, if he was going to, she asked Fredricks where the microphones and cameras were hidden, waited for the technicians to appear. After a moment Myra said, "You guys got it down pat. I'll say that for you. The outfits. Your little gold badges. Notebooks. Way you ask questions. Like you've been doing it forever. Anyone didn't know otherwise would think you were real investigators. How long did it take you to rehearse this? Fooled the shit out of me. I mean the hell out of me. Sorry 'bout that, Marty. But you got me on this one. You really did. I know Craig helped set this up. Just wait'll I see him. Boy, has he got it coming." And Myra, trying to smother her laughter and only slightly successful at it, said for the fourth time, "You don't have to answer . . ." Myra shook her head. "Jesus, I can't believe I fell for this."

It was only after Myra's laughter began to subside, when it dropped down to a few incredulous grunts and she had regained her composure, that she realized no one in the room was laughing. Had not in fact been laughing at all. Just staring at her as if she was a curiosity on display. And once she realized that, realized there was something else, she brought herself upright on the couch, emerald eyes searching Marty's face and saying, "Marty? This is a joke. Right?"

Letting Myra's green eyes hold his own, Marty said, somewhat reluctantly, "No one is laughing but you, Myra."

"Me. The primary murder suspect?" Looking at all of them now, incredulous green eyes sweeping across impassive, unsympathetic faces. "You can't really be serious?"

"Not even primary, Miss Cross," Fredricks said. "*The* suspect."

"*The* suspect?" Myra jumped up from the couch, pushed through Pearson and Baker until she reached Marty French's desk, and, leaning halfway across it brought a burning pair of green eyes, flared nostrils, and a face flushed red with the blood of anger just inches from his face, saying, "What is all this shit, Marty—*the* suspect? They're not interviewing anybody else in the department? Just me? What the hell is going on? Two months ago you had the Bobbsey Twins in here saying I was the bride of Osama bin Laden." Extending her arm behind her but not turning around, she said, "Now it's the Andrews Sisters there accusing me of homicide just because I fucked some guy we all know. That illegal? What the hell's this all about, Marty—Fuck with Myra Cross Month? You running a PD's office or a goddamn dog-and-pony show?"

Baker said to Myra's back, "Not just *a* homicide, Miss Cross. A double homicide. We think you killed the girl too." That spun Myra around. She pulled herself away from Marty's desk, her face grown cold with frown lines, knotted eyebrows, bulging jaw muscles, and full pouty lips barely open.

"Double homi—Oh, please!" Incredulous disbelief slipping out from under her words. Myra hesitated a moment. She folded her arms across the shelf of her breasts, began pacing slowly across the width of the office between the couch and Marty French's desk. Not looking at anyone in particular but her voice strident and clear, its undertone of hostility unmistakable, she said finally, "You guys in the DA's office got something against me? Dillon Lester pushing this? Pissed off because I wouldn't fuck him? Because I know Dillon for what he is, a little rat-faced asshole who hasn't got the balls a newborn baby has." And she brought her eyes up from the floor, first to Pearson, then to Baker, holding his eyes, saying, "Everybody gets a turn, huh? That what this is all about—pressure me so he can get laid by Myra Cross, put his name on the bulletin board alongside half the department I've wrapped my legs around." And realized for the first time it may very well be true. Jesus, close to half. Not really knowing, but wondering just how many that would be. What she did know about was the DA's bulletin board from Bruce's pillow talk about her reputation. You were a "made man" if you got your name added to the "List of Achievement," as they called it. Code word for getting laid by Myra Cross. Myra shaking her head now, like she was agreeing with what she was saying. "Oh, yeah. I know all about the 'List of Achievement' in your office. You guys looking to do the same," Myra said to Baker, who was trying not to show his expression of surprise but knew it was there and that Myra had seen it. "Get your turn with the slut, add your name to the list?"

Sheila Cooper spoke from the couch and said rather forcefully, "I wouldn't discuss anything personal, Miss Cross. You're a suspect in a double homicide. Don't let them goad you into discussing anything personal. Don't volunteer any information. Keep any comments you have on the facts."

Because she was seething with indignation she didn't say it, but Myra appreciated Sheila Cooper's advice. Keeping her grounded during the attack. Professional to professional. Girlfriend to girlfriend. Well, maybe not girlfriend . . .

Myra said indignantly, "All right. And just what *are* the facts that have so convinced everyone I'm the one and only suspect. I'd like to know." Looking first at Fredricks, then Pearson and Baker. Dismissing Marty French altogether. Grunting cynically and trying to laugh, bleed off some of her anger, the fear and panic she could feel developing. But she was all laughed out now, the humor hard to summon. "Go on," Myra said, challenging the room. "Ask me anything you want. I've got nothing to hide. You may see me as a slut. Well, all right. Whore of the nineteenth floor." And tried to remember who'd given her that label, or if she'd labeled herself. "But that doesn't mean I'm an ax-murderer. So you go right on. Whatever you want to know."

Fredricks jumped at the bait. "You said you left Mr. Marshall's condo sometime between two and two-thirty. That correct?" Myra said it was.

"What time did you come back?"

"Come back? I haven't been back since. I told you, I broke off with him that night."

"You didn't come back an hour later with a bouquet of flowers? Ask the security guard to buzz Mr. Marshall's unit, send you through when he answered? That your story, Miss Cross?"

"Bouquet of flowers? No, I didn't come back with any flowers. I went straight home."

"You saying you didn't buy any flowers that night from Gibson's Flowers on Figueroa and Seventh?"

"I did not."

Fredricks removed a slip of paper from his inside coat pocket, unfolded it, and held it out to Myra. "Then I suppose you don't recognize this receipt for the seventy-five dollars you paid. Your signature at the bottom there. See . . . on the bottom, your name, Myra Cross."

"May I see that, please." The squeaky voice on the couch extended a razor-thin arm and intercepted the receipt ahead of Myra. The eyes behind the rimless glasses studied the paper, then looked up at Myra expressionless, thin delicate fingers handing the paper almost reluctantly to Myra. Myra staring at it blankly at first, then her face twisting in a violent knot of unattractive lines. It was a receipt from Gibson's Flowers, dated for Monday, Myra's name scribbled at the bottom. Practiced. A good likeness. But not good enough.

Myra said, "My name. Not my signature. Handwriting expert will prove that."

"Maybe. Maybe not," Fredricks said.

"I've never been to that flower store in my life."

Pearson said, "So you say. Flower shop's video surveillance tape is very clear. And the salesclerk who sold you the flowers ID'd you from your employment photo, passport photo, and one taken from Mr. Marshall's condo." To Sheila Cooper he said, "We did a photo lineup. A six-pack. Mixed her photo in with six other women. Witness ID'd Miss Cross." Myra remembering Bruce enlarging several pictures he'd taken of her when they'd first started going together. His favorite he kept on his bedroom dresser, a candid close-up photo of her standing by the window, reading liner notes on a Dizzy Gillespie CD, Myra looking directly at the camera and smiling. Well, considering he was an amateur, it was a good picture. Thank God she'd resisted his effort to photograph her in the nude. Although if she hadn't met Jason Rice . . .

"So did the security guard in Mr. Marshall's building," Pearson was saying to Sheila Cooper. "Picked her photo out of another six-pack we set up. Said he spoke with Miss Cross when she returned, offered to carry the flowers up to Mr. Marshall's unit for her." And to Myra he said, "You deny all that?"

"Larry. Spoke to me when I left, yes. But I never came back."

"Well," Fredricks said, "maybe the surveillance video will jog your memory."

Myra said, "I'd love to see it. See who's impersonating me."

"So would I, Detective." Squeaky whistle-voice coming from somewhere on the round pixie-like face sitting atop a puppetlike stick figure. "And the one from the flower shop also."

"You will, Counselor." Fredricks scribbling on his pad, not looking up.

Baker said, "You own a gun, Miss Cross?"

Myra said, "I most certainly do not. I'm afraid of guns."

Baker withdrew a piece of paper from his coat pocket, unfolded it, and said, "So you're saying you didn't purchase a nine-millimeter pistol, a Glock, from Gun Rack West out in Whittier two months ago?" He handed the paper to Sheila Cooper. Sheila Cooper holding it for a moment, handing it over to Myra but looking at her this time, Myra not sure what she was thinking. Until she read the paper. "I suppose that's not your signature either," Baker said.

Another receipt from a store she'd never been to. Her address. Social Security number. Birthday. Same scribbled signature that was practiced but not perfect. Whoever it was had been well coached. Myra wondering how they got her personal information, trying to remember if she'd ever lost her wallet, credit cards, driver's license. But couldn't come up with anything. Then too, if the police could get her driver's license and passport photo, so could criminals. She shook her head, handed the paper back to Baker.

"Only time I go to Whittier is for court appearances. I wouldn't know where Gun Rack West was if you drew me a map and showed me pictures."

"You came back clean on the FBI check," Baker said, cocky and confident. "Salesman remembered your red hair when you came back to pick it up."

"You'll need more than red hair to make me out to be a serial killer."

Sheila Cooper said, "Gun store would have a surveillance camera. When will that tape be available?"

Baker said reluctantly, "Camera wasn't working that day, unfortunately. But he ID'd Miss Cross from a six-pack with different photos." And to Myra he said, "But if it's not your gun, Miss Cross, how do you explain your prints on it? Osmosis? They just attach themselves out of thin air? Want to help us out here?"

Now, that got to her. Myra's mouth snapped open, but the shock kept any words from coming out. Finally she found her tongue and said somewhat hoarsely, "On the gun? My fingerprints were on the murder weapon? But how's that possible?"

Fredricks laughed facetiously. He said to Myra, "Usually happens when you hold a gun, Miss Cross." And to Sheila Cooper he said, "Ballistics proved the same gun that was used to kill Mr. Marshall was also used in the Roberts killing. About an hour apart." And to Myra he said, "No one else's prints on the weapon but yours, Miss Cross."

The tiny egg shaped mouth on Sheila Cooper's face opened and the squeaky voice that slipped out said, "May I see the ballistics report, please."

"Certainly." Fredricks withdrew another piece of paper from his jacket pocket, larger than the first, and handed it to Sheila Cooper. He said, "Miss Cross's prints were all over Mr. Marshall's condo, which, in and of itself, is not incriminating since she'd spent considerable time there. But her prints on the gun used to kill both Mr. Marshall and his girlfriend suggests the motive was a crime of passion. The signed receipts, along with eyewitness accounts of her presence at both the flower shop and gun store, the security guard eyewitness and surveillance tape of her movements in and out of the attorney's condo complex that puts her at the crime scene right smack in the middle of our time line—all of this is more than enough evidence for us to charge Miss Cross with the murders of both Mr. Marshall *and* Rosalie Roberts."

Sheila Cooper studied the report a moment longer than she'd studied the receipts from the flower shop and gun store, saying to Fredricks as she handed the report to Myra, "Are you formally charging Miss Cross?"

"I am."

"Without an eyewitness lineup?"

"We'll arrange a lineup before her arraignment."

Aware for the first time that she was trembling, Myra stared at the report, but not really concentrating, lost now in the shock of hearing familiar words but not wanting to believe they applied to her— . . . *charge Miss Cross with the murders of* . . . —and realizing now the enormity of what was happening. Knew now that she'd been framed. By whom and why. Taking on Napoleon Booker's defense had proven a fatal decision. Her sense of fair play and moral obligation. And her ego, thinking she could go it alone, that she could outwit them with the law. Realizing now too late they *were* the law. Whoever "they" were. That she was out of her league from the get-go. She'd been set up along with Napoleon Booker. And knew exactly what was coming next. They were going to arrest her and send her to prison. Maybe to her death. This couldn't be happening to her. It just couldn't. Not to Myra Cross—longtime member of the County Bar Association, highly respected defense attorney with the Office of the Public Defender. It just couldn't be happening. It just couldn't.

But it was.

Myra suddenly felt sick to her stomach and had to suppress the urge to vomit. She became dizzy, her legs weak and numb. She was barely able to keep her body upright and had to work at not collapsing, backing against Marty French's desk for support. This had to be a dream. It had to be. A nightmare from all the cocaine she snorted. And in this respect Myra was right. But only half right. Because what happened next wasn't a dream. What happened next was truly a nightmare. In broad daylight. Reality style.

Roy Fredricks, homicide detective with the Rampart Division, said to Myra, deputy assistant public defender, "Myra Cross, you are hereby charged with two counts of first-degree murder," withdrawing from his belt a pair of blunt steel handcuffs, noisy in the way they clinked together, turning around to include Marty French as a courtesy in the same motion. Marty French sitting impassively behind the desk, his chin still on the brace of clasped hands, raising a pair of eyebrows along with his shoulders in a show of resigned acceptance, surprised but trying hard not to show it. Putting emotional distance between himself and the proceedings, thinking how best to do damage control, salvage his department's reputation. More specifically his own reputation. Thinking how it was going to read in the morning edition of the *LA Times*, a member of the PD's staff charged with a double homicide in a love triangle. Tabloid fodder for the masses. Jesus, that's all he needed. Fredricks turning back to Myra and grabbing her wrist, bringing it down and behind her back, snapping one handcuff shut around Myra's wrist, bringing her other arm around her back, cuffing its mate.

Sheila Cooper's stick frame suddenly rose from the couch the way a praying mantis unfolds itself from a tree branch.

"Whoa, there, Detective," she said to Fredricks, Fredricks checking the handcuffs for tightness behind Myra's back. "I assume you have a warrant?"

"You assume correct," he said, and Myra watched as Fredricks withdrew a piece of paper from his jacket, slapped it into the palm of Sheila Cooper's hand like it was a scalpel being passed to a surgeon. Fredricks reminding Sheila Cooper a capital crimes warrant carried no bail.

Opening and closing the warrant without reading it, Sheila Cooper said, "But is it necessary to arrest her at this moment, Detective?" Myra half listening, standing helpless in the middle of the office, hands shackled behind her back, head of red hair hanging down in the humiliation of shock and disbelief, all the fight gone out of her.

Fredricks said, "It is."

Pearson said, "She's being charged with a capital crime, Counselor. A double one eighty-seven. Now is as good a time as any."

Sheila Cooper said, "Yes. But I'd prefer to surrender my client personally. Miss Cross is a respected public figure with considerable responsibilities. She'll need some time to put her affairs in order. Marty?"

Marty French came off his brace of clasped hands, leaned back in his chair. Pencil flipping between his fingers, his tongue making sucking noises with his teeth as he thought about it. Figured the best way to buy his reputation some time was to go along with Sheila Cooper. But God, he didn't want to.

"Miss Cooper is right," Marty said convincingly. "I'd want to handle this professionally without jeopardizing the rights of our clients. She has an enormous caseload. We'll need time to transfer her cases," he said, knowing Craig McInnis was on top of every case Myra had.

Baker said, "I'm worried about her being a flight risk."

Sheila Cooper said, "Don't be. She'll surrender her passport. And if that's not enough of a guarantee we can call the State Department and cancel it."

Baker said, "Not on the weekend, you can't. Besides, we already have her passport. We searched her condo earlier today." And he pulled out another piece of paper from his jacket waving it in the air just long enough for Myra to glimpse it before handing it to Sheila Cooper, the alternate PD lawyer knowing it was a search warrant, not bothering to read it. "But I still consider her a flight risk."

Searched her condo? Aw, shit. Myra heard that through the fog of shock. Panicked at the thought they would have found her stash, charged her with possession. But in the same instant relaxed, remembering the reason she was so on edge: she'd exhausted her entire supply of dope—rocks, primos, the purple bubblegum weed, Swisher Sweets, and Blunts—in the three days of bingeing. She'd intended to replenish her supply today after work, make contact with her dealer, one of the maintenance men who worked the high-rise criminal courts building at night.

Sheila Cooper said, "Why? If you have her passport . . . ?"

Baker said, "Because there's plenty of countries she could go to that don't require passports."

"I think she needs to be in jail to protect the public safety," Pearson the midget black detective said, looking up at the thin, shapeless lawyer towering above him, both hands in his pockets, pulling his coat away, showing the Cracker Jack gold badge and nine-millimeter on his belt. Little-man syndrome exerting his authority. Pushing the envelope beyond his color. "What makes a woman lawyer any different than a woman garbage collector, you commit a double murder?" And Pearson knowing the answer to that one was race. Special consideration for white girls accused of double homicide. Get time to put their affairs in order before going to jail. Dress up. Go out to dinner. Dancing. Show up in a limousine to surrender. She was a black girl, they'd cuff her in the middle of taking a dump, take her to jail in the back of a black and white, let her put her affairs in order behind bars. "Law says if you're charged with a capital crime, you go to jail. Why there's no bail attached," Pearson went on. "Cut and dry, way I see it. You can't do the time, don't do the crime. Do not pass go. Go straight to the gas chamber." Judge, jury, and executioner all wrapped up in a carbon-colored package the size of a jockey. Dress him up in uniform, cap on his head, stand him out in front of the criminal courts building. Let people pet him as they walk by.

Baker seemed to be thinking about it. He said to Sheila Cooper, "How much time are we talking about?"

Sheila Cooper said, looking at her watch, its face a dinner plate of scattered remnants on the bony wrist, "It's Friday. We'll surrender her this time Monday. Four-thirty. Department One Ten, superior court or Rampart station. Your call."

Baker said to Pearson, "You okay with this—Monday four-thirty?" Not having to, but giving the midget black man some say in the matter.

Pearson said, "On a capital case, a double one eighty-seven, she wants to go party first? Hell, no, I'm not okay!" He seemed to want to go on but couldn't find the right words, so he just strutted back and forth with his hands in his pockets like Little Caesar. All he needed was a cigar.

Marty French said from across the desk, "We'll guarantee her appearance, Detectives."

Pearson thought about that for a moment and shook his head reluctantly. He said, "Monday at four-thirty is nonsense. I'm not in the habit of giving capital murder suspects weekend passes. You surrender your client Sunday morning, Counselor. Nine a.m. sharp. Rampart." Throwing his jockey-sized weight around. Not looking at Marty French but at Sheila Cooper, both hands plunging deep in his pockets, his short body rocking back and forth from heel to toe for more height, playing the role but knowing in truth his words lacked any authority, were impotent in the same manner he was impotent, because Baker was the top dog and he, Pearson, little more than a feral runt. You could tell he wasn't happy.

Sheila Cooper looked at Marty French. Marty French nodding, resigned. She said to Pearson, "Rampart. Sunday morning at nine, then."

Baker said to Fredricks, nodding his head, "Let her go." To Myra he said, "Have a nice day," as the cuffs sprung open, her arms swinging free again. Saying it in a way he hoped she'd remember if she ever beat the case, give him a chance to get his name on the List of Achievement.

If Myra heard him, she didn't reveal it. She was rubbing the strange discomfort out of still-numb wrists and thinking about prison, that once she surrendered she'd never see daylight again, and wondering if she'd hold up. Thinking if she could be Lil' Kim's cell mate, she might learn how to sing.

CHAPTER 15

"YO, MISS CROSS! HEY! Miss Cross, S'up?" Napoleon Booker's diamond ring tapping hard against the glass of the Mercedes passenger window. Myra raised her head slowly from the cradle of arms covering the steering wheel, vacuous green eyes feeding a waterfall of tears down a face streaked with makeup. She looked over, saw the cherubic face in the dim light of P3's parking structure, lowered the window, and, dabbing wet eyes with a handkerchief, looked away. Without asking, Napoleon slid into the leather seat beside Myra, closing the door. "Sorry I'm late. Tried to get here by four like you wanted, but Shaniqua's car went into meltdown mode, know what I'm sayin'—say, you been crying. What happen? You lose a case or something?"

"I wish it were that simple, Napoleon," Myra said, not looking at him, the handkerchief turning her face into a canvas of makeup. Not wanting to tell him, anyone really, but knowing she had to and not knowing how. "I . . . I don't think . . . what I'm trying to say is . . . that . . . well, I can't . . . Jesus, this can't really be happening. It can't."

Napoleon said, "What can't be happening, Miss Cross? You have a fight with my business partner. A lover's quarrel. Something like that?" Napoleon smiling, letting on he knew or thought he knew about the two of them. "'Cause that ain't nothin' to cry over, Miss Cross. He an older man. Set in his ways. Something you have to get used to, that's all. And—"

"Nothing like that, Napoleon. Something much worse, I'm afraid," Myra said in a voice barely audible, shaking her head, still playing artist with her face, not looking at Napoleon. "I can't . . . I can't . . . represent . . . you anymore, Napoleon." The words coming out in unpolished bits and pieces, as if being chipped away from a rock quarry one by one. "I . . . can't . . . they won't let me . . . not just you. I can't represent . . . anyone . . . anymore. I . . ."

Napoleon looked at her. "Why you talking crazy, Miss Cross . . . can't represent me? *You* my lawyer. Ain't gonna be no other lawyer represent me. Tell the muthafuckin' head man myself, I have to." Napoleon grunting deep in his throat and shaking his head. "Can't represent me no more. That some bullshit." Napoleon's face turning cold and mean and confused in the frown that covered his face, wondering now if she'd sold him out and not wanting to believe it but maybe . . . ?

Her soft, quiet voice forcing the words out, Myra said. "You don't understand. It's not that I don't want to, Napoleon. Not that at all. It's . . . it's . . . I'm . . . they're . . . oh Jesus, Napoleon, they're . . . they're"— trying to get up courage to say it, as much for herself as Napoleon— "they're sending me to jail," Myra said finally, familiar words sounding strange and alien, turning to look at him now and Napoleon seeing her anguish and truth in the endless flow of tears coursing down her face, not understanding it yet but knowing now she hadn't rolled over on him. Knowing too there was something else, something more ominous in the tone of her voice, in the way she said it.

Napoleon said, not seeing it yet, "Sending you to jail? You being transferred? What?"

Myra looking away again and saying, "I'm being accused of murder." Just like that. Saying it. Trying to get used to saying it. To get familiar with the words. Accused of murder. As if she was talking about someone else.

Napoleon said, "Murder? Who you kill?" Still not seeing it and sounding silly, knowing she hadn't killed anyone. But knowing too if she said it, there must be something to it.

Myra, shaking her head, managed to say absently, "They say I killed Bruce. Some girl. Jesus, Napoleon, you got a joint on you?"

Not embarrassed at asking now, her professionalism and pride gone with the memory of snapping handcuffs. Hoping her presumptuousness about Napoleon Booker was right and if so, that he wouldn't be offended.

He wasn't. Just surprised it took her so long to ask.

"Bruce? Who's Bruce?" Napoleon pulling out a handkerchief of joints in a routine practiced a thousand times for a thousand junkies and lighting one, handing it to Myra, Myra drawing the herb deep into thirsty lungs, waiting for the buzz to put out the fires ravaging her brain.

"Lawyer in the DA's office."

Napoleon frowned, thinking about it. He said, "TV said something about a lawyer, girl killed in his garage few days ago. That you?" Myra nodded and said it was.

"Why they think you did it?"

"Bruce was my ex. We spent time together. I don't know."

Bruce. Napoleon looked at Myra. Wondering if she'd told his business partner about Bruce. Decided whether she did or didn't was his partner's business. But giving it a little more thought all the same and finally seeing it now, connecting the dots. Big dots. With blue uniforms and gold badges that said LAPD mobsters. Napoleon nodded in agreement with his own conclusions and sucked air through his teeth.

He said to Myra, "Muthafucka! Set you up, didn't they? You know it's about me, don't you? About those same LAPD gangstas protecting their seven million Benjamins we been trackin'. Figured we might get some evidence put them in a trick bag. They stop you, they stop me, know what I'm sayin', Miss Cross?"

Myra did. Absolutely. But didn't think there was much she could do about it. Not before Sunday, when she'd have to surrender. Explaining to Napoleon there was no bail. She'd be confined for the duration. That Craig McInnis would take over his case.

Napoleon didn't hear the part about Craig McInnis. He heard Sunday and said, "Sunday? Aw, hell no! You need a lawyer."

"I have a lawyer," Myra said. "The department provides one."

Napoleon pulled out a cell phone, flipped it open, and punched in a number. "You not hearing me, Miss Cross. We need a lawyer. A real lawyer. 'Cause you ain't going to no jail. Not on Sunday or any other day. We ain't goin' out like that. Know what I'm saying?"

Myra Cross didn't hear the "we." She heard the part about not going to jail and said, "I agreed to surrender, Napoleon. Not much I—"

Napoleon raised his hand, waved Myra silent, spoke into his cell phone. "Yo. Scarecrow is down." Flipping the cell phone closed, he said, "Can't help what you agreed to, Miss Cross. Ain't gonna be no surrendering to no kinda jail on Sunday. Now we wait. Business partner call. Take it from there."

Scarecrow is down. The secret code. Like a Flash Gordon ring in a box of Wheaties.

• • •

"How did my prints get on a gun I've never owned?"

Myra exhausted and spent, having recounted the events of the day, sitting next to Napoleon, the two of them crammed into the tight space of the *Prince*'s kitchenette booth, Gerald Seymore seated across from them. An ashtray of spent joints, three half-empty glasses, and a half-filled pint of Johnnie Walker Red on the table. Gerald Seymore listening intently, leaning forward on the table with both elbows making the space between them even more claustrophobic. His Van Heusen satin striped long-sleeved shirt, gold monogramed cuff links as much at home on his yacht as in the Century City law office. The yacht's cabin was, if anything, a miniature clone of the Century City office. A narrow, elaborate redwood-paneled space with brass fixtures in place of artwork and a large clock in the shape of a mariner's wheel over the transom. Divided its entire length by a sunken walkway fed at one end by stairs leading up to the deck, the other end disappearing behind closed doors. The cabin's height was at best six feet. The walkway was interrupted at its center by the prodigious structure of the yacht's mast, which coursed up and vanished into the ceiling. On one side was a long padded bench bracketed at each end by a wall of shelves holding books, charts, and maps. On the other side a thimble-sized kitchenette elevated nearly two feet above the walkway. And on both walls curtains drawn tight across a pair of tiny portholes shutting out the night. The single light that hung from the deck ceiling above the kitchenette table swung back and forth in tandem with the rocking motion of the *Prince*, throwing first one face, then another into moments of restless shadows. The creaking noises from the yacht's weight straining against the ropes holding it secure in the marina against the occasional surge of water into the slip, the water making slapping noises against the bobbing hull.

In the criminal court's underground P3 parking level, Myra and Napoleon had waited seventeen minutes in silence until Napoleon's cell phone rang, Gerald Seymore instructing Napoleon to bring Myra to the *Prince* at nine that evening. Myra not objecting but hungry, the two of them eating from a Burger King drive-thru to kill four hours, sharing a joint as dessert. Myra not wanting to go home to a condo she knew detectives had tossed.

And now, after two hours of discussion in the yacht's cabin, Napoleon ferreting out the essence of the case against the two of them for Gerald Seymore, seeing more clearly now just what lay before them, how he and Myra had been set up, tied together in a criminal conspiracy germinating from within the LAPD, and the seven million dollars at its core. "They" were thinking well ahead of him, Napoleon admitted reluctantly. Anticipating all his moves the way a chess master lays out all the possible moves of his opponent in advance, plans his countering strategy. And reminding himself if the drug dealer–turned–Muslim father had taught him nothing else about playing chess, it was that you had to think for two people—yourself and your opponent. That was how you won the game.

Or lost.

He'd forgotten that. Forgotten the words of his father—*You're smart, Napoleon. Got a chance to make something of your life. But don't ever forget how to use the streets. You ever get backed against the wall, you be ruthless if you have to . . . street smarts save your life.*

And while it was not necessarily in Napoleon Booker's nature to be ruthless, it had on rare occasions been necessary. Like what happened with Chandra, his homey's girlfriend. He'd been robbed of drug money by rival dealers on three different occasions. Nearly killed on two. Close to twenty thousand dollars a pop. Napoleon knew there had to be a leak in his posse. Someone was dropping a dime on him after each transaction, but he couldn't figure out who. So he set up a sting operation, arranged a series of buys from the Mexicans in Watts, and on each one gave out false locations at the last minute to all but one of his posse. It was dangerous, sending trusted lieutenants into hostile neighborhoods alone and without backup to empty locations. But it finally paid off. Just before one of the buys it was his dog Wiggyboy's turn to be sent out to a false location. But Wiggyboy was arrested on outstanding tickets. And since Wiggyboy's girlfriend Chandra was a trusted member of the posse who'd been carrying and trafficking for them, he changed his mind and gave her the true location of the buy instead. But it wasn't Chandra who showed up. It was a rival gang, and Napoleon knew he'd found the leak. He didn't say anything to Chandra right off. He waited until Wiggyboy was released from doing his ninety days of three hots and a cot, told him what had happened. Wiggyboy didn't want to believe Chandra was playing them, but the proof was irrefutable. Napoleon never asked, and Wiggyboy never said, but in less than a month's time Chandra lost an eye in a vicious knife attack by an unknown assailant that left her face horribly disfigured. After that, Napoleon Booker was never robbed again.

Now that time had come to be ruthless and use street smarts again. Up to now he'd followed Myra Cross's recommendations to the letter. All for nothing. Now he'd have to do it his way. No one was going to save Napoleon Booker but Napoleon Booker. He had nothing to lose now. He'd have to start thinking on his feet. Start taking penitentiary chances if there was any chance of surviving. It was no longer a matter of *thinking* like the criminals in the LAPD— it meant *acting* like them. He knew that now. Knew too that he needed Myra Cross. That their destinies were tied together. He saw it if Myra did not. And so did Gerald Seymore. For the moment she was in a funk. He could understand that—white girl a victim of a corrupt system black folks had grown up in. But she'd come out of it. He'd see to that, with a little help from his business partner. Myra had balls and what he had in mind would take a woman with balls. It might not work with her. But it would absolutely not work without her.

Or Gerald Seymore.

"Simple enough," Napoleon said after a moment. "Probably stuck a gun in your hand that time they broke in your condo, knocked you out."

"You said they asked if you owned a nine-millimeter," Gerald Seymore said. "A Glock?" Myra nodded and said yes, they did mention a Glock. She'd forgotten that.

Napoleon said, "Guarantee you it's mine."

Gerald Seymore said, "No odds on that."

"What do I do now?" Myra said, sense of desperation leaking out around her words. "How in God's name do I get out of this?"

Napoleon looked at her. And realizing this woman was frightened and thinking only of herself, he was not offended. "You mean how *we* gonna get out of this, don't you?" he said. "Don't forget we tied up together with the same rope."

Myra touched Napoleon's arm, squeezed it for a second of apology, and said, "Yes, of course, Napoleon. How do *we* get out of this. Forgive me. Please."

Napoleon said, "You scared, huh?"

Myra turned to look at him, unblinking green eyes speaking

silently in a terrified face breaking into tears again, her head dropping into a cradle of arms on the table, sobbing. "Oh, God, I can't believe this—going to jail for something I didn't do."

Napoleon said, "I know exactly how you feel."

"If they convict me it means the rest of my life behind bars—"

"Or worse," Napoleon said to Myra. To Gerald Seymore he said, "Be of help we keep her out of jail, business partner." Calling him that because it was the nature of their relationship. Business partner the only way he addressed Gerald Seymore. "Extra pair of hands come in handy. Help dig our way outta this shit. Know what I'm sayin'?"

Gerald Seymore, shaking his head, said to Napoleon, "A double homicide. No bail on a capital charge like that, Napoleon."

"Ain't talking about bail, business partner."

"No. What, then?" Gerald Seymore said perfunctorily, not picking up on it.

"What happens she don't show up Sunday morning like she supposed?"

"We already tried for an extension," Myra said, raising up from the cradle of arms, working at composing herself, delicate fingers wiping away tears, not picking up on it either, where Napoleon was going with it. She said, "Someone got a Kleenex, paper towel, something?" From his coat's breast pocket Gerald Seymore pulled out a powder-blue handwoven silk handkerchief embroidered with the initials GS, handed it to Myra, holding her hand gently a second longer than necessary during the transfer, until she caught his eyes and smiled briefly. "Sunday was all they'd give me," Myra said, Gerald Seymore's blue handkerchief working the corners of her eyes.

"I guess ain't nobody at this table listening to me," Napoleon said. "I said, what happens she don't show up Sunday morning at nine?"

Gerald Seymore seemed to think about it for a moment. He poured himself a shot of Johnnie Walker Red, leaned back in the tight confines of the booth, and said, "On a failure to surrender? Since they've already got a warrant, they'll come looking for her." But thinking about it now, beginning to see where Napoleon was going with it.

Napoleon said, "They find her. Then what?"

"Nothing," Gerald Seymore said. "They'll arrest her, put her in jail. Twin Towers most likely."

Napoleon nodded as if agreeing and said, "No bail anyway, right?"

Realizing now just what Napoleon Booker had in mind, Gerald Seymore brought the glass to his lips slowly, holding it a few seconds before drinking, then smiled for the first time that night.

"You're saying she's got nothing to lose?"

Now it was Napoleon's turn to smile.

In the moment of absolute silence before Myra finally caught on, a bell rang on a distant mooring buoy, the high-pitched blare of an approaching yacht's air horn. She said, "Oh, now wait a minute. What are you guys saying?" Through a tear-streaked face twisted in anguish, she looked incredulously first at Napoleon Booker, then Gerald Seymore. "That I shouldn't turn myself in? I can't do that. I'm an officer of the court. I gave my word."

"Hate to tell you this, Attorney Cross, but your word don't mean shit," Napoleon said, respect for her title still there. "Not no more, it don't. You a murder suspect now. And all that being an 'officer of the court' as you say . . . well, you can forget all about that. It carried any weight, you wouldn't be sitting here worried about turning yourself in. Know what I'm saying? They gettin' ready to fry your little flat white butt right along with me, I don't get us outta this shit."

"But I'm not a criminal, Napoleon," Myra said. That idealism not wanting to give up, raise the white flag.

"That's right, Miss Cross. You keep telling yourself that," Napoleon said. "But while you playing games with yourself, keep remembering how them detectives treated you like the criminal you say you ain't. How you felt they put them cuffs on you this afternoon. What it felt like you didn't have no more control of your life. Way them detectives looked at you, not wantin' to believe nothing you said. Yeah, you keep on tellin' yourself you ain't no criminal. Then ask yourself how come they think you is. Know what I'm sayin'?"

Truth has many faces and many disguises. Some pretty. Some ugly. And some unrecognizable. Napoleon's face was cherubic and pleasant to look at. But the truth that came from his lips was incomprehensible, ugly, and virulent.

"But my reputation, Booker," Myra said. "I can't just not surrender, break the law like that. Become a fugitive." Myra looking at Gerald Seymore now for an ally, for validation that her idealism was a more powerful truth than what Napoleon Booker was offering. But she got nothing from the familiar face a foot away, now expressionless, gray eyes staring back impassively.

Suddenly Napoleon's arm slammed down hard on the table, shot glasses and the fifth of Johnnie Walker Red jumping.

"Goddammit, Miss Cross, pull that red head of yours outta the sand and smell the roses. All that shit about reputation and honor don't count no more. Can't you see that? You staying outta jail only chance we got. 'Cause I got something in mind get us up outta this. But I need your help to pull it off. Do it together as a team. We don't, you being a fugitive won't really matter. Know what I'm saying."

Myra looked first at Napoleon, then Gerald Seymore. "But going on the lam. Being hunted like that. How would I ever have a chance at a fair trial when that's brought up?" she said, like this was an old Edward G. Robinson gangster movie.

"Fair trial? Who in the fuck are you kidding? Fair trial . . . ?" Calmer now but grabbing her chin, pulling her face around to his, Napoleon went on, "Miss Cross, ain't gonna be no fair trial. They gettin' ready to send you and me to the chair. 'Lectric chair, you know . . . kind that sends volts through your body, make you come in an orgasm just before your heart stops beating. Yeah, that kind.

Straight up. And those eyes, red hair, and titties you got ain't gonna work on the executioner. You feeling me on this, Miss Cross?" And he nodded his head to give his words more emphasis.

Myra looked at the near-empty shot glass in front of her. She picked it up and drained it. "I just don't see how my going on the run is gonna get us out of this."

"Because no lie can live forever. Truth crushed to earth shall rise again," Napoleon said.

"Martin Luther King," Gerald Seymore said.

"You learning, business partner. You ain't there yet. But you learning," Napoleon said.

"But to become a fugitive . . . ?" Myra looked at Napoleon. "I go and do that, they sure will convict me. I'm not a criminal and I refuse to act like one."

Myra reached across the table and took Gerald Seymore's hands in hers, brought them to her cheek.

"I can't do this," she said. "Go on the run . . . ? You can understand that, can't you? Tell him, Daddy." Myra squeezing Gerald Seymore's hands tightly, her sharp painted fingernails biting into palms of soft flesh.

"Yes, Daddy," Napoleon snapped. "*Tell* me." And looking at Gerald Seymore as he spoke. "Tell me what kinda chance we got way it's stacked against us. You a lawyer, speak her language. So you do like she said, *tell* me, 'cause you must know something I don't. Know what I'm saying."

Gerald Seymore shot a harsh, angry stare across the table at Napoleon's face. But only for a moment. The lines on his face soon softened and he brought his gaze to Myra, her beauty still evident behind a tear-streaked face of anguish and tension. He remembered their day aboard the *Prince*, their night together at his mansion, the following day by the pool. He'd begun to care for her, more than he'd intended. Their relationship was built largely on sex. Her phenomenal intellect was obvious. Already he didn't want to lose her.

"You wouldn't look good in prison stripes, Myra," Gerald Seymore said. "Napoleon's right. You've got nothing to lose. This is as good as it gets."

Myra pulled Gerald Seymore's hand away from her mouth, but still holding on to it. "But I haven't got a choice. Sheila Cooper says the law . . . ?"

"Forget about Sheila Cooper. Forget about the law."

"What I got in mind, everybody got a role," Napoleon said. To Gerald Seymore he said, "Business partner, you intelligence. Your job is to get us some four-one-one. Straight up."

Napoleon detailed a complex shopping list of information he felt was necessary to prove their innocence. A reluctant Myra added to it. And all the while Gerald Seymore weighing the danger against the benefit to his reputation if it went sour. He listened to the shipboard sounds of marina living: the surge of water in the slip, waves slapping against the *Prince*'s hull, never-ending creaking of the lines securing the yacht to the dock, occasional bell on a distant mooring buoy. And wondered if his decision to help would bring it to an end.

With both elbows on the table, monogrammed cuff links gleaming in the dull glare of the swinging light overhead, Gerald Seymore leaned forward on the table, closing the gap between them.

"Make sure this is everything you need," he said. His words were cold and harsh and without emotion and matched the chilly, unflinching stare that bored into them. "If I do this for you," he went on, his words measured and calculated and well thought out, "there's no going back. Not for me. It means calling in a favor. A big one. If it blows up in your faces, I don't know you. Either one of you. And this meeting never took place. We clear on this? Good. You'd better be. And understand this too . . . what we're doing is not a game. We get one shot. You sink or swim on this one shot. You swim, I'll join you. You sink, you drown alone!" Letting them know in no uncertain terms that his loyalty was not a given. Not for drugs and not for sex.

Myra listened to gangsters plan her life on the run. One a black streetwise closet genius. The other white and privileged but morally bankrupt, hiding behind the respectability of Ivy League credentials. Working together in a tenuous alliance like barracuda and shark.

"Just what's my part in all of this?" Myra asked Napoleon.

"We ain't there yet, Miss Cross," Napoleon said. "But your turn's coming. Big time. Need to get you squared away first. Said you have to report to work tomorrow . . . right?"

Myra said she did. To help Marty French and Craig McInnis transfer the cases. Knowing all she'd really be doing was cleaning out her desk and the closet, dealing with Clara's rumor mill, having polite but awkward conversations with PD staff in the corridors. Playing it off with Sheila Cooper, making final arrangements for a surrender she wouldn't keep.

"Put you into hiding tomorrow night, then," Napoleon said. "So don't drive your Benz to work. And don't take a cab. Take a bus. Don't pack no clothes neither. In case they be watching your place, think you gettin' ready to bail. I'll pick you up from the office when . . . ?"

"Don't pack any clothes? I've got to have clothes, Napoleon."

Napoleon looked at her in amazement. White girl running from the law worried how she gonna look. "Don't worry about that," Napoleon said. "Get you some clothes from Shaniqua."

"Shaniqua?"

"Yeah. Shaniqua," Napoleon said. "What time I pick you up from work tomorrow?"

Myra guessed between three and five. She asked where she'd be hiding. Napoleon said not to worry about it. Someplace cops would never think to look. She'd be comfortable, but it wouldn't be a suite at the Hilton Hotel.

Napoleon pulled out his cell phone, spoke to someone he called Money, gave him directions to the marina, agreed to meet him at the entrance. Napoleon poured himself one last shot of Johnnie

Walker Red, lingered a few minutes to tie up loose ends, telling Gerald Seymore he'd call with Myra's location once she was safe and wanting to know when did he think he'd have something. Gerald Seymore said Wednesday at the earliest. This was not something you rushed. It had to be finessed. Napoleon seemed to agree, nodded and slid out from the cramped quarters of the *Prince*'s kitchenette, worked his way around the base of the yacht's mast, and headed toward the forward bulkhead. He stopped at the bottom of the stairs, grabbed the railing to steady himself against the water-bed motion of the *Prince*. He said to the two of them, but more to Myra, "Best you enjoy your last night of freedom. Know what I'm sayin'? I'm gone." And he disappeared up the stairs, the yacht swaying as he leapt off the deck onto the dock.

Myra looked across the table at Gerald Seymore, took his hands in hers, and caught his slight smile, the sparkle of anticipation behind his eyes.

"Yeah," Myra said over her shoulder to Napoleon Booker's shadow. And to Gerald Seymore, her emerald eyes fastened on his face, five delicate fingers stroking his cheek, she said, "I know just what you're saying. Don't I, Daddy?"

But Daddy was too busy unbuttoning Myra's blouse to answer.

CHAPTER 16

"AM I THE ONLY ONE concerned about this?" Neil Sanford was speaking to the Gang of Five, three of them a loose knot of blue uniforms seated on battered chairs about the cluttered workbench. Calvin in Adidas sweats and Nike Air Max. Stepolini in dress slacks, trendy open-collar Van Heusen without cuff links, Kenneth Cole boots. The two of them camped on improvised seats of ten-gallon drums. They were in the shed of Manuel's Junkyard, tired and irritable and not wanting to be there for Neil Sanford's hastily called midnight meeting. Power wrenches and mariachi music beyond the door. The whine of tow-truck wenches dropping off battered cars.

Blank, disinterested stares, not the kind of response Neil Sanford had anticipated. After a moment of silence, when they'd all settled down, he removed his glasses and rubbed fatigue out of a pair of gray watery eyes, thinking drugs or booze the only possible reason they might not read it his way. Going over in his mind how best to present his concerns about the recent turn of events— Napoleon Booker making bail, Myra Cross not surrendering and going on the run, and what, if any, the connection might be. And finally just telling them outright and waiting for their reaction. Each one looking at the others, their expressions saying, he got us out of bed for this shit?

"No connection," said Gilbert Monroe from the corner. "The bitch didn't wanna go to jail, plain and simple. Figured she buy herself a little more time before doing the Martha Stewart bit. Way I see it, she figures she's got nothing to lose. There's no bail anyway.

Have a little last-minute fun before going beddie-bye. In her shoes can't say I wouldn't do the same."

Darryl Brigham said, "You must have awfully small feet." Everyone laughed. Even Neil Sanford.

"Why are you so worried about her, Neil?" Stepolini said after the laughter died down. "She'll be in custody before the week's out."

"I'm not so sure of that," Neil Sanford said. "And it isn't just her that concerns me. It's both of them, her and the nigger, Napoleon Booker." Saying it like Calvin wasn't even in the same room. Calvin just sitting there in his blue Adidas sweats, Nike shoes, slouching with attitude. He fronted his anger but sold out his integrity for a share of seven million dollars in blood money. Blood he spilled.

"It's 'nigga'," Calvin felt prompted to say. Tolerating the white boys only because they hated black folks as much as he did. "'Nigger' is burnt out," he said, "old school. The correct pronunciation, for your information, is 'nigga.' The emphasis is on the letter *a*. Nigg-ah. Way the Chinese say 'ah-so.'" Calvin being facetious and starting to laugh now, the others joining in, tentatively at first, but then, seeing Calvin was all right with it, more boisterously. "You gonna insult me, be ghetto correct about it."

Here we go again. Malcolm X clone without the X. "I stand ghetto corrected," Neil Sanford said sarcastically, patronizing the jelly bean stuck in their midst and regretting now that he was, wishing there was a way to get rid of him quietly and casting a pair of solicitous eyes over to Stepolini, who read them clearly. "*Nigg-ah. Emphasis on the* a." Neil Sanford went on with a derision Calvin missed. "I wouldn't want to insult you with a name you deem offensive. Please accept my apology." Neil Sanford looking at Calvin but not smiling now, Calvin's black thing wearing thin.

"Yazza, massa," Calvin said, not seeing Neil Sanford was through with it and ready to move on. "I's 'cepts yo 'pology." And still laughing, he slid off the ten-gallon drum and started dancing a jig, jumping about the tight space with an awkward set of moves somewhere between *Riverdance* and breakdancing. Calvin showing them the kind of nigga they all hated. But too dumb to realize he was that kind of nigga himself.

The trouble with Calvin James was, he never knew when to quit. The minstrel show lasted through several seconds of laughter and a few of complete silence before Stepolini said, "All right, muthafucka. You've had your fifteen minutes of fame. Now sit your Sambo ass down."

Calvin bristled. He stopped his routine, looked over to Stepolini, and said, "S'pose I don't wanna sit down, Italian stallion. Suppose I just wanna keep on dancin' and dancin' and dancin'. You know us *nigras* 'jes love to dance."

Stepolini didn't say anything. He just looked at Calvin. Not giving him anything. But catching Neil Sanford's look and thinking about it. Thinking about it real hard.

"You short of money," Monroe said, "we could pass the hat around, take up a collection." His laughter drawing more from the group.

Calvin still didn't get it. He looked at Monroe. At all of them. "Day I need you white muthafuckas' charity be the day I die." And not realizing how close to prophesy he'd come.

Neil Sanford was tired of Calvin. His never-ending racial point of view. He said forcefully, "You don't wanna be here, Calvin, you can leave. Otherwise sit down." Calvin hated being told what to do. Especially by white boys. So he didn't respond to Neil Sanford right away, took his time before he went back to his perch on the drum.

"What I wanna know is how the little punk got someone to put up a quarter mil," Darryl said to Neil Sanford.

"More than that," Neil Sanford said. He'd only just found out, right after they'd taken care of Rose, when he'd learned Myra Cross had gone to Mexico with Booker.

"Yeah, but who'd put up that kind of money for a little punk nigga gangbanger like him?" Calvin asked.

"What we'd all like to know," Monroe said.

242

"Has to be drug money. And that's illegal. The court can't accept drug money for bail!" Darryl suggested.

"It wasn't drug money," Stepolini said.

Darryl said, "What do you mean it wasn't drug money. You sweat the bondsman?"

Stepolini nodded. "He said it was clean. It came from a trust."

"That doesn't tell me shit," Calvin said. "These little punk niggas got all kinda ways of cleaning up their money. A trust funded with drug money is still illegal for a bondsman to accept."

"It came from a blind trust that Bank of America certified was established thirty years before Booker was born," Stepolini said. "So what does that tell you?"

"That it's old money," said Monroe.

It told Darryl that all he could do was whistle. And so he did.

Neil Sanford said after a moment, "Now you see why it concerns me."

Darryl said, "So? Get a court order, force the bank to reveal the source of the trust."

Neanderthal with shit for brains.

Neil Sanford said, "You have any idea what it would take, going up against Bank of America? And on what grounds? A blind trust set up a generation before Booker's own mother was born. Talk about making ourselves look stupid." Then reminded himself they were cops.

Monroe said, "I still don't see why you think the kid's bail and the hottie failing to surrender are related." Monroe standing and stretching and yawning, no apology for wanting to go, working his way around the bench to the door.

"Don't you think they are? I mean, look at it," Neil Sanford said. "We set up the drug dealer on a case he can't possibly beat. And what happens—he bails out. We set up his PD on a double homicide case we know she can't beat—she doesn't surrender. She goes on the run. Now, taking each one separately, it doesn't mean much. But *we* know the two are tied together. And my guess is by now they've figured that out. Unless we're dealing with real imbeciles, which I doubt." And beginning to wonder about his partners, why they couldn't see it like he did. "In addition, I'm thinking that whoever they got to put up the kid's bail also knows they're tied together."

"So?" said Monroe when Neil Sanford had finished, hand on the door, ready to leave. He pushed it open a crack, let in noises of power tools and echoes of mariachi music. Blue light occasionally flickered from the carbon arc welder. "Who cares they see the connection. Nothing they can do about it. And for sure the hottie can't do shit, now she's a fugitive. The evidence'll send them both away permanently, get the heat off our backs. Wasn't that the whole purpose of this operation?"

Neil Sanford said yes. But he hadn't anticipated Booker being able to bail out, the PD becoming a fugitive.

"I still don't see what worries you," Monroe said, sentiments of agreement mumbled around the room, yawns of fatigue signaling Neil Sanford was losing them.

Neil Sanford guessed he'd have to spell it out for them.

"Hold up a sec, Gil," Neil Sanford said, waving his hand. "Hear me out. Let me give you a hypothetical. You tell me what you think. You don't agree, I'll let it go. That fair? Yes . . . ?"

Monroe thought about it, looked around the room at familiar disgruntled faces waiting for his decision. He bails, they bail. Monroe looked at Neil Sanford, shrugged his shoulders in a what-the-hell attitude, pulled the door shut, found a nearby ten-gallon drum, and looked at his watch.

"Give you five minutes, Neil. Then I'm outta here."

"Five minutes is all I need," Neil Sanford said, relieved. "Okay. Now, then, let's suppose the PD's on the run because she's figured it out. The money source knows that too, is working with whomever to keep her hidden. Maybe even Napoleon Booker. Who knows. But I can guarantee you, regardless of who's helping her, going on the lam like she has is no sudden impulse based on fear. Don't kid yourselves. This is well planned and calculated."

"How do you know that?" Monroe said.

"Because I know the type," Neil Sanford said.

Monroe was not convinced. Neither were the others in the room.

"Meantime," Neil Sanford went on, pushing the stone uphill like Sisyphus, "the three of them are putting together a team to dig up evidence that'll get 'em off the hook. And remember, anyone with access to three hundred grand from a blind trust has an unlimited amount of money to spread around to informants. And I'm not talking about a couple of hundred dollars here, couple of hundred there. We have to assume they're gonna spend thousands, tens of thousands, hundreds of thousands if necessary. And with that much money on the streets, I don't have to tell you guys how much information it can buy, how dangerous that makes them. See, that's what really worries me. The money. Informants will roll over on their own children for that kind of money. Make up stuff if they have to. Point a finger at everyone and anyone who even looks at them the wrong way. And to say nothing of satisfying old grudges . . ."

Neil Sanford let that settle for a moment. He looked around and knew he had their attention now. At least some of them. Outside, someone was singing along in Spanish with a mariachi song on the radio, a melodic lament with shouts and screams peppered throughout. Karaoke Mexican style.

Monroe jumped off the drum, opened the door, and shouted, "Hey, Manuel, you chili-eating wetback, turn that shit down, why don't you?" He returned to his seat knowing he hadn't heard him, that the mariachi music with the karaoke sing-along would play on. And it did, but he felt good telling them anyway.

Darryl said, "But the only information they could buy is in this room. You saying someone here is for sale?" No one was thinking of leaving after that. And Monroe stopped looking at his watch.

"Of course not," Neil Sanford said. "Remember, this is just a hypothetical. I'm only guessing what they're up to. Keep this in mind also—the press hasn't got wind of this just yet. So many suspects fail to surrender, unless it's a celebrity, it doesn't get reported. But the PD could change all that."

"How you figure?" Darryl said.

Cro-Magnon man. Right at home with the dinosaurs. Couple of eons too late.

Neil Sanford took a deep breath, tried hard not to show his irritation.

"Suppose the press picks up on it. The PD might even alert them. The news turns her into a celebrity, takes the case nationwide, pretty young lawyer crying frame-up, gets a lot of sympathy, everyone and his brother starts investigating, puts the case and everyone involved under a microscope, looking for cracks—remember what happened to Mark Fuhrman in the OJ case, girl in the Kobe Bryant case . . . ? You guys with me on this now?"

"Way I see it," Calvin said, "Fuhrman was a Klansman. Should've known not to put his cracker-white ass on the stand. And as far as snowflake and Kobe—? Shit, everybody knows white boys set him up. 'Cause ain't no nigga 'spose to have money *and* the Hugh Hefner American Dream."

Ignoring Calvin, Neil Sanford said, "Let's suppose for a moment that I'm right. That it happens just the way I've laid it out. Just for the sake of argument. What do you think we should do?"

Darryl said, "This *is* a hypothetical, right? You don't really know the reason the PD skipped."

Neil Sanford said yes, it was just a theory. He said in truth he didn't know why the PD didn't turn herself in. But he knew the type. Knew the thinking, the reasons for running. From thirty years' experience as a detective. Thirty years' experience and a gut feeling.

Calvin said, "I say split the seven mil now and leave the country. Build me a house in Rio."

Jesus. The man hadn't heard a word he said. The dumb fuck.

Neil Sanford said, "The United States has an extradition treaty with Brazil. Any other bright ideas?" Shutting Calvin up with knowledge that made him look as stupid as he really was.

For the most part Stepolini had been quiet. Now he came to life. After thinking about it for a moment, he said, "Be helpful we knew where the PD was hiding. Get to her before they catch her, lock her up."

That's what Neil Sanford was waiting to hear. He tried to hide his smile but failed miserably.

Darryl said, "I agree with Paul. But what do we do that's any different than the shields already looking for her? I'm sure they've already talked to the Booker kid. The PD's family, friends she might turn to?"

Calvin said, "I say we arrest that little nigga and sweat his ass. If he knows where she is, time I get through with his black ass, we'll all know."

"Yeah, that too. But I have something else in mind," Stepolini said. "Got an idea might help us find her. Something we can do the shields on the street can't . . ." And he stopped to think about it.

Neil Sanford said, "Paul . . . ? Something that'll hold up?"

"Don't know if it'll hold up. But if it smokes her out of hiding, who cares," Stepolini said. "We get to her, we get to the money source. We get to the money source, well, who's to say what happens to Myra Cross. If you get my meaning."

Neil certainly did. And so did the others, nodding their heads in agreement, but not really knowing what they were agreeing to and anxious to find out.

Over the din of karaoke mariachi music and the distant hum of power tools, Neil Sanford said, "All right, Paul. It's your show. Let's hear it."

"I'm thinking we need a hostage or two," Stepolini said.

Darryl said, "Hostages?" Like the word was foreign to him.

Stepolini looked at Darryl and said, "You asked what we could do different. I say hostages. Shields on the street may have talked to them, tapped their phones, put one or two under surveillance in case she makes contact." Stepolini shook his head, like the cops on the beat were wasting their time. "I say we snatch a few relatives, sweat 'em real hard. They may or may not know where she is. They don't, let the word out through informants . . . see what happens."

His eyes brightening, Monroe said, "A trade. She comes in from the cold, to us, we let the relatives live. She doesn't? Oh, well, as the kids say. I like it."

Darryl held back for a moment, thinking about it, warming to it the more they discussed it.

"Where we gonna keep 'em? Hostages," Monroe said.

"Where do we keep the money?" Stepolini answering a question with a question.

Neil Sanford thinking if he had three more like Stepolini, he could rule the world.

"Okay," Calvin said. "We can start with the little gangbanger Booker. I find his little punk ass, muthafucka tell us shit he didn't even know he knew. Know what I'm saying?" Waiting for Stepolini to give him the word.

But when it came down it wasn't what Calvin had thought.

"We can, yeah," Stepolini said. He turned to Darryl. "Darryl, can you track him down, bring him in? Charge him with peeing in his pants or something?"

At this Calvin jumped off the drum, incensed, jaws tight with rage.

"Darryl? Aw, hell no. I'll bring the little nigga in."

"No. It'd be better if Darryl did," Stepolini said.

"Why?"

"'Cause I said so, Calvin. That's why. You've got too much of a hard-on for him. We might not ever see the kid alive."

Calvin stood in front of Stepolini, eyes even, hands on his hips, their faces so close Calvin could see Stepolini's nose hairs.

"'Cause *you* said so?" Calvin making the biggest mistake of his life, letting his overinflated ego have a life of its own. "Who the fuck are you?" Looking now over to Neil, who gave him nothing.

"Get out of my face, Calvin," Stepolini said. "I said for Darryl to bring the kid in. Way it's gonna be."

"Get out of your face? Muthafucka, I haven't started to get in your face yet!"

"I'm the wrong person for you to fuck with tonight, Calvin. Back off, all right?" And Stepolini knowing he wouldn't. Knowing what was coming next, that Neil Sanford had given him the word, letting him carry it.

Calvin backed away, throwing up his hands the way wannabe gangsters issue a street challenge.

"Oh, so it's like that, huh? What you gonna do, I don't back off? Huh? You gonna shoot me, you Guinea muthafucka?" Calvin beat his chest with both hands, like Tarzan calling for a backup of jungle animals. All he needed was the cry. "Well, come on, then," Calvin went on, his suicidal tidal wave of self-loathing beyond the point of no return. "You the Italian stallion. Just do it! 'Cause I'm right here in front of you, and I ain't gonna move a muthafuckin' inch!" Tarzan. Black Tarzan. Big ego, prehistoric brain. "You got the balls, you shoot me, right here, right now!"

Which is exactly what Stepolini did. Without moving from his perch on the ten-gallon drum, he slipped the snub-nose .38 out of his ankle holster and fired point-blank into Calvin's chest. Five times. The .38 cracking loud and sharp like the snap of a whip. Its force sending Calvin staggering back in a few seconds of wide-eyed disbelief, long arms windmilling for balance as he stumbled into the workbench, holding on just long enough to look at his chest, the blue Adidas jacket slowly turning crimson. Calvin James doing his last minstrel show, staying in character and saying with his last angry breath of life as he crashed to the floor, "Guinea Muthafucka, you—"

Stepolini replaced the .38 back in his ankle holster, eased himself off the ten-gallon drum, and walked over to Calvin's lifeless form. "Should've worn his vest. Especially if you gonna talk shit," he said to Neil Sanford.

Rolling Calvin's body over with his boot, Stepolini laid out what each cop was to do, like nothing had ever happened. Nobody paid attention to the crumpled corpse on the floor. When they'd all signed off on Stepolini's plan, they left the shed together for the noise of the chop shop. They found Manuel stripping a stolen Honda, his face shield illuminated by the sun of a carbon arc welder. Stepolini, shouting over the mariachi music, told Manuel his place was filthy, if he didn't clean it up they'd put the health department on him. And by the way, there was a dead body in his shed. Get rid of it. There was a Yukon parked somewhere outside. He could have it. No questions asked.

Neil Sanford and Stepolini stopped to talk for a minute by Stepolini's Crown Victoria. Neil saying to Stepolini, looking through the driver's-side window to the magazine on the passenger seat, "What're you reading?"

"New *Playboy*. Picked it up at the Seven-Eleven on the way over. Haven't read it yet."

Neil Sanford saying to Stepolini, "I like the interviews, myself."

Stepolini said, "Hottie's ain't bad either."

"Yeah," Neil Sanford said, "but you seen one, you've seen 'em all."

But he hadn't. Not yet.

CHAPTER 17

MYRA CROSS HID FOR TWO WEEKS in a converted ante-room of the Heavens Rest Funeral Home on Broadway in South Central LA. Napoleon Booker had picked her up from work that Saturday evening in his mother's Hyundai and whisked her off to begin life as a fugitive. He was right, it wasn't a suite at the Hilton. It was a room filled with seventy-five years of antique clutter that resembled an ancient Egyptian tomb that had been broken into one too many times. It was a room used to prepare corpses for burial, relegated now to a storage room, after Heavens Rest fortunes had increased and they expanded the seventy-five-year-old black-owned landmark facility with a new wing that included a more modernized preparation room, larger viewing room, and an even larger chapel. With its only access through the casket viewing chamber, the room was windowless and cold. Extremely cold. Its floor and walls were covered in lusterless green tiles. Capped plumbing fixtures protruded from spaces where cast-iron sinks once lined the walls. And from the ceiling hung long-spindled electrical fixtures with dusty metal shades that once illuminated a row of porcelain preparation tables. The room was buffered on one side by the refrigeration unit that was still in use, where the deceased were stored until their services. On the other side was a garage that housed a six-car fleet of limousines. There was a small bathroom and shower where security personnel were housed when it was first decommissioned as a prep room. And carved out of the clutter: room for a makeshift bed, a cluster of old chairs around a small table with fresh remnants of take-out in paper plates, the odor of fish filling the air.

"You got a nice body, Miss Cross." Napoleon Booker turned pages of the week-old *Playboy*, gazing at Myra in the surf of Cancún, stretched out on the sand with her finger in her mouth.

"My opinion, of the three with your clothes off this is the best one. Photographer's the bomb."

"Jason Rice," Myra said.

"Yeah. Way he set it up, framed you on the sand, ocean in the background. Boy's got an eye."

Napoleon turned the pages, put his fingers on a photograph of a black woman sitting nude in a dentist's chair, holding a drill.

"Long-legged sister from Miami be a close second if she wore less makeup," Napoleon said, his index finger tapping the photograph to make his point.

Seated on the bed and wrapped in the warmth of a down comforter, Myra scooted to the edge and stared at the spread of the dentist.

"You're just saying that because she's black, Napoleon," Myra said, and turned the pages to another spread that featured a CPA from Chicago, a well-endowed but overly made up brunette reclining on top of a desk, working a calculator. "Now, I think this girl is every bit as pretty as the dentist."

"Sure you're right. She's a dime. Do my taxes any day of the week," Napoleon said. "But you need to understand in some cases, color is relative to beauty. See, in black women, their dark color is the attractive element. The core aesthetic." Napoleon turned the pages back to the dentist from Miami and said to Myra, "Like this sister here. She's real dark. That's what makes her so pretty. That and them long legs she got. What ruins it for her is all that makeup. Way I see it, excessive makeup tends to draw the eye away from that aesthetic, her color, which is her true beauty."

"The core aesthetic," Myra said. From Rembrandt to core aesthetic. Myra wondered if there was anything Napoleon couldn't speak on.

"Yeah," Napoleon said, "core aesthetic. See, in your case, Miss Cross, the red hair is your core aesthetic. Them big boobs you got just enhance it. But it's the red hair key to you bein' so fine. Know what I'm sayin'?"

Myra didn't know if she could agree with him on that point. "Well," she said. "Not saying you're wrong, but nobody ever asked me if I gave good red hair. I suppose red hair might be a turn-on for some men. But I'm not about to get a breast reduction for the sake of core aesthetics. Trust me."

"They real?" Napoleon Booker looking at the *Playboy*, then at Myra. Myra flung open the comforter for an instant and glanced down at the bulge beneath her jacket, smiling.

"Mother nature's very own."

Playboy's Professional Women's issue hit newsstands one week after Myra went into hiding. Myra wanted to call Jason Rice to thank him for his work, but Napoleon said it was too dangerous. The FBI most likely had checked her phone records and gone through her computer, recovered her e-mails, and if they hadn't contacted individuals directly, they probably tapped their phones. In all likelihood Jason Rice would be one of them.

And most certainly her parents. Which was why Napoleon and Gerald Seymore had addressed that possibility before the start of her fugitive status. Myra had called home one last time to explain things.

"Something's come up, Mom," Myra had said to her mother, trying not to sound too apprehensive and not sure she was succeeding. "About a case of mine. I can't go into details, but there's going to be a lot about me in the news in the coming weeks. And it really won't be wise for you and Edward and Nathan to be around when that happens."

"Why not?" her mother wanted to know.

"Because it's going to be a lot of bad publicity, Mom. That's why," Myra said. "It's a high-profile case. They'll try to involve you and anyone I know if they can."

"You said 'they.' Who is 'they,' Myra?" her mother said.

"I can't go into that, Mom. But you've got to listen to me. Please. This is the kind of publicity and the kind of people you have to be afraid of. I can't tell you why. But you do. There's a lot more to it that I can't explain. But you guys can't be around when it breaks. You need to understand that. Like I said, I can't explain why. But this is serious. You'll just have to take my word on it, Mom. Okay?"

"How serious?" Myra's mother asked.

"Serious enough that I need the three of you to take a cruise for a few weeks."

"Cruise?" her mother blurted out. "Myra, we just came back from a cruise. What in heaven's name kind of crazy talk is this?"

"I can't explain it now, Mom. You'll just have to trust me. I wouldn't be asking you to do this if there wasn't a good reason. Believe me."

"But another cruise? Even if we agreed, if I could talk Edward into it, we haven't got that kind of money, Myra."

"Don't worry about the money, Mom. Everything's been arranged. You just get packed. Airline tickets and cruise package are on their way to you as we speak."

"Suppose Edward doesn't agree?"

"Mom. When has Edward not agreed to anything you ever wanted?"

"Well, what about your brother. I doubt seriously if he'll go along with something like this."

"I've already talked to Nathan, Mom," Myra said truthfully, the conversation with her brother just minutes before ending with his enthusiastic agreement. A break from his chiropractic practice just what he needed.

"I just don't understand, Myra," her mother said. "I never did like the idea of you being a lawyer. A criminal lawyer at that. Having to deal with all those criminal lowlifes. If you were going to be a lawyer, why couldn't you do civil law and file class-action lawsuits. Or work for a big corporation. Something safe. Why couldn't you have picked a less hazardous profession. Become a chiropractor like your brother, or an engineer like your uncle Arthur—"

"Mom," Myra interrupted. "We've been over this countless times before. It was my decision, remember? I happen to enjoy my work. Just trust me on this, okay? This is something you and Edward and Nathan *have* to do. You don't have any choice. You have to go. And by the way, once you're on the ship, you'll meet a couple of very nice people. A Mrs. Booker. And Shaniqua. Be sure to tell them hello for me when you see them. Mom, I gotta run."

"Shaniqua?" Myra's mother said.

"Love you dearly, Mom. 'Bye."

Myra wondering now, going through the pages of *Playboy*, just what her mother was thinking about her photo spread. Myra knew it would be available on board the ship. Her stepfather, Edward, most certainly had seen it, brought it to her mother's attention.

"What's keeping your business partner?" Myra said to Napoleon. "I haven't heard from him since our last meeting on the *Prince*. Have you?"

"He's around."

"You think he's seen this?" Myra pointing to the magazine and saying, "You think it turned him off, seeing me like this?"

"He seen it," Napoleon said absently, reading an article about Norman Mailer. "He ain't got no problem with it. So don't be worrying. He's taking care of business and that's more important than jacking off to a photograph. He'll be here tonight. Guaranteed."

Myra pushed herself back across the bed, folded her bare legs underneath, and pulled the comforter tight. She sat up against the wall, sipping a Sprite.

The first leg of Myra's flight to avoid prosecution had been to the South Central apartment on Sixty-first Street and Western Avenue where Napoleon and Shaniqua lived. The outside was not impressive, a two-story apartment complex of chipped stucco whose front was covered by gang graffiti and that hosted a front yard of dirt made barren by the numerous children playing behind the safety of a worn-down wrought-iron fence. Inside was another matter. The apartment was small but well maintained. There wasn't a great deal of furniture, but it was neatly arranged. Brightly colored handmade curtains covered the windows, a portrait of a black Jesus and select African-themed artwork hung on the walls, and a large throw rug with a design pattern of African kings covered the floor. Myra knew, even before she met Shaniqua, that she'd misjudged her.

When Shaniqua first emerged from the kitchen, extending a soft hand and warm, genuine smile of welcome to greet her, when there was none of that jealous, neck-moving "Who are you, snowflake, and why's this nigga got you up in my house, bitch?" attitude she was expecting, Myra felt a twinge of shame. For Shaniqua was a very soft-spoken girl, still possessed of that girlish look betraying her almost twenty years of age. She was dark complexioned, with delicate African features, full, pouty lips fronting a smile of gleaming straight teeth. A head of freshly done cornrows tapered into a neck-length curtain of beaded braids. She had a chest every bit as ample as Myra's, a tiny waist, and well-developed hips and calves. She wore flats, a plain, simple blouse and skirt, the skirt long enough to be decent, short enough to be a touch revealing. The smell of frying steak drew Myra's attention to the small table neatly set for three. A nearby empty high chair prompted Myra to ask about Napoleon II. Shaniqua said he was sleeping. She disappeared into the bedroom and returned a moment later carrying a one-year-old, a cherubic clone of Napoleon Booker, sleepy-eyed and rubbing his eyes, not really ready to wake up yet but fascinated now by the presence of an unfamiliar guest. He reached out to try to touch Myra's head, Myra extending her arms toward

Shaniqua, who didn't hesitate to hand him to her. She dropped to the couch and laughed as Napoleon II's fingers pulled her hair. Shaniqua's cooking was magnificent. Shaniqua was pleasant and engaging during dinner, but not talkative. She never mentioned Myra's situation. Myra's guess was that Napoleon had already told her what was going on.

They left the apartment at midnight, Myra almost reluctant to leave the cocoon of warmth she felt in Napoleon's family, the play of Napoleon II's tiny hands now at home in her hair. And wondering if she'd have Shaniqua's patience and skill if she ever had a son. Taking Myra into the bedroom after dinner, where she had prepared a small suitcase of clothes and toiletries, Shaniqua laid out items on the bed she thought Myra could wear. The clothes were clean and freshly scented from washing and ironing. And if Napoleon hadn't told her where they were going or why, he must have told her it would be cold, for in addition to a pillow and several sheets, she produced a number of blankets, including a down comforter. Myra sensed it was Shaniqua's only comforter, Shaniqua's eyes betraying reluctance to give it up, that Myra had to take it. Myra thanked Shaniqua for everything.

Myra wrapped herself in the comforter and picked at remnants of the take-out Napoleon had brought, now familiar nightly fare they simply labeled numbers 1, 2, 3, 4, and 5. Tonight was number 4, fish from Stevie's on the Strip. Number 1 was Domino's Pizza; 2 was KFC; 3 was Chinese; 5 was Mexican. It wasn't so much the repeat take-out that was hard. It was being locked up in a chilly, claustrophobic windowless room lit only by the dull glare of two shaded sixty-watt lamps, passing time with no point of reference and no company. She had a portable CD player, small portable TV, combination VHS-DVD player, an even smaller and ineffective electric heater, and a growing stack of old magazines. A cell phone was there for emergencies only. Days and nights passing into one another, seamless and without definition. Occasional screams of hysterical sadness seeped through the walls from the casket viewing chamber. The drone of power tools and chatter from the mechanics servicing the limousines filtered through the wall from the garage. The distant playing of a pipe organ during services let Myra know it was daytime, if she wasn't watching *Oprah*. And having seen no daylight for two weeks bothered Myra more than anything else. Well, almost.

Not having sex with Gerald Seymore for two weeks topped the list. Fantasizing about Daddy as she masturbated twice a day just wasn't doing it. And coming to realize that this was the way of life in prison—years on end without the familiar touch of men. The very thought she'd either become celibate—if that was even possible—or the more likely possibility of being another woman's stuff was so repulsive and depressing that Myra would break down in tears, wondering if it wouldn't be better to take her own life than to surrender it to a lifetime of purgatory.

Napoleon, who up to now had been Myra's only visitor, said the only time she could come out was after midnight, when he brought her the take-out meals. She would leave the hiding place for the casket viewing chamber, a room only marginally warmer than her own, walk its length to a door that opened into the garage, and from there walk through a door to the parking lot, let Napoleon in. Napoleon wore a security guard uniform Myra assumed was fake. Napoleon saying it was and it wasn't, that the funeral home's owner was a customer and owed him. She'd be safe as long as he owed him. If he paid off his debt, they'd have a problem. But considering the monkey on his back, that wasn't likely. And when Napoleon left, she could stay outside no more than a few minutes at a time, just in case someone hopped the fence and wandered across the parking lot as a shortcut home. Just long enough to smoke some bubblegum weed. Or a primo. Maybe freebase a rock. Sometimes the two of them smoked a joint together just outside the garage door after she'd eaten. Talking with each other about fragments of their lives, Napoleon about the drug dealer–turned–Muslim father, Myra about her mother, the dream of becoming a TV talk show host, her plans for *Myra's One Night Stand*.

Napoleon looked at his watch. He said, "Business partner be here shortly. Said he had what we needed."

"Finally," Myra said. Coming back from the wall to the table, finishing up the last bit of gumbo. "What took him so long? He was supposed to have it a week ago."

"You impatient," he said, not looking at her. "I understand that. This can't be no picnic. But now that business partner got what we need, won't be much longer. Trust me."

Myra pushed herself away from the table and back up against the wall, enveloped in the down comforter. She said, "I can't tell you how many times I've heard that in my life. From men, mostly."

"You ever been with a black man, Miss Cross?"

"I beg your pardon?"

"A nigga," Napoleon said. "You ever had a boyfriend was black?"

Myra's face betrayed no surprise. She said, "Relax, Napoleon. You're not my type. You're too young, to begin with."

Napoleon smiled.

"Don't flatter yourself, Miss Cross, thinking I'm trying to hit on you. White girls available at the snap of a finger, I want one."

Don't flatter yourself. Now that's something no man had ever told her.

"Why would you? Shaniqua's all the woman you'll ever need."

"Sure, you right. But my needs ain't why I asked the question."

"Really. Why, then?"

"'Cause you just seem so down with black folks. That's why. I just figured maybe you spent some time in a relationship with a black man, you know, got a sense of the experience. Different perspective on race. Know what I'm saying?"

She thought about his question and started to say no. Then remembered a three-month fling years ago, when she was in college, when she'd shed Richard and was partying like there was no tomorrow. They'd played Oregon State and won, tight end Nathaniel Brown's last-second touchdown making him king for a day. Any girl he wanted for the asking. The entire campus was euphoric.

Nathaniel Brown came to her sorority house party that night with other team members. An ink spot on a sheet of white paper. She'd focused on Nathaniel Brown from the moment he walked in the door. Myra, her eyes locked with his, took his arm in hers and guided him through the crowd of handshakes and back-slapping accolades toward the bar. She offered him the rest of the beer she was drinking when he came through the door. She hung on to his arm as a protection from a gathering swarm of sorority sisters. A few beers later, Myra suggested they leave to find someplace they could be alone. They went to his place and fucked all night. The following morning she discovered an attraction to his intellect. Ironically pressure from his mother, a longtime civil rights activist, pulled them apart in three month's time. He called Myra and broke it off with the lame excuse that he just wasn't ready to get serious. Serious? That had to be a joke. All she wanted was a fuck buddy and study partner.

"Whatever happened to him?" Napoleon asked. But his cell phone rang before Myra could answer. "Business partner's at the door," he said, jumping up and leaving the room. "Time to go to work."

Two minutes later and with Napoleon following, Gerald Seymore entered Myra's hiding place and winced almost immediately at the cold in his tailor-made Pierre Cardin suit. He carried an oversized briefcase. Myra came out from under the comforter and threw her arms around his neck.

"Oh, Daddy," she said, and kissed him profusely. "I thought you'd forgotten all about me."

"I may be many things. Forgetful is not one of them. Especially about a redhead who likes jazz and says 'yipes' like Marilyn Monroe."

Myra's blush, barely visible in the dim light of the three lamps, was one of relief. She relaxed her arms from around Gerald Seymore's neck, led him to a clearing on the bed, dropped down beside him, picked up the *Playboy*, and turned to the spread.

"How do you feel about this?" Myra said. "I know we talked about it. But actually seeing it now, I was worried that maybe you'd be turned off by it—you know, all my stuff on display like this." Myra leafed through the spread absently, not looking at him.

Gerald Seymore smiled easily and shook his head. "It's not every day a man gets to see a naked fugitive."

Myra giggled. "And to think you've actually touched one."

Gerald Seymore said, "And can't wait for an encore."

"Well, Mr. Seymore," Myra said, her chin going up haughtily, "I only take my clothes off for the camera"—she giggled again—"and when I go to bed." Now she was looking at him and smiling, her hands rubbing his arm and back. Myra pulled the down comforter around the two of them, Gerald Seymore shrugging it off, saying he was okay, that she needed it more then he did, swinging it back across her shoulders.

Napoleon, waiting for the reunion to end, his patience thinning, pulled a chair up to the table and interrupted. "What you got for us, business partner?"

"Quite a bit, actually."

Without moving the briefcase from the floor, Gerald Seymore sprung the locks and withdrew a thick manila folder that he placed on the table, untying the string that bound it closed.

"It seems this entire thing with you, Myra, and Booker here started several months back when the DA's office received a letter from the hospital administrator of Braskin State Mental Institution. Marilyn Cartright, a woman who'd been committed there against her will because of the effects of PCP, kept insisting he forward a $100 bill along with a note to the DA she'd written about a bank robbery. But since she was paranoid and suffering the effects of PCP, he blew it off as just a typical unrealistic request by a mentally disturbed patient. He put the note on her chart. He couldn't forget about it, though, because the patient kept insisting. He finally sent it just to shut her up. Well, as it turned out, this patient, Marilyn Cartright, aka Princess, was a hooker with a mile-long rap sheet and a paid informant. She'd been used a number of times by undercover detectives investigating drug dealers. In the note she made all kinds of crazy claims, about being followed by the FBI, detectives she worked for, drug dealers she informed on. She claimed her food was being poisoned, things the doctors say are typical of paranoid mental patients. But one thing in the note struck the DA as curious—she claimed to have gotten high with Calvin James, a cop from Central Precinct whom she alleged bragged about having lots of money due him from a bank robbery he and his buddies pulled four years ago."

"The S and L in Santa Monica . . ." Myra said. "But why would he incriminate himself? Give her money from the robbery? Reveal something like that to an addicted hooker of all people . . . ?"

"Remember, they were getting high together. So what does that tell you?"

"Birds of a feather, that's what it tells me. Sounds like maybe he had something on her. Something he felt would keep her silent no matter what he told her. Gave her $100 hush money. And if she's sending letters to the DA about him, it means he did something she didn't like, or thinks he did or wanted more money. Or maybe it was like the hospital administrator said, she was just plain crazy from the PCP and was making it all up."

"All of the above. None of the above. Take your pick. Princess also claimed in her note that James's 'buddies' were other cops— she didn't name them—cops she'd partied with in their off-hours at a rented house out in Culver City. They'd have hookers and all the drugs you wanted."

Gerald Seymore hesitated.

"And?" Napoleon said, waiting. Myra doing the same.

Gerald Seymore shook his head as if regretting to do so.

"And nothing," Gerald Seymore said. "That's all the letter said. That and a lotta undecipherable nonsense about her being followed by the CIA and wanting the DA to put a stop to it. She did give the address of the party pad, though."

"You see the letter?" Myra asked.

"Got a copy right here." Gerald Seymore pulled out a sheaf of paper covered on the front and back in a crudely printed, disjointed script covering every bit of writing space.

Myra and Napoleon scanned the note together. "They talk to this Princess?" Myra asked.

"Can't talk to a dead woman," Gerald Seymore said. "She got into an altercation with another patient and was strangled in her sleep. Just about ten days ago. It's still under investigation."

Napoleon said, "Why am I not surprised?"

"Here's the cooker. The DA assigned the investigation to none other than your ex, the very late Bruce Marshall."

Myra looked up abruptly, eyes wide open.

"You've got to be kidding." Myra trying to recall if Bruce had ever said anything that alluded to his investigation. He was always tight-lipped about everything except his libido. "Talk about a guy who could keep a secret. Give him an Oscar posthumously."

"It seems Marshall's investigation traced the $100 bill to the S and L robbery. It also turned up James's running buddies, four cops with high IA profiles for police misconduct, all of which they've beaten—individually and collectively. Two of them, Brigham and Monroe, were involved in your arrest, Napoleon." Gerald Seymore's eyes swinging to Napoleon and holding. "Calvin James was present but he isn't mentioned. The other two, Paul Stepolini and Neil Sanford, round out the rat pack. Last two names mean anything?"

Napoleon thought about it, then shook his head. "No one I ever heard of."

"Well, it seems because of the many IAs of these guys, the DA had a question about the three fifty-seven they claimed was in your car. The same three fifty-seven used in the S and L homicide. He just didn't think you'd be that dumb to carry it around on your person that long so as to incriminate yourself."

"DA knows I was set up by these jackboot muthafuckas. I'm gonna carry 'round a three fifty-seven in my car four years with no prints—what I'd do, wear gloves every day?"

"And if that had been all the evidence, the three fifty-seven, he was ready to kick it out. 'Cause it just didn't feel right. And he knew it wouldn't feel right to a jury. But he couldn't ignore the money. Not a quarter mil with serial numbers traced to the S and L robbery and seven point five million still missing."

Napoleon looked at Gerald Seymore levelly in the eyes and said, "I had that kind of bank, I'd put it in a private vault, keep it safe way you white boys do till they could arrange to launder it. And you know that's exactly what I'd do, don't you, business partner? 'Cause you know all about that."

Gerald Seymore not saying anything, but sending a hostile gaze from the folder to Napoleon, not appreciating being called out like that. It wasn't the fact Napoleon was speaking from truth, it was having truth thrown in his face, reminding him of who and what he was. And realizing now it was too late to change his image.

Myra listening to the street crook and the Ivy League crook talking about the way they do business. Daddy and the hustler.

"It gets even better," Gerald Seymore said after a moment, his ego settling down, angry eyes finally dropping from Napoleon's face to the folder. "Marshall's investigation seemed to stall after a while. Despite the DA pressing him to move ahead with his investigation, Marshall was always hesitant to go to a grand jury, saying he felt he still needed a stronger case. He kept putting off any indictment until he could see the outcome of LAPD's own IAs. But they were so numerous and never-ending he could never get anything to hold water. Or so he claimed. This made the DA suspicious. So they put Marshall himself under investigation. That investigation suggested

Marshall must've been financially compromised at some point, put on the payroll to stall or mislead the investigation. He took nine trips to the Cayman Islands in less than a year. Going to a different bank each time. His last trip, two days before he met you, Myra, in Cancún."

Myra sat back from the table, shaking her head in disbelief. She said, "I swear I never knew anything about that. Stupid little old me." Myra saying truthfully it was hard to believe she'd been taken in that easily.

"You were in love," Napoleon said. "But not with Mr. Marshall. With yourself. You selfish, Miss Cross. See only what you wanna see in a man. Sex and ego blind you to everything but the ceiling."

"Oh, please!" Myra said. But truth was truth. She considered the risk of letting Gerald Seymore love her and if his love would ever be enough. Yes, she said to herself, Napoleon was right. She began to cry.

She looked at Napoleon, but his face was stone and gave her no quarter.

Gerald Seymore handed Myra his handkerchief, waited for her to compose herself.

"At some point, however," Gerald Seymore said, "shortly after the Cancún trip, Marshall must have gotten a conscience and stopped taking the money. Or, he got greedy and wanted more. Or the fact another assistant DA had been assigned to help him with the investigation. Who knows. But at any rate Marshall suddenly announced he was ready to move ahead with his investigation. Take it to the grand jury and try to get indictments." Gerald Seymore then looked at Myra and said, "Far be it from me to judge you, Myra," he said, "but maybe it was you who turned him around. You said he wanted you to move in. Make him an honest man."

"He never mentioned the honest man part."

Gerald Seymore raised his eyebrows and smiled.

"Whether or not Marshall began to suspect he was under investigation, we'll never know," Gerald Seymore went on. "He wanted authorization to use a wire, had scheduled another interview with the witness up at the mental hospital, and was working with LAPD's IA investigator when—"

"They blew up Miss Cross's car by mistake," Napoleon said. "They'd already set me up to take the heat offa them. But once they realized Miss Cross knew the gun was planted, the investigator had the evidence—they killed him. Set up Miss Cross here with my Glock, her prints, and a double—Rosalie what's-her-name—to kill Mr. Marshall. Then with the same gun took what's-her-name out like Monday-morning garbage. Ho in the hospital the last witness, so you know they gonna snuff her. Take no prisoners and leave no witnesses. I know the story from there, business partner."

"So it seems you do," Gerald Seymore said. He leaned back from the table as if there was no reason to go on, that there was nothing else to say.

"How'd my prints get on the gun?" Myra asked.

"S'plained that to you before, Miss Cross," Napoleon said. "Whichever one knocked you out probably stuck the gun, *my* gun, in your hand." And to Gerald Seymore he said, "You get the serial number of the murder weapon?"

"I most certainly did." Gerald Seymore reached in the folder, withdrew another sheaf of paper, and handed it to Napoleon. Napoleon glanced at it for an instant, withdrew a small envelope from his rent–a–security guard jacket, and, along with the paper, pushed it across the table to Gerald Seymore, saying, "See, it don't match!"

Gerald Seymore opened the envelope, unfolded a piece of paper, studied both for as long as it took to blink, and said, "Identical."

"Knew that. Used my gun to set up Miss Cross," Napoleon said. "White boys smart."

Gerald Seymore said, "Calvin James is black."

His eyes suddenly brightening, Napoleon's head snapped up.

He said to Myra, "Remember . . . back in jail . . . I told you was a black cop asked me about the money, night I was arrested?" All the pieces of the puzzle fitting together now.

"I guess there's just no accounting for a crook's color, is there," Myra said.

"Naw," Napoleon said. "You can take the nigga out the thug life, but you can't take thug life out the nigga."

"They said they had a video of me entering Bruce's building," Myra said.

"Got a copy of that too," Gerald Seymore said, and from the briefcase on the floor he pulled out a VHS tape that they played several times, all in agreement that the double was smaller, thinner, shorter, older, and dumber than Myra Cross. The disguise of flowers that hid her face would be something they could challenge if necessary, Myra hoping it wouldn't be, but in her mind already planning what she would say, the words she would use to discredit the tape's authenticity.

Myra looked at Gerald Seymore. "So what's the next step, Daddy?"

But Daddy wasn't in charge. Napoleon was. He said to them both, but more to Myra, "Remember, I said everybody got a role to play in this. Business partner done his part. Now it's up to you and me, Miss Cross." And for the next hour he laid out the plan they were to follow in minute detail, every facet well thought out and organized.

When he had finished, when it was out there for Myra to see, for her to realize and understand it was the only option left, that both Napoleon Booker and Gerald Seymore had signed off on something that was irreversible, had in fact committed her to an act in which she had no say and from which there would be no second chances if they failed, Myra Cross was stunned. Her dull green eyes suddenly came to life, snapped wide open in an uncontrolled surge of energy, eyebrows raised and furrowed on a face now twisted and distorted into a countenance of incredulous disbelief, her skin covered in a chilly web of goose bumps, not from the funeral home's refrigeration unit but from the very thought of the plan already in the works.

"You can't really be serious—kidnapping? My God, Napoleon, that's a felony!"

Napoleon didn't even think about it. Not once.

He said, "It sure is."

CHAPTER 18

THE BANNER HEADLINE of the *LA Times* read, **FUGITIVE PLAYBOY CENTERFOLD SOUGHT IN DOUBLE HOMICIDE.** The *Playboy* photo of Myra standing in front of the bookcase was opposite a photo of Condoleezza Rice speaking before the UN. The byline below Myra's photo read:

> *The* Times *has learned that a warrant has been issued for the arrest of Myra Cross, an attorney in the Office of the LA Public Defender. Cross, who currently appears in the buff in "Playboy" magazine, is being sought in connection with a double murder. Assistant DA Bruce Marshall, rumored to be Cross's lover, was found shot to death in his downtown Bunker Hill condo two weeks ago in what investigators believe was a crime of passion. Investigators theorize that when Cross discovered his involvement with another woman, Rosalie Roberts, she killed Marshall, then sought out Roberts, whom she shot to death in the parking garage of Marshall's condo. According to detectives familiar with the case, recovery of the murder weapon as well as other forensic evidence ties Cross to both homicides. Cross, who rose to notoriety on her handling of the Ralph Raymond case, failed to surrender to authorities as agreed and has been a fugitive on the FBI's most wanted list for the past two weeks. Her recent appearance in "Playboy" has . . .*

Neil Sanford rubbed tired eyes, handed the newspaper to Darryl Brigham. Darryl in plainclothes, seated in the passenger seat of the Thunderbird, drew deeply on the joint and held it, the car stuffy with the odor of weed.

"This is exactly what you were afraid of," Darryl said, squeaky voice exhaling, his hairy wrist reaching up and cutting off the dim overhead light plunging the Thunderbird into the flickering shadows of a moonless night. He folded the newspaper and set it on the seat between them. "But who knew the hottie would be in *Playboy*? You see the issue? Man, what I wouldn't give. You see the rack on her? Lord Jesus."

They were parked on the darkened shoulder of the Boyle Heights Twentieth Street underpass, noise of occasional traffic passing overhead filtered down. It was nearly midnight and they'd been parked for just over thirty minutes, waiting for Monroe and Stepolini. Stepolini's plane from Phoenix had landed over an hour ago. Neil Sanford talked to Stepolini by cell phone, said there'd been developments, told him where and when to meet once he'd arrived. Neil Sanford looked at his watch and rubbed his eyes again, more out of habit than necessity. In the shadows of the underpass, heavily weighted deep, puffy sacs under bloodshot eyes, his face sagging under a road map of frown lines not as much from age as from a lifetime of deceptions that required putting out one fire after another because he could trust no one else.

It wasn't the *Playboy* issue so much that bothered him. It was the fact the *LA Times* had picked it up. It had taken them fourteen days. With this exposure Myra Cross would be a cause célèbre in fourteen hours: CNN. *America's Most Wanted*. FOX News. *Newsweek. Time*. He could maneuver the situation if left alone to do so. But now the looming publicity was threatening to undermine everything. After the *LA Times* story broke, Neil Sanford spent a sleepless night going over minute details of the double frame step-by-step in a frantic search for holes. Holes he knew were bound to surface under intense media scrutiny if he didn't get to

Myra Cross and Napoleon Booker before their benefactor's money got to someone else: Mark Gerragos, Gloria Allred, Melvin Beli, F. Lee Bailey, and Tom Mesereau. Lawyers with the clout and cash to find the holes, destroy the detectives' credibility the way they did Mark Furhman.

And their search had not gone well. Darryl had been unable to locate Napoleon Booker. Not even his mother, who they felt would've been excellent leverage. And Booker's mother herself was now missing, Darryl reporting she had abruptly taken a leave of absence from her job. "Without pay," he was told by her supervisor at the West LA DMV office where she worked. No explanation given. He'd gone to her house only to find it locked down. The utilities shut off. Newspaper canceled. Mail put on an "indefinite vacation hold" according to the carrier.

Indefinite. That meant she wasn't coming back anytime soon.

"What about his baby's mamma," Neil Sanford asked Monroe after he'd arrived with Stepolini, Stepolini pulling the Crown Victoria to a quiet stop in front of the Thunderbird, both walking back in the gloom of the underpass, sliding one after the other into the backseat of the Thunderbird, Neil Sanford turning around in the driver's seat to face them, arm around the headrest.

Gilbert Monroe shook his head. Pulled out a joint and lit it, drew the herb in deep and held it for the buzz.

"Shaniqua Jones," he said, exhaling slowly, switching the roach to his left hand, his right going into the jacket pocket, pulling out a piece of paper. "Is gone. Long gone. Baby too. Apartment is empty. Utilities cut off. She called the welfare department and told them to cancel her welfare check, that she was relocating out of state, but didn't say where. No forwarding address according to the post office."

Neil Sanford said, "When did this take place?"

"About ten days ago, give or take a day," Monroe said. "I contacted her mother. A Jesus freak who didn't know shit from Shinola. She last talked to Shaniqua a month and a half ago. Tried to get her back in church. Said the girl's association with the Booker

271

kid is the devil's work. I told her I couldn't agree more. Contact me if she heard anything."

Darryl said, "Girl on welfare canceling her check—what does that tell you?"

"She ain't coming back anytime soon," Monroe said. "Older sisters hadn't heard from her in months. Of course they're all crack addicts, so maybe she wanted it that way."

Neil Sanford said to Darryl, "When did Booker's mother take off?"

"Within the same ten-day time frame."

"What about you, Paul," Neil Sanford said to Stepolini. "What's happening on your end with the PD's family?" Stepolini sat there in the darkness, his head outlined in profile, silhouetted by the vague ambient light of the rear window as he gazed silently at the night beyond his side window, seeming lost in thought and not paying too much attention.

Now he turned his head back around, ran ten fingers through a shock of wavy black hair, brought Neil Sanford's image back into the focus of jet-lagged eyes.

"Ten days ago," Stepolini said to no one in particular, running his tongue over his front teeth, thinking about it, trying to access its significance, to make some sense out of it. "The PD's parents left Phoenix for their cruise."

"Cruise?" Darryl asked.

"What the neighbors said."

"You believe that?" Neil Sanford said.

"I did," Stepolini volunteered, "until I tried to talk to her brother. He's a chiropractor in Tucson. He's gone too. He turned his practice over to a colleague. Didn't say anything about a cruise. Just that he was taking some time off, that he didn't know how long he'd be gone, but it would be awhile. The colleague thinking awhile meant an early retirement, that he might not ever return." Stepolini paused to think about it some more. "Yeah, just about ten days ago."

Neil Sanford sucked air through his teeth and turned back around. It was not the kind of news he wanted to hear.

Darryl said, "Maybe it's just a coincidence, all of them being gone like that."

A coincidence? Jesus. What did these guys think with. Unbelievable.

Neil Sanford said, "Nobody in his right mind would believe that, Darryl."

Darryl, tired of Neil Sanford's insults, taking it personally and trying hard not to let it show, said, "All right. What *do* you believe, if it isn't coincidence?"

Neil Sanford took a deep breath, thinking about it.

"Everyone we targeted to lean on is gone," he said. "And all at the same time. Not one or two together like you'd expect to see if it was coincidental. But everyone connected to both our suspects, everyone on the list, suddenly vanishing at the same time. A coincidence? I don't think so. No. No, this was well thought out and executed. Someone with a lot of cash and organization. You remember what I said before, about the one thing that worried me the most, about them having access to an unlimited amount of cash, and how dangerous that could be? Well, now you see what I mean. It's as if they were peeping our hold cards, reading all our moves in advance."

Darryl Brigham liked to beat a dead horse. He said, "Well, I don't know that I go along with that. Booker's mother's a church-going woman. Her kid's breaking her heart, going up for the rest of his life on a one eighty-seven beef. I could see she'd be embarrassed. Want to relocate elsewhere. Make a fresh start."

"Black women don't abandon their children," Neil Sanford said, "good, bad, or crazy. All the years I worked the ghetto, I know that about niggers if I don't know anything else." Neil Sanford caught Darryl's stare in the flash of light from a passing car. He said facetiously, "These people we're talking about have a broken heart—they all decide to move away on the same day?" Neil Sanford wanting to ask Darryl if he was really that dumb and knowing he was. Instead he just said, "You really believe that?"

That sarcasm again. Like nobody had a brain worth anything but him. Darryl didn't say anything. But you could tell by his silence he didn't like it. He just stared at Neil Sanford in the shadows, returned the half-finished joint to his lips, and took a deep breath.

Monroe said from the backseat shadows, "So you're saying, Neil, they're both holed up somewhere out of town or out of the country with their families. That it? We can stop looking?"

Neil Sanford shook his head. "No indeed." He rubbed his eyes and turned back around, arm gripping the headrest again.

"Just their families are gone," Neil Sanford said. "Booker and the PD are right here in town. I guarantee you."

"What makes you think that?" Stepolini said.

"Looking for evidence to clear themselves. What I'd do if it was me. Remember, we have to assume they know it's a frame and probably figure was us who framed them. Which is why we have to be extremely vigilant from this point on. Without anyone to lean on, our only hope is to find them before they come down on us. And all this publicity won't make it any easier."

Darryl fully opened slow-moving, half-closed lids and said, "You mean they're out there somewhere looking for *us*?"

Neil Sanford hated dealing with the retarded. "They already know who we are," he said. "But with unlimited cash to spread around they'll go all out. Do anything to get the frame off their backs—tapping our phones, hiring PIs to follow us around town, talking to people we know, checking our bank accounts. To say nothing of what they're spending on informants. So be very careful what you say to informants."

"So you're saying the hunters have now become the hunted?" Stepolini said.

Neil Sanford said, "You'd better believe it."

Because he knew it was true.

• • •

GILBERT MONROE'S CHEVY IMPALA pulled into the under-ground garage of the Simi Valley condominium complex he'd occupied for the past seven years. He'd moved to the sterile all-white LA suburb of Rodney King's Simi Valley after ten years of apartment living in another all-white LA suburb, Moorpark. Pres-sured by ever-rising rent and his then-girlfriend Teresa, who insisted they needed a two-bedroom and why couldn't it be a condo. Monroe didn't like to spend money, was cheap and wasn't afraid to say so. Teresa convinced him that with the right down payment, the monthly payments on a condo would be the same as rent and would make him money in the long run because of appre-ciation. But when Monroe refused to add Teresa's name on the title, she gave him back the key and left. So he populated the condo with a series of dysfunctional women who were hookers, shot dope, or drank. There would be no one waiting for him tonight because he was between women.

Perhaps because he was thinking about that, about being nearly forty and being alone and no one waiting to greet him when he turned the key and opened the door, perhaps because he was just tired from the eight-hour grind at the precinct that turned into twelve hours because of added hours driving around searching for Napoleon Booker, and Neil Sanford's insistence they meet under the Twentieth Street overpass—he didn't notice the uncharacter-istic dimness of the lighting in the garage, the absence of two of the four bulbs that normally illuminated the parking facility. Nor did he pay any particular attention to the gray-paneled van parked in the space next to his own. Monroe stepped out of the Impala, opened the trunk to retrieve his tennis racket. He heard a slight noise behind him, thought it was the familiar click of a door open-ing, and rose up to look around.

It happened just that fast.

What he saw as he straightened was the last vestige of dim light as a cloth sack suddenly covered his head with darkness, its draw-string pulled tight around his neck. In the same instant, before he could react, before he finally realized what was happening—that he was being robbed, perhaps about to be killed—he felt several pairs of strong muscular arms suddenly encircle him at three differ-ent levels, completely immobilizing him: one pair around his upper chest, pinning his arms down tightly to his side, another set around his waist, and a third pair going around his legs, the tandem lifting him off the ground and beginning to carry him across the concrete in short, hurried steps. There were no other sounds. No one spoke. No whistles. No snapping of fingers. No telltale odors of cologne or cigarette smoke. In those few panic-filled seconds, he realized it had been planned and rehearsed. Professionals.

With great effort he tried to move, twisting and turning his two-hundred-and-ten-pound body violently against the forces that held him, but they were unyielding. He tried to yell, to call out, saying, "Hey, what . . . ?" then suddenly felt something pressing down over his face, smothering his screams, a hand he first thought was trying to suffocate him but then realized was holding some-thing firm over his nose and mouth. And Monroe noticed then a familiar smell—sweet and pungent—but realized too late it was chloroform. Despite his head twisting violently from side to side, the hand remained firmly clamped over his face, the chloroform seeping effortlessly through the cloth sack. But he had to breathe, and knew that when he did, each breath would take him deeper into unconsciousness.

Trapped in a sack of darkness, his strength and consciousness ebbing, he was scarcely aware of being laid on his back, the arms that imprisoned his torso relaxing, the slight jogging motion of the van as it traveled up the incline and onto the street. All Gilbert Monroe wanted to do was sleep.

And that's exactly what he did.

CHAPTER 19

THE FIRST SENSATION Gilbert Monroe experienced was the nausea from the lingering effects of the chloroform, its bittersweet aftertaste caught on the edges of his tongue, otherwise dry as cotton. When he made an effort to move, he couldn't. His arms and feet were frozen. Something was a heavy weight on them. He couldn't make a fist. Some time passed and he was finally able to bring his head upright, blink away the cloudiness of blurred vision, and see that he was in a thimble-sized room with cement-block walls, a low ceiling, no furniture, no windows, one door, and that was lit from above by the dull, flat glare of a single fluorescent light. It looked like a public storage space or abandoned warehouse.

He was strapped to a chair by thick cords of rope and reams of wide leather belts. The chair in which he was seated was pushed up chest-high to the edge of a wide metal table, and both arms, from the elbows forward, were somehow attached to the table and hidden from view by a large bulky item covered in its entirety by a blanket. And seated directly across from him were two figures he recognized: Myra Cross and Napoleon Booker. Their faces were pale and washed out in the flat illumination of the fluorescent light. Seven men wearing hooded ski masks and holding a factory of handguns stood behind them.

"What the hell's going on?" Monroe said thickly, working his tongue to bring moisture to dry lips.

"Feeling better, Gilbert? May I call you Gilbert? Or do you prefer Gil? Okay, Gil. Little water here should help." Myra Cross filled

277

a paper cup with water from a pitcher, holding it to Monroe's lips, letting him sip until he shook his head.

"Where the hell am I?"

"You know who we are, Gil?" Myra said.

Monroe didn't have to think about it. Neil Sanford had called it—they were still here in LA. Right under their noses. The drug dealer and PD working together, just like he said.

"And *what* you are—criminals wanted for murder. Untie me!" Looking at the strange apparatus covering his hands, trying to move them and failing.

Monroe still now, light sweat across his forehead. He stared at Napoleon and Myra.

"I don't know what the hell you two think you're doing," he spit out, harsh words wrapped in the emotion of rage, "but you'd better well untie me. And do it real quick. I'm a cop. The police. You can't do this to me."

"What Denzel said in *Training Day*," Napoleon said, reaching over and checking the ropes, satisfying himself they'd hold.

"What?"

"You see the movie? Thought every cop saw *Training Day*. Anyway, Denzel a crooked cop like you. End of the movie he gets caught in the jungle, niggas gettin' ready to take him out. He says, 'I'm the *po-lice*!' same as you. Like that suppose to protect him." Napoleon broke out in a laugh that was joined by the chorus standing behind him. "I'm the police. Yeah, right."

"Nigger, I don't give a fuck about any movie. You and the woman here, Miss Cross, need to untie me before all hell breaks loose!"

"Already broke loose," Napoleon said. "You just ain't felt it yet." He smiled at Monroe from across the table, made another check of the ropes.

"You like that, huh? Callin' people nigger to they faces. 'Cause you know it makes 'em mad, makes 'em wanna hit you, and you hopin' they do so you can go upside their heads. But they can't 'cause you the *po-lice*! And if they do, you in white-cop heaven, huh. Get to do your Rodney King dance on their head 'cause you got the power. Guess wearing a uniform and badge makes you brave, huh. Give you another set of balls make up for the ones you ain't got. Makes you feel invincible. Makes you—"

"I don't show at the station tomorrow, gonna be an army come looking for me!" Monroe spit out. Little punk-ass nigger talking shit to him like that. Who the fuck does he think he is . . . ?

"I was gonna say makes you feel like Superman. But I can see now, they make you dumb and blind, 'cause just in case you haven't noticed, you all tied up and shit. Ain't a chance in hell you gonna leave here alive 'less I say so, and you still got nerve to call someone a nigga to they face. Either them extra balls ain't working, or you just plain stupid."

Monroe staring at Myra now, but his words meant for Napoleon. "Fuck you, nigger! *And* your nigger gangbangers," he said. And to Myra, but softer and with less intensity, he said, "Would be in your best interest, Miss Cross"—addressing her that way, regardless of what Neil Sanford said, feeling she still deserved it—"to convince your associate there to untie me. Give yourself up. Let me take you in. I'll put in a good word for you, say you cooperated, that it was all his idea." Jerking his head in Napoleon's direction but his eyes still on Myra. "You haven't got a chance of getting out of this," he went on calmly, "and taking me hostage as a bargaining chip won't get you anywhere," he said in truth. "Because when it comes to hostage negotiations with a murder suspect, in this case two murder suspects"—and he shook his head in Napoleon's direction—"if it comes down to it, I'm expendable," he said again in truth. "You need to understand that." And again he looked briefly at Napoleon. "Both of you."

Myra, incredulous eyes staring at Monroe, feigned a sigh of exasperation.

"You haven't heard a word he said, have you, Gil?"

Haven't heard a word? That stopped him cold. He couldn't have heard her correctly. The PD taking the nigger's side? Against him? A cop? What on earth . . . ?

"What?"

"Mr. Booker was trying to help you, Gil. Trying to explain your situation, and you just blew him off like he wasn't there."

Monroe grunted. "Are you on drugs, Miss Cross? I've heard that about you. Heard lotta things about you, in fact. Like how famous you are in the DA's office," he said, and waited.

The list. Badge of honor. Or dishonor? Nothing else to do but smile.

Myra said to Monroe, "Am I on drugs? That's all you have to say? Nothing else? I'm insulted, Gil." And still smiling, she turned to Napoleon. "You're right. He's deaf, dumb, and blind."

Napoleon stared at Monroe and shook his head.

Myra said, "For your information, Gil, this isn't about you being a hostage."

Monroe's eyes brightened with curiosity.

"No? Don't tell me." Monroe in denial but cynical, trying to be hard. He said, "I'm strapped to a chair. Got some kinda shit keeping my hands down. Holding me against my will. Now if that ain't the definition of a hostage, suppose you tell me what is?"

"Well," Myra began slowly, the way they'd gone over it, "Mr. Booker and I were hoping you'd help us clarify a few things. For example, we'd like to know who set us up. No, wait. I said it wrong. We know who set us up. What we want to know is why. No. That's not right either. Because we know why we were set up. I guess we just want to know about the money."

Monroe laughed. "I don't know what you're talking about."

Myra turned to Napoleon. "He doesn't know what we're talking about."

"But he knows all about you and the DA, huh?" Napoleon said.

Myra said to Monroe, "You mean to say you don't know anything about the seven and a half million dollars missing from the S and L you guys hit four years ago? You don't know anything about the guard that was killed, the gun you planted in Mr. Booker's car? The men you hired to kill my investigator when you discovered we had pictures to prove the gun used to kill the guard had been planted? And then once you removed Mr. Booker's gun from his car, the gun that was really in the car, you put my fingerprints on it, then used it to kill Mr. Marshall and Miss Roberts? You mean to say, Gil, you don't know anything about that? That what you're saying?"

Monroe looked at Myra with cold, penetrating eyes and shook his head, but the laugh took effort. His eyes shifted now to the strange apparatus that covered his arms.

"Will you get whatever this is off my arm, please?"

Napoleon said, "Please?" and looked at Myra. "Now that's a first for a cop." Back to Monroe he said, "Gotta help us first."

Monroe said, "I'm afraid the only way I can help is you let me go and I surrender the two of you to the DA. Say you cooperated."

Myra said, "I'm sorry to hear that, Gil. I really am. We were hoping you'd cooperate, roll over on Neil Sanford and the rest of your police Mafia friends, Stepolini, Brigham, and James, cut yourself a deal, let us off the hook, and join Raphael Perez in the Witness Protection Program. You'd be right at home with him."

Whoa! Neil called this one too. In a move that did not go unnoticed, Monroe's eyes came wide open in surprise at the mention of his partners, thinking if she knew anything more, they'd all be in jail and the pretty little PD with the nice rack, red hair, and green eyes would be on *Oprah*. He looked up at Myra, thinking about it.

"You've got to be joking."

"I wouldn't joke about a thing like this, Gil," Myra said.

Monroe just stared absently at Myra, at her chest, not really aware he was doing so.

Myra said, "So what you're telling us, Gil, is that you'd be willing to die so your friends can enjoy your share of the money. That what you're saying?"

Monroe's eyes stayed open, moved from her chest to her eyes. He said, "Die? What are you talking about?"

Pushing her chair away from the table and standing up, beginning to circle the table in a slow, casual pace, heels clicking on the concrete floor, Myra said, "Well, it's like this, Gil. You and your buddies got Mr. Booker and me in a frame we can't get out of. Not unless you help us, and you said no. So that means we have no real choice. If I'm gonna go to prison for two murders I didn't do, then I may as well go for one I did. Wouldn't you agree, Mr. Booker?"

Napoleon said, "Sure you're right, Miss Cross."

Monroe grunted and shook his head. He said, "Yeah, right. I'm so scared." Still glancing occasionally at the object under the blanket that covered his arms.

"You need to be, Gil." Myra turned to the group standing behind her and said, "Any one of you got a gun I can borrow?" And she took the Beretta nine-millimeter from a hooded gangbanger who withdrew it from his waist and handed it to Myra. She racked the slide and laid it on the table the way they'd rehearsed it. She was not comfortable with this part of the plan, the gun, but hoped it didn't show in her slow pacing around the table. "If you don't change your mind and cooperate with us, Gil, I'm afraid I'll have to blow your brains out," Myra said, she hoped with conviction, the way she and Booker had rehearsed it. Killing wasn't part of her nature: at nine years old she'd watched her brother shoot a bird with a BB gun and was sick to her stomach the entire day; at fifteen her cocker spaniel got out of the yard and went barking up to the mailman, the mailman pulling out a steel pipe and beating the cocker spaniel to death right there in front of her, Myra inconsolable for a week. "Keep in mind," she went on, playing it out and failing miserably at being hard-core, "I've got nothing to lose, really." She said it as if she was addressing a women's tea party. "I'm going to prison anyway. And like I said, it's just as easy to go to jail for a murder I did do as it is for one I didn't do."

Monroe, his eyes on the Beretta, raising them now to read her

face, to see if the threat behind the green eyes matched the empti-
ness of her voice and realizing it did, had to work at not laughing.
He said, "You're bluffing, lady. You haven't got it in you to kill
someone in cold blood. So you can stop all this posturing 'cause you
aren't gonna do a goddamn thing to me."

And Myra knowing that he was right, that she didn't have it in
her to just kill someone outright, even if going to jail was
inevitable. He was right, she was just posturing, putting on a show,
and remembered she'd warned Napoleon that she might not be
able to pull it off, but he'd insisted she try, that it was all part of the
plan.

Myra turned once again to the enforcers standing in loose
groups behind her.

She said, "Is there a silencer for this gun?" And feeling incredi-
bly stupid saying it, the words leaden on her tongue, her mouth dry
in the process.

The gun's owner stepped forward for the second time, grabbed
the Beretta from the table, attached the silencer, and handed the
gun back to Myra. Myra having to work at supporting its weight with
one hand the way she'd practiced, her hand visibly shaking as she
turned the gun toward Monroe and fired. Twice. The Beretta making
a dull hissing sound like a high-pressure air hose. The rounds missing
Monroe by a margin he knew was intentional but coming closer than
he would've liked, splintering the wood beam that ran vertical from
the low ceiling to the uncarpeted concrete floor.

Monroe barely flinched. He just turned his head around toward
the beam, real casual like, not really able to see it and not caring.
Then came back around to Myra, shaking his head, leaded eyes a
pair of cold stones slowly closing and opening, just staring at her.
Taking his time.

Poker-playing time.

"You wanted me dead, I would be," he said, reading Myra's
impotence like yesterday's newspaper, cool and unfazed about it.
Too much experience not to know a bluff when he saw one.

Napoleon jumped up from the table, cursing. Knocking his chair away and waving his arms in a fit of agitation. He startled Myra, the Beretta hanging loose in limp fingers, empty green eyes blinking in a state of unrehearsed confusion.

"We wasting time, Miss Cross," he shouted, realizing now that the cop had seen through her sham threat. Napoleon wondering now whatever possessed him to think he could pull off a Pygmalion with Myra Cross. She'd blown it. Big time. Napoleon questioning now if she'd be able to carry out the last part of his plan. That once they'd finished with Monroe, the rest was on her. She'd be on her own then, wouldn't have him to bail her out like he was getting ready to do now. And if she blew that, if she couldn't pull it off, neither of them would see tomorrow's sunrise. "Man don't understand we serious," Napoleon said. "Time we showed him." And Napoleon snatched the blanket from off Monroe's arms, saw his head drop down, his eyes suddenly narrow in confusion at what he saw.

Two items on the table.

A meat cleaver. And a paper cutter. Not a school paper cutter—a large industrial paper cutter like they have at Kinko's. Gilbert Monroe's hands were palms down and flat across the surface, his wrists held down by a crudely fashioned metal U-joint bolted underneath. His fingers, spread apart and stretched across the cutting edge of the blade were encased in a transparent plastic mold, a see-through glove of sorts that prevented any movement.

Napoleon said, bringing angry African lips close to Monroe's cheekbone, his lips foaming slightly with a trace of spit, "Maybe my partner here, Miss Cross, ain't got it in her to fuck you over. All right. That's her. But I'm different, see. I'm one of these little street niggas you kick around don't give a fuck. Kill me! Like she said, if we gotta go to jail for people we didn't kill, may as go for one we did. You feeling me on this, Five-O?" Napoleon Booker looking in the cop's eyes to see the confusion, the beginnings of fear. He said, "But before I do that, I'm gonna fuck you up real bad, see just how much you can take, you don't tell me what I wanna know. Understand me, Five-O?"

Monroe not sure but thinking now this was good-cop, bad-cop time. His frantic eyes sought out Myra's face, but she gave him nothing but a blank stare. Eyes back to Napoleon, the paper cutter, the meat cleaver, and he realized the bad cop was serious. Monroe started to speak, saying, "Say, what . . . ? Oh, now wait a minute. You—" But he was cut off midsentence when a gangbanger, moving behind him on Napoleon's signal, stuffed a white cloth in his mouth.

"Minute's too long, Five-O," Napoleon said. "I'm the impatient type." And in almost the same instant Napoleon slammed down the handle of the paper cutter. He had to stand up, put his hundred and eighty pounds of weight on it, and the paper cutter's blade sliced easily through the soft thickness of the transparent plastic mold, the plastic mold making a high-pitched squeezing sound, like a balloon only half filled with air and about to pop. Then the blade making a harsh grating sound as it sheared through the bedrock of bone, the mold suddenly filling with blood and falling to the floor with Gilbert Monroe's pinky finger, stream of blood spurting from the amputation site liked a water pistol, spraying the metal table, catching Napoleon's pants, Shaniqua's blouse just above the waist. A gangbanger rushing to the table with a handkerchief, pressing it against the red geyser in a futile effort to stem its flow.

That fast. Napoleon Booker, the executioner.

Myra's lusterless green eyes suddenly came open in shock, not wanting to believe what she just saw. God! He did it. Just like that. Cut off his finger. Like it was a loose thread on a cheap suit. Lied to her. Told her it was just a prop for effect. But he did it. Had planned to do it all along. And so easily. No show of emotion. Not even giving the cop time to speak, to say whether he'd cooperate or not. Just chopped the man's finger off. Jesus! Myra knowing now that if Monroe refused to cooperate, she would become an accessory to murder—a moot point given the circumstances. Still, knowing Monroe's execution could be part of Napoleon Booker's plan, that he was willing and capable of carrying it out, was not something she'd anticipated. And Myra didn't know what to say, or if she should say anything, her mouth hanging open and staring with unblinking, vacuous eyes at the amputated finger on the floor, blood dripping down around it in a steady stream from its reservoir above spreading slowly across the top of the metal table.

Monroe's head swung wildly in uncontrolled spasms on its tether, like a flag caught in a brisk wind. His face contorted into a mosaic of gargoyles, bulging eyes wide open in a blaze of disbelief and fear, a forehead of perspiration, stinging moisture filling his eyes a testament to the pain. Even muffled by the gag, the scream in his throat accompanied by a network of distended neck veins was chilling.

Napoleon said, "You ready to talk to me, Five-O?" And he pulled the gag out of Monroe's mouth, filling the room with the deafening cry of pain and profanities.

"Ooooww!" Monroe half screamed, half cried. "You cut my finger off, you little punk-ass nigger! I ain't gonna tell you shit! Ooooww, God, it hurts!"

Napoleon said, "Wrong answer."

Monroe screaming profanities, his head twisting and turning in pain until a gangbanger's arms grabbed it, held it steady, his mouth trying to stay closed but opening to scream because it was so painful, spitting and foaming in a last attempt at defiance as Napoleon wedged the gag back into his mouth.

"I guess you from Missouri, huh?" Napoleon said, unmoved by the intensity of Monroe's muffled scream he instinctly knew was a litany of familiar profanities, racial insults, and threats he'd heard a thousand times from a thousand cops. "I got to show you," he said, and the hundred-and-eighty-pound frame with the black skin and neatly manicured cornrows brought the paper cutter's blade down for a second time.

Myra nauseated now and wanting to turn away and vomit, but holding it in, closing her eyes for an instant but not long enough to miss Monroe's bloody ring finger fall to the floor in its plastic tomb, his muffled scream, more desperate in its intensity than before, reaching across the short space between them.

"You ready to talk to me, muthafucka, or do I gotta turn you into a quadriplegic? 'Cause I can cut off body parts till ain't nothin' left but your head. And this take care of that."

Napoleon picking up the meat cleaver, playing with it, balancing it in his hand like it was a gun and getting a kick out of Monroe's suffering, his eyes bulging wide open and laced with a spiderweb of tiny red arteries. And drenched in sweat, a face of unrecognizable distortion made even more startling by its flailing back and forth, rapid, deep, coarse breathing desperate in its force through a pair of flared nostrils.

Napoleon bringing his ear close to Monroe's neck and saying, "I can't hear you, Five-O. You'll have to talk louder. Okay?" Waiting, then saying, "No? Suit yourself, then." And the paper cutter's blade coming down a third time, Monroe's middle finger joining its mates in the bloody pile on the floor. Blood was now flooding the table, spilling unchecked like a waterfall from every edge, the gangbanger playing paramedic snapping his fingers for more handkerchiefs. Napoleon saying to Monroe, "You ready to talk to me, muthafucka? Yeah? No? Oh, well, number four." But this time, as Napoleon's hand went for the paper cutter's handle, the cop's head fluttered from side to side in a frantic no, wide, bulging eyes speaking desperately for the muffled scream that couldn't. Napoleon hesitated long enough to say, "Yeah? Do I understand you correctly, Five-O—you ready to speak with us, answer some questions we got? If so, we get finished, might even take you to a hospital, get your fingers sewed back on. What you do after that your own business. I don't give a fuck, I get what I want. Know what I'm sayin'?"

If he had to think about it he didn't take long. Monroe nodded. But not with a great deal of enthusiasm and not with the kind of gratitude for an end to torture one might expect. And his eyes, stinging with tears of pain, still held a reservoir of resentment and malignant hostility for which he was unrepentant.

The Beretta still dangling from her limp fingers, Myra was standing motionless in a gathering pool of blood, vacuous eyes looking off, scarcely aware of what was being said, desperate for anything to numb the sheer horror of Gilbert Monroe's torture and her complicity in it. Wanting to close her eyes and cover her ears to block out the sights and sounds alien to her existence, to pretend it wasn't happening, but knowing that it was, that she was as much a part of it as if it was her own hand pulling down on the guillotine. Wanting to turn and walk away but knowing it was too late. Instead, she let her mind take her away from the torture chamber, the chilling sound of the paper cutter slicing through tissue and bone, the torrent of blood, amputated fingers, muted screams of excruciating pain. She took herself out of the room, back to the sun-drenched beaches of Cancún. Warm ocean waves washing over her nude body. Jason Rice's camera. And to the south Atlantic, trying to imagine her parents, her brother, Mrs. Booker, Shaniqua, and little Napoleon all having dinner together on the high seas, playing shuffleboard and enjoying themselves. But the sudden silence in the room and Napoleon Booker's commanding voice interrupted the fantasy, brought her back to a true reality show.

"I take this gag out your mouth," he was saying to Gilbert Monroe, "you gonna tell us all about you and these other muthafuckin' Five-O gangster pals of yours—Brigham, Sanford, and Stepo-what's-his-name—who set me and Miss Cross up behind this bank robbery. You understand? You start talking shit, I'm gonna play Paul Bunyan on your ass with the meat cleaver." And waited.

Monroe, in a final act of resistance, seemed to think about it, taking his time, looking off, assessing the situation and weighing options that were slim to none. The PD, he decided, was not really the problem. Thinking to himself she'd lost her nerve early on, probably before they'd even grabbed him. She either wouldn't or couldn't help him, that was obvious. But she wouldn't hurt him. He was sure of that. But this little punk, Booker, on the other hand, was another matter altogether. This little muthafuckin' gangbanging nigger was crazy! The nerve, cutting off his fingers like that! And it was his show. All the way. The PD just along for the ride. And that meat cleaver—little punk-ass nigger drug dealer was really gonna do it—cut off his head like he did his fingers. The way they killed hostages in Iraq. And wouldn't blink an eye doing it. Cold, sadistic little muthafucka. Kind of like Stepolini, whom he'd never really liked. Yeah, this little baby-faced nigger was really going through with it if he didn't talk. He could see it in the cold, hard eyes, hear it in the angry voice totally devoid of compassion. Talk about underestimating somebody. Of course they wouldn't be able to use what he'd tell them, not in court. He'd say he was coerced and forced. Look at my hands, he'd say, see how many fingers they cut off. But would his partners believe him? And if they didn't, may as well join up with the PD on the run. And in that same instant of revelation, he felt the throbbing bite of pain in his hand and decided, hell, he couldn't really take much more, that life with seven fingers was something he'd have to adjust to. Trying to imagine a future in the Witness Protection Program, if it came to that. Playing golf with Raphael Perez. And figuring it might not be that bad if they let him have cable and a couple of whores from time to time. Finally, having made his decision in the few seconds allotted him and without looking up, he answered Napoleon Booker in the only way he could. He nodded yes.

Flushed with victory and smiling, Napoleon straightened up, turned to Myra, and said, "Business partner on first. I'm on second. Looks like you on third, Miss Cross. Five-O ready to talk. Say you wanna be a talk show host? This be good practice for what you gotta do tomorrow night."

And it was. Absolutely.

CHAPTER 20

TRACI LORDS on an eighty-inch Mitsubishi screen—*Sex Fifth Avenue*. Traci larger than life, but very young and underage, doing what made her famous—giant boobs and long tongue reaching out from the screen like 3-D. All you needed were the glasses and bail money. And on surround sound, loud moans and screams of enjoyment you couldn't be sure weren't genuine. But the raucous noise from her audience of three sounded like ten and was absolutely genuine. Neil Sanford, Darryl Brigham, and Stepolini in plainclothes, drinking Coronas and Heinekens, and munching chips, Stepolini smoking a joint and passing it around.

They were in the party pad. A small four-bedroom stucco house in Culver City, part of a post–World War II housing development that sprung up in the shadows of MGM's back lot. Baldwin Avenue a narrow street ending in a cul-de-sac. The party pad set off at the dead end with no backyard, but a view overlooking the steep incline of a wide concrete drainage channel that wound its way through Los Angeles to the Pacific Ocean, where it ended just south of Marina del Rey. An eyesore strewn with dry brown weeds pushing up between the unrepaired cracks and refuse of weekend Super Bowl parties. Its isolation the perfect place for the Gang of Five's drug parties and sex orgies. Shuttered windows all the way around. And just enough low-end furniture on cheap carpets over linoleum floors to make it comfortable for men whose definition of comfort was brutality. And for the women they brought there to use and abuse who'd never known anything else.

All eyes and ears glued to the underage fifty-foot woman in the throes of an ear-splitting orgasm that sounded more painful than pleasurable, the laughter and derisive shouts at Traci Lords continuing unchecked. Until Darryl Brigham knocked his near-empty bowl of chips on the floor, bent down, saw colored toenails in expensive open-toed shoes and a pair of beautifully shaped bare legs he thought at first was an apparition. But rubbing his eyes didn't make them disappear.

Frowning, he stood up slowly, empty chip bowl shaking in his hand.

"Guys," he said, repeating it a second time, and a third, until he got their attention away from Traci Lords's marathon orgasm and they turned around.

That's when the laughter stopped.

No one had seen her enter, heard the key turn quietly in the lock, the door open and close softly. And now Myra Cross standing there behind them, holding a small handbag and wearing a blouse unbuttoned down to her nipple line, showing an abundance of cleavage, short, tight-fitting skirt with ruffled hemline hitting midthigh. Myra's face beginning to show the strain of a life on the run: three weeks of constant vigilance, nights of sleepless apprehension, and the stale diet of tasteless fast foods. But makeup perfectly applied to cover shadowy circles under two darkened caves of eyes grown dull and fatigued. And below a cap of untended red hair a worried forehead of frown lines dancing between a pair of ragged and unshaped eyebrows.

Total shock the only way to describe it. Three pairs of unblinking bloodshot eyes on wide-open blank faces. Darryl the only one standing and holding the bowl of chips, still shaking and not aware of it. Stepolini seated on the edge of a chair, holding his Corona in one hand, a half-smoked roach in the other, both frozen just inches from his mouth. And Neil Sanford catatonic, twisted uncomfortably around in his chair like a Rodin statue, staring at Myra Cross with a pair of tired watery eyes not wanting to believe what they saw. But seeing is believing.

Complete silence. Except for Traci Lords. And you couldn't really say the groans and moans were articulated speech as such.

Looking up at Traci Lords, Myra said, "I didn't know orgasms lasted that long. Jesus, if they did, the country would grind to a stop. Who'd ever want to get out of bed? Anyone going to offer a girl a seat?"

No one spoke. No one moved. Just their eyes following Myra as she moved around and past them to an empty couch, dropped down on a cushion of worn vinyl, and crossed her legs in the *Basic Instinct* pose.

Stepolini thinking, *What the fuck . . . ?*

Darryl thinking, *Jesus, look at that rack.*

Neil Sanford thinking, *If it seems too good to be true, it probably is. Or is it?*

Myra Cross thinking, *Maybe the talk show host wasn't such a good idea.*

Trying to calm her nerves, she'd smoked three joints and a primo earlier that night while waiting in the van. The same van used to kidnap Monroe. After being certain Monroe wasn't going to bleed to death, and leaving him in the care of the seven gang-bangers, Napoleon had driven Myra to the Culver City address and parked a block away where the party pad could be watched, see what time Monroe's buddies would arrive after his call earlier that day. The call made from a cell phone Napoleon held to Monroe's lips with one hand, meat cleaver in the other hand, held high over Monroe's arm. And Monroe in agonizing pain it took great effort to suppress, managing to tell them he was bringing three girls by later that night who wanted to party. Stepolini arriving first around eleven. Neil Sanford and Darryl arriving together thirty minutes later. Napoleon not letting Myra leave the van for at least thirty minutes after everyone was there. Give them a chance to loosen up with weed and beer. Make her job easier.

Easier. That had to be a joke. Getting them to talk. Monroe had told them everything. Not that they hadn't figured most of it out ahead of time. But it was nice to have the blanks filled in. Still, his confession on tape, revealing as it was, was forced and Monroe would say so the moment his fingers were sewn back on. They'd known that from the beginning. What they needed now was corroboration from his accomplices. Confessions that were not forced or coerced, the final part of Napoleon Booker's plan. Using what Monroe had told them in an effort to get them to talk. And that task fell to Myra. If she failed, there would be no light at the end of the tunnel. And if she failed miserably, well, no need to think about that.

"You guys aren't very sociable," Myra said, breaking the ice, bringing them out of their collective trance. "Considering how much you've fucked up my life. Thank you very much."

Darryl was the first to find his tongue. He moved to a chair across from Myra, dropped down, empty chip bowl still shaking in his hand.

"What are you doing here?"

"Now, that's a question, isn't it?"

"But we don't know you." Darryl waved his free hand about the room. "Nobody in this room knows you. What are you doing here?"

Myra shook her head and looked at them. Incredible. She just grunted.

"I need a joint first." And as she'd been instructed, she started plowing through her purse, cursing, finally turning it upside down and dumping out its contents on the sofa: cell phone, Palm Pilot, Kleenex, compact, cosmetic case, key chain, lighter, a paperback book of Stephen King's *Pet Sematary*, miniature digital recorder, thirty dollars in cash and change, and three joints.

Four quick tries with a lighter programmed not to work.

"Light, anyone?" Myra looked up.

Darryl jumped up, almost too eager, it seemed. Held out his lighter, his eyes having a hard time pulling themselves away from her chest, Myra drawing the herb in deep, waiting for the buzz before exhaling.

"Why am I here, I believe was the question," she said, and looked at them. Darryl first because he was still in her face with the lighter, realizing he was really more interested in her chest than why she was here. Then at Stepolini, Stepolini not quite sure what was happening but cool enough about it to know if he was patient, whatever was up would become clear, sipping his Corona, drawing on his own joint. Myra thinking Stepolini was the one to watch out for, his coolness masking his killer instinct, more handsome in his photograph than he was in person. Neil Sanford's tired eyes staring back at Myra, Myra seeing the confusion in his eyes, knowing he should be able to see it too but couldn't.

Darryl said, "You gonna tell us?" He looked at his watch, saying to no one in particular, "Where the hell's Monroe?"

Myra said, "Who, Gil? He's all tied up at the moment. Said to tell you he'll take a rain check."

Stunned, the three of them stared at Myra. What the hell was going on—the PD they set up a fugitive now, and busting in on them like this and saying she knew Monroe? Wanting to ask how'd she know about the house, where'd she get a key? Then, as if on cue, Darryl and Stepolini turning to Neil Sanford for a collective response, Neil Sanford lowering his Heineken to the table, settling back on the couch, thinking about what to say.

"Oh? You know him?"

"Gil and I go back a ways."

"Really. And just how far back would that be?"

"Far enough."

"Why should I believe you?"

"Gave me the key," Myra said, and her fingers picked through the pile on the couch, held up the key chain. "How do you think I got in?"

"Doesn't prove shit. Could've had a locksmith do that."

Hardball. Monroe had said Neil Sanford was like that.

"I would say call him. But like I said, he's all tied up right now."
Neil Sanford said, "Paul . . ."

Stepolini replaced his joint with a cell phone and waited.

He said to Neil Sanford after a moment, "Voice mail," and to Gilbert Monroe's voice mail he said, "Monroe, what the fuck is going on here?" Trying to talk over Traci Lords moaning and groaning in her hourlong orgasm and putting a finger in his ear. "If you know anything about giving someone a key, you get this message, call me back yesterday. Something's going down with a redheaded bitch that's got your name on it!"

The three cops staring at Myra, waiting.

Myra said, "You know, Gil is really a nice guy once you get to know him. In fact, he's such a nice guy that he's had a change of heart. He really doesn't want to see me go to jail."

Stepolini said, "The fuck are you talking about, Red?" Her new nickname.

Stepolini mashing out the blunt in an ashtray and moving up to the edge of his seat in the same motion, his hand dropping down low to his boot, eyes shifting to Neil Sanford for the word. But Neil Sanford was shaking his head slightly, wanting to know more, needing to see it clearly first.

Myra picking up on it, aware now of just how close she was, how dangerous these people really were, had to work at hiding her fear. Feeling her heart jump in her chest, her pulse quicken, the first inkling of sweat under the mop of red hair, hoping it didn't show. She had to move quickly, try to get them to talk, and seeing now that wasn't going to happen because they weren't convinced about Monroe.

She said, "Well, maybe I have something else here that will prove Gil and I are good friends." She rummaged through the pile on the couch for the second time, picked up the miniature digital recorder. The only thing that wasn't in the script was little Traci Lords. "Do you think we could put the adolescent on mute?"

Stepolini said, "Why, Red? Does it bother you, getting fucked like that?"

Myra said, "Not ordinarily. No. But I have something I'd like for you to hear. It's not nearly as exciting as our girl there, but it's definitely more interesting."

Stepolini took a deep breath, picked up the remote, and plunged the room into silence, freezing Traci Lords with a dick in her mouth.

"Thank you." Myra set the digital recorder down on the end table, hit the Play button, and waited for all hell to break loose.

Monroe's voice: " . . . *and Calvin all up in his face, talking smack. So Paul shot him. Just like that. Put five slugs right in his chest. You shoulda seen Calvin's face as he went down, his expression. Man, that was funny.*"

Myra's voice: "*Paul. You mean Stepolini?*"

Monroe's voice: "*Yeah. Paul. Did the girl too. Rosalie. We called her Rose. We partied with her a lot. I don't think he wanted to kill her. He kinda liked her. But Neil said she had to go. He couldn't trust her after she'd killed your boyfriend, Marshall.*"

Myra's voice: "*Neil. That's Neil Sanford?*"

Monroe's voice: "*Yeah. Neil.*"

Myra's voice: "*But why Bruce . . . ah, Mr. Marshall? I don't get the connection.*"

Monroe's voice: "*Marshall was on the take. He knew about the bank robbery from Princess . . . that's the prostitute informed on us, the one Calvin shot his mouth off to. Neil approached Marshall, offered him a piece of the action if he'd stonewall the investigation for a few years, let the leads go cold, publicity about the case die down . . . was gonna give him half a mil. But Marshall wanted cash up front or he wouldn't go along. So we all forked over a grand a month from our IRAs . . . each one of us. After a year he wanted more, two grand a month. Christ, we'd've been broke something happened . . . say we couldn't get to the seven mil or something. So Neil said he had to be eliminated. But the Mexican Paul hired blew up the wrong car . . . yours, I guess. Something 'bout the same license plates . . . you guys had similar plates, huh? Yeah. Anyway, Neil figured it was only natural Marshall would tell you*" *all about it after that happened, you know, pillow talk. So he figured out a way to get rid of both of you . . ."*

Myra's voice: *"By putting my prints on Napoleon Booker's gun?"*

Monroe's voice: *"Calvin did, yeah. When he broke in your place, knocked you out. We hadn't known about the custom gun rack in the Mustang when we first busted Booker. The plan was just to set him up to get the heat off us once we realized Marshall might roll over on us. Then we discovered Booker's Glock hidden in that custom gun rack he made. All the investigators missed it, it was so well done. Jesus, if you'da got those pictures to court, the DA would've known we planted the three fifty-seven. And if that happened it wouldn't have taken long to figure we planted the money too. 'Course I guess you already knew that."*

Myra's voice: *"So you killed Ray, my investigator?"*

Monroe's voice: *"Paul did. Rather, the dope addicts he hired did. Then Neil saw a chance to use Booker's Glock, solve two problems at the same time."*

Myra's voice, cracking slightly: *"Ray was a really nice guy."*

Monroe's voice: *"Yeah?"*

Myra's voice: *"Tell me about the robbery. Who killed the guard? Paul?"*

Monroe's voice: *"No. That was Calvin. With the three fifty-seven we planted on Booker. Calvin was supposed to watch him, make sure he didn't try anything while we were loading the money. But he shot him anyway, stupid-ass muthafucka. He claims the guard went for his gun. But we knew that was bullshit. Because the guard was in on the deal. Make him some extra cash for his retirement down the road. But I blame Neil for that. He set the robbery up, said he had an inside contact but never told us who it was. Security reasons, he said. He knew how Calvin was . . . look at him wrong he'd kill you. Especially another black person. This racial thing he had for his own people. The guard was black, I mention that? He was. You want my opinion, I think . . ."*

Myra reached over and hit the Stop switch, plunging the room into silence. And waited. If it was going to work, it would be now. It just had to. If it didn't . . . ?

No one speaking. Not really knowing what to say. Myra trying not to let her apprehension show, but her heart racing at Triple Crown speed. She picked around the pile on the sofa, nervous fingers finding another joint and holding it, waiting.

It seemed they all turned to Myra at the same time, staring at her in amazement or disbelief, Myra couldn't tell which. But Stepolini's stare the most chilling—cold, brutal eyes telegraphing his thoughts better than any words. He was the first to speak, never taking his eyes off Myra but intending his words for Neil Sanford, saying, "Dirty muthafucka. Dirty little fat-ass muthafucka. I never trusted him, Neil. I told you that. Had a feeling about him same as I did about that nigger, Calvin."

Darryl said to Myra, "How'd you get him to say that, hold a gun to his head?"

Myra said, "Actually, I sat on his face. Can I get a light, please? Someone . . . ? Anyone? All right." And Myra, not knowing why but feeling it was right, stood up and walked the short distance to Stepolini, the Italian's eyes in the unsmiling face glued to Myra's green eyes, the green eyes coming to life now and holding him in check as she approached and bent down, her cleavage bulging, taking his lighter from the end table, drawing in deep on the joint, replacing the lighter, and saying, "Thanks."

Taking her time back to the couch, dropping down and crossing shapely bare thighs below the tight ruffled skirt and waiting.

Darryl said, "So, you got Monroe to roll over on us. His word against ours. Why should anyone believe anything he'd say?"

Myra said, "The court will believe him." Myra lying, bluffing the way Napoleon scripted it. "They'll also believe Manuel when he shows them where he buried Calvin's body." Myra drawing in deep on the joint and watching their expressions change. "It's there on the tape, you want to hear it," she said, exhaling, squeaky voice from the weed clearing. "You know Manuel, don't you?

Manuel's Junkyard on Alameda?" Myra knowing this was truth, knew as she spoke the words that police already had Manuel in custody, were combing the chop shop for evidence.

"Should've buried that nigger ourselves," Darryl blurted out. "Stupid-ass wetback Manuel. Threaten to deport his ass, no telling what he'll say." Admitting to something and not aware of it.

Myra Cross—cleavage all but popping out of Shaniqua's blouse, big sexy legs crossed, six-hundred-dollar open-toed Jimmy Choo shoes dangling from the painted tips of delicate feet—almost choked at the admission. Finally. Sensing she was on the verge, that they were right there, one little push all that was needed. Myra getting comfortable now and beginning to think she could do this. Her pulse beginning to slow, the joint relaxing her now, perhaps more than it should have.

"Then there's the serial number of Booker's Glock. Imagine what the DA will say when he opens Booker's safe-deposit box, finds a copy of the serial number of the Glock he stole six years earlier." Myra saw three pairs of eyebrows rise at the same time. "Don't ask me why he did that, I couldn't tell you. But he did, and he'll cop to possession of a stolen gun. No problem there. But how's the DA gonna explain my prints on that same gun, a gun I had no access to because Mr. Booker was incarcerated—osmosis?"

Myra looking at them, feeling her confidence return, the apprehension starting to drain itself away. Watching their blank, bewildered faces beginning to sense things getting beyond their control, listening to the PD punch sewer holes in the frame they had thought was airtight, but not so sure now and not really knowing what to say or do.

Stepolini pulled the .38 from his boot and stood up. His eyes still glued to Myra, he said, chillingly and without contrition, "You know, Neil, I think it was a mistake to have Rose kill Marshall. If we'd been thinking, we could've set it up so he and Red here were together. I could've gone in, shot 'em both together, made it look like a murder suicide. It would've been a lot cleaner and a lot less complicated, and it wouldn't have been necessary for me to kill Rose."

Stepolini's feelings for Rose not lost on Myra, but she kept her eyes on the .38 as he walked slowly toward her, the green eyes following the .38, going up in her head and rotating out of focus as she felt the cold touch of the gun's barrel against her temple.

Stepolini said, "As it is, there's one-half of that equation I can still eliminate. I don't know what effect it'll have on Gil, but it'll give me an intense sense of pleasure." Like killing was a sport, on the same level as the World Series or Super Bowl.

And Myra giving the Italian nothing, surprising even herself, showing no fear . . . no apprehension. No movement except to inhale deep on the joint and somehow maintaining her composure, the weed giving her a false sense of security, perhaps. Myra couldn't be sure. And as she so often did when faced with adversity, she took herself out of the room and away from the threat of death, back to the beaches of Cancún, the south Atlantic, in bed with Gerald Seymore . . .

Neil Sanford suddenly realized something. A truth. Or at least he thought he did. He stood up and shouted, "Wait, Paul! Put that away and don't say anything! Both of you. Don't open your mouths! If she got Gil on tape like that, she can do the same to us. Think about it—Gil calling us like that, telling us to meet him here, and the PD showing up in his place. Walking in here with a key like she owns the place. Her on the run and turning Gil like she did. How'd she get to him like that? I'll tell you how—because she's working with IA. She's got to be. And probably the DA's office as well . . ."

Myra came back from Gerald Seymore's bed and a ten-second orgasm just in time to hear Neil Sanford say, "We're being set up, can't you guys see that? This whole thing about her being on the run is nothing but a sucker play. A trap! You think if the DA's office had this much information we'd still be sitting here watching Little Miss Muffet there give head? Not on your life! Not unless . . ." Neil

Sanford hesitated, thinking about it, trying to make the pieces fit. He pointed to the end table. "Grab that recorder, Paul. Get rid of it."

Stepolini scooped the recorder off the table, dropped it on the floor, brought the heel of a heavy Timberland boot down hard, crushing it. The heel turning back and forth, grinding it, tiny fragments of metal and plastic scattering across the floor.

"Unless what?" Darryl asked, waiting. "You were saying . . . ?"

"Not unless she's wired," Neil Sanford said.

At this Myra couldn't help but laugh. "Wired? Jesus. You guys are really paranoid, aren't you?" But no one laughed with her.

Stepolini said, "Take off your clothes, Red." Not asking, commanding.

Myra stood up from the couch and, looking Steoplini levelly in the eyes, said, "Would you like to frisk me?" Having fun with them now, practicing her skills as a talk show host like Napoleon had suggested, but not like he'd scripted. "Better yet," Myra went on, taking the last draw on the joint, reaching down to mash it out in an ashtray, "why don't one of you undress me, satisfy yourselves I'm not wired." Looking at Darryl as she spoke, knowing he'd be the one to do it. "All right, then, you want, I'll start," Myra said, and unfastened the two buttons of Shaniqua's blouse, let it fall open, and said, "Darryl, if you'd do the honors . . ."

It took Darryl all of two seconds to comply, the hulky cop rushing over too fast and too eagerly, pulling the blouse out of the skirt and off Myra's shoulders. And while his clumsy fingers fumbled with her bra clasp, Myra unfastened and worked the short skirt with the ruffled hemline, straps of delicate thong panties down long, shapely legs. And if you didn't know better you would think her moves well rehearsed and choreographed. But they were not. They were the natural moves of a woman instinctually sexual. Her breasts full and supple once free of the Victoria's Secret bra, Myra stepped out of her clothes and stood before them on three-inch heels, naked and unashamed. In fact rather proud of her body, enjoying the chance to exhibit it and not at all self-conscious or bothered by their lecherous stares. Myra, her arms slightly bent and held out from her sides, turned full circle, smoothly, and posed in the process as if on a modeling shoot. In reality she was, if nothing else, practicing for her close-up. She had the audience. All she needed was the camera.

Myra looking at Traci Lords frozen on the screen, wondering if this was how she got her start in the porn business, doing strip shows for dirty old men. Wondering too if there was really any difference between them. Both had fucked more men than they could remember: Traci Lords for money. Myra Cross for the orgasm. Neither had ever fucked for love. And in that sense, Myra was thinking, they were sisters under the flesh. Both whores. On different levels, of course. But whores nonetheless.

Incredible what a mesmerizing effect a really attractive woman can have on men. Especially up close and personal. Close enough to reach out and touch. Neil Sanford, Darryl Brigham, and Paul Stepolini were speechless. Traci Lords may have been there on the screen with a dick in her mouth. But Myra Cross was standing butt naked right there in front of them. Darryl thinking *Playboy* hadn't done her justice. And Jesus, would he like to do her. Man oh man.

"Are we satisfied yet? Yes? No? Not sure? All right . . ."

Myra bending over, hands on her knees, wiggling her butt in the degrading way she'd seen black girls do in rap videos. And turning to look at them but getting no answer from a trio still entranced by the very fact of her presence.

"If there's a wire, fellas, it's up my ass. And you'll have to pay before you look."

And not waiting for any comment or instruction, Myra began to dress. Perhaps because of her *Playboy* celebrity status or her arrogance—Myra wasn't sure which—no one moved to stop her. She didn't feel they would, though she could tell Brigham was thinking about it. Seriously. Still, she managed to dress unmolested. And once she was dressed and back on the couch, no one really seemed to know what to say. Even Neil Sanford, the wind gone out of his sails because there was no wire, was speechless.

Myra said at last, "Well, then, what say we get down to business, shall we?" And waited.

"You mean you wanna fuck?" Darryl was salivating.

Stepolini said, "What are you talking about, Red? What business? Or we just supposed to feel so scared by Monroe's confession we accompany you to the DA's office, turn ourselves in, get the charges against you dropped. What?"

Myra drew in a deep breath of exasperation she made no effort to conceal. Dealing with imbeciles was a lot of work. She guessed she'd have to spell it out for them.

Myra said, "Maybe I don't want the charges dropped."

CHAPTER 21

TRACI LORDS WATCHED the whole thing unfold with a dick in her mouth.

They heard it. Heard it but didn't believe it, what she said about not wanting the charges against her dropped. It had to be the weed. Or she was crazy. Make a comment like that. This whole thing with her being here didn't make any sense.

Neil Sanford was thinking about it. Then suddenly his face turned into a mask of incredulous disbelief. He finally saw it. The way a new bulb lights up a darkened room.

Moving forward on the couch, he said to Myra Cross, "Well, I'll be . . . So *that's* it! You sneaky little cunt, you!" And couldn't believe it had taken him this long, that he hadn't picked up on it from the beginning.

Stepolini and Darryl looked at the Godfather to share his revelation.

"What?" Stepolini said.

Neil Sanford said, "She's here for the money. That's what this whole thing's about, isn't it, Miss Cross?" Calling her that and not really sure why. "The money?"

Myra knew she needed more, that they hadn't said quite enough to fully exonerate her and Napoleon. So she'd departed from Napoleon's script with one of her own. She clapped her hands together lightly and smiled.

"Take off the dunce cap and go to the head of the class. Hip hip hooray. We finally have a winner."

Stepolini, still not with it yet but getting there, said to Neil Sanford, "Money?" And to Myra he said, "You need money to leave the country? What?"

Myra unwound from the couch like Mata Hari, moved past Stepolini to his lighter, lit the last joint, and, hoping it would be enough, held it in deep and turned to face him, unafraid now and exhaling in his face. She'd have to spell it out for him, but carefully, because he was trigger-happy and it wouldn't take much to provoke him.

"I'm your new partner, Mr. Stepolini," Myra said, and saw Stepolini's expression go from blank to stupid.

"Partner?" Saying it like the word was in a foreign language.

"That's right. I'm replacing the late Calvin James."

"Says who?" Stepolini frowning, trying to follow the action. But struggling with dementia.

Darryl saw it before Stepolini. He jumped up from the comfort of his chair and said, "Aw, now wait a minute. Wait just a minute!" Looking over to Neil Sanford to confirm his understanding, Neil Sanford just looking at him, raising his eyebrows as an answer. "If she's talking about what I think she's talking about," the cop went on, "that's bullshit! I got three years to go, and I ain't giving her shit! Not a goddamn muthafucking dime!"

Neil Sanford laughed for the first time since Traci Lords stopped groaning and moaning. "It seems," he said with some amusement in his voice, "that our Miss Cross here has decided it would be better to be a rich fugitive than a poor public servant. Have I got it right, Madam Public Defender?" Sarcastic, but respecting her title.

The .38 still in his hand, Stepolini finally getting it now and looking at Darryl, saying, "The seven mil? That's the money she's talking about?" And turning back to Myra he said, "Lady, you must be crazy. I should've killed you outright myself instead of going along with Neil over there and his crazy plan to frame you and the Booker kid. Had it my way, I'd have blown your brains out way I did Sambo."

Myra said, "And Rosalie?" and knew immediately she'd touched a nerve.

In a rare display of emotion, Stepolini seemed to hesitate a moment. Staring at her, cold, brutal eyes appraising her face, red hair, her green eyes.

"That was my mistake. But I'm gonna correct it right now." And Stepolini brought the .38 up to Myra's face.

Neil Sanford said, "Not here, Paul. The noise . . ."

For some reason Myra did not feel herself in any real danger. The weed perhaps, or sensing in Stepolini that something about her reminded him of Rose. She just reached up, and with the back of her hand gently pushed against a wrist that yielded without resistance, the .38 moving away from her face and falling to Stepolini's side.

"Yes, Paul, not here. Besides, I'm not your problem. It's the money you have to worry about."

"What are you talking about?" Darryl said. "Why do we have to worry about the money? We've got seven and a half mil tucked safely away, we're just biding our time until we can spend it."

"Yes," Myra said. "In the vault downstairs." She knew this was true from Monroe, and felt comfortable saying it. "Actually, it's closer to seven point two and change if you deduct the two hundred fifty grand you planted in Mr. Booker's car."

Darryl said, "It was a good investment. We knew he couldn't explain it away."

Stepolini said, "Go on. You were saying, about the money . . . ?"

"But you need the combination locked in the safe-deposit box at the bank where the Gang of Five has its account." Monroe had told her about that too, what they called themselves. "And just in case you don't know it, that seven and a half mil you have all tucked away is money you can't spend."

"Not for three more years," Darryl said.

Myra looked at Neil Sanford. "Three more years? That what

you told them, Neil—the statute of limitations would expire in three years?"

Something in the way she asked the question bothered Darryl. He said, "Yeah, three years. What about it?"

Myra said, "Ever heard the term 'special circumstances,' Darryl?"

Darryl nodded and said yes, of course he had. But he didn't really.

Myra walked away from Stepolini, began pacing in a small circle in front of Traci Lords, the way she would do in a courtroom, occasionally making a point to the jury with her arms, only now drawing deep on the joint and holding it. She said, exhaling slowly, not really looking at anyone in particular, "The statue of limitations only applies to how long an agency has to prosecute you. It does not apply to ownership of money. As far as a bank or S and L is concerned, it's never anyone's money but theirs. Now, having said that, in the ordinary commission of a capital crime, that is, a felony—in this case bank robbery, an S and L to be more precise—the statue of limitations for prosecution runs anywhere from five to seven years, give or take a few years, depending on whether it's federal or state. And if that's all it had been, a simple robbery, you'd have been in the clear when the statute of limitations expired. Unfortunately, the Gang of Five wasn't that lucky. The law clearly states that if, during the commission of said felony, a homicide occurs, such as what happened in your case when Calvin killed the guard, a 'special circumstance' is attached to the charge, making it a death penalty case. And as everyone in this room knows, or should know, there is no statute of limitations on murder. Everybody with me so far? Good." Myra looking at faces astounded by Basic Law 101. "Now, then, what about the money? Is the bank going to send a posse out to find you after five to seven years? Probably not. Not if all you spend is ten or twenty bucks. But try and put a quarter million with those serial numbers in Bank of America and see how fast they come knocking on your door. And I daresay Obi-Wan Kanobi here"—and Myra turned to face Neil Sanford, his face flushed with anger—"has suggested you lay low—don't show off, start grandstanding, or living beyond your means with Rolls-Royces and Donald Trump mansions. Which is probably good advice. That's how thieves get caught—buying million-dollar homes on LAPD dollar-a-day salaries. Way I see it, fellas, whether you spend the money today or ten years from today, it's still the bank's money and they'll want it back. Maybe not right away. But if any of those serial numbers turn up, whether tomorrow or a millennium from now, they'll come calling. Trust me."

Myra watched two expressions change sourly with the education she'd just given, and realizing now that Neil Sanford had lied to them, Darryl and Stepolini turned to face him.

Stepolini said, "Neil, that true? What she says . . . ?"

Neil Sanford looked like a constipated man trying to take a crap. The bitch was smart, he thought. Smarter than he was. And shrewd, peeping his hold card like that, letting on he'd been lying to them. What the fuck, he'd had no choice. These idiots had no discipline or patience. First thing they'd have done was go crazy with toys, just the way she laid it out. Draw a big circle on their chests that said "Look at me, I'm rich and I only make forty thou a year before taxes, ha-ha-ha. Guess where I got it from." Jesus, they'd all be in jail by now if he hadn't concocted that lie about the statute of limitations. Nothing but shit for brains, these guys.

After thinking about it, not wanting to admit it but having no choice, Neil Sanford said, "It was good advice, like she said." Thinking on his feet like that, making Myra Cross an ally.

Anger filling out his words, Darryl said, "Well shit, goddamn, Neil. If that's the case, we're fucked! You shoulda told us. What the hell do we do now?"

"Well," Myra said, "you could do what we're planning to do, leave the country."

"We, huh," Neil Sanford said ruefully. "I figured you and the Booker kid were in this together. Didn't I say that, guys? The two of them working together?" Neil Sanford looking to save face. Redeem his tarnished image, if it wasn't already too late.

Myra said, "Booker? Guys, give me a little credit here. No, I'm going away with Gil. Your buddy. I told you he doesn't want me to go to jail. And he's not a bad-looking guy, really. We get along great, I'm telling you."

Darryl said enviously, "So you said. You sat on his face."

"Hey, nowadays a girl does what she has to do. We're going to a country where tax evasion is not a crime, a place that has no extradition treaty with the United States and whose banks don't care where the money comes from. Just as long as it's the almighty US dollar."

"Where?" Stepolini asked, cynical. "North Korea?"

"Good heavens, no! I'm a warm-weather girl. I like to walk around in bikinis." Winking at Darryl, she added, "Or nothing. Which brings me back to the point at hand, why I'm here—to get my share of the money. Gil's too, while I'm at it. All two point nine of it. So we can hightail it out of here."

They just looked at one another. And at Myra.

Stepolini said, "We don't go along with this, what? Gil talks to the DA?"

"He can't talk to the DA if we're living overseas."

"Going anyway, huh. Money or no money," Stepolini said, not quite believing it but wanting to. "Now, isn't that nice. True love. The crooked cop and crooked lawyer going off into the sunset arm in arm. A perfect Hollywood ending. Will wonders never cease. Almost makes me want to cry, except I'm fresh out of tears." And beginning to get a kick out of it.

"Look," Myra said. "You're sitting on money nobody can spend here in the states unless . . ." Myra hesitated, thinking how she wanted to present it, make something she knew nothing about sound believable.

"Unless . . . ?" Stepolini said.

"I'm here to offer you a deal," Myra continued, then paused long enough to look at Stepolini, to read the feeling behind his eyes. "I've got a way for you to get your money in less than thirty days and not have to spend the rest of your lives looking over your shoulders every time you spend five dollars, terrified some hungry little Treasury agent or bank manager will recognize the serial number and come calling." All of them paid close attention now. "Someone who can make your money legal. Can take your portion, move it out of the country to a foreign bank of your choosing, wash it, bring it back in clean as a whistle." She said it the way she imagined Gerald Seymore would say it.

Twirling the .38 like the cowboy he was, Stepolini said, "Thirty days, you say? Work with me on this, Red, so I can see the picture more clearly. Now then, as I understand it, you want us to turn over our share to you, sit back and twiddle our thumbs until you return it. Meantime you and Gil Judas are stretched out on the beach somewhere between here and Antarctica." Stepolini laughed sarcastically and said, "Red, do I look like I have the word 'stupid' written on my forehead?"

Myra wanting to say yes, he did. In capital letters. That he really was that stupid. They all were. And not just written on their foreheads but all over their faces. Instead she said, "Not to me. To an associate. Someone with experience in offshore money matters."

"A money launderer," Stepolini said, as if referring to a cockroach that needed exterminating. The pot calling the kettle black.

"Of course you can always take a chance," Myra went on, undeterred. "It's your money. Handle it any way you like. I just thought we might accommodate each other, that's all. You want to spend your retirement years looking over your shoulders every time you buy a pack of cigarettes, that's on you. I'm offering you a way to get your cash in thirty days. Not thirty years from now. I figure that ought to be worth Calvin's share."

Darryl didn't have to think about anything. He said, "I like the idea of thirty days, Neil." And to Stepolini he said, "What do you think, Paul. Thirty days? Oh, yeah. I can go along with that. I sure can."

Stepolini tossed a glance in Neil Sanford's direction, his allegiance to the aging general still there but slipping now in the wake of his deception.

With some levity in his voice he said, "You know, Neil, we wasted a lotta time framing the Booker kid. We didn't have to. In hindsight we didn't have to do any of the stuff we did. We didn't have to kill Marshall or Rosalie, or even Princess for that matter. All we needed to do was talk to our girl Red, here. She'd have made a hell of a lot better partner than the jigaboo. Don't you think?" The backhanded compliment the only one Myra would ever get from Stepolini. Stepolini not really expecting Neil Sanford to answer him. He just continued twirling the .38 around his index finger, waiting.

Neil Sanford sat thinking about it. A long period of silence in fact. Trying to put the pieces all together, to see if the girl's reasoning was sound, still not completely convinced she was as crooked as she sounded. But then, a lot of lawyers were crooked . . .

The thirty-day option might be worth exploring. Not the whole amount. Just a portion, to see if it worked. If she was wrong—and there was still something in his gut telling him she was—if she was just bullshitting them, well, then he'd turn Stepolini loose on her. Track her and her turncoat lover down to whichever country they lived in. And handle it. Both of them.

Neil Sanford stood up for the first time that evening. He stretched tired, aging arms and legs and said, "Have to sleep on it, Miss Cross. How long you plan to be around?"

"Long enough for your answer, or they arrest me. Whichever comes first."

"Have your answer tomorrow. That be soon enough for you?"

"Tomorrow night. I don't travel during the day," Myra said, and began gathering her items from the couch in preparation to leave, not really sure she had enough but running out of options now.

She was suddenly very tired. The dope was wearing off. Her arms and legs grew weak. Her thinking became more scattered, the stresses of the past three weeks taking their toll. Myra knew she had to quit now, to get out of the house before she slipped up, made a mistake, and said something that would tip them off.

Her heart started to flutter in her chest and her pulse quickened. It took effort to stand.

"By the way," Myra said, "Monroe mentioned it on the tape, we didn't get to it, but who made that horrible-looking gun rack for Calvin's three fifty-seven you stuck in Booker's Mustang?"

The trio laughed in unison.

With a certain amount of pride in his voice Darryl said, "I worked on that goddamn gun rack all night long to get a three fifty-seven to fit. You didn't give us much time. When you filed the motion to suppress the gun we figured you knew it was stolen, but we didn't know how you knew. We never thought to look, see if it would fit. We would've never been able to make the exchange with the three fifty-seven if we hadn't seen the photos from the investigator."

"Yeah, Ray," Myra said. "He was a great guy." Hoping there was enough indifference in her voice to cover her anger. "Oh, well. Life goes on. Gentlemen, guess I'll be on my way."

No one tried to stop her as she approached the door.

"I'll walk you, you like," Darryl said, offering to carry the handbag, Myra declining. She reminded him that she was a fugitive, that they were searching everywhere for her and it would put anyone seen with her in danger if she was arrested. Darryl said he could understand that and appreciated her caution. Myra forced her lips into a tight circle and blew him a kiss.

Myra stepped off the porch into a chilly Culver City night. She started down the walkway on a pair of unsteady legs.

"Hey, Red!"

Myra froze as Stepolini's voice, lethal and commanding, thundered from behind, catching her just as she reached the sidewalk. Terrified now that they may have discovered the ruse, and knowing if they had, if she hadn't pulled it off, the price she would pay. Or perhaps Darryl had convinced them to bring her back for sex. Remembering the way he looked at her when she was undressed, his thinking after a while that she was just like them and chomping at the bit to fuck her. And would have too, if she hadn't brought up the fact of Neil Sanford lying to them and distracted him with talk about the money. Oh, God, Myra thought, praying she hadn't blown it.

Napoleon had warned her it could happen if she wasn't careful, like in the torture chamber when she blew it with the gun. And if it happened this time, the consequences would probably be fatal. She'd be on her own. He'd wait for her in the van but couldn't rescue her if it blew up in her face.

She turned around slowly, not knowing if she'd face an execution or gang rape.

It was neither.

It was Stepolini walking briskly toward her, his arm extended, a shiny black object in his hand.

"Forgot your cell phone," he said. "No honest-to-goodness fugitive should leave home without one." He handed it to her and added, "See you tomorrow."

Myra's heart nearly stopped at the thought she'd left it behind, the single most important piece of equipment in the whole operation. Myra thinking Jesus, making that kind of mistake, she must really be tired. Thanking him, she turned and walked slowly down the block, heels of the Jimmy Choo shoes tapping lightly on the concrete, not daring to look around to see if she was being followed. She turned at the corner, saw the waiting van, heard its engine start, saw its lights come on as she approached, Napoleon swinging open the passenger door, pulling away from the curb as she slid into the seat and somehow found the strength to fasten her seat belt.

They didn't speak for several minutes until Napoleon had put the van in light traffic going east on Slauson Boulevard, past the deserted Fox Hills Mall.

Myra said to Napoleon, "You wouldn't by any chance have any coke, would you? A primo? A rock? Anything. Something to pick me up. I'm just out of it."

"Yeah, you look it," he said, and pointed to the glove compartment. "Ought to be something in there."

The glove compartment yielded a half-smoked primo and a lighter, Myra bringing the cocaine in deep, waiting for the electricity to fire up her brain.

Napoleon said, "Let me see your cell phone." Myra, reaching in the handbag, handed it to him, trying to imagine what she would've said if she'd left it at the party pad.

Napoleon looking at it, flipping it open, holding it to catch the streetlight through the window, and smiling in the darkness.

"Three hours. Damn, still got battery life. We get to the mortuary I'll remove the transmitter, hook your shit back up proper. You sure nobody noticed anything? Suspected it was on all the time?"

Myra said no, she didn't think they did.

"Let's see if this transmitter and James Bond spy-shit equipment we installed worked," Napoleon said. "See how much of the meeting was recorded on business partner's receiver." He pulled out his own cell phone, punched in a number, and said, "Scarecrow is down."

Napoleon Booker's cell phone rang in three minutes.

"Talk to me." There was a long interval of silence before Napoleon said a word. There was no radio announcer and no music playing. Only the soft humming of tires on rough pavement, occasional blare of horns from passing cars. And when he finally spoke, it was in a tone not uncharacteristically subdued, but more stoic and emotionally uninvested. "Really! Money for spy shit well spent, huh? But I think Miss Cross needs to hear it from the horse's mouth." He handed the cell phone to Myra, saying, "New technology's a bitch when it works. Know what I'm sayin'?" Like it was the outcome he expected all along and was no big deal.

The primo not quite there yet, Myra took the cell phone and said, almost in a whisper, "Daddy?"

Gerald Seymore said, "Hi, baby. It worked beautifully. It picked up the entire conversation. Every word, crystal clear. There's enough on this tape to exonerate both of you. I play this for the DA in the morning, they'll cut you guys loose so fast you won't know what hit you."

"You wouldn't kid me, would you, Daddy? Not about this, you wouldn't. You're not just saying it to make me feel better?"

"No, Myra. I wouldn't kid you about a thing like this. The nightmare is over, honey. You performed magnificently. There's so much here, these guys are all looking at retirement on death row. Trust me."

Myra said, "My parents . . . you'll tell them I'm okay? That I—"

"You can tell them yourself. Their ship reaches Buenos Aires in two days. With any luck you can talk to them directly. Your brother said to tell you he won five hundred dollars in the casino. Says he may give up being a chiropractor and get a position on a cruise ship."

Life coming back in her voice now, Myra said, "He always did like to gamble. Let me tell you—neither you nor Napoleon will ever know just how frightened I was. You just don't know!"

"I know you were, honey. But you pulled it off beautifully. You really did. And by the way, I've got a hunch you and Napoleon may be in for a finder's fee, the bank gets its money back. Ten percent of whatever's recovered is the going rate. Maybe even more. I'll know more after my meeting."

"Daddy, I miss you," Myra said.

"I miss you too, Myra. I really do. Napoleon's taking you back to the safe house. I've still got a couple of hours' work ahead of me, get this tape duplicated, prepare for my meeting with the DA tomorrow. I'll meet you there later tonight, if you're up to it. Okay? But I have to warn you, Myra, once this is over, I'm not letting you out of my sight. Even if it means putting you in handcuffs."

"Well, now—handcuffs. A little S and M action, huh? I'll bring the whips and chains."

"Myra. That wasn't what I meant."

Myra drawing on the primo, getting back into it, her voice stronger, saying, "Wait till you see the casket I've picked out, Daddy."

"Casket? No reason to plan your funeral, Myra. I told you, this'll all be over by tomorrow."

Myra giggled and said, "Who's talking about a funeral? I'm talking about a casket to make love in."

"Myra, really, now. You're sounding very kinky."

Myra didn't answer Gerald Seymore right away. She was thinking about her future, in what ways it might change. Or might not. Thinking about her mother, always critical and never satisfied with anything she'd done, the lingering bitterness over her father's abandonment an inpenetrable wall between them; little Traci Lords, child porno star; Clara with the long nails, a weight problem, and an attitude; Marty French's secretary, Lorna, at peace with her ugliness, her money, and no life; and Shaniqua, a girl with no vision or expectations beyond tomorrow, but loving and selfless to a fault. Women who were products of their own doing, or someone else's, but creatures of habit. All of them. With no plans to change and no apologies for not doing so.

She drew on the primo one last time, shuttered at the buzz when it came. Myra Cross understanding now that at the end of the day, when all was said and done, nothing had really changed. Society in general and men in particular would still see her as the lawyer with the red hair, big boobs, drug habit, unquenchable sexual appetite, and genius IQ—in that order. Like it or not, Myra Cross was what she was.

"Oh, Daddy," Myra said, schoolgirl giggle still in her voice. "Don't be such a prude. We're gonna have the best sex ever in the casket."

And they did.

EPILOGUE

FEDERAL INDICTMENTS WERE ISSUED for all members of the Gang of Five.

Neil Sanford was arrested while on duty at LAPD's Central Division Precinct.

Paul Stepolini attempted to flee the country in his yacht, but was wounded in a shoot-out with the US Coast Guard who intercepted him at the three mile limit.

Before he could be apprehended, Darryl Brigham fled the country to Mexico in his plane. Charged with unlawful flight to avoid prosecution, he was extradited back to the states by Mexican law enforcement officials who acted on a warrant issued through the US embassy in Mexico City.

Gilbert Monroe was arrested in Queen of Angels Hospital while undergoing surgery to reattach his fingers. Following surgery, the sheriff's custody unit transported him to the jail ward of Los Angeles County General Hospital, where he was held until trial. He was offered a deal by prosecutors who allowed him to plea down to a lesser sentence in exchange for his testimony against Neil Sanford, Paul Stepolini, and Darryl Brigham. The three were tried and convicted on multiple counts of robbery, murder, extortion, assault, and conspiracy to commit murder with special circumstances. They are now in California's San Quentin prison awaiting execution on death row. Gilbert Monroe is currently residing in another state under the Witness Protection Program.

Gerald Seymore negotiated the dropping of all charges against Myra Cross and Napoleon Booker, Napoleon pleading guilty to possession of a stolen gun and sentenced to time served with no probation.

Immediately after their exoneration, Myra, Napoleon, and Gerald Seymore flew down to Buenos Aires, where they joined relieved family members on board the cruise ship and where, just before the ship's departure for Capetown, the captain married Myra and Gerald Seymore in a quiet ceremony on the bridge.

Their return thirty days later was to an unprecedented storm of publicity surrounding Myra's ordeal that made her a celebrity. Her picture appeared on the covers of every major magazine in both the United States and Europe. *Playboy* commissioned Jason Rice to shoot more photos of Myra for a centerfold. She was a guest on *Oprah*, interviewed on *Larry King Live*, and appeared on FOX News's *The O'Reilly Factor* with Martha Stewart and Gloria Allred for a discussion on how women are treated by a male-dominated criminal justice system.

Myra never returned to the public defender's office. She handed in her resignation to Marty French and formed Cross, Seymore, and Booker, a multimedia entertainment conglomerate whose first venture, *Myra's One Night Stand*, made its debut on the FOX TV network opposite Jay Leno and David Letterman. It was the highest-rated new show in the history of late-night television.

At Myra's insistence, Napoleon Booker took the college entrance exam. His SAT score was 1580 out of a possible 1600 and resulted in a flood of scholarship offers, all of which he rejected in favor of becoming the head of Cross, Seymore, and Booker's music division.

The S and L never did pay a finder's fee on the seven point two million dollars that was recovered.

FIC   Jefferson, Roland S.
JEF
             One night stand.
c.1

$24.00

30207100010449

DATE		
	WITHDRAWN	

Property of Nueces County
Keach Family Library
1000 Terry Shamsie Blvd.
Robstown, TX 78380

WITHDRAWN

BAKER & TAYLOR